SO-ARY-809

The PATRIOTS

JACK CAVANAUGH

The PATRIOTS

RiverOak®
Good News in Fiction

COOK COMMUNICATIONS MINISTRIES
Colorado Springs, Colorado • Paris, Ontario
KINGSWAY COMMUNICATIONS LTD
Eastbourne, England

RiverOak® is an imprint of
Cook Communications Ministries, Colorado Springs, CO 80918
Cook Communications, Paris, Ontario
Kingsway Communications, Eastbourne, England

THE PATRIOTS
© 2005 by Jack Cavanaugh, second edition,
previous ISBN 1-56476-428-1.

First edition published by Victor Books in 1995 ©.

All rights reserved. No part of this book may be reproduced without written
permission, except for brief quotations in books and critical reviews. For
information, write Cook Communications Ministries, 4050 Lee Vance View,
Colorado Springs, CO 80918.

Printed in Canada

1 2 3 4 5 6 7 8 9   Printing/Year.   10 09 08 07 06 05

Cover Design: Jeffrey P. Barnes
Cover Art: Ron Adair

Unless otherwise noted, Scripture quotations are taken from The King James Version.
Italics in Scripture quotations have been added by the author for emphasis.

Library of Congress Cataloging-in-Publication Data

Cavanaugh, Jack.
  The patriots / Jack Cavanaugh.
    p. cm. -- (An American family portrait ; bk. 3)
  ISBN 1-58919-067-X
  1. United States--History--Revolution, 1775-1783--Fiction. 2. American loyalists--
Fiction. 3. Boston (Mass.)--Fiction. I. Title.
  PS3553.A965P38 2005
  813'.54--dc22
                                2005019520

To my wife, Marni—

my greatest inspiration,

my greatest encourager,

my greatest temptation when I should be writing.

ACKNOWLEDGMENTS

To John Mueller and Barbara Ring—this is the third book you've critiqued for me. It's a special friend who will go the extra mile like the two of you have.

To Kim Garrison and Karen Stoffell—your enthusiasm for the series encourages me to write; thanks for your time and comments on the manuscript.

To Greg Clouse—it's hard for me to decide which I like better about you, your editorial skills or your friendship; both are top notch.

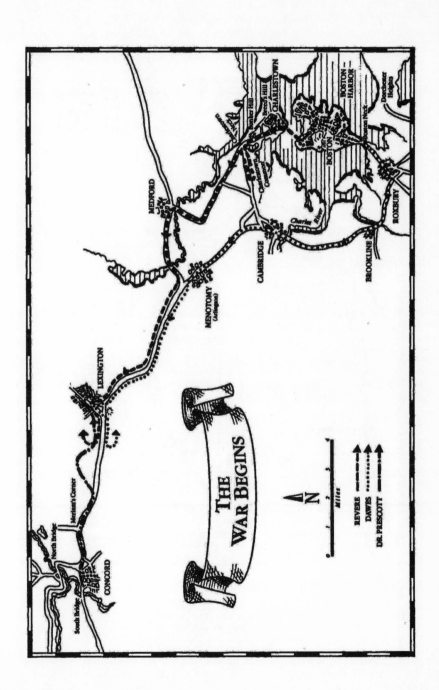

THE WAR BEGINS

N

Miles

REVERE
DAWES
DR. PRESCOTT

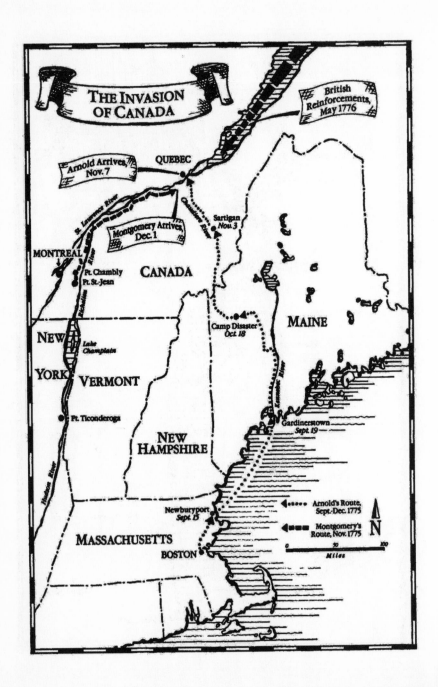

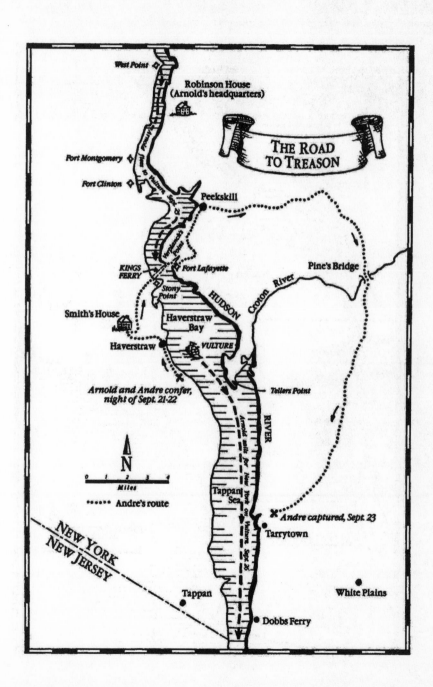

West Point

Robinson House
(Arnold's headquarters)

THE ROAD
TO TREASON

Fort Montgomery

Fort Clinton

Peekskill

KINGS
FERRY

Fort Lafayette

Pine's Bridge

Stony
Point

HUDSON

Croton River

Smith's House

Haverstraw
Bay

Haverstraw

VULTURE

Arnold and Andre confer,
night of Sept. 21-22

Tellers Point

RIVER

N

0 1 2 3 4
Miles

••••••• Andre's route

Tappan
Sea

Andre captured, Sept. 23

Tarrytown

NEW YORK
NEW JERSEY

Tappan

White Plains

Dobbs Ferry

1

"TRAITOR!"

"Liar!"

Jacob and Esau Morgan stood nose-to-nose—jaws set, necks strained, faces flushed, eyes brimming with fury. Except for their clothing, they were mirror images of each other. While Esau wore silk, Jacob wore breeches made of dark-brown woolen broadcloth.

"Jacob, sit down! Esau, you know better than to behave like this! We have guests!" A voice heavy with authority boomed from the head of the dinner table.

Anne Morgan glanced at her husband, Jared, the source of the thundering sound. The salt air and sun had not been kind to his skin over the years, baking it until it was brown and leathery. Even so, he was ruggedly handsome. His blue eyes could still dance with that look of mischievous fun that first attracted her to him. And although his hair was white and thinning, he was still virile and full of life, a man not easily ignored.

Good, she thought. *Let him handle the boys this time.* Inwardly, she corrected herself. *Boys. They're hardly that. The*

*twins are over thirty now. Still, whenever they're in the same
room they invariably fight with each other like little boys.*

His orders unheeded, Jared gave a grunt, pushed himself
away from the table, and stood. The old sea captain was accustomed to barking orders from a standing position; to him, seated
orders carried no more weight than an invitation to tea.

As he stood, the heads of the Morgans' three dinner guests—
John Hancock, Dr. Samuel Cooper, and Sam Adams—swiveled
from the combatants to Jared, then back to the combatants again.
They wore an amusing assortment of expressions. Hancock's
eyes were half-closed in elevated detachment. Seated between
Anne and Mercy Morgan with his hands in his lap, he wore the
expression of a bored nobleman, the kind one might see on an
upper-class lord crossing the street to avoid a common street
brawl. On the other side of the table, closest to Jared, the
Reverend Samuel Cooper, dressed in the traditional black clothing with white cravat and clerical bands, was caught up in the
conflict. Unlike Hancock, his eyes were sharp and eager. With a
nod in Jared's direction he seemed to be encouraging his host to
exert his fatherly authority to quell the dispute. Of the three dinner guests, Sam Adams was closest to the fight. With Dr. Cooper
on his right and a standing Jacob Morgan on his left, the expression on Adams' face was almost comical. He looked like a little
boy in worn and stained brown clothes watching a circus act. His
eyes were wide and anxious, his mouth formed a silly grin. He
was relishing the fight. More than that, had the circumstances
been different, he clearly would have enjoyed rolling up his
sleeves and jumping into the fray.

"Jacob, listen to me! I'll not have you acting this way in front
of our guests!" Jared bellowed. "Esau, don't make me come down
there and separate the two of you!"

Anne stifled a smile—not at her husband's use of his "captain's

voice," but at his choice of words. Out of respect for the presence
of their minister, Jared's vocabulary was noticeably restrained.
Anne doubted he would have used these same words had he been
aboard ship, though he had never been one to use the foul language
so often associated with men of the sea. Just then an odd thought
struck her. Other than his restricted vocabulary, this wasn't anything
unusual for her husband. Having spent years aboard ships sailing to
and from China, living in cramped quarters for months at a time
with little or no privacy, certainly he'd been called upon to mediate
a fair amount of disagreements, squabbles, and brawls among his
crews. The difference tonight, however, was that these weren't
sailors who were scuffling—they were his sons; and their disagree-
ment wasn't aboard ship—it was at the dinner table in the presence
of several notable members of Boston society.

"Jacob! Did you hear me? Esau, I'm talking to you!"

*Separate commands, one for each boy. Good. Jared hasn't
forgotten.* From infancy it took separate commands to discipline
the twins. They had never been able to share anything, not even a
verb in a sentence. They had to be told separately to be quiet, to
quit hitting, to sit still and pay attention. Even then, getting them
to leave each other alone was always a monumental effort. Anne
knew. She'd had to do it often enough while her husband was
thousands of miles away at sea. But lately, they'd stopped heed-
ing her altogether. Once they began debating colonial rights, they
became delirious with passion. It was like they were out of their
minds with fever. They said things they couldn't possibly mean.
Irrational, crazy things. Try as she might, there was nothing Anne
could do to break the fever's grip on them. And it scared her.

Tonight, however, Jared's volley of words broke through
and reached its mark. At the end of the table, Esau backed
away. He glanced at his father, then his mother. Anne shot him
a disapproving scowl, the kind naughty boys get from their

mothers when they misbehave. To Anne it didn't matter that he was a fully grown man. *The boys are acting like children; they deserve to be treated like children!*

Esau apologized to their guests. "Forgive me if I've offended you," he said. He took his seat.

Jacob didn't budge. He remained frozen at the corner of the table, hands clenched, towering menacingly over his twin brother.

"I said, sit down, son!" Jared balled his own hands into fists, placing them on the table and leaning on them in the direction of his unrepentant son.

Opposite Jacob, seated next to Hancock, sat Mercy, Jacob's wife. To this point she had shown little interest in the brotherly spat. She'd seen it hundreds of times before. While Jared, Anne, and the three dinner guests suspended their meal pending the outcome of the standoff, Mercy helped herself to a second portion of veal and happily carved it. Now that Esau was seated and Jacob was the sole recipient of his parents' displeasure, Mercy swallowed a bit of meat and said dryly, "Jacob, dear, do sit down. You're spoiling the party."

For an agonizing minute Jacob Morgan clenched and unclenched his fists. Then, without taking his eyes off his brother, he lowered himself into his chair. Not until he was fully seated did he look away. When he did, he let out a snort of disgust.

At the head of the table, the host pulled himself upright. He stood tall for several seconds—a signal to his sons not to act up again. Then he offered apologies to his guests and everyone resumed eating. No one looked up. The only sound heard at the dinner table was the clink and scrape of silver utensils against china plates.

The dinner had been arranged the previous Sunday. Following the worship service, Dr. Cooper pulled Jared aside. Citing the need for privacy, the minister led Jared to a small room where, to the sea captain's surprise, Hancock and Adams were waiting for them. His surprise stemmed from the fact that these two highly visible revolutionaries were still in the city. Adams had frequently been warned by friends that he was in danger of being seized by British military authorities, clapped in irons, and taken to England to be tried as a rebel. It had been rumored that Adams and Hancock had fled Boston.

After Jared exchanged brief pleasantries with the two men, Dr. Cooper took charge of the gathering. He requested that Jared meet with the three of them within the week to discuss something of the utmost importance. Cooper didn't allude to the subject matter, and Jared trusted his pastor enough that he didn't ask. Jared invited the three men to join him for dinner on Wednesday. Adams and Hancock looked anxiously to Cooper. They were concerned for their safety. Cooper gave them an assuring nod, and the meeting was set.

It wasn't until later when Jared informed Anne of the arrangement that he learned of Esau's unexpected presence for dinner that same night. While Jacob and Mercy Morgan shared the large Boston mansion with Jared and Anne, Esau lived in Cambridge at the Morgan family's home on the Charles River. When Anne learned he had business in Boston that Wednesday, she invited him to come for dinner.

Given the difficulty of un-inviting people, Jared and Anne proceeded with their dinner plans, hoping their sons would behave themselves. The problem, as Jared saw it, was Adams. He was the hero of the Sons of Liberty—men like Jacob—and the bane of loyalists—men like Esau. To forestall preliminary hostilities, Jacob and Esau were told nothing more than the family was expecting additional guests that night. When John Hancock and Sam Adams appeared rather mysteriously through a rear entryway, Jacob was elated. Esau was furious.

At the table, Anne stole a glance at her husband as he lifted a crystal goblet to his lips. She and Jared had come so far since the night he climbed the tree outside her bedroom window in Cambridge and clandestinely listened to her sing love songs. Back then things were so simple. They were young, idealistic, foolishly in love. They owned nothing. Jared had few interests and even fewer prospects for a profession. Now look at him. He was one of the richest merchants in Boston. Leading citizens—on both sides of the colonial conflict—sought his advice. God had been good to them.

The very house in which they lived was a testimony to God's grace in their lives. Once the property of a mortal enemy, it became Jared and Anne's love nest. The reminder of those uncertain days caused Anne to shudder involuntarily. It was true God had delivered them from their enemies, but the price of victory was high. It had cost Jared's father his life. Daniel Cole, a ruthless merchant, had had Benjamin Morgan killed in an attempt to gain control of the Morgan family's meager investment shares in his company. When that attempt failed, the greedy merchant deceived the dead man's wife—Jared's mother, Constance—into marrying him. It took the united effort of Jared; his older brother, Philip; and sister, Priscilla, to defeat the scheming merchant, but not before losing nearly everything they owned. Ironically, it was Cole's death that had restored their fortune with added measure. To protect his business from hostile takeover attempts, Daniel Cole had placed all of his holdings in his wife's name. When he died, Constance turned over all his assets to her children.

Jared and Priscilla parlayed Cole's money into a substantial family empire through the China trade. Priscilla orchestrated the business while Jared sailed the ships. Philip—returning to the Narragansett Indian reservation to marry his sweetheart—chose to be a silent partner. He used his portion of the family income for missionary enterprises among receptive Indian tribes.

Following their wedding, at Constance Morgan Cole's request, Jared and Anne shared the spacious mansion formerly owned by Daniel Cole. It was here that the twins were born. And it was here, when the twins were fifteen years old, that the Lord called Constance Morgan home to heaven.

Over the years, Jared and Anne redecorated the house to reflect their interests and successes. The huge pewter kettle that once hung garishly over the front door—a testimonial to Cole's wealth made through the pewter industry—was the first thing to go. Room by room the mansion became less of a legacy to an ostentatious, greedy merchant and more of a personal museum testifying to Jared's world travels.

In the dining room, the Morgans and their guests sat at a Chippendale table made of imported mahogany. The dinner setting included crystal from Waterford, old English silver, and fine porcelain plates from China. Silver candlesticks adorned each end of the table, while a crystal chandelier illuminated the center from high overhead. Immediately behind Anne's side of the table was a fireplace, which featured several Chinese porcelain vases on its mantel. The vases provided a balance for the portrait on the wall, that of Sir Amos Morgan, a heroic English seaman who had distinguished himself in the battle against the great Spanish Armada during the days of Queen Elizabeth. The admiral, Jared learned during a trip to London, was an ancestor of his through Drew Morgan. Jared was quite fond of the portrait. He shared a love of the sea with his ancestor. And though he would have brushed aside the thought, he and the admiral had something else in common. Both were men of honor. While Sir Amos Morgan made a name for himself in Queen Elizabeth's court, Jared Morgan had established himself as a respected merchant in Boston. The three dinner guests at his table were evidence of his status. John Hancock was possibly the wealthiest man in the city,

Dr. Cooper was a respected man of God, and Sam Adams was a powerful politician. Jared sat comfortably among them.

Hancock was the first to break the uneasy silence following the twins' outburst. "If it's any comfort, madam," Hancock dabbed the corner of his mouth with a napkin as he turned and addressed Anne, "your sons merely reflect the turmoil presently in Boston." Sensing a correction from Adams, Hancock hastened to add, "More correctly, in *all* the colonies, even as far south as Georgia. This, of course," he nodded in Adams' direction, "is due to the excellent work of Mr. Adams' committees of correspondence."

Adams graciously returned the nod without discontinuing his chewing.

Anne was not impressed with their display of mutual appreciation. "It gives me no comfort, sir," she replied softly. "I raised my sons to exhibit better manners at the dinner table, regardless of what all Boston—or the whole world for that matter—is doing. And quite frankly, the turmoil, as you so describe it, frightens me to death."

"But you will agree, my dear madam," Adams said, quickly swallowing a bite, "that this great debate is unavoidable. Our most sacred freedoms hang in the balance! Surely you can grasp the scope of what we are fighting for! The future of countless generations is at stake!"

Jared jumped into the conversation before Anne could respond. "I can assure you, gentlemen, that my wife is fully aware of the significance of what is happening. However, it seems to me, Mr. Adams, that you have already concluded that our fellow countrymen in England will acquiesce to our demands—something they have been most reluctant to do. Or are you suggesting that our colonial militia is strong enough to force our will upon Parliament? If that is the case, I urge caution. For I fear that if we fail, our situation will be far worse than it is presently."

Anne placed her hand on top of Jared's. "Dear husband, I believe Mr. Adams was addressing me." Turning to Adams she said, "As for my position in this great debate, as you call it, I have not yet come to a conclusion as to which side I favor, although it has claimed a large portion of my prayers as of late. However, my position regarding family dining is well defined—there shall be no debating politics here. This table is my haven from this great storm. And I intend to defend my tiny island of peace with every fiber of my being. Surely, Mr. Adams, you can grasp the importance of what I am fighting for!"

Adams conceded to his hostess with a smile. "Rarely do I hear opinions stated with such clarity, madam. Consider your island safe from political intrusion."

The conversation at the table fell silent once again, and Anne shooed away a twinge of guilt like she would a fly. It wasn't like her to reprimand guests. But she wasn't going to let these men who were turning Boston upside down do the same thing to her household.

The political differences between England and her American colonies loomed over every aspect of life in Boston. Like an avalanche, it threatened to sweep up everyone and everything in its path. Anne knew she couldn't stop it, but that didn't mean she was going to abandon her family to the inevitable without a fight. But hers was a losing battle, and she was growing weary of it.

At first, while Jared was at sea, Anne Morgan refused to allow the boys to discuss colonial grievances anywhere in the house. Then, upon Jared's return as he got caught up in events, she was forced to give ground. Still, she succeeded in persuading them to confine their arguments to Jared's study. This lasted less than a week. The debate soon spilled into the hallway, then the sitting room, and the dinner table, where she took her final stand. She'd lost the house to the insanity, but she refused to surrender the dinner table. And until tonight, the boys and Jared had conceded to her this tiny island. Tonight, however, the shadow of the avalanche threatened Anne Morgan's final refuge.

Anne looked down the table at her sons. It wasn't the debate that frightened her; it was the hatred behind the words. What would happen to her sons when the debaters exchanged their words for musket balls? It wouldn't be Mr. Adams or Mr. Hancock or Dr. Cooper who would line up against the British regulars. It would be Jacob and Esau. And what about Jared? Could he stay out of the fight? She doubted it. Her husband was not one to sit idle in a time of crisis. He'd always been an active man with an adventurous life. Somehow, even though he was past his sixtieth year, he would find a way to get involved. So let Masters Hancock, Cooper, and Adams think her an unkind hostess.

"Well, I, for one, am grateful that Anne has rescued us from this *dreadful* discussion!" The sprightly voice came from the far side of Hancock. "After all, gentlemen," said Mercy Morgan in a playful tone, "you all should know there are certain things one does not do at a dinner party. Did you forget what you were taught as young lads?"

With a mischievous smile Mercy straightened herself in her chair, sitting dramatically prim and proper. Not until she was certain all eyes were upon her did she launch into a recitation that was familiar to all Boston schoolboys:

"Never sit down at the table till asked," she shook a dainty finger in lecture fashion, "and then only after the blessing! Ask for nothing; tarry till it be offered thee. Speak not. Bite not thy bread, but break it. Take salt only with a clean knife," she picked up her knife in demonstration, "dip not thy meat in the same." She gave a playful scowl. "Hold not thy knife upright but sloping, and lay it down at the right hand of the plate with the blade on the plate."

This was typical Mercy Reed Morgan. She loved to entertain and was most alive when she was the center of attention in a festive room filled with guests. Three years younger than the twins, she had caught their attention at a party. And, as in everything else, it became a contest between the boys who would win her favor—a contest that took on a life of its own, developing in ways no one could have foreseen from the outset.

Normally, Anne thought her silly. But tonight, Mercy's merriment was a welcomed distraction. Hancock particularly enjoyed her etiquette lecture. Smoothing the wrinkles from his black satin smallclothes and adjusting his white silk stockings from his knees down to his red morocco slippers, he adjusted his position to watch her performance. Dr. Cooper, on the other hand, looked only mildly amused. And Sam Adams paid scant attention to her. His preoccupied stare gave evidence to the fact that he was still engaged in the debate in his mind. Jared and the twins were all smiles. They never seemed to tire of Mercy. It was the expression on Esau's face that concerned Anne. He was still in love with Mercy. Anne could see it in his eyes. Although Jacob and Mercy had been married ten years, this wasn't the first time Anne had caught Esau longing for his brother's wife. She prayed that Jacob would not look in his brother's direction right now. For if he did, another fight would break out. She was sure of it.

Mercy continued her lecture. "Look not earnestly at any other person that is eating!" She lowered her head and shot coquettish glances at the guests. Hancock laughed hard and clapped his hands when she looked at him. "When moderately satisfied, leave the table." Mercy patted her waistline contentedly. "Sing not! Hum not! Wiggle not! Spit nowhere in the room but in the corner...."

At this, even Adams let out a guffaw.

Mercy looked pleased she'd won over the politician's attention. She demonstrated each succeeding exhortation with exaggerated expressions and movements. "Eat not too fast with greedy behavior! Eat not vastly but moderately. Make not a noise with thy tongue, mouth, lips, or breath in thy eating and drinking. Smell not thy meat, nor put it to thy nose. If thy meat offend thee, throw it not under the table!" Lifting the cloth, she tossed an imagined piece of meat under the Chippendale table. Her performance concluded, she folded dainty hands in her lap and assumed an angelic countenance, the practiced pose of a perfect lady.

John Hancock's enthusiastic applause prompted polite handclapping from the other dinner guests. Mercy accepted their applause with humility. It too was part of her act.

Next, Dr. Cooper did his part to provide a topic of discussion other than politics. "As you might expect," he said to Hancock and Adams, "Jared and Anne have an exquisite collection of porcelain from China. These plates, for example."

Dutifully, Adams and Hancock looked past the veal and vegetables on their plates at the design. The enameled porcelain plates were white with red, turquoise, and black enamel designs painted over the glaze. Pagodas adorned the center of the plates drawn in black atop a blue wash. Around the rim of each plate four similar pagoda sketches were separated by square cartouches painted in red, each containing indecipherable inscriptions. Although china had generally replaced pewter at most tables in Boston for special occasions, the Morgans' china was among the finest in the city.

"Lovely," Adams said.

The wealthy Hancock studied his plate but looked unimpressed.

"Anne!" Dr. Cooper said excitedly. "Show them your vase … you know, the robin's egg one."

Anne looked to her husband. He nodded.

Moments later she returned cradling a delicate porcelain

vase. It was almost two feet tall with a narrow, bottlelike neck. The sides extended from the neck with a broad sweep falling gently inward at the base.

"It's called Shiwan ware," Jared said. "It's Anne's favorite piece."

If Hancock was unimpressed with the plates, he was mesmerized by the vase. It had a finely sparkled blue and lavender glaze that pulsated with color, looking very much like ...

"A robin's egg," Dr. Cooper said, smiling broadly, "just as I said."

"May I?" Hancock rose and held out his hands.

Anne gently passed the vase to him. For several moments he turned it 'round and 'round, admiring the dance of colors beneath the glaze. His appreciative appraisal pleased Anne.

Samuel Adams leaned toward Dr. Cooper and whispered. Cooper nodded.

"My dear Mrs. Morgan," Dr. Cooper said rising from his seat, "as usual, you have been a wonderful hostess. Although we'd love to enjoy the pleasure of your company longer, Mr. Adams and Mr. Hancock have pressing business." To Jared he said, "May we retire to your study?"

Hancock handed the vase back to its owner. The appreciative wonder in his eyes was gone, replaced by the hardened look of a man about to transact business. The other men rose from the table simultaneously and filed after Jared into his study, leaving only Mercy and Anne.

Mercy gave her mother-in-law a wry grin and left the room.

Cradling her porcelain vase, Anne Morgan stood over a table littered with bits of uneaten veal, mutton, and a smattering of vegetables. Puddles of drink rested at the bottom of crystal goblets. She was not fooled by the men's claim to pressing business. It was nothing more than an infantile excuse to continue the debate. As if to confirm her assessment, the sound of angry voices drifted from behind the closed door of Jared's study—the debate had resumed with full intensity. Anne hugged the vase to her breast. Her momentary peace was nothing more than a fragile illusion, infinitely more fragile than the vase in her arms. Despite her most determined efforts she knew the avalanche would rumble through her house and sweep away Jared and her sons.

It was then that the full impact of what was to happen hit her, bringing with it a horrible, sickening feeling. She struggled to maintain her composure, not to give in to her fears, to tell herself that there was still hope. But no amount of reasoning could dispel the fear. Just like the fear that masqueraded as a monster under her bed when she was a little girl, this one was impervious to reason. She couldn't chase it away. And the longer she stood there, the stronger it became. Anne began to weep as her fear took shape. Unwanted details added to its chilling power over her. She didn't know how; she didn't know when; but somehow she knew, she just knew that this was the last time her family would all sit at the same table together. The avalanche would claim a life. Maybe more than one.

Anne sniffed angrily. She told herself it was just a feeling. It had no substance. But she didn't believe herself.

2

In some ways, Jared Morgan's study was no different from other merchants' studies in Boston. Books lined the walls, encased in elegantly carved cabinet shelves with glass-paneled doors; a small desk with a variety of papers protruding from rows of cubbyholes was pushed against one wall near a window; a sofa and several covered chairs were gathered into an informal group slightly off center in the middle of the room; and a chandelier with eight candles served as the main source of light after dark. Personal treasures included the family Bible, displayed in open fashion on a small mahogany table, and a chessboard and pieces set in the ready on an end table. The game once belonged to Jared's first sea captain, a man by the name of Devereaux, commander of the pirate ship *Dove*. He thought he'd lost it forever when the *Dove* sank, only to receive it years later as a present from his fellow tar James Magee, who had managed to salvage it. It was difficult even now—over four decades later—for Jared to hold the watermarked pieces of the game without getting nostalgic, or emotional, or both.

What made Jared's study unique was that it had a distinctly

Chinese flavor. The wallpaper had a green tint to it, featuring tree branches, bamboo shoots, and leaves. There were porcelain figurines scattered about—a dragon roared atop one end table while a pair of Chinese warriors graced the fireplace mantel. In addition to the figurines, a variety of porcelain bowls and vases was lying about, also from China.

As the English colonials debated their relationship with the mother country, Chinese emperor Ch'ien-lung seemed to preside over the clash from on high. Leaning against the fireplace mantel, Jared glanced up at the portrait. It was a gift from a fellow merchant—Jared's counterpart in China. The man in the picture was seated. He wore a long red robe with enormous sleeves that completely hid his arms and hands, which were resting comfortably on his rather substantial midsection. The emperor sported a black mustache that cascaded past his lips and fell well beyond his chin. Another dangling growth of hair protruded from his chin like a stalactite. The emperor's eyes hid behind narrow slits that, along with thin black eyebrows, plunged at a steep angle toward the bridge of his nose. His expression was solemn, befitting his royalty. The fourth emperor of the Ching dynasty, he was the present ruler of China.

Jared wondered what the Chinese emperor would do to men in his kingdom if they were discovered plotting against him.

"I strongly disagree!" Adams shouted. "Parliament has made its intentions clear. They want nothing less than to enslave us!" He stood opposite Esau with one hand on his hip and the other making his point. The extended finger shook from palsy.

The sides of the debate were uneven. Esau alone argued the loyalist position against four revolutionaries. For the time being, Jared remained neutral, a position that was becoming increasingly difficult to maintain.

The scene before him was more of a political mugging than a

debate. Hancock, Cooper, and Jacob had already taken their turns attacking Esau. Now it was Adams' turn. Jared couldn't help but be proud of his Oxford-educated son, even though he didn't share all of Esau's opinions. Though the boy was holding his own against superior odds, at the moment he was facing his toughest opponent. Sam Adams was an experienced debater and one of the city's toughest politicians. When it came to promoting the Whig agenda for independence, Adams was Boston's champion. Dispensing with reason, he was a master at enflaming the emotions of the populace. More succinctly, he was a political arsonist. His tools were biting wit and caustic commentary.

Looking at Adams, you wouldn't have guessed he was a powerful political force. He was a plain man of middling stature with a strong Roman nose, who looked like he could use a new set of clothing. Others in Boston and England were less kind in their assessment of him. One American painter who knew Adams well was said to have remarked that if he wished to draw a picture of the Devil himself he would get Sam Adams to sit for him. Of course, Adams' enemies circulated this anecdote freely.

The remaining revolutionaries in the room arrayed themselves behind their champion. Hancock slouched in a chair, his fingers forming a steeple, the tip of which tapped his lips. Dr. Cooper sat stiffly at one end of the fruitwood sofa, the other end previously occupied by the standing Adams. Jacob leaned forward on the edge of his chair, ready to spring to Adams' defense should he require it. Jared doubted the veteran politician would need Jacob's help.

"For eleven years Parliament has treated us shamefully!" Adams shouted. "I believe the most rancorous envy and venom swells in the veins of those tyrants of London. It's a well-known fact that extreme corruption is prevalent among all orders of men in that old rotten state! And that corruption stands in contrast to the glorious public virtue that has been proudly demonstrated in every colony of our rising country. Parliament has made it clear that they regard the American colonies as nothing more than a ready source of revenue. That makes us slaves, working this great land for their profit! Well I, for one, will tolerate it no longer! We are freemen! And I will do all that is within my power to keep that corrupt nation from dragging us to ruin with them!"

Dr. Cooper pounded the sofa's arm in agreement. "Here! Here!" he cried. Hancock nodded solemnly. Jacob smiled triumphantly.

Despite being outnumbered, Esau showed no sign of surrendering ground to the more experienced debater. Even as a boy Esau had always thought for himself. He examined both sides of an issue, drew his own conclusions, then acted upon them regardless of what anyone else was doing or what they thought or said of him. It was a trait that served him well in his youth, keeping him from the more foolish predicaments in which his friends and brother often found themselves. But Jared feared that the same self-determination that had served Esau so well in his youth might be his downfall as a British loyalist. Passion ruled the streets. Individualism was not in fashion. And heaven help any man or woman who did not readily join the prevailing opinion.

Esau squared his shoulders in response to Adams. He was more plump than his twin brother, spending a majority of his time hunched over ledgers while Jacob worked all day on the wharf. Both boys had thick brown hair, bushy eyebrows, broad noses, and clefts in their chins. Neither wore facial hair. And while Esau wore silk suits and powdered wigs, Jacob was more comfortable in leather breeches with his natural hair tied back. Generally, Esau's eyes were softer and more pensive; Jacob had the flashing eyes of a zealot. Tonight, however, it was Esau's eyes that were flashing as he responded to Adams' interpretation of Parliament's intentions.

"Do you think, sir, that Great Britain is an old, wrinkled, withered, worn-out hag, that every scoundrel that walks the street may insult with impunity? You will find her a vigorous maiden and with spirit and strength sufficient to chastise her undutiful and rebellious children. I have recently returned from England, sir, and can truthfully say that your measures have yet to produce your desired results—Great Britain is not intimidated. She has already a considerable fleet and army in America; more ships and troops are expected soon; every appearance indicates a design in her to support her claim to maintain control of the colonies with vigor."

Placing one foot in front of the other, Esau moved into an attacking posture. "Consider, sir," he said, "is it right to risk the valuable blessings of property, liberty, and life to the single chance of war? Of the worst kind of war—a civil war? A civil war founded on rebellion? Without ever attempting the peaceable mode of accommodation? Without ever asking a redress of our complaints from the only power on earth who can redress them? When disputes happen between nations independent of each other, they first attempt to settle them with ambassadors; they seldom run hastily to war till they have tried what can be done by treaty and mediation. I would make many more concessions to a parent that were justly due him, rather than engage with him in a duel! But we are rushing into a war with our parent state without offering the least concession, without even deigning to propose an accommodation. You, sir, have employed your pen and exercised your abilities in recommending measures which you know must, if persisted in, have a direct tendency to produce and accelerate this dreadful event. May God forgive you. And may He give you repentance and a better mind!"

Instantly Jacob was on his feet, demanding that Esau apologize to Adams. It took Adams and both his friends to keep Jacob from doing violence to his brother. After several tense moments Jacob was persuaded to return to his seat.

Jared shook his head and sighed softly. He found it ironic that his sons would have such passionate opinions on the current state of affairs while he remained so undecided. He'd spent many waking hours and several sleepless nights trying to figure out which side was right. On the one hand, he despised the capricious acts of Parliament that seemed intent on ruining the colonies. More than most men, he had every right to be angry. As a shipping merchant, his family had been hit doubly hard—taxed as consumers and restricted as suppliers. Yet on the other hand, armed revolt against his own country was unthinkable. He was an Englishman and proud of it. His many travels to other countries— the Caribbean, Africa, India, and China—merely confirmed his pride. In Jared's mind the British system, with all its flaws, was the best system of government in the world, and the thought of being a subversive, of plotting to overthrow his own government didn't sit well with him. Not at all.

Even so, how long could he defend his country's leaders when they enacted legislation that threatened the very existence of the colonies? If there was one point in which all Boston merchants were in agreement, it was this—something had to be done! But what? Should they follow Adams and take up arms? Jared was angry enough to fight, but reason argued against it. How could they win? Britain had the finest fighting force in the world; the colonies' army consisted of ragged, unkempt volunteers in loosely formed militias. Could they defeat the redcoats? It would take a miracle. And if they fought the redcoats and lost, what then? What measures would Parliament enact against the defeated colonies? Jared didn't like to think about it.

The very idea of armed resistance seemed so far-fetched, it bordered on the ridiculous. The colonies were notorious for their inability to get along with each other. If England's stabilizing force were removed, there would be anarchy! Every colony would form its own government, and soon America would be like Europe, a continent of countries continuously warring and feuding with one another.

And who would lead Boston? Sam Adams? Not likely. He and his kind were best at inciting unrest and revolution. With his rhetoric, Adams had stockpiled explosives throughout the colonies, and now he was lighting the match. But how does one stop a series of explosions once they're ignited? When the time came, could Adams and his friends stop the revolution they started? And then could they build a lasting peace and a stable government? Jared shook his head. When he thought of Sam Adams, peace and stability did not come readily to mind.

For Jared, armed resistance was shortsighted. It was easier to destroy a house than it was to build one. It was this fear of anarchy that kept him from embracing the colonial call to arms.

Jared's attention was pulled back to the debate as Esau leveled a steady finger at his brother while addressing Adams. "See what you're promoting? Violence! Well, let me tell you, Mr. Adams, your vitriolic generalizations regarding Parliament may work with the unlearned dockhands, but not with thinking men!"

The truth of Esau's statement hit a nerve, and the only thing that kept Jacob from charging out of his chair again was Adams, who, with outstretched hand, motioned for him to remain seated. It was common knowledge that Adams was most effective with laborers of limited education, men like Jacob and his coworkers.

While Esau had inherited his grandfather's love of learning and had an extensive education at Harvard and later at Oxford, Jacob disdained academics, preferring taverns and the company of dockworkers to campuses and academicians. In one respect this particular difference between the twins made life simpler for

Jared. He was able to employ both his sons in his merchant business yet keep them far apart from each other. Jacob worked on the docks. Esau assisted his Aunt Priscilla with the financial ledgers and company records.

"The simple facts are these, Mr. Adams," Esau continued. "Less than twenty years ago when the French and the Indians were threatening our colonies, we were quick to remind Parliament that we were Englishmen. They sent us supplies, munitions, and troops, without which we never could have survived the onslaught. If it were not for our fellow Englishmen across the sea, we would be speaking French today! That is, if we were still alive. And who paid the expense for these troops? Parliament! And who profited from the increased shipping traffic? Colonial merchants like Mr. Hancock and my family! And now that the war is over and England is on the brink of financial ruin, we turn our backs on them like ungrateful children. When they request we repay a portion of the war debt, what do we do? We take up arms against them! I ask you, Mr. Adams, does goodwill travel only one direction across the Atlantic? How can we as Englishmen in all good conscience hold out an open hand when we're in need, yet reply with a closed fist when we're asked to do our part for our country?"

Adams bristled at Esau's suggestion that England, not the colonies, was the wounded party in this dilemma. "Young man," he said, "this is not a matter of ingratitude. You use terms to describe Parliament that have little resemblance to the truth of the matter. Had Parliament treated us as Englishmen, we would have readily done our part and more! No, this is not a question of loyalty, it is a question of equal representation. Parliament did not request our aid, they demanded it. Without involving us in their discussions, they levied us with taxes. Like a cutpurse they reached into our pockets and took our money without so much as asking us for it! I ask you, sir, have we forfeited our right as Englishmen to representation simply because we live in New England? I say no! Do we currently enjoy the same rights that are enjoyed by other Englishmen? Again, no! The result? The representatives in Parliament have conspired to enact a series of laws exclusively applicable to us and not to them."

Adams' palsied fingers emerged one by one as he counted off colonial grievances:

"First, there was the Currency Act. With one stroke of the legislative pen Parliament ruled that our paper money was no longer legal tender. How are we to pay our debts if our money is no good? Then, knowing we have precious little gold or silver of our own, Parliament made it illegal to export bullion from England to America. The result? We are expected to assume a large portion of the war debt with a decreasing supply of money.

"Next, they passed the Sugar Act to raise more revenue. Raising revenue, of course, is well within their right. But did they also have to abrogate our rights as Englishmen to enforce the action by substituting crown-appointed judges for juries, and declaring suspected violators guilty until proven innocent? You see, young man, it's not a matter of money, it's a matter of citizenship. We're losing our rights as English citizens."

Esau began to say something, but Adams held up his hand and stopped him.

"I'm not finished," he said. "Then there was the Stamp Act, the heaviest blow of all. It required that every legal document must bear a registered seal. Of course, we were expected to pay a fee to have this official seal affixed to our documents—another tax! This tax applied to newspapers, pamphlets, almanacs, playing cards, and dice. Did we have any voice in the law that levied this tax? No! It was something Parliament did to us. And if we object to this law? The act stipulated that we would be tried—not by a

jury of our peers—but by a government-appointed judge! And so
we were stripped of another right of citizenship."

Adams held up a fourth finger. "Next came the Quartering Act
declaring that our public inns, alehouses, unused buildings, and
barns could be used by troops without our consent. Immediately
following the bill's passage, Parliament pulled all English troops
from the western regions and filled our cities with them. Our
cities are bulging with the increased military presence, and once
more, we had no voice in this decision."

Adams' thumb was used for the fifth point. "Then new taxes
were levied on glass, lead, paints, paper, and tea. We were
informed these products could be imported only from England
and duties had to be paid in silver or gold."

Another hand and another finger (this one was raised with a
smile). "Of course, then there was the Tea Act in which
Parliament passed legislation to save the struggling East India Tea
Company at our expense. In effect, Parliament attempted to
establish a monopoly by favoring those merchants who could
pass their loyalty test. Of course, we didn't let them and that tea
is now at the bottom of the harbor."

"A shameful affair!" Esau burst in. "Didn't you realize that by
your thinly disguised Indian raid you would force the king's hand
when you dumped the tea into the harbor? When we resort to
anarchy, turmoil, and bloodshed, we're admitting to the civilized
world that we're unable to manage our own affairs! I was in
England when the king responded to your unconscionable tea
party. Have you heard his response? To quote him: 'We must master them or totally leave them to themselves and treat them as
aliens.'"

"I prefer he do the latter," Adams said with a smirk.

"Can't you see what your ill-considered acts of anarchy have
done?" It was Esau's turn to raise fingers. "One, as punishment,

Boston's port has been closed to all shipping until the East India Company has been compensated for its tea and the required duty on it has been paid. Two, the governor's powers have been increased so that at his discretion he can ban public meetings. Three, officials charged with crimes of violence will be shipped to England for trial. Fourth, now troops not only have the right to occupy taverns and empty buildings, but private homes as well! Mr. Adams, your acts of violence have backfired! You have not made things better for us, you've made them worse! We haven't regained our rights, we've lost more!"

A wide smile crossed Sam Adams' lips. It was genuinely warm with no trace of rancor or ill will. "It is evident you will not be one of my converts tonight, Mr. Morgan," he said. "All I can say in my defense is that I pray daily that heaven will guide our course through these troubled waters."

An unsmiling Esau replied: "To quote Mr. Locke—whom you revolutionaries seem to revere so highly—'He that appeals to heaven must be sure that he has right on his side.'"

Cooper rose, stood close to Jared, and said in a low tone, "There's still the matter of business to discuss and"—nodding slightly toward Esau—"I'm afraid it's rather confidential."

"Esau, Jacob," Jared said, "if you'll excuse us."

"Jacob can stay, if he wishes," Cooper whispered.

Jared shook his head. "It's better this way." He held the study door open for his sons. Esau bowed politely to each of the guests. When he reached the doorway, his father stopped him. "Will you be returning to Cambridge tonight?" he asked.

Esau nodded. "A new student is moving into the house, a truly gifted lad. I promised to be there when he arrived."

One of the first victories Jared, Philip, and Priscilla had over their nemesis Daniel Cole was to repurchase their family home in Cambridge along the Charles River. Even though Philip chose to live among the Narragansetts and Priscilla and Jared had houses in Boston, they decided to keep the house on the Charles in the family. It was Philip's suggestion to use it as lodging for select students from Harvard. It seemed a fitting tribute to their father, Benjamin Morgan, who had been a tutor at the college for many years. The house was well equipped with a library, and each student had a separate room complete with desk for study. The Morgans hired a staff consisting of a cook, a maid, a groundskeeper, and a tutor whose duties included supervising the boys in residence. Esau managed the estate for the family. He kept a room there as well as one in Boston. When his time allowed it, he loved nothing more than to involve himself in the students' late-night discussions as they prepared for exams.

"We're scheduled to meet with Priscilla tomorrow afternoon to go over the books. Will you be back in time?"

"My business in Cambridge will be brief." Esau said goodnight to his father and left.

Jacob's departure was delayed by Sam Adams. Jared stood in the doorway and waited for him. Adams held Jacob's arm just above the elbow and was whispering in his ear. Jacob was nodding in understanding.

Just then a flurry of movement at the end of the hallway caught Jared's eye. Esau had reached the entryway. There was a rustle of skirts as a feminine arm reached out from the drawing room and pulled him in. He emerged a few moments later with a slight smile on his lips. The smile vanished as he glanced down the hallway toward the study. Esau said good-night again to his father and hurried out the front door. Mercy emerged from the drawing room. She nodded at Esau, said good-night, and hurried upstairs. Jared turned back into the study to find Jacob standing in front of him.

"Good-night, Father," Jacob said. His face had the look of

urgent business on it. He rushed past his father, down the hall, and out the door.

"I sent Jacob to the Green Dragon Inn," Adams said in way of explanation, though Jared didn't feel any was needed. "Some gentlemen are waiting for me there. Jacob was good enough to offer my apologies and explain the reasons for my delay."

Jared smiled inwardly at Adams' use of the word "gentlemen." The Green Dragon Inn was a popular meeting place for the Committee of Safety, an organization with an infamous reputation for very ungentlemanly-like conduct. Most members were common laborers, dockworkers, sailors, and the like. They were fond of revolution rhetoric, which Adams gave them in large doses, and fonder still of late-night activities such as hanging public figures in effigy, rousing public figures from their beds to harass them, and taking part in an occasional tar and feathering.

"Jared," Dr. Cooper placed his hand warmly on Jared's shoulder and spoke in fatherly tones, "quite simply we need your help."

"I'm listening," Jared said.

Dr. Cooper deferred to Adams for the actual request. The Boston politician cleared his throat, looked up at Jared, and said, "We need you to go to London and keep an eye on Franklin for us."

"*Benjamin* Franklin?"

Simultaneously, Jared's three dinner guests nodded.

3

The four men returned to the informal grouping of chairs. Adams and Hancock shared the sofa; Dr. Cooper and Jared occupied the two chairs facing the sofa.

"You want me to spy on Benjamin Franklin?"

"We don't want you to spy on anyone!" Dr. Cooper responded, his hands and arms swinging wide in a gesture of openness. "We need an objective observer in London. Someone who can keep us informed regarding the actions and mood of Parliament. And we believe you're the man for the job. It's as simple as that."

Objective observer. Jared mulled over the words. What they were asking him to do still sounded like spying to him. He shook his head, declining their request.

"Do you remember the scandal of a few years ago," Cooper asked, "the one when Governor Hutchinson's private letters became public?"

Jared nodded. "Stating his belief that well-born gentlemen should rule over the lower classes?"

"Precisely," Cooper affirmed. "If you'll also recall, the governor's comments prompted public demonstrations and unrest."

"And rightly so," Adams added emphatically, leaning forward, "because the comments threatened our rights to a representative government!"

"Hear! Hear!" Hancock added.

Cooper gave the zealots a stern look before continuing. "Although the revelation of the letters helped us publicly," he said, "they hurt us internally."

"How so?" Jared asked.

Dr. Cooper looked at Adams and Hancock on the sofa before responding. Jared got the impression that Cooper was about to reveal a piece of information that the three of them had not agreed to reveal before now. Adams nodded a single nod and Hancock fidgeted to get on with it, so Dr. Cooper pressed forward.

"The letters were obtained clandestinely by Franklin in England," he said.

Jared nodded. "That much I already know. It cost him much of his popularity in England and the office of postmaster general for the colonies."

"What you *don't* know ..." Hancock burst in impatiently.

Cooper's upraised hand cut him off. "What you don't know," he said, "is that Franklin stipulated specific conditions regarding the use of the letters. No copies were to be made, they were to be shown only to a few influential colonial friends, and the letters were to be returned to England."

"The contents of those letters had to be made public!" Adams thundered.

Jared was beginning to understand. It was Adams who read the incriminating letters to the Massachusetts House of Representatives. And it was Hancock who first claimed to have obtained a printed copy of the letters, which, for the sake of fairness and accuracy, were then compared with the originals.

Dr. Cooper continued with a soft, even tone. "Consequently, a rift has developed between us," nodding specifically at Adams with his head, "and Franklin. And we feel he is no longer a credible source of information for us. And more than ever, we need an accurate source of information in England. That's why we've come to you. You are a respected merchant both here and in England. All we want you to do is to go to England, offer your assistance to Dr. Franklin regarding colonial merchant interests, and report back to us the things you see and hear."

Having pleaded his case, Cooper sat back and awaited a response.

Jared Morgan rose from his chair and wandered over to a small round mahogany table that stood a few inches higher than his knees. The tips of his fingers played lightly on the table's edge as he gazed vacantly across the room, deep in thought. The three dinner guests followed his movement with their eyes, allowing him this moment of silence, quietly aware that there was no ready response to what they were asking him to do.

Jared's hand absentmindedly moved to the Bible that lay open atop the mahogany stand. It was the Morgan family Bible, brought over from England by his ancestor Drew Morgan in 1630. A coveted heirloom, it was the symbol of the Morgan family's faith. It seemed fitting that this Bible—which had seen so much history—was in the room at this moment. For Jared's answer to these men would determine the future history of the Morgans for generations to come.

The time for him to make a decision had come. He could avoid it no longer. Would the Morgans remain British, or would they side with the rebellion and commit themselves to an uncertain destiny?

Jared's fingers brushed across the Bible's pages, momentarily distracting him. This Bible had once been the property of the

infamous Bishop Laud of London. He had presented it to Drew
Morgan so they could send coded messages to one another while
working to expose and destroy nonconforming Puritans. Then
something happened that changed everything. God got hold of
Drew Morgan. His eyes were opened. For the first time he saw
clearly Laud's evil intentions compared to the sincere faith of the
villagers he was persecuting. In that moment, the Puritans gained a
convert and Bishop Laud lost an operative. And his Bible, the very
one that lay open on this table, the one that had once been used as
a tool for espionage, became Drew's guidebook for living and the
foundation of everything for which the Morgans stood.

When Drew fled to America, he brought the Bible with him.
Then, mysteriously, the Bible disappeared, along with Drew's son,
Christopher, who was a missionary to the Indians. The Bible was
forgotten. An entire generation of Morgans never even knew it
existed. Then by accident, Jared's father happened upon Drew
Morgan's diary, discovered in someone else's attic. The diary told
of the Bible's existence and its importance to the family. It
became Benjamin Morgan's personal quest to find the missing
Bible and return it to family hands. After much research, he
believed he knew the location of the missing keepsake.
Unfortunately, before he had a chance to test his theory, he was
murdered. Philip, Jared's older brother, took up his father's quest
and found not only the Bible, but also an aged Christopher
Morgan—Drew and Nell Morgan's firstborn son—still living
among the Indians. Philip fulfilled his father's dream of restoring
the Bible to the family. In a ceremony similar to the one in which
Drew gave the Bible to his son, Philip presented the Bible to
Jared, charging him with the responsibility of the Morgan's spiritual heritage. It was a responsibility that humbled Jared at the
time of the ceremony and still humbled him more than thirty
years later.

A white bone-lace cross rested snugly among the Bible's pages. It was the handwork of Drew's beloved wife, Nell. Born and raised in the little village of Edenford, it was there she and Drew met and fell in love.

A sudden realization brought Jared back to the present. This current crisis wasn't the first time the Morgans were at odds with British authorities. *What would Drew Morgan think of all this talk of revolution?* Jared wondered. *Would he do what Cooper and Adams and Hancock were asking him to do?*

"I'm not a politician, nor am I a lawyer," Jared said. "And I know nothing of the procedures of Parliament. I'd be lost."

"Not necessary," Adams replied. "All you have to do is listen, observe, and report back. We'll know what is important and what is not."

"It won't work. Franklin won't confide in a man he's never met."

As an intimate friend of Franklin's for years, Dr. Cooper offered to write a letter of introduction. The letter would state the reasons for Jared's presence in London; namely, to represent the merchant's point of view and to assist Franklin in his duties out of consideration for his age and failing health.

Again Jared objected. "I'm only three years younger than Franklin."

"Age itself is not the issue," Hancock replied. "You're in much better health than Franklin. Besides, your age might prove beneficial, Franklin might more readily confide in someone closer to his own age."

The room fell silent. Jared's gaze fell once again upon the Bible on the mahogany table. He could feel the eyes of Cooper, Adams, and Hancock on his back.

"I'm your friend and your minister," Dr. Cooper said softly. "We wouldn't be asking you to do this if it weren't vitally important to the survival of our country." A pause emphasized his last two words. *Our country.* Not England. The three men in Jared's study no longer considered themselves Englishmen. "Jared, it's time you decided which side of this conflict you're on."

Again there was silence.

Which would he be—an English patriot or an American patriot? Jared's fingers flipped the pages of the Bible. Book names flashed before him—Exodus, Numbers, Joshua, 1 Chronicles, Psalms. And Jared knew what he had to do.

The family Bible had given him the answer that to this point had been so elusive. Jared didn't find his answer in any particular text, but in the panorama of history represented in the accumulated books of the Old Testament. The books that flashed before him were united in a single theme: freedom. It was for freedom that God led the Israelites out of Egyptian bondage. And this theme was not restricted to the Old Testament. Didn't Jesus preach in a synagogue, announcing that He came to set the prisoners free? And what of Paul's impassioned epistle to the Galatians? Didn't he teach that it is for freedom that Christ had set believers free? And, if Jared remembered correctly, the apostle also included a warning to believers not to allow themselves to become enslaved again. Freedom! It was God's will that His people live in a land of freedom.

All the elements on the mahogany table seemed to confirm Jared's answer with a resounding *Amen.* It was for freedom of religion that Drew Morgan fled to America carrying this very Bible. It was for freedom from bondage to sin and death that Jesus died on the cross—so elegantly symbolized by Nell's cross of lace. The Bible on the table spoke to Jared Morgan in a clear voice. Its singular message was freedom. The cry of God's people from the straw pits of Egypt. Freedom. God's plan for His people from the beginning of time. Freedom. The foundation of the Morgan family's spiritual heritage. Freedom. In a soft, almost inaudible voice, Jared said, "All right. I'll go to England."

When Jared told Anne he was sailing immediately for London, she didn't say a word. That's how he knew she was angry.

After seeing his guests to the front door, Jared climbed the stairs to the second-floor bedroom. The covers on the four-poster Chippendale bed were turned down. It was unoccupied. Anne, dressed for bed, sat at a small desk in the corner of the room.

The unadorned, natural beauty of his wife never failed to stir him. The vision of her loveliness had been his sole comfort for countless nights at sea. Anne's soft red hair fell loosely over her shoulders; the fair complexion of her cheeks and hands reflected the flicker of the candle that provided illumination for her writing. Even as a mature woman, Anne's face had maintained the innocence of youth. However, as Jared discovered more than once over the years, it was a mistake to equate her look of innocence with a lack of determination or will. She was a thin woman of medium height and a wonderful mind. The best times of Jared's life were spent with her. That's why it was so difficult for him to tell her he was leaving.

Several loose sheets of paper lay scattered randomly under the sheet upon which Anne was writing. Candles at the desk's corners cast crisscrossing shadows across the pages. The scratching of quill against paper was the only sound in the room. This was Anne's favorite time of day—between dinner and bedtime. It was this time she set aside for her poetry.

It hadn't always been this way. Her writing at night was a practice born of fear. Over the many years Jared was away at sea, even before they were married when Anne lived with Jared's sister, Priscilla, night was a fearful time for Anne. It was at night—after the last of the good-nights was said and before sleep overcame her—that Anne felt most vulnerable, most alone, most afraid. For a while she tried delaying the nightly fear by prolonging her conversations with Priscilla. This proved to be an inadequate solution to her problem. How many nights a week can one talk to the point of exhaustion? So Anne tried another tack. She tried hastening sleep by jumping into bed, slamming her eyes shut, and forcing herself to escape from the world of fear and darkness into the world of dreams, only to find that the border between waking and sleeping was impervious to direct assault.

That's when she had a revelation. She realized that those who sought sleep rarely found it, yet those who tried to escape sleep's grasp were inevitably overcome by it. Like a warrior who just discovered his enemy's secret hideout, Anne devised a plan to use sleep's own fickle nature to trap it.

Each night she would prop herself up in bed with a tall stack of books on the nightstand, determined to stay awake and read through the night. With vigor she would launch into the pages. It wasn't long before she would feel the tug of drowsiness on her arms pulling the book down. Her plan was working. Like a sparrow perched on the bedpost, sleep was near. Her next step required caution and patience, lest she frighten it away.

Propping her book against bent legs, she ignored sleep. She continued reading. She read until she could no longer remember anything in the previous paragraph and the words on the page were no more than meaningless smudges of ink. From the bedpost to the covers, sleep was inching toward her. But Anne knew better than to make any rash movements now. Many people, fooled at this point, think that sleep is about to overtake them. So they set aside their book and put out the candle, only to find themselves moments later fully awake in the darkness with sleep having flown off into some corner, perched high and out of reach, mocking them.

Anne wasn't going to let sleep play this game with her. It was her plan to make sleep want her so badly, it would have to swoop down and forcibly carry her away. She continued reading.

She read aloud, speaking the words until her lips mumbled incoherently. She waved sleep away, struggled in its clutches, fought if off, until finally, it overcame her. This was how Anne Morgan tricked sleep into overpowering her on the long, lonely nights when Jared was at sea.

After a while, Anne discovered she could achieve the same goal by writing instead of reading. One night while reading the Bible, specifically the Psalms, an idea for a poem came to her. Wanting to capture the idea before it got away, she rose and scribbled her thoughts on a piece of paper. Satisfied she'd recorded enough of the thought for her to remember it the next day, she returned to bed only to realize that although she was finished with the idea for the night, the idea was not finished with her. As she lay in bed, several new insights occurred to her, but before she got up to write them down, sleep waylaid her. For several long moments, she fought it off. But, true to its nature, the more she fought sleep, the greater was its power until finally she succumbed. The next day when she attempted to recollect her unrecorded thoughts, she discovered that they were gone forever.

A poem was lost, but from the experience a nightly habit was formed. Anne learned that by working on her poetry before bedtime, her work drew her spirit closer to God and closer to her absent husband. Writing poetry quieted her spirit to such an extent, she no longer needed to resort to trickery to get to sleep. Warmed by her thoughts of God and her love, she found she could slip across sleep's borders with little effort. This hour of writing before retiring became her most productive time. So she continued the practice even when Jared was home.

It was this special time that Jared interrupted with his disquieting news that he was sailing for England. Anne lay down her pen. Her face was expressionless as she weighed with apprehension the prospect of another long stretch of nights alone. She rose and walked to the window beside the bed overlooking the garden, her back to Jared.

"Anne, can't we at least discuss this?"

With a thud, Jared's sea chest pounded the floor behind him, delivered to the room by a house servant. Sensing the mood in the room, the young black slave made a hasty departure.

Anne turned and stared at the sea chest. "What's there to discuss? You've already made your decision. Have a pleasant journey, Captain." She turned back to the window.

"It's not like that at all, Anne," Jared said. He paused, hoping she would ask him to elaborate. She didn't. So he elaborated anyway. "I know I promised to stay home after my last trip. And I meant it. But I didn't anticipate this development. This is different!"

He paused again. Still, she didn't bite.

"It's different," he explained, "because I'm not going as a captain, I'll be a passenger. It's not a company trip, it's a diplomatic trip."

Anne's curiosity was aroused. She turned to face him. She had assumed that Dr. Cooper, Adams, and Hancock came to ask Jared to ship munitions and powder from the Caribbean to the colonies for the anticipated rebellion. It was no secret that militias throughout the colonies were stockpiling weapons and supplies in little towns like Medford and Concord. Last September General Gage's troops had marched to Medford and seized the munitions stored there. Word around the docks was that the Committee of Safety was looking to increase the number of munitions shipments to replace what was lost.

When Jared first spoke of England, Anne knew her assumption about munitions shipments had been incorrect, but she was so angry about his leaving again, the destination really didn't matter. But Jared's role in the trip intrigued her.

"A diplomat?" she said.

Jared suppressed a smile. He had her attention, that was all. Now he had to convince her that the trip was unavoidable. "More specifically, an aide to Dr. Franklin."

"That doesn't make sense. Why you?" she asked. "You're a ship's captain, not a diplomat."

Her comment bruised Jared's professional ego. He considered pointing out that being a ship's captain required a great deal of diplomatic skill—initiating and maintaining good relationships with suppliers, negotiating contracts with sailors and arbitrating their differences at sea, appeasing port officials, and so on. But convincing her of his qualifications wasn't the task at hand. So he simply said, "Dr. Franklin is more than able to handle the diplomacy. I will assist him in matters related specifically to merchants."

A thin smile broke across Anne's face. She looked impressed. "I didn't know you knew Dr. Franklin," she said.

"I don't."

"Then why did he request you to be his aide?"

Jared looked down and wet his lips. "He didn't. Dr. Cooper, a good friend of his, thought I could be of service to him." He shrugged. "I know it doesn't make sense, but I really can't say more than I already have. Believe me, should things get worse here in Boston it's better that you don't know all that's going on."

Anne's smile faded. Her hands drew up to her waist in anger, one hand alternately rubbing the other. She resented it when men treated women like children. It was a resentment she learned from Priscilla, Jared's sister, who had always been any man's intellectual equal. "How long will you be gone?" she asked tersely.

This was the question Jared was dreading the most. "I don't know," he said. "There is no definite timetable." His furrowed brow pleaded with her to be understanding.

"I see." Anne looked down at her nervous hands until she became consciously aware of what she was doing. Then, instantly, she dropped them to her sides, angry with herself for revealing her anxiety. She turned away from Jared, toward the window.

"Anne!" Jared pleaded. Moving to her, he placed his hands on her shoulders and gently buried his face in her hair. Its fragrance was warm and sweet. How many nights at sea had he endured the creaking of the ship, braced himself against the damp, bone-chilling sea, and dreamed of being this close to Anne, wondering if he would ever smell her hair again? Not until this moment did Jared realize how much he didn't want to go to London. But it was not a matter of choice, he reasoned, rather a matter of duty. "This isn't something I want to do," he whispered. "It's something I *must* do. Anne, it's my hope that in some small way I can do something that will help us avert an armed uprising against England. At least, that's my hope."

"Do you really think that's possible?" she asked softly, but not warmly. "Look at what happened at dinner tonight. Our sons nearly came to blows! All the while Adams and his crew were inciting them. With all the inflammatory remarks in the newspapers, the market, and the churches, do you really think men like Samuel Adams will be content with a negotiated peace?"

"I've got to try," Jared replied. He felt Anne shudder. He encircled her with his arms, holding her against him, resting his lips on the nape of her neck. He could feel her trembling.

"I'm frightened, Jared," she said. "After dinner I had this awful feeling that it was the last time we would be together as a family. I can't explain what made me feel that way. But it was strong. So strong."

Jared pulled her close to calm her. He whispered: "It's all right to be scared. I'm scared too. We'll just have to pray that God will see us all through this."

No response.

With his cheek pressed against the back of her head, his lips almost touching her ear, Jared prayed. "Lord," he said aloud, "You know Anne deserves better than this. She has suffered too many nights alone already. She deserves to have a husband who is home more than he is away. And Lord, You know my heart. I want nothing more in life than to spend the rest of my days with her. But for reasons known only to You, You have placed us in these uncertain times; our streets are no longer safe; anger and hatred are our common fare; and our colony, our family is balanced precariously on the edge of warfare. We don't know where all this is leading, Lord. But we know this: We are in Your hands."

At this point in the prayer Anne's cheek rested on Jared's forearm. It was warm and moist with tears. To Jared it served as a signal that she had joined in the prayer with him. From the early days of their marriage this had been their custom—in matters of importance to pray together sooner rather than later.

Jared continued: "And dear Lord, I pray for Jacob and Esau. Should the conflict escalate and we find ourselves at war, I pray that You will keep them safe. And Lord, I pray for wisdom in this decision regarding London. My sincere desire is that I might promote peace for our country. But if my going injures the one I love more dearly than life itself, the price of the task is too high. Please, Lord, show me Your will. Amen."

When Jared finished his prayer, Anne voiced one of her own: "Dear God, give my husband a safe journey. May he be instrumental in bringing peace to our troubled colony. From the beginning we have placed our lives and our sons' lives in Your hands, and we'll not be taking them back now. And please, Lord, if it be Your will, bring Jared home to me soon."

Jared and Anne Morgan busied themselves with collecting the necessary clothing for Jared's impending journey. As Anne walked past the window near the bed, a movement outside caught her eye. It came from the shadows along a tall, snow-laden hedge in the garden. Anne moved closer to the window to get a better look. Everything in the garden was still. Large moonlit patches of snow rested heavily upon the hedges, showing sagging holes where it had melted. The walkways were well trodden with footprints. But she could see no movement. Maybe it was her own reflection in the window she'd seen.

Then, just as she was about to turn back into the room, she saw someone half-walking, half-running down the garden path, coming toward the house. By the build and stride of the dark form, she could tell it was a man. He was looking from side to side. Just as Anne was about to call out to her husband, she recognized who it was. *Esau! What was Esau doing sneaking around at night? Hadn't he left the house over an hour ago for Cambridge?* Suddenly, a cloaked figure darted from the shadows. The corner of the cloak lifted, revealing a flash of white. Mercy, still in her dinner dress. Grabbing Esau by the arm, she pulled him into the shadows, and the garden was still again.

4

He heard her giggling before he saw her. Then, there was a whooshing of skirts, the moonlit flash of a white dress peaking from under her cloak, a petite hand pulling on his arm, and the next thing he knew he was standing in the shadows of the frozen garden hedges within inches of a giddy Mercy. Even in the dark her eyes sparkled and her smile flashed gaily. Her chest rose and fell excitedly from the sudden exertion. Her breath vaporized in short, quick puffs. Without releasing his arm, she gazed upward into his eyes. Her perfume acted like a narcotic, dulling his senses—especially his good sense that, had it not been temporarily incapacitated, would have reprimanded him for meeting her in the family garden at this late hour. *What if someone saw them?*

"Where have you been?" she scolded him playfully, her lower lip extended in a mock pout. "I've been waiting out here in this frigid weather *forever!*"

Esau hadn't noticed the cold, warmed by the rush of excitement he felt in anticipation of his rendezvous with Mercy. "You knew I'd come," he said.

An impish grin formed on her face.

"Why did you want me to meet you here?" Esau asked the question only because it was the natural thing to say at this point. Truth was that he would have met her for no reason at all. He would do anything just to be alone with her like old times, before she and Jacob married.

"Do I *have* to have a reason?" Mercy teased.

It was Esau's turn to smile. He shook his head.

His response was the right one. Mercy rewarded him with a smile and a wink that made Esau's head spin dizzily. There was something about this woman that intoxicated him. She'd always had this effect on him, from the moment they first met. Now, almost a dozen years later, her power over him had not diminished one bit, even considering that for ten of those years she had been Jacob's wife.

Every time Esau thought of that unpleasant reality, he seethed with anger. It never should have been this way. Mercy was his! The only way Jacob could get her was by stealing her! An act of treachery for which Esau would never forgive his brother. Never.

"I just *had* to talk to someone!" said Mercy. "Jacob's off with that *stupid* Committee of Safety doing *whatever* it is they do all night long." At the mention of Jacob's name, Esau stiffened noticeably. Mercy, feeling his response, leaned against him. Her bosom pressed against his arm. As she knew it would, her warmth and nearness melted Esau's anxiety away and brought his full attention back to her. "I just needed someone to talk to," she cooed, "and you're such a good man to let me prattle on so."

Without so much as a pause, Mercy launched into a diatribe critiquing that night's dinner party with Dr. Cooper, Adams, and Hancock. This kind of social commentary was not uncommon for Mercy Reed Morgan. She was an opinionated social butterfly, accustomed to being the center of attention at any gathering, large or small, formal or informal. Even her enemies—mostly women who envied the fawning attention men paid her—reluctantly placed her at the top of their guest lists. They knew that for their event to have a chance for success, Mercy had to be there.

Poor Abigail Hunter discovered this law of Boston society the hard way. The homely daughter of a wealthy printer, she set out to prove that there was such a thing as a Boston party without Mercy Reed Morgan. For six months Abigail planned the gathering, hiring the best musicians, importing the finest food and drink, and spending more time on the guest list than a newly elected prime minister would spend forming his cabinet. The night of the gala event, everything was arranged to perfection—the lights were bright, the colors cheerful, music wafted gaily through the rooms; and when the venerable Benjamin Franklin arrived from Philadelphia, Abigail Hunter beamed victoriously.

Unfortunately, her victory celebration was premature. It was still early in the evening when Mercy's absence was noticed. Like a fire, the rumor spread from one clump of guests to another that her absence was not an oversight, but intentional. By dinnertime the whispers had progressed to speculation. *What had poor Mercy done that Abigail would hate her so?*

As the guests assembled at the table, Miss Hunter strove valiantly to direct conversation away from the missing Mercy. Her efforts were in vain. Not even the venerable Dr. Franklin—whose dinner anecdotes were legendary—could turn the tide of conversation in Miss Hunter's favor. One by one, the guests took turns relating his or her favorite Mercy Reed Morgan story. Abigail's dinner soon took on the appearance of an Irish wake! Mercy Reed Morgan was more than just absent; it was as if she had died! The stories told of her grew to mythical proportions. Mercy's stories were funnier, her antics more outrageous than they ever were originally. It wouldn't have surprised Abigail if someone proposed they canonize Mercy and make her the patron saint of the Boston social scene! And if Mercy was a martyr, Abigail was to blame.

Early the next day a contrite Abigail Hunter appeared at the Morgan house, apologizing profusely for her rude behavior. Mercy graciously, if not a bit smugly, forgave her. She didn't say as much, but the way Mercy saw it, Abigail had done her a wonderful service. Mercy couldn't have advanced her own reputation in a single night as greatly as Abigail Hunter did for her by not inviting her to the party. From that night on, Mercy Reed Morgan was the preeminent authority in Boston in all things social.

"Wasn't dinner tonight *absolutely boring?*" Mercy cried, still clinging to Esau's arm. "All men ever talk about anymore is this *ridiculous* revolution! It makes me *absolutely ill!*"

Mercy absolutely loved the word "absolutely," almost as much as she loved overemphasizing words or phrases in her sentences to demonstrate her feelings.

Esau couldn't get enough of her. He didn't mind that she was simple, arrogant, and conceited. Mercy wore these traits well—more than that, she paraded them around for all to see. Maybe that's why Esau loved her so much; she was confident and free, but most of all she was fun.

"Must we *always* talk of war?" Mercy complained. "The topic always makes everyone so angry!" Tugging on Esau's arm, she continued, "And you and your brother were *absolute bores* tonight with your idiotic fighting! Why can't things be like they were? Why can't we have a party without it turning into a *moronic* political debate?"

"I was wrong," Esau said softly. "Please, forgive me."

"Yes, you were wrong!" Her eyes flashed angrily, but only for a moment. Then she softened. "But at least you're *sensible* enough to admit it."

Their eyes met. Even in the shadows of the garden at night, sparks of light danced in them. Esau had never known a woman

so stunning. Long black hair framed a soft porcelain-white complexion. Full lips parted slightly as he leaned toward her.
Suddenly, she broke away.

"Oh my, it *is* freezing out here, isn't it?" she exclaimed, wrap-
ping her cloak tightly around her. She reached out, touched his
cheek with a warm hand, and said, "You are such a dear for listening to me prattle on like this. Jacob never has time to talk, he's
either too busy or too *angry*." Bouncing up on her toes she gave
him a peck on the cheek. "You're always here for me when I need
you, aren't you?" she said. "Good-night!"

With a rustle of skirts she was gone, and Esau was left standing
alone in the cold. This is the way it had always been between him
and Mercy. So near, yet out of reach. But it wouldn't always be so.

"Don't you know by now, my love?" he said. "I'll always be
here for you."

But only the bushes heard him.

Like most young ladies of the time, Mercy Reed made her public debut at age sixteen. The youngest of twelve children, and the
only girl born to Richard and Patience Reed, her father doted on
her from the day of her birth. A Philadelphia tailor with a long list
of wealthy clients, Richard Reed's greatest pleasure in life was
making ballroom gowns for his maturing daughter.

Mercy wore the first of her father's elegant creations to a
Philadelphia ball, that year's premier social event. Her gown was
a French design, blue and white with a low, square neckline and
fitted bodice, trimmed with ribbons, bows, and ruffles, featuring
a polonaise skirt over a frilled underskirt. A white powdered wig
with side ringlets and a pearl necklace complemented the tailor's
masterpiece.

For many young women, such a gown would appear ostentatious, the gown being more striking than the woman wearing

it. Not so with Mercy. The two were equally striking. The sparkle in Mercy's intensely black eyes was a perfect match for the shimmering glint of the pearls; her porcelain complexion and thin, graceful neck and high cheekbones were as much the envied fashion of women as was the French style of her dress; the bold strokes of the low-cut bodice gave testimony to a young woman who was confident with the powers her gender had over men.

The center of social life for the colonies, Philadelphia was a fitting location for Mercy to make her debut. From her initial entrance, she took the social scene by storm. Within a year, she had become one of Philadelphia's reigning socialites, well known in all the prominent drawing rooms and ballrooms in town, and a formidable opponent in the battle of wits, a favorite pastime among Philadelphia's privileged class.

From this exalted position, naturally Mercy Reed had her pick from hundreds of suitors representing nearly every colony in America, which was exactly her intention. Having her fill of sharing limited resources with eleven older brothers, Mercy's one goal in life was to marry wealthy. In her quest, she narrowed her choices down to two men—the Morgan twins of Boston.

She first saw them from across the room at a party in Philadelphia, but didn't actually meet them until several months later when she was in Boston for the spring ball. Much to her delight, she found them both overeager to gain her attention, to please her, or simply to make her laugh. In a word, they were smitten. Mercy liked smitten. It gave her every advantage.

She thought the twins attractive; either one would make a fitting consort to wear on her arm at future social gatherings. Since they were identical, she didn't have the dilemma of one being better looking than the other, and because they were brothers, they were also equal in the matter of inheriting the family's vast wealth. The tiebreaker came down to personality. By far Esau was the more polished of the two, having been to Harvard and accustomed to interacting with the educated and social elite. But manners and breeding could at times be boring and stuffy; that's where Jacob came in. His slightly crude behavior had a naughty fascination for her. His conversation and humor were ribald, which Mercy found delightfully shocking. But then, Jacob tended to carry his crudity too far and would often become offensive and boorish. Which always brought her back to Esau.

It was Mercy's firm commitment to wealth and fine living that finally tipped the balance in Esau's direction. She reasoned that his superior education and social standing destined him to become the head of the Morgan clan once the captain passed on. So it was decided. She would woo Esau into marrying her. But no sooner had she arrived at this conclusion when Esau announced he'd been accepted into a two-year program of study at Oxford and would be sailing for England shortly. Mercy was faced with a new dilemma—wait for Esau or fall back to choice number two?

Mercy's plight was solved by Esau. Much to her delight, before leaving for England, Esau rushed to her side, professing his ardent desire to marry her and take her with him. His father, however, disapproved. Captain Morgan had counseled him to conclude his studies first, then marry. And although Esau professed to see the logic in his father's counsel since his studies would give him little time to lavish attention on a new bride, and their accommodations and social life in England would be meager at best, if it meant losing Mercy to any other man, he'd defy his father and whisk her away to England; or, if she preferred, he wouldn't go at all!

Shrewdly, Mercy encouraged Esau to go alone to England. She promised to wait for him. She reasoned it was wise to promote goodwill in the family by making the elder Morgan happy. This bit of unselfishness on her part now could very well reap larger dividends in the future when the captain's will was read. She would just have to think of this setback in investment terms. Two years of patience in exchange for a lifetime of wealth. A suitable return.

The longer Esau lingered in his good-byes to her—begging and begging her to wait for him and continuously pledging his faithfulness to her—the more she knew she'd made the right decision. All she needed to do was wait two years and all her planning would pay off.

At first the letters from England arrived in bunches, dated one, sometimes two or more a day. Then, as the school year progressed and the curriculum load exacted its toll on Esau's time, Mercy received a letter a week. But what a letter! Each one was crammed full of the poetic longings of the lovesick student.

Jacob saw Esau's absence as his opportunity to win Mercy's heart. He called on her frequently, sent her gifts, volunteered to escort her to social functions, and even tried his hand at poetry, but only once. Publicly Mercy did not discourage him. After all, she reasoned, Jacob would soon be her brother-in-law and she had to keep peace in the family. Besides, Jacob looked like her absent Esau, though he didn't act like him, and having a handsome beau on her arm was better than no beau at all.

Privately, Jacob's plodding attempts at romance were tiresome. His efforts were met with cold resolve. Jacob soon realized that competing against his absent brother for Mercy's affections was more difficult than if Esau were in the room with them. It was like doing battle with a martyr. In his absence, Esau could do no wrong; he was perfect in Mercy's eyes.

Jacob was growing desperate. One year had already passed. He couldn't let another six months pass without dethroning Esau.

Given that much time, Mercy would surely have her absent suitor knighted or maybe even canonized.

He was working on the docks when the plan came to him. The *Cumberland* had just arrived from England, bearing, with its cargo of household furniture and silver tea settings, the weekly letter from Esau to Mercy. The dockworker entrusted to deliver the mail had just finished ribbing Jacob about his brother's letters being so timely. He boasted that the letters were a convenient reminder that payday was only two days hence. Another coworker added that it would be more profitable for Jacob to spend extra time on the docks, for he would certainly get more from the paymaster than he ever would from Mercy Reed. Jacob brushed aside the rude humor like he would an insect. It was a way of life on the docks. Then the idea hit him. *What if the letters didn't come every week? What if they stopped coming altogether?* An idea began crystallizing in his brain, an idea that just might get Mercy Reed to marry him.

The complete plan didn't form overnight. It took several weeks. But then, it was the most complicated and devious plan Jacob Morgan had ever attempted. He was careful not to act in haste. The risk was great, but then so was the reward.

The first step was the easiest. Stop Esau's letters from reaching Mercy. Jacob bribed the dockworker who handled the mail, who was more than willing to profit from one of Jacob's pranks against his brother.

When the letters stopped coming, Mercy was angry. She was unaccustomed to feelings of neglect. It was a new experience for her and she didn't like it. Then, after two months without letters, she grew concerned. Something was wrong. At least Jacob was there to comfort her. He agreed with her. It wasn't like Esau to be so inconsiderate. There had to be a reason why he was no longer writing.

The second and third steps were costly, but Jacob was more than willing to pay the price. He knew that a mere lack of letters would never tumble the exalted Esau from his pedestal in Mercy's mind. It would take hard evidence delivered by credible sources. Jacob hired credible sources in a tavern near Harvard. He needed educated men to complete his plan. The first man he hired was an actor.

The second step involved a carefully orchestrated chance encounter. Howard Franks introduced himself to Mercy at a party as a man recently returned from England, Oxford specifically. Upon hearing of his close proximity to her beloved, she naturally inquired if the recently returned Franks had any news of an Esau Morgan. Most certainly, came the actor's reply; why the last time he saw his good friend Esau was at a celebration honoring the former Bostonian's betrothal to Lady Levy of the Berkshire Levys.

Naturally, Mercy was devastated by the news. And once again, Jacob was there to console her.

The third step was the knockout blow. Whereas the absence of love letters raised suspicion, and the false testimony of Howard Franks was enough to shatter the saintly image of his absent brother, Jacob had to ensure that the breakup of Mercy and Esau was immediate and irrevocable. The third step came in the form of a letter, two letters actually.

One letter was from Howard Franks to Jacob. In the letter, Franks expressed his deep regrets that the news of Esau's engagement had such an unfortunate effect on a lady as fine as Mercy Reed. Had he only known of her relationship with Esau, he would have held his tongue rather than injure her in this way. His stated objective in this letter was twofold: Would Jacob convey his sincere regrets to the lovely Mercy? Secondly, he was enclosing a letter recently received from Esau, showing his true nature. It was Franks's stated hope that Jacob could use the information to show Mercy how fortunate she was to escape from such a wretch.

Enclosed was the forged letter purported to have been written by Esau to Franks. Jacob had paid a pretty sum to have it forged, using Esau's diverted letters as samples for the forger. In the counterfeit letter, the Oxford scholar proclaimed himself to be happily wed. He counted his good fortune to have met Lady Levy; otherwise he might have been joined to a Philadelphia tart who fashioned herself a lady but, compared to the regal Lady Levy, had all the charm of a frontier trapper. He mentioned that his wedding was being kept from his parents who had earlier expressed their concern of his getting married before he finished his schooling. As soon as he earned his degree, he would inform them. At such a time, their objections would be moot, and they would most certainly welcome his refined lady from England into the family with open arms.

The finishing touch on the letter was an uncharacteristic stroke of brilliance for Jacob. In the text, he had Esau ask Franks to do whatever possible to keep Jacob away from Mercy. Esau's reasoning was that although he no longer had any use for her, neither did he want his brother to have her.

The letter drove Mercy into Jacob's arms. Distraught, terribly wounded, and confused, she verbalized her venomous thoughts to him. He listened, consoled her, took a few castigating shots at his brother himself, and when the moment was right, expressed his love for her in uncharacteristic tenderness. Together, he proposed, they could see this through. Within a month Jacob and Mercy were married.

Mercy's decision to marry Jacob was not totally emotional. She reasoned that she could do worse than marry Jacob. First, there was his family's wealth. She'd already grown so accustomed to thinking of it as her own, it was difficult for her to imagine giving it up. Then, the best way for her to get even with Esau would be to marry his brother. Year after year, she would be in the position to make his life miserable. She was already formulating in her mind possible scenarios, the first of which was to let it be known publicly that it was *her* decision to choose Jacob over Esau. She pretended to know nothing of Esau's supposed marriage to Lady Levy. This way it would appear that *she* rejected *him*.

Mercy's switch from Esau to Jacob and the suddenness of the wedding surprised Jared and Anne Morgan, but not unduly. Their impression of Mercy was that of a social bee flitting from one flower to the other. To them, the greater surprise was that she would willingly limit herself to one man through marriage. Another concern was her lack of spiritual depth. Although she was known to attend church, she'd shown little evidence of the Christian graces. Plus, they knew there would be problems when Esau returned home. Little did they realize the enormity of the crisis they were about to face.

Esau learned of Mercy's wedding through a letter from his mother. In her correspondence, Anne described in innocent detail the wedding ceremony, held in the family garden. She concluded with a note of motherly advice. Knowing that Esau had expressed feelings for Mercy in the past, she hoped that upon his return he would be a good Christian and join the family in congratulating Jacob and his new bride.

The collapse of Magdalen's Bell Tower upon Esau could not have crushed him more completely than did his mother's letter. At the time he received it, he was more in love with Mercy than ever. True to his word, he had forsaken all other women, living a semi-monastic life and dreaming of the day when he and Mercy would become man and wife.

From the beginning, Jacob knew his deception would ultimately be discovered. He had prepared himself to endure his

father and mother's insufferably long tirade in which they
denounced him, expressed their disappointment, and bombarded
him with a seemingly endless list of questions, all of which could
be answered with the same answer. He did it because he loved
Mercy. And he was prepared to endure the ravings of his brother.
If fact, he was looking forward to it. Making his brother angry had
always given him a perverse sense of pleasure.

The final success or failure of his plan rested not with his parents, or with Esau, but with Mercy. How would she react when
she learned she'd been tricked into marrying him? Of course, he
hoped he would be able to convince her that his one motivation
was his love for her. That he couldn't imagine life without her.
That he would have done anything—*anything!*—just to have her
for his wife.

As it turned out, Jacob understood Mercy better than he or
anyone else could have imagined. When she discovered his trickery, she was hurt, but not as hurt as when she thought that Esau
had spurned her. Maybe it was because she expected less from
Jacob, so it was easier to be disappointed by him. Then there was
the fact that she was a Morgan. She liked that. Divorce was hardly
a consideration; to do so would place her on the social level of a
prostitute. The fact was, she'd made a play for the best and
wound up with second best. She could live with that. Too much
was at risk to try to undo what had been done. Besides, there was
something romantic about a man who would go to such great
lengths to marry her.

Esau couldn't bring himself to forgive his brother. He didn't
fault Mercy. She'd been deceived and trapped. His only consola-
tion was his hope that God would make things right. Striking
Jacob with a bolt of lightning was preferable, but Esau chose to
let God handle the specifics. He was willing to wait. Someday,
Mercy would be his wife.

For more than a decade Esau waited and prayed. The fact that Jacob and Mercy were unable to produce children in that time was for him an encouraging sign that God did not favor their union. He contented himself with brief, clandestine encounters with her. They were innocent enough, but the control was all Mercy's. She seemed to enjoy having a suitor as well as a husband. She would always agree to meet him; sometimes it was she who arranged the rendezvous. She permitted talking and flirtatious touching, but no more. The moment Esau showed the slightest sign of serious romance, she fled.

Now, late in the second month of 1775, as Esau left the garden to return to Cambridge, he renewed his prayer that God would dispatch some form of violence against his brother. *Maybe something good can come of the increased hostilities in the colonies,* Esau thought. *Especially since Jacob runs with a violent crowd. Hostilities can lead to war. People die in war.* Esau prayed that if an armed uprising ensued, one of the first casualties would be his brother, Jacob. Then Mercy would finally be his.

5

Boston's North End was a compact, tight region. Except for the slopes of Copp's Hill, which were surmounted by a burying ground and a windmill, the North End was heavily populated, chiefly by merchants who had their dwellings, warehouses, and wharves in close proximity and by shipbuilders who preferred the convenience of living close to their yards. It was here a ferry normally transported travelers to and from Boston and Charlestown. Tonight, a heavily armed detachment of redcoats from the 29th Regiment, commanded by a thin-faced lieutenant with a saucy tongue, had shut down all passage across the waterway.

Having been turned back from his intended route, Esau did his best to rein in his surging anger. It wasn't the delay that upset him so much, he kept telling himself. True, he was irked that he'd been forced to ride back through the city at this late hour and take the longer land route to Cambridge. But what really angered him was the taunts, threats, and innuendoes of an overzealous, foul-mouthed lieutenant and his band of redcoat ruffians. Instead of merely informing Esau that the ferry was closed, the lieutenant thought it necessary to force Esau to dismount at gunpoint. Then, with a bevy of musket barrels leveled at him, he was pummeled with questions. *Where was he going? Why was he out so late? Why was he alone? Was he a minuteman? Why should they believe him?* As Esau answered the lieutenant's questions, the officer nervously thumped him on the chest with the barrel of a loaded pistol, occasionally interrupting Esau with asides to his companions that he hoped the pistol wouldn't discharge accidentally, an unfortunate event, he claimed, that would cause him no small amount of embarrassment.

The lieutenant's second volley of questions was more belligerent. *Where were the colonials stockpiling ammunition? Where were the Sons of Liberty meeting tonight? Who were they targeting as their next victim?*

No matter what Esau said, no matter how many assurances he gave the lieutenant that he was a devout loyalist, the redcoat officer insisted on calling him a Liberty Boy, all the while thumping Esau's chest with the deadly end of his pistol. The interrogation lasted nearly an hour, after which the lieutenant allowed Esau to remount and return in the direction from which he came. As he rode away, the other redcoats shouted obscenities and yelled at him to inform the Liberty Boys that musket balls, bayonets, and nooses were the inheritance of traitors.

Not until Esau was well out of sight did the shouting stop, leaving only the solitary clop-clop-clop of horse's hoofs on the cobblestone along a bared wheel rut in the street, echoing up and down the narrow row of houses. The sides of the street were still heavy with snow, as were the ledges and steps and the tops of the lampposts. A dense fog from the harbor was snaking its way up the side lanes, spilling into Prince Street, skating across the snow from one edge of the street to the other. It scrolled up the sides of the brick buildings, swirling ever upward around the lamp poles, circling the glass-encased candles as if it were seeking a way to get in and douse the light and plunge the street into darkness. Droplets trickled down the lamps' glass panes like tears, as though they were weeping over the fog's assault.

Esau shivered. The heavy moisture accumulated on his hat and overcoat and face. A drip formed on his forehead and streamed down the ridge of his nose. At the tip it swung precariously over his lips. Esau wiped it away with a shaking hand. Not until that moment did he realize how much the encounter with the soldiers had rattled him. He took a deep breath. His chest shook involuntarily. *Stop being so childish!* he scolded himself. *They may have played the brute, but they didn't injure you!*

But they could have. And though Esau didn't want to admit it to himself, he knew the soldiers wanted to hurt him. Like a gathering storm, the mounting anger of England's frustration with her colonies was etched on their faces. It was as if they were begging Esau to give them an excuse—any excuse at all, thank you—to kill him. Killing a colonist would be so satisfying for them; through his death their tension would be relieved and they would feel so much better. But Esau refused to oblige them, choosing to be inoffensive in his every word and deed. He figured he had better things to do with his blood than to allow these men to paint the street with it.

Had Esau not restrained himself, it wouldn't have been the first time British soldiers' frustration had boiled over to the point of violence. The senseless killing on King Street nearly five years previous had given the colonials an occasion to gather every March 5 to memorialize the deaths of their fellow rabble-rousers, making martyrs of mobsters and further heightening tensions in the city. The annual event, orchestrated by Sam Adams, induced decent men on both sides to act like hoodlums. Like the British lieutenant tonight. A fellow Englishman. Esau wondered whether under different circumstances—say, if they'd met at Oxford instead of the end of Prince Street—he and the lieutenant might have become friends instead of antagonists.

Just then, an odd thought struck him with such force that he laughed out loud. The sound of his baritone voice echoed up and down the empty street. *Imagine what the lieutenant would have done to me had he known I dined tonight with Sam Adams!*

"HOLD!"

Torches borne by men appeared from everywhere. With the sound of crunching snow, from every side street and alley and doorway, they rushed at him; dark figures, causing the carpet of fog to swirl angrily about them. Esau's horse reared.

"HOLD, I SAY!"

Two oversized dark men seized the horse's bridle. Esau was hemmed in all around. A squat man wearing a tricorne hat approached. The flickering torch he held cast light and shadow on a grisly face—his left eye squinted shut while a vicious scar stretched across the cheek below it; his nose was bulbous, his whiskers patchy, and his teeth, the few remaining, were black.

"And where might ye be heading?" he asked.

Esau glanced around him. Men with tattered linen shirts, felt hats, and coarse cloth breeches looked up at him. Those whose faces he could see were hard as granite.

"I don't see that it is any of your business, sir," Esau replied.

His use of the word "sir" brought a grin to the grisly face and prompted whistles and catcalls from some in the crowd.

"It sounds to me like ye might be a man of letters."

Esau didn't reply.

"Cambridge, no doubt."

"Oxford."

"Ah! An Oxford man!" the squinty-eyed interrogator called out as if he were impressed, which set off a chorus of derisive cheers. "Me? I'm a Cambridge man myself!"

A burst of raucous laughter. The heavy odor of rum wafted all around Esau. He worried the leather reins nervously with his thumb, looking for a chance to bolt.

"No doubt," the squat man shouted over the others, "you'd be a close personal friend of King George!"

Esau was silent. His eyes darted. There were so many of them.

"I said, no doubt ye be a friend of the king!" the stout man shouted at him. He was growing agitated. "Are ye a friend of the king or no?"

There was silence. Every man waited to hear Esau's answer.

Esau sat proudly in his saddle, refusing to be intimidated by ruffians. His eyes engaged those of his interrogator. With a calm, clear voice he said, "I am."

A huge, ugly grin split wide the interrogator's face. He said viciously, "Git 'im, boys."

From all sides, angry hands lunged at Esau. Men jumped high to grab his arms, his shoulders, his hair, anything they could reach. Esau tried to spur his horse. No response. The next thing he knew he was pulled from his horse and slammed face first to the ground. It seemed like hundreds of hands and arms swarmed over him, pinning him down. His cheek was smashed against icy-wet cobblestones. His arms were yanked behind him and bound tightly with coarse rope; likewise, his legs were tied together. Then he was lifted like a sack of grain and thrown into an open cart that emerged from an alley. Surrounded by shouting, drunken torchbearers, Esau Morgan was paraded like a circus bear to a warehouse on the wharf.

※

"This meeting of the Committee of Safety will come to order!"

The squat, scarred interrogator who had confronted him on Prince Street pounded an equally scarred wooden table, using an old leather shoe for a gavel. The pounding sound echoed high above in the warehouse rafters. Men of all sizes and shapes gathered around him, some leaning against the half-dozen or so wooden pillars that supported a balcony, others sitting on stacked crates or sacks of grain. The immediate vicinity was lit with torches, fading to black deeper into the bowels of the cavernous building. An acrid odor permeated the room, overpowering the rum smell that had been so rife on the men's breath when they captured him.

The recognized chairman of the proceedings had doffed his tattered tricorne and laid it at the corner of the table. As talking gave way to his pounding, the stout man ran stubby fingers over a scalp that resembled a fallow field. With the same hand, he wiped his nose and hitched his pants before beginning.

Esau stood a few feet in front of the table, his hands and feet still bound. He wobbled unsteadily. With his feet bound together, remaining upright required constant effort; a lack of concentration, or any sudden movement, would find him toppling over with nothing to break his fall, which, considering the company of men surrounding him, seemed the least of his concerns.

"We'll make this simple," said the stout man. "Curse the governor, curse Parliament, and curse the king, and we'll count you among us as a patriot and let you go. Refuse, and we'll provide you with a new set of clothes that you can wear proudly with all the other chickens in Boston."

So that's what they had in mind for him. Tar and feathers. Now he recognized the pungent smell that hung so heavy in the air. It was tar.

Careful to maintain his balance, Esau did his best to glance around the room, looking from face to face, searching for some visible sign of compassion or hope, or possibly even a familiar countenance to whom he could appeal. The eyes that stared back at him were cold and unfriendly. Most of them, like the redcoats at the ferry, looked eager for an excuse to do him violence. Others, he couldn't see at all. They stood too far from the light. They could see him, but all he could see of them was their shadowy forms. One in particular, a black visage, reminded Esau of a hooded executioner.

"You would be doing an injustice to harm me," Esau replied in a loud voice. "For I am a patriot!"

The stout man's mouth fell open. All manner of expression drained from his face, a comical sight indeed. Esau's response was unexpected. The stout man didn't know what to do next. You could see the thought forming behind worried eyes: *Had he detained the wrong man?* He glanced nervously past Esau into the shadows. Just as Esau thought. The empty-headed spokesman was someone else's puppet. Esau strained to look over his shoulder, to see who the stout man was looking to for instructions. Try as he might, he saw no one he recognized.

"Look at me and explain yourself!" the stout man shouted at him. "You're no patriot!"

"Ah, but I am a patriot," Esau replied. "And a finer patriot you'll never see. Should you form a just idea of the immense wealth and power of the nation I serve, you would tremble at the foolish audacity of your pygmy minds. Another summer, and everyone in Boston will come over to my opinion! I feel for the miseries hastening upon my countrymen, but alas! They must thank their own folly for their unfortunate blunder."

With screwed-up face, the stout man blinked his good eye once, then twice, trying to make sense of Esau's response. The unlearned man's stupefied expression crystallized Esau's resolve to a course of action. He no longer cared what these unwashed, ragged, rum-soaked simpletons threatened to do to him. He refused to be intimidated by them.

"I'll make this simple," Esau said, mimicking the stout man's opening words. Looking into the faces of the men leaning against the pillars and sitting on the grain sacks and perched on the edges of crates, he yelled, "I am an *English* patriot! Curse all traitors to the crown! God save great George our king!"

They descended on him with a fury. Shouting. Cursing. Knocking him to the ground. Hands tore at his clothes, ripping them off, stripping him naked. Like a carcass picked apart by vultures, Esau was powerless to stop them. A stab of pain ripped through his shoulder as someone, in his zeal to remove Esau's shirt, dislocated his arm. Esau could barely hear his own screams over the shouts and curses of his attackers.

Then, by signal, they all backed away. Hot mops of tar plunged toward him, the first one hitting him square in the chest. Esau screamed again as the black pitch seared the skin on his chest, then his arms, his legs, his face. His eyes began to roll upward into his head as the pain of the burns and his separated shoulder pushed him toward the precipice of unconsciousness. The shouts and jeers of the men faded into the background of his awareness as chicken feathers were heaped upon him.

For the second time that night, Esau was loaded into the cart. His moans were drowned out by drums and fiddles as he was paraded up and down the streets of Boston to the tune of "The Rogue's March." Cautious men and women in their night clothes peered at the spectacle through barely cracked shutters. Some, eager to participate, dressed and joined the procession.

The procession made several stops, usually at taverns. While the celebrants refilled their flip-mugs with ale, Esau would be dragged from the cart and charges of disloyalty would be read, after which he would be whipped. Sometimes, they would ask him to offer a defense against the charges. He never did. He knew that anything he said would only be used to further injure or humiliate him. Besides, it was too painful for him to speak. His thirst was incredible. His lips were dry and swollen, and his tongue stuck to everything it touched. He couldn't begin to form words. Taking his silence as an admission of guilt, his accusers would then load him into the cart again, and the procession would continue.

The patriot parade made its way to the Liberty Tree. It was here prominent officials were regularly hanged in effigy, or grievances against King and Parliament were read and posted. The cart bearing Esau was positioned under a sturdy limb. A rope with a noose was thrown over it. Two men helped Esau to his feet, and the noose was placed around his neck, after which the two men jumped from the cart.

With crusted pitch on his eyelids, it was difficult for Esau to keep his eyes open for any length of time. But he was able to open them long enough to see the rank hatred on the faces of the men and women gathered around him. They were eerily silent, anticipating the command that would end his life. Torches flickered. The wind gently rustled the branches of the Liberty Tree. A horse whinnied. Esau stared at his fellow colonists and they at him.

"What say ye now, English patriot?" The stout man broke through the front line of witnesses. "Do ye recant and curse your king, or do ye hang?"

Esau lowered his eyes. There was no fight left in him. His flesh was raw, gouged by the brittle edges of the tar every time he moved. His throat was scratchy and parched. The chilly night air stung the red stripes on his back. What did it matter? In moments he would be dead, transported—if what he'd read in the Bible was true—to a far better world than this.

"Answer, man!" the stout spokesman shouted. "Or I'll order the cart pulled!"

Raising his head, Esau fought to open his eyes. That's when he saw him. He just opened his eyes and there he was, standing on the edge of the crowd. Jacob. His brother. Jacob's arms were folded casually. He leaned to one side and said something to the man next to him, who chuckled in response. Esau recognized the man next to him too. Not by name, but by location. The man next to his brother was one of his attackers on Prince Street. Esau had also seen him sitting on a crate at the warehouse. He was one of the men who had done this to him.

The stout man flushed red in the face, cursing Esau and threatening to give the order to pull the cart away unless he answered.

Esau said not a word. He couldn't stop looking at his brother. Tears wet the feathers on his cheeks; they mixed with the pitch in the corners of his eyes and burned mightily, but Esau fought back the pain and kept his eyes on his brother.

The cart was never pulled. The crowd dispersed. And Esau Morgan was dumped in a heap at the base of the Liberty Tree.

The massacre on King Street as described in the annual March 5 speeches bore little resemblance to the actual event. Actually, the hostilities began several days before, on Friday, March 2, when a group of British soldiers, redcoats from the 29th Regiment, went to a ropewalk, a spacious area set aside for the making of rope, looking for work. It wasn't uncommon for British soldiers to take on part-time jobs to supplement their meager pay. But the colonials didn't like it since the soldiers accepted jobs for less than the going rate. This was just one of many things to which Bostonians objected regarding the troops in their city. Other complaints included rude off-duty behavior, noisy drill practice during church services, drunkenness, and chasing after colonial women.

On this particular day at the ropewalk, ropeworker Samuel Gray told British soldier Patrick Walker that if he wanted work, he could clean Gray's outhouse. The soldier took offense at Gray's remark and rushed at him. Gray fought him off. A short time later Walker reappeared with eight or nine soldiers of his regiment carrying clubs and challenging the workers to a fight. The workers obliged with superior numbers, and again the soldiers were forced to retreat. The soldiers returned a third time with thirty more men. There was another fight, but the results were the same. The soldiers were chased away.

Three days later, the residents of Boston awoke to find the buildings, trees, and fences littered with notices, purportedly signed by British soldiers garrisoned in the city. The notices proclaimed that any further insolence toward the troops would provide grounds for attacking the perpetrators. The posted notices threw Boston into an uproar, though most people dismissed them as forgeries. It didn't make sense that a regiment would announce intended illegal activities, then sign their names to documents that could later be used as evidence against them.

In reality, they were the product of the cunning minds of Sam Adams and his Loyal Nine, a select group of radical rebels whose intent was to sweep Boston clean of redcoats. The thinly disguised notices that greeted the residents of Boston on the morning of March 5, 1770, would not accomplish their goal; this was not the purpose of the notices. Like the loading of a cannon, it was merely one of several steps. With demonstrations and speeches and late-night vigilante justice, Adams and his men had packed the barrel of Boston emotions with powder and shot. The notices merely primed the weapon. It was now ready to go off. All they needed was a spark.

They didn't have to wait long.

That evening a crowd of boys pelted the British sentry on King Street with snowballs. In itself, this was nothing unusual. Pelting sentries was a recognized pastime for colonial youngsters.

And, in keeping with the usual course of events, the sentry sent his attackers scampering. Normally, this would have been the end of it. But, because of Adams' propaganda, many colonists were now convinced they were in danger of massacre from British troops. Word spread quickly that an armed British sentry was harassing defenseless colonial boys. A fire bell was rung and the people of Boston swarmed toward King Street.

The square of the customhouse was soon filled with a swearing, turbulent mass of men armed with planks torn from a demolished butcher's stall and clubs and jagged pieces of ice and any garbage they could find laying about the street. Among those responding to the call were Samuel Gray, who had initiated the brawl at the ropewalk three days earlier; Crispus Attucks, a huge mulatto and veteran of a score of riots; James Caldwell, a ship's mate; and Patrick Carr, a seasoned Irish rioter. Other fire bells were now ringing. Scores of men were running through the icy streets, shouting threats at British soldiers, cursing and calling them bloody-backed rascals and scoundrel lobster-backs.

At the customhouse, the British sentry, still standing guard in his box, wasted no time in loading his musket, fixing his bayonet, and sending for emergency reinforcements. While the dense crowd showered him with a hail of snowballs, lumps of ice, and street refuse, a detachment of soldiers under the command of Captain Thomas Preston marched double-time through the moonlit streets to his rescue. Preston ordered his men to fix bayonets and load their muskets as they positioned themselves in front of the building.

A merchant by the name of Richard Palmer approached Captain Preston. "I hope you do not intend they shall fire upon the inhabitants," he said.

"By no means, by no means," Preston replied.

Taunting the soldiers, the mob pressed forward. "Fire, why

don't you? Fire! You cowards! You dare not fire!" Some of the Boston youths shouted provocative insults as they tapped the soldiers' muskets with sticks, daring them to shoot. "Fire!" they shouted. "You can't kill us all!"

Suddenly, one of the soldiers was knocked to the ground by a lump of wood. The crowd shouted for him to fire. Somewhere, behind the line of soldiers someone shouted, "Fire! Fire by God! I'll stand by you whilst I have a drop of blood! Fire!" Scrambling to his feet, the soldier raised his musket and pulled the trigger. Within seconds the other soldiers opened fire too.

Instantly Captain Preston jumped in front of his men, waving his sword. "What did you fire for?" he cursed at his men, striking up the gun of one of the soldiers who was reloading his weapon. But the damage was done. Five men had been killed or mortally wounded. Among them: Samuel Gray, Crispus Attucks, James Caldwell, and Patrick Carr.

Captain Preston and his men were put on trial for murder. Defending them were Josiah Quincy and John Adams, Sam Adams' second cousin. During the course of the trial, it was significant that the notices posted around Boston the morning of the riot were not introduced as evidence against the defendants. After two and a half hours of deliberation, the jury returned its verdicts. All but two soldiers were acquitted. The two who were not acquitted were found guilty of manslaughter, not murder. They were branded with the letter *M* on their thumbs and permitted to rejoin their regiment. Captain Preston was acquitted in a separate trial.

Sam Adams lost no time in making the most of the "bloody work on King Street." Only one of the victims, Patrick Carr, was denied the sweets of martyrdom by Adams because while on his deathbed, Carr absolved the soldiers of all blame. Articles were published condemning the quartering of troops in populous towns. Ministers preached sermons on such texts as the "Slaughter of the Innocents." Engravings were made portraying Captain Preston standing behind his men, waving his sword and ordering them to fire. The townspeople voted that March 5 would be set aside annually to commemorate the massacre on King Street. On that day a speech was to be delivered followed by a public exhibition at the site of the massacre. The exhibition depicted the innocent bystanders; the troops; the order to fire; and the slaughtered victims, who were portrayed as decent, hard-working, innocent men.

Jacob Morgan stood shoulder to shoulder with Sam Adams watching the residents of Boston pour into the Old South Meetinghouse for the annual Massacre Oration of 1775.

"It's as you suspected," Jacob whispered to Adams.

"No doubt they've come to beat up a breeze," Adams replied.

He was referring to a large number of British officers and soldiers represented among the audience. It was no secret that the British regiments regarded this annual oration as a deliberate insult. They particularly disliked the frequent references to the "bloody massacre" of March 5. In previous years, speakers used the phrase as an emotional bludgeon against the military presence in the city. Rumor had it that this year the soldiers would not tolerate this waving of the bloody shirt.

With deliberate strides, Adams mounted the platform and approached the black-draped pulpit. "Welcome, friends!" he called out cheerfully, looking directly at a large group of soldiers. "As moderator of this annual commemoration, I would like to invite all our soldier friends to take these seats up here." He motioned to the first few rows. "We want you to feel welcome."

The soldiers looked at one another quizzically. *Why would Adams direct them to the best seats in the house?* There was a moment of hesitation as whispers scurried back and forth; then a few of the larger soldiers, as if on a dare, strutted boldly to the front row and sat down.

Adams had returned to his place next to Jacob. The younger man's puzzled expression drew his comment. "It is a good maxim in politics, as well as war," he said, "to put and keep the enemy in the wrong."

When the time arrived for the ceremony to begin, Joseph Warren, the speaker of the day, mounted the pulpit clad in a Ciceronian toga. Accompanying him on the platform were Adams, Hancock, and Cooper. Jacob Morgan watched from floor level at the side of the platform.

At first, Warren seemed unnerved at the number of soldiers seated in front of him. He stammered something about their large numbers, then shot a glance to his compatriots behind him. Their calm attitudes seemed to settle him. Warren threw himself into a Demosthenian posture, with a handkerchief in his right hand and his left hand in his breeches, and began his speech.

His wasn't the most eloquent speech ever delivered on this day of commemoration, nor was it the most memorable. Joseph Warren began and ended safely, his restraint being the most obvious element of the address. He was careful not to risk a riot by waving the bloody shirt and never once referred to the events of that night five years previous as the "bloody massacre." When Warren finished, there was some polite applause and a smattering of groans. He retreated to the rear of the platform and sat down amid a mixture of cheers and hisses. Any danger of a free-for-all between civilians and soldiers seemed to dissipate.

From his vantage point beside the platform, Jacob had listened to Warren's speech with a sinking disappointment. In his opinion, Warren had capitulated to the soldiers' intimidation tactics with their inflated attendance. Jacob wished Sam Adams had been chosen for this year's speech. Adams wouldn't have shrunk back in fear.

As if to confirm Jacob's assessment, throughout the speech Sam Adams squirmed and tensed and grimaced every time Warren built to a point, then backed away from it. Jacob's neck and shoulders ached from the strain of just watching Adams' tension.

After Warren finished, Adams, acting as moderator, proceeded to the pulpit. "The thanks of the town should be presented to Dr. Warren," he said, "for his elegant and spirited oration." He paused for applause. "And in keeping with Dr. Warren's fine address, another oration should be delivered on the fifth of March next ..." Adams paused again, this time for effect; he didn't continue until all was silent, and when he did, he shouted ... "to commemorate the *Bloody Massacre* of the fifth of March, 1770!"

Officers leaped to their feet crying, "O fie, O fie!"

Jacob and his fellow patriots cheered and whistled.

Suddenly, panic erupted in the galleries. In the midst of all the din, the officers' cries of "O fie!" sounded much like "Fire! Fire!" Expecting musket fire, the crowd poured out into the street through every door and window of the meetinghouse. To add to the confusion, a regiment of British regulars happened to be passing outside at that very moment. When the patriots indoors heard the beating of drums and tramping of feet, they concluded they were about to be slaughtered in the meetinghouse.

Jacob Morgan leaped to the stage and pulled Adams aside, sheltering the politician with his body. Several of the British officers seated on the front rows advanced toward them. Jacob could see their thoughts reflected in their eyes and sneering grins. *Why not take advantage of the the confusion? Surely there are bound to be some casualties. Wouldn't it be a pity if Sam Adams was counted among those injured or killed in the riot?* But before they could mount the platform, Jacob rushed Adams out a back exit to safety.

Miraculously, no one was trampled in the stampede, and at last, order was restored. The meeting broke up without further incident.

The next day, Sam Adams—typically—declared that the soldiers, not the civilians, had been the ones in danger at the meeting; that had it not been for the patriots' self-control, not an officer or soldier would have left the meetinghouse alive.

6

"My, aren't you the *wicked* one?"

The lyrical tone in her voice indicated she was not displeased. Mercy stood with her back against the closed door of her bedroom, a dainty hand resting on her chest. Though it was mid-morning in the middle of a workweek, she was dressed in finer attire than many women could afford for a ball. Her full skirt stretched over stiff petticoats; elbow-length sleeves with cuffs were adorned with lace frills.

Esau stood in the center of the room a few feet from her, his hat in his hand. His free hand fidgeted nervously, alternating between smoothing wrinkles in his velvet breeches and worrying the middle button on his waistcoat. Although it had been over two weeks since the tar-and-feather incident, portions of his hands, neck, and face were still shaded black; other portions of his skin were red or scabbed from the burns, and a distinct odor of tar lingered about him. At the moment, however, none of this seemed to matter. He was alone with Mercy in a room that—though it was Jacob's bedroom too—showed little evidence that anyone lived there but Mercy. He knew he was foolish to be there. But if all went as planned, this day would be the end of secrets and hiding and the beginning of a new future with his beloved.

Mercy whispered, "I'm *flattered* by your bravado, Master Morgan, but I *must* insist you leave here immediately. Jacob is right down the hall in your *father's* room! If he should return ..."

"I know. I'll make this quick," he whispered back. Esau struggled momentarily to put his thoughts into words. "Mercy," he began hesitantly, "come to England with me."

"*Whatever* are you talking about?"

"Run away with me. Tonight. We can go to England and make a new life for ourselves. Just you and me. I have it all arranged. First to Philadelphia, then to England. Think of it, my love! We can be together, like we were meant to be!"

"Oh my!" Mercy fluttered a hand in front of her face. It was a practiced gesture that she often used at parties whenever a handsome gentleman flirted with her. She learned that a display of mock embarrassment usually encouraged the *paramour du jour* to continue his flirting, usually with greater boldness than before. For once, however, her practiced gesture was driven by real emotions. Esau was serious and she didn't know what to do. "Oh my," she said again, slumping against the door. "I don't know what to say. I ... I ... really, just don't know what to say."

"Say yes." Esau took a hesitant step forward, his face twisted in a goofy grin.

"This is so uncharacteristic of you, Esau. I've always been able to count on you to be the sensible one."

"Perilous days demand great risks, my love. Besides, there is no future for us here. In England we can build a new life. We can change our names. Start over. Have a family."

All gaiety and pretense drained from Mercy's face. The sparkle left her eyes. The impish curve of her lips was gone. She was plain, and it startled Esau. He'd never seen her like this.

Never. There had always been some element of Mercy that was animated ... lively ... glimmering. But at this moment there was none of that. Mercy Reed Morgan looked like an average woman approaching middle age.

"I can't go with you," she said flatly.

The scene before him was unnerving. Esau's butterfly was withdrawing into a cocoon. He had to stop her. Grabbing her by the shoulders, he stared hard into her eyes as if he could revive her animation with sheer willpower. "Don't be afraid, darling," he pleaded. "It will be all right. We'll make it all right!"

Mercy lowered her eyes to the floor.

"Is it the money? This house? Is that what's stopping you? I know I'm asking a lot, darling, but we can build our own business. Together we can make a fortune! Soon you'll be the envy of all the lords and ladies in England! Think of it, my dear! Not just colonial Philadelphia and Boston—compared to England, they're nothing! The finest families in London and Oxford and Southampton will know you and adore you as much as I do!"

Her eyes blinked slowly, dully, almost as if she were in a stupor. Esau wanted to shake her. *Who was this woman? This was not his Mercy. His Mercy was a sprite. A fairy. A young doe romping through the woods on a spring day.*

"I never should have ..." she mumbled, "so long ... I should have ..."

Placing a cupped hand under her chin, Esau lifted her head. She closed her eyes, refusing to look at him.

"Whatever it is that is frightening you, we can face it together!"

Her eyes still closed, she mumbled, "I can't ... go with ... you."

"Mercy, listen to me!" His voice was stern. "It doesn't matter that you're married to Jacob. If he hadn't tricked you, you never would have married him in the first place! And I don't believe

God honors a marriage based on lies and deception. The fact that you and Jacob are childless is proof of God's disfavor! I'm sure of it!"

He placed his blackened palms on her velvety, pale cheeks.

"Look at me!" he said. "Look at me!"

Slowly, she opened her eyes. As she did, tears fell upon Esau's burned hands.

"Jacob can't give you children," he pleaded. "I can! God will honor our marriage because our marriage will be based on love!"

Mercy stared vacantly into his eyes.

"Just say you'll go with me. That's all you have to do. I'll do everything else. We'll be halfway to London before Jacob even misses you."

"I'm carrying Jacob's baby."

Esau's heart stopped cold. He pulled his hands from her face. This couldn't be true. She must be mistaken. He shook his head in disbelief.

"Yes, Esau," Mercy insisted. "I'm with child."

Esau's mind raced from thought to thought, searching for bits of medical knowledge, folklore, something, anything that would create doubt or prove her wrong.

"Why ... um, who else ... why hasn't Jacob said anything?" he asked.

"I haven't told him yet." Esau's eyes lit up at this revelation, so she hastened to add, "I just haven't found the right time, what with all the committee work he's been doing. I plan to tell him soon. Today."

"He doesn't need to know!" Esau exclaimed. "And the baby need never know! If we go soon, you can have your child in England. We can raise him together. I can be his father. As long as you're his mother, I'll love him as if he's my very ..."

"Esau, stop it! Stop it!" Mercy grabbed the sides of her head in agony. "Stop it ... stop it ... it's all my fault ... I never should have ..."

She slumped to the floor. Her petticoats bunched all around her. She looked almost comical, like a little girl playing dress-up in Mother's clothes.

"I never should have led you on," she said between sobs. "It was selfish of me. I knew it, but I did it anyway. I craved the attention you gave me, the way you would risk family and public humiliation just to talk with me in private. But, until now, you never pressed for anything more. I had the best of two worlds. I had a husband *and* a suitor. And now look what I've done ... all these years ... look what I've done to you. I'm so sorry."

"But you love me," Esau insisted. "I've always known you loved me!"

Mercy shook her head back and forth.

"Why are you doing this, Mercy? Our love for each other will never die!"

Angry eyes shot up at him. "What will it take to get through to you?" she cried, careful to keep her voice low. "Why are you forcing me to hurt you? I'm a leech, all right? Do you understand that? I've been feeding off you. But I don't love you. Not anymore. Do you hear me? I don't love you!"

Jared was in an ugly mood. Five times in two weeks his plans had changed. First he was going to London, then he wasn't, then he was going again, then he wasn't. Yesterday he learned the trip was on again. Politicians. If he had a choice of tangling with politicians or a hurricane, he'd choose the hurricane. Both, of course, were known for their wind, and both were nearly impossible to predict. The difference between them was integrity. You knew where you stood with a hurricane. In all his years at sea, Jared never once met a hurricane that claimed to be his friend just before it tried to dash him against the rocks.

It didn't help his mood that he was waging an internal war over his own integrity. He didn't want to go to London. The more he thought about it, the more he didn't want to go. But he'd given his word. He'd go. But he hadn't promised to be happy about it.

The thing that bothered him most about going was leaving Anne at such a perilous time. It wasn't safe to walk the streets of Boston anymore. As Esau proved, if the Tories didn't get you, the rebels would.

Esau hadn't said much about his tar and feathering. He failed to identify any of his attackers. Either that, or he simply refused to identify them. Jared tended to believe the latter. And deep inside Jared couldn't help thinking that Jacob had a part in it. How much, he didn't know. But it was too much of a coincidence for him to believe that Esau was picked at random by Adams' mob the same night verbal hostilities were exchanged between them in his study.

Jared threw the last of his shirts into a seabag that was sitting on his bed. This was the second set of clothes he'd packed. His trunk sailed without him after the first aborted trip, and only a fool would count on it still being there by the time he finally arrived. As he pulled the rope that drew the bag closed, he glanced over at Jacob slumped in a corner chair. Jacob was being stubbornly uncooperative. Jared had asked him point-blank whether or not he had anything to do with the assault on Esau. Jacob's response was as clear as bilgewater, and smelled as such. He claimed that as a minuteman he had sworn an oath not to divulge any information discussed in the meetings. Certainly, he'd argued, his father could understand the importance of loyalty to one's mates. Jared's rebuttal that family concerns outweighed any oath made to tavern-mates fell on deaf ears, as he knew it would.

Sensing he would get no further information from Jacob on this matter, he changed the subject.

"While I'm gone, I'm counting on you to protect the family. Esau is needed in Cambridge. I want you to escort your mother and Mercy whenever they step outside this house. It's not safe for them to be alone on the streets."

Jacob straightened himself in the chair. "I won't be here," he said. "I'm leaving."

"What?"

"I won't be here. I'm leaving shortly myself."

"To go where?"

The look on Jacob's face indicated he didn't wish to divulge his destination. Probably another tavern secret. But the look on his father's face convinced him to reevaluate. He said, "Lexington. I'm going to Lexington."

"What on earth for?" Jared shouted. "What in Lexington is more important than your wife and your mother?"

Jacob was noticeably displeased that his father was questioning his value judgments. He chose to answer anyway. "I'll be accompanying Mr. Adams and Mr. Hancock," he said.

Jared's eyes rolled heavenward.

Jacob was on his feet. "Don't treat me like a child!" he shouted. "Whether you want to admit it or not, we're on the verge of war. And at least I'm man enough to get off the fence and fight for my country!"

"Is that how you rationalize abandoning your wife and mother?" Jared shouted back.

"And how did you rationalize all the times you left Mother and us to sail to God-knows-where?"

"Boston was safe in those days! By leaving I wasn't endangering your lives!"

"And the only way Boston will be safe again is if we drive the redcoats into the sea! The best thing I can do for my family's safety is to hasten that day."

Jared pulled his seabag from the bed and slammed it to the floor. "And you'll hasten that day by becoming Samuel Adams' lackey?"

"Unlike other men, Mr. Adams is not double minded. He is the one man who sees most clearly what must be done. More than that, he does whatever is necessary to bring about change."

"And he needs you to help him do that?"

"He has requested I accompany him for his personal safety."

"And what prompted him to choose you?"

"I protected him at the massacre oration."

Jared shook his head and sighed heavily. "And Mr. Adams' safety is more important than the safety of your mother and wife?"

Jacob's hands flew up in exasperation. "I could ask you the same question. Is your trip to England to spy on Franklin's questionable representation of the colonies more important than the safety of your family?"

"I'd rather not be going," Jared said. "But I gave my word."

"So did I," said Jacob.

The two men stood facing each other. Jared's hands were on his hips; Jacob's arms were folded across his chest.

Finally, Jacob said, "I'll ask Masters and Hawley at the warehouse to check on Mother and Mercy daily."

Jared nodded. "They're good men."

Jacob ambled uncertainly toward the door, unclear as to whether or not their conversation was concluded. "I need to pack," he said. "And to tell Mercy good-bye." He reached the door and looked back. His father was angrily tossing the seabag back onto the bed, pulling furiously at the rope. It was like this every time he packed. It would take him three or four times before he'd get everything he needed into the bag. Jacob took his father's lack of attention as a dismissal and walked down the hallway toward his bedroom.

"Jacob's coming!" Mercy squealed from the floor as heavy footsteps became louder in the hallway.

"I won't leave you like this!" Esau insisted.

Mercy looked at him like he was insane. "He'll kill you!" she said.

Esau looked around for a place to hide.

"No, out the window! The trellis!" Mercy insisted.

Esau ran to the window just as the sound of footsteps stopped outside the door. He stuck his head out and immediately pulled it back in. "It won't hold me!" he said in a strained whisper.

The latch clicked and the door pushed open, but just a crack, hitting Mercy in the rump.

"Mercy?" It was Jacob's voice.

Mercy motioned furiously at Esau to climb out the window. He did. The door closed, then opened again with the same results. Mercy held her place.

"Mercy, what's going on?" Jacob was speaking into the door's open crack. "Why are you sitting on the floor?"

"I'm … I'm …" Mercy stammered.

Esau's legs dangled out the window. He balanced his midsection on the windowsill, searching blindly for a foothold.

"Just a minute, darling!" Mercy called.

Jacob, impatient as ever, closed the door and pushed again, this time with enough force to scoot Mercy forward several inches.

Esau had found a foothold. The window framed his upper body like he was a portrait on the wall.

"Don't push, darling! You're hurting me! Just give me a minute and I'll let you in."

"Mercy, is something wrong?" The voice didn't belong to Jacob. It was Jared's. Apparently he'd heard the commotion and come to investigate.

All that could be seen of Esau now was the top of his bobbing head. A moment later he was gone. Mercy stretched a leg out and flipped up the edge of a throw rug. "I'm getting up," she called out. She reached for the latch and pulled herself up, making it appear to be more laborious for her than it actually was.

"Mercy, are you all right?" Jacob called.

On her feet again, she lifted the right one from the ground and hopped on the left. Steadying herself with the edge of the door, she took a small hop backward and opened it. Jacob was the first one through, with a worried Jared close behind.

"Clumsy me," she laughed self-consciously. Pointing to the rug, she said, "I must have tripped." Mercy placed her right foot on the ground, as if to straighten the rug, and winced.

"You hurt yourself!" Jared cried.

Instantly, the two men jumped to help her, one on each side, and gently assisted her to the bed. Mercy did a masterful job of acting hurt, a testimony to her years of performances in ballrooms all across New England. Once she was seated, Jacob fell to his knees in front of her and reached under her skirts.

"What are you doing?" she asked frantically.

Jacob looked puzzled. "Checking your ankle to see how bad it is. You might have broken it!"

Mercy shook her head and waved him away. "It's not broken," she said. "Probably only a sprain—a small one at that."

"At least let me check," Jacob insisted.

Jared, sensing that his being there was a source of embarrassment for Mercy, excused himself. At the door, he stopped. "You're sure you're all right? I can send for the doctor."

Mercy insisted that wouldn't be necessary.

Jared eased the door shut.

"It doesn't seem to be swelling," Jacob said, probing her ankle.

Mercy yelped and winced and whimpered as would be expected of one who had just suffered a sprained ankle.

"Doesn't look too bad," Jacob concluded. He stood. "But you need to be more careful. And stay off that ankle for a few days. Give it time to heal."

A twinkle appeared in Mercy's eye. Having narrowly escaped getting caught with a man in her room had stirred her blood. She was rapidly returning to normal. "It looks like you'll have to be my nursemaid," she said playfully. "Two, maybe three days and nights of your constant attention and I just may recover."

Jacob was only half-listening to her. He was bent over a chest of drawers pulling out clothes and stacking them in the crook of one arm.

"What are you doing?" she asked.

He glanced up. "Going to Lexington. Don't know for how long." Reading the displeasure on her face, he added, "Mother can help you with your ankle."

"And what or who is in Lexington?" Her tone was icy.

Jacob shrugged. "Sorry, can't tell you. Committee business." He straightened up, his arms loaded with shirts and breeches. "It's really for your own good," he said. "The less you know, the better."

"When will you be back?"

"I already told you. I don't know."

Mercy sat rigidly on the edge of the bed. This was just like Jacob. With no thought for her, he'd go off for a night or a day or on a trip. With him it was always important. Something had to be done and he was the only one who could do it.

"I'd tell you if I could!" Jacob insisted.

She folded her arms tightly across her chest. Two could play this game. If he wasn't going to confide in her, she wasn't going to confide in him. As far as she was concerned, he could be the last one to know she was going to have a baby. Let him stay away six or seven months and come back to find a baby in her arms. It would serve him right!

Jacob resumed packing. He recognized his wife's posture and her pursed lips. She was angry with him; he'd be lucky if he heard another word from her before he left. He sighed. He didn't have time for this, he thought. Rumors in Boston were rampant. The redcoats were up to something. The number of their drills had increased; they'd shut down traffic across the harbor; they'd tightened security at the neck, Boston's thin attachment to the mainland. Normally, he'd beg and plead with Mercy to forgive him for being a brute. But he had to get to Lexington. He'd just have to endure her anger and make it up to her when he returned.

While Mercy stalled Jacob upstairs, Esau reached the ground beneath her window and raced toward the front of the house. As quietly as he could, he pressed the latch of the front door and slipped inside. With the door eased shut behind him, he tiptoed toward the stairs and his room.

"Esau? Is that you?"

Anne Morgan called to her son from the drawing room.

"Yes, Mother," he called back. "It's me."

"Could I bother you for a moment?"

Esau reversed his course and walked to the drawing room, all the while straightening his clothes and trying to calm his rapid breathing from the run around the house. He entered the room to find his mother sitting in a chair by the window. Her dress was bright yellow, but modest; when it came to clothing, Anne Morgan's artistic flair usually manifested itself in color rather than a preponderance of ribbons and bows. A small table bearing an open Bible lay in front of her. There was an identical chair on the other side of the table. Esau associated the cozy setting with his Aunt Priscilla. Whenever she came for a visit, it was here the two women inevitably chatted for hour after hour.

"You're a more accomplished Bible student than I am," his mother said. "Could you help me with this passage?"

His breath almost under control, Esau smiled and walked over to her, chuckling inwardly at her self-denigration. For a woman who had never spent a day in a classroom of higher learning, his mother knew the Bible better than most ordained ministers.

"This passage here." An elegantly thin finger pointed to the verse. She leaned back in her chair, allowing Esau room to read it for himself. "John 1:47," she said as he bent over the Bible, "Philip just found his brother and was bringing him to Jesus."

Esau read aloud: *Jesus saw Nathaniel coming to him, and saith of him, Behold an Israelite indeed, in whom is no guile!* He nodded. "All right, I recognize the passage. What do you need help with?"

She motioned him to the chair opposite her. He sat down. "I seem to recall that there is an interesting history behind that word *guile*. But that's all I remember. Do you recall the background to this word?"

"Fish bait!" Esau answered. "The word means fish bait. It can also be translated 'deceit, cunning, treachery.' Jesus was saying that Nathaniel was a man who did not practice deceit."

"Fish bait!" Anne placed her finger on the verse as she looked at it again, sounding out the definition for herself.

Esau nodded at her, pleased he could be of assistance.

"Thank you, son. It's good to know all those years of study have paid off for you."

Esau rose and headed for the stairway again.

"One more thing ..." Anne called out after him.

He stopped and turned toward her.

"Was that you who ran by my window a few moments ago? I was sure you were already upstairs."

Esau's mind searched frantically for a plausible response, one that would place him outside and bring him around the house empty-handed. "Well, actually, I stepped out of the house for a few moments...."

Anne Morgan sat primly in her chair, listening innocently to the beginning of his tale. But the feature that caught Esau's attention was his mother's finger. It was still resting on the Bible, pointing to the word that meant fish bait.

He stopped his fabrication midsentence. "Mother," he said, "how long have you been reading from the gospel of John?"

"Well, let me see now," she said, "how long ago was it that you ran past my window?"

Esau returned to the chair opposite her. "What are you trying to tell me?"

"Oh, I'm not trying to tell you anything, dear. I thought I'd let God's Word do my talking for me."

"Do you think I'm doing something I should be ashamed of?"

"Son, I'm your mother, not your judge. My prayer for you is that you will find the happiness God wants you to have. You're a good man. And if I have learned anything about God during my lifetime it is this: He rewards faithfulness, never bitterness or jealousy or deceit."

For a long minute Esau stared at the floor. He thought of Jacob and Mercy. It was deceit that got Jacob his wife. The tactic seemed to work well for his brother. But he knew that argument wouldn't hold water with his mother, so he kept the thought to himself. Slowly, he stood, averting his eyes from his mother's.

"I saw you and Mercy in the garden the night of our dinner," she said.

This revelation startled him.

"And I saw the way you looked at her at the dinner table that night. You still love her, don't you?"

He said nothing.

"Esau, she's a married woman! Give her up. I'm confident God has a wonderful woman for you, but He can't help you find her until you surrender your infatuation with Mercy."

Infatuation. The word wedged in Esau's mind in a most uncomfortable way. He *loved* Mercy. It was love, not infatuation, that drove him. And, to use his mother's own source of authority, didn't the Bible teach that love never gives up?

"Well," Anne said, "I can see by the look on your face that I'm not getting through to you. Esau, just promise to think about what I've said." She looked at the scar tissue and black residue on his hands. "I know you're a fighter. I simply pray that God will grant you wisdom to know when to fight and when to turn away."

In his mother's comments, Esau saw a chance to change the subject. "Speaking of turning away," he said, "what would you say if I told you I was seriously considering moving to England permanently?"

It was Anne's turn to lower her eyes. "I'd miss you," she said. "And although the thought had never crossed my mind, at the same time I'd have to say I'm not surprised. Your fierce loyalty to England puts you in constant danger here. Between us, I must confess I have a difficult time thinking of myself as anything but an Englishwoman." She paused to take a deep breath. Looking up, she said, "Have you told your father?"

"No, not yet."

"Then I think it best you tell him now before he leaves." She rose and straightened the front of her dress. "The Lord alone knows when the two of you shall ever see each other again. May I go with you?"

Esau smiled. "I'd like that."

She reached out and touched his forearm. "And please promise to think about what I've said. Don't give up on God, son; He hasn't given up on you."

Esau broadened his smile and patted her hand affectionately. But he didn't promise.

※

Jared's seabag hit the floor with a thud as Anne and Esau walked through the door.

"Finished packing already, dear?"

Jared mumbled incoherently. He'd just tied the bag for the third time.

Anne passed the conversation to Esau. "Father, I have something to tell you," he said.

"Better make it quick, or my ship will sail without me." Sarcastically, he added, "Unless the trip has been called off again."

"I'm thinking of moving to England. Permanently."

Jared straightened himself, looked at his son, then turned toward the wardrobe, searching the bottom of it for a forgotten item. With his head in the wardrobe, his words sounded like they were coming from the bottom of a well. "Don't be a fool. There's nothing for you in England."

"There's nothing for me in America!" Esau retorted angrily.

Emerging from the wardrobe, Jared examined a pair of shoes he'd retrieved, then threw them back. "Everything that is anything is here in America!" he shouted. "Your family, the business. Stop being so self-centered and think about others for once in your life!"

Esau replied with measured tones, struggling to restrain his mounting fury. "I am thinking about the family," he said. "About our family's future. If the rebels persist in their present course, they will force Parliament's hand and the colonies will be subjected to military rule. By siding with the rebels, we could lose everything! Just maybe, if I can prove myself a loyal Englishman, when that day comes, I'll be able to salvage at least a portion of what we own!"

"It's too late for that," Jared retorted. "The die is cast. Our ancestors fled from English oppression and gave their lives to build everything we hold dear. It's time to fight for what is rightfully ours; politically if possible, with muskets if necessary."

Esau shouted, "I can't believe you've allowed yourself to be brainwashed by all this revolutionary drivel."

"This is *our* land!" Jared shouted back. "The future of the Morgans is in America, not England. And any Morgan who refuses to fight for his country is no better than a deserter! Do I make myself clear?"

※

Just then, a door flew open with a crash as Mercy and Jacob's argument spilled into the hallway. Jared snatched up his seabag and left the master bedroom; Anne and Esau followed.

Mercy: Go then! And if I'm not here when you get back, don't come looking for me!

Jacob: You'll be here. End of discussion.

Jared to Esau: We'll talk more of this when I return.

Esau: By then it may be too late.

Jared: Is that a threat?

Anne: Jared, don't be so defensive. Hurry along, you'll miss your ship.

Mercy: I never should have married you in the first place!

Jacob: Isn't that just like you? You think every man in the world would feel lucky to have you for his wife.

Anne: Jacob, are you leaving right now too?

Mercy: Yes, he's leaving ... he's leaving me all alone and ..."

Esau: Do you want me to look in on you and Mother occasionally?

Jacob: Look in on Mother, but stay away from my wife!

Anne: Now, Jacob, he didn't mean anything by that.

Mercy: At least someone's concerned about me.

Jared: Can we clear this hallway? I'll miss my ship!

Jacob: Looks like you're doing just fine to me; you're not even limping! Look, everyone! A miracle! Or is there something you're not telling me, little miss actress?

Mercy (weeping): I can't believe you think I'm not in pain. If that's the way you feel, well, I hope you never come back!

Jared: Can I please get to my ship?

※

Minutes later the Morgans' upstairs hallway was empty. Mercy was in her room, crying. Esau was headed back to Cambridge, Jared to the wharf, and Jacob to Lexington. Anne returned to her seat in the drawing room. She was not alone. Her guest was the same horrible feeling that had haunted her the night of the dinner. The feeling that something dreadful was about to happen and she could do nothing about it. She fought the feeling the only way she knew how, with prayer.

She began, "Lord, when I am weak, You are strong...."

7

The British march on Lexington and Concord was not unexpected. Military surprise in those days was about as rare as a toast to King George's health at the Green Dragon Inn. Both sides were riddled with spies. So when the British regulars set out to raid the stockpiled munitions at Concord and arrest the notorious Adams and Hancock at Lexington, Paul Revere had already warned the two towns of the impending strike three days previous.

It was no surprise to the Concordians that something was afoot. In March the townspeople had escorted two of General Gage's spies and their collaborating Tory friends out of town when they were caught mapping the roads, locating the hiding places of the munitions, and taking the political pulse of the town. And when the Congress met in Concord on March 22, the most immediate problem facing them was that of false alarms. Everyone expected the British regulars to march on Concord; they just didn't know when it would happen. It was a time of dread suspense.

A threefold plan to sound the alarm was devised. The moment the time of deployment was known, Revere would cross over to

Charlestown by rowboat and from there ride to Concord sounding the alarm; Robert Newton, a young sexton, was posted at the North Church to flash the alarm signal to waiting patriots across the shore—one light if the British were traveling overland by way of the Boston neck, two lights if they crossed the water to Charlestown—so that if Revere didn't make it, at least the signal would. As added assurance, William Dawes, a rotund shoemaker, set out by the land route to carry the message to the anxious towns.

On the afternoon of April 18, British Lieutenant Colonel Francis Smith received orders to head the expedition that night. The troops, comprising nearly six hundred men, were told they were leaving by their sergeants putting their hands on them and whispering gently in their ears. They were then led out the barracks the back way and marched in silence to the common where they were stealthily loaded onto boats at 11:00 p.m.

As the troops were crossing over to East Cambridge, two lanterns appeared in the North Church steeple. Dawes had already passed the British sentries on Boston's neck, and Revere had rowed across to Cambridge ahead of them, then borrowed a horse from Deacon John Larkin, and was sounding the call to arms. Revere had been tipped off by a groom who had overheard some young officers joking in the stables about riding out to Concord that night.

The British expedition was doomed to failure. The men and women of Concord had already worked through the previous night to remove the arms and ammunition by ox team to new hiding places in Acton, Stow, and in the woods and outskirts of the town.

Jacob Morgan shivered in the cold outside Rev. Jonas Clark's house in Lexington. Without releasing his musket, he wiped his nose with the back of his hand. Cold weather always affected him that way. It was nearly midnight. He and three other men had volunteered to stand watch outside the house to safeguard the persons inside, notably Samuel Adams and John Hancock. Until a short time ago, it had been a quiet evening. But now they could hear in the distance church bells ringing and muskets being fired. It could be just another false alarm, but then it could also be the real thing. When they first heard the bells, Jacob and the other sentries had conferred and decided that until they knew more, it was best not to wake up those in the house. One of the sentries, a younger man with a full red mustache and beard, spoke an octave higher than he normally did; another stammered a lot and kept drying his palms on his breeches. Jacob wondered if the tension inside him was manifesting itself in an equally obvious way.

Pounding horse's hoofs caught his attention. Coming closer. A laboring horse and his rider could be seen at a good distance because the moon was full and bright enough to cast shadows. Jacob raised his musket and watched. The rider was coming straight at him. He was alone.

"My name's Revere!" the rider shouted. "Sound the alarm!"

The sentry with the full beard came running forward. "We have orders that the residents of this house are not to be disturbed by any noise," he said.

"Noise!" Revere exclaimed. "You'll have noise enough before long. The regulars are coming out!"

Within minutes the church bell sounded the alarm, militiamen grabbed their firearms and hurried in the night toward Lexington common. Adams and Hancock were roused from their slumber as was their host, Rev. Clark. An impromptu meeting was held at the dinner table. Express rider Paul Revere was invited in, as was Jacob, at Adams' request.

Jacob remained standing while the others pulled up chairs.

Although Revere didn't seem in any great hurry, Jacob wouldn't have been able to sit still. Standing, he thought, would make his fidgeting less noticeable, and he wouldn't have to surrender his musket. He positioned himself facing the door.

Prompted by Adams, who wanted to hear every detail, Revere launched into an account of his ride thus far. He was an average-size man with straight brown hair. What stood out to Jacob was his strong hands and thick wrists, which seemed natural enough for a silversmith. Although they'd never met, Jacob had often heard of the man at committee meetings.

"Two friends rowed me across Charles River, a little to the eastward where the *Somerset* man-of-war lay," Revere began. "They landed me on Charlestown side, and I went to get me a horse."

Hancock interrupted: "Surely the *Somerset* had sentries posted. How did you manage to slip by them?"

Revere shrugged and grinned. "Have you seen how full the moon is tonight? I thought for sure we'd be spotted, even though we'd taken extra precaution to quiet the oars."

"Extra precaution?" Adams asked.

The grin widened. "A friendly young lady lent us her petticoat with which we muffled the oars."

The mental image of a young woman donating her petticoat to the revolutionary cause sent Hancock to howling. He slapped his knee several times.

"When we reached shore," Revere continued, "Colonel Conant and some friends of his were there to greet us. He had seen the signal in the church tower and was anxious to know what was happening. I learned from him that British officers were patrolling the roads between Cambridge and Concord. Of course, we expected this, but I thanked him anyway. Then I went to John Larkin's house. He loaned me a very good horse, and I set off for here. By then it was almost eleven."

A pewter mug of ale was set in front of the express rider. He interrupted his narration long enough to take two long draws from the mug. Adams drummed his fingers impatiently.

"I rode over the neck at a slow canter until I reached the fork in the road. I took the left road to Cambridge across that flat marshland there."

"Charleston common," Jacob filled in while Revere took another drink. He nodded as he swallowed, indicating that Jacob's identification was correct.

"Where that iron cage is with the bones in it," Revere added.

Years before, a slave named Mark had murdered his owner. The slave was executed and his body left hanging in an iron cage to serve as a warning to other slaves.

"Just past the cage, I spotted two redbacks under a tree. I identified them by their silhouettes—their holsters and cockades gave them away. One of them spurred his horse to come after me. So ..." Another drink emptied the mug. Revere signaled for a refill. "I turned sharply and galloped away. He tried to cut me off, but got bogged down in a mud hole. I got clear of him and went through Medford, over the bridge, and up to Menotomy. In Medford, I awakened the captain of the minutemen. After that I alarmed almost every house until I reached here."

The front door swung open. Jacob snatched up his weapon, then lowered it when he saw the familiar red beard of the other sentry. With him was William Dawes, who had ridden the land route, waking up the countryside with the news that British troops were on their way. After Dawes refreshed himself, the two express riders continued on to Concord.

By 2:00 a.m. about 130 patriots had gathered on the Lexington green. Forty-five-year-old Captain John Parker, a veteran of Rogers's Rangers in the French and Indian War, was in command. Adams sent Jacob out to the green to learn their plan.

The minutemen talked over the situation and concluded they would not fire upon the troops unless first fired upon. Parker sent scouts to locate the approaching redcoats and report back. The minutemen stood in groups and chatted to pass the time, shifting weight from one foot to the other and rubbing their arms and shoulders to fight off the chilled night air. Maybe it was the stillness of the night, but their laughter and banter were noisier than usual. When none of the scouts returned with fresh news, the minutemen disbanded with orders to reassemble at the sound of the drum. Some went home, others to nearby Buckman Tavern for a warming mug of rum.

Just before daybreak, Thaddeus Bowman, the last scout Parker sent out, raced into town with the news that the regulars were near. Captain Parker's drummer beat out the alarm, and minutemen came running back to the green. While Parker lined his troops up double file on the green, Jacob hurried back to Rev. Clark's house. Adams and Hancock readied their things for escape.

Just as they were at the point of leaving, Paul Revere returned to Lexington on foot. He told Adams and Hancock how, just after leaving Lexington, he and Dawes were overtaken by Samuel Prescott of Concord, who had spent the evening courting a lady friend in Lexington and was returning home. Prescott asked the two express riders if he could assist them. At each house they came to, the three roused the inhabitants.

Halfway to Concord they were stopped by a British patrol. Dawes made a dash for it. He made it to a farmhouse where he fell off his horse, then escaped by foot. Prescott managed to jump his horse over a low stone wall and got away to Concord. Revere was ordered to dismount. He was questioned, and his horse was taken. Then he was allowed to go free. His journey, which began with a clatter of hurrying hoofs, ended with a trek on foot back to Lexington through the burying ground.

With the British regulars only two miles away, Adams and Hancock, accompanied by Revere and Jacob, made a hasty retreat on horseback through the woods toward Woburn. Although in his heart Jacob knew he was doing the best thing by staying with Adams, he hated to leave Lexington. He had been aching to fight redcoats for years, and now that an opportunity presented itself, he was running in the opposite direction of the action. With a glance back at the green—Captain Parker was pacing up and down the line of minutemen, giving them instructions—Jacob reached down, grabbed a bag of clothing, slung it over his shoulder, and followed after Samuel Adams.

They hadn't gone far when John Hancock remembered he'd left a trunk packed with valuable papers at the tavern, papers that, should they fall into British hands, could hurt the patriot cause. Jacob volunteered to ride back to Lexington and hide the trunk at Rev. Clark's house. Revere was sent with him, not because Hancock didn't trust Jacob, but because the trunk was large. It would take two men to spirit the trunk away in a timely manner. So Jacob and Revere doubled back. Adams called after them to stay long enough to observe what was happening and then bring him back a report.

It was five o'clock. The stars had faded, and the morning sky was turning from flat gray to blue as Jacob and Revere reached a mist-enshrouded Lexington. Although buildings blocked their view of the common, the drums and fifes of the British troops could be heard distinctly. Jacob's heart raced, his pulse quickened, and his senses took on a sharp edge. He felt more alive now than ever before in his life, as if he had been born for this moment.

He remembered when he was younger hearing stories of battle bravery during the colonial wars against the French and Indians. There was something in the stories that captured his imagination. In war, it seemed to Jacob, crucial decisions determined life and death; friendships were deeper; life was reduced to a simple formula—do whatever it takes to stay alive.

When Jacob was fourteen, he ran away to fight the French, without giving much thought to provisions and shelter. He supposed he'd join up with a band of colonial soldiers who would readily recognize his fierce determination and invite him to join them. For three days and nights he tramped through the forest carrying his father's musket, after which he returned home hungry, tired, and angry. He was angry because in all that time never once did he see a Frenchman or Indian. When his father returned a few days later from an extended voyage, Anne turned Jacob over to him for discipline. Jared was rather lenient. After all, other than severely fraying his mother's nerves, no real damage was done. And Jared remembered what it was like for him at that age, including an incident in his life involving his father's musket, some wolves, and an unexpected night's stay in the forest.

Over the course of his life, Jacob's thirst for the heady brew of battle never diminished. And as hostilities in Boston increased, life became so much simpler—black and white, right and wrong, us and them. The covert activity of the Sons of Liberty and later the Committee of Safety gave him a cause to live for, but more important, gave him something to do. Let the others debate their endless debates; Jacob was a man of action. And with British troops marching on Lexington, the last thing he wanted to do was ride away from the fight with Sam Adams to Philadelphia and the convening of another Continental Congress where men stood in hallways and talked and talked and talked.

As the roll of the British drum beat the call to arms, Jacob could hear Captain Parker instructing his double file of thirty-eight men to let the British pass by. With a quick glance out the tavern window, Jacob saw about forty unarmed spectators standing on the common watching their husbands and sons prepare to meet the redcoats.

Revere and Jacob located Hancock's trunk and carried it to the Clark house, entrusting the good reverend with the task of hiding it safely away. Hurrying back to the tavern ahead of Revere, Jacob took up an observation post. He desperately wanted to join Captain Parker's minutemen on the common, but he was reminded of his duty—to observe and report back to Adams.

The light infantry led the redcoats onto the common. These were soldiers chosen for their dash and boldness in skirmishes. The grenadiers were in the rear. Each one was over six feet tall and looked even taller with their pointed hats shaped like cathedral windows; they were picked not only for their height, but also for their strength. Moments before, Major John Pitcairn had ordered them to prime and load their muskets and fix their bayonets. After doubling their ranks, he ordered their advance at double-quick time. From atop his horse, Pitcairn shouted to the light infantry: "Soldiers, don't fire! Keep your ranks! Surround and disarm them!" The trotting soldiers began the hoarse, familiar shout of an advancing British battle line.

Captain John Parker, concerned for the safety of his greatly outnumbered men, ordered them to give ground to the regulars, to disperse. Repeatedly, he told them not to fire. Some turned and walked away. Others, like Jonas Parker, a man well into his sixties, stood his ground.

The British troops rushed furiously forward, yelling, "Villains and rebels, disperse! Disperse! Lay down your arms! Disperse!" In their fury and zeal, their lines began to break. After a night of delays, wading waist deep through bogs, and marching more than a dozen miles, they were hungry, damp, chilled, and caked with mud. Having lost all discipline, they rushed madly after the rebels.

Suddenly, a shot echoed through the common. At its sound the now disorderly line of redcoats fired a volley. Major Pitcairn spurred his horse forward, furiously slicing his sword downward in the signal to cease fire. To no effect. His men raged out of control, unable to hear the shouting of their commander.

Old Jonas Parker fell, hit by a musket ball. To Jacob's horror, an infantryman finished off the old man with a bayonet thrust.

A few Americans returned fire. Smoke swirled around the village green, making it difficult to see what was happening next. While the redcoats continued to fire, the balance of the British troops arrived. Seeing the confusion on the green, British Colonel Smith ordered his drummer to beat assembly. The staccato roll of the drum broke through the din of battle, recalled the redcoats, and restored order.

As the British soldiers returned to their lines and the smoke lifted, Jacob pressed forward from his position to count the casualties. Eight colonists lay dead; another nine were wounded, most in the back. Jacob's heart pounded in his chest, his blood raced. He fought the urge to level his musket at the back of a retreating redcoat, to exact a measure of revenge. Instead, he snatched his firearm and rushed to report the event to Adams.

The morning of April 19, 1775, had barely begun. The British had been in Lexington less than half an hour. But in that time, the whole complexion of the colonial struggle against England changed. For Jacob, the debate was over, as were the late-night covert pranks under the cloak of committee activity. Everything was out in the open now. They were at war.

With his back to the town, Jacob galloped after Adams. Behind him he could hear the British troops firing a victory volley and shouting the traditional three cheers for a successful engagement.

When Adams heard Jacob's report, he exclaimed: "Oh, what a

glorious morning it is!" Seeing Jacob's startled reaction, he added, "I mean for America."

News of the Lexington skirmish spread quickly from town to town. As the British troops marched the straight six-mile road to Concord, invigorated by the action, warmed by the sun, and inspired by the fifes and drums, Jacob traveled at a leisurely pace with Adams and Hancock. Scores of farmers from nearby towns passed the trio, going the opposite direction, toward Concord, toward the fight.

Adams babbled happily on to Hancock, who rode next to him but was preoccupied with thoughts of his own. Jacob trailed behind them, unsure as to what his role would be in Philadelphia. When Adams first asked him to travel with him and be his protector, Jacob thought it was the most important thing he could do to forward the cause of the revolution. Now he wasn't so sure. It made sense that Adams would not allow himself to be caught in towns that came under British attack. That being the case, in place after place, battle after battle, Jacob would find himself in a similar position—his back to the fighting, riding away. He looked at the farmers who passed him going in the direction of the fighting. Young, old; of every conceivable size; some well outfitted, others with little more than a linen shirt, dirty breeches, and an aged musket and powder horn. Yet they were similar in one respect. There was a look of urgency in their eyes and a determined set to their jaws. Knowing they would line up against Britain's finest, knowing they might not ever return to their farms and their loved ones, yet they marched into danger. They were going to fight for their land. Their country.

"Jacob? Jacob!"

The persistent call of Sam Adams broke through his thoughts. Jacob reined to a halt just before he ran into the back of Adams' mount. For nearly a minute, Jacob waited for Adams to say what was on his mind. Adams, seemingly in no hurry, waited until two men, heading toward Concord, passed them by. One was older, the other younger than Jacob. From the similarities in facial features and the gait of their walk, Jacob guessed they were father and son. Their patched clothing indicated they were poor people; the boy wore no shoes. Adams tipped his hat politely to them. Not until they were out of earshot did Adams speak to Jacob.

"You want to join them, don't you?" he asked.

Jacob turned and looked at the father, who was growing smaller as the distance between them increased. "I have a job," he said. "I've made a commitment to protect you."

"You've made a commitment to serve your country," Adams replied.

Jacob turned to the statesman. He wasn't sure what to say. Was this a test of his loyalty?

With a twinkle in his eye, Adams reached out and slapped him on the shoulder. "Shoot a redcoat for me," he said.

"But what about ..."

"Go!" Adams insisted. "I only wish I was young enough to join you. I'd love to get one of those lobster-backs in my sights." Adams leveled a pretend musket in the direction of Concord.

Jacob felt a rush of blood to his head. He slipped from his mount and handed the reins to Adams.

"Wish I could give the horse to you, but it's not mine to give. Now, hurry, or you'll miss all the action!" Adams stretched out his hand.

Jacob pumped the politician's hand twice and turned back to Concord.

By the time Jacob Morgan reached Concord, he had learned something about himself. He learned he was younger in mind than he was in body. His thirty-year-old frame, though fit from long days loading and unloading on the docks, was suffering as he approached the edge of town. His legs cramped and his chest burned.

Falling in with a band of men who were circling the edge of town, heading toward the North Bridge, he learned that the red-coats had reached the center of town at eight o'clock. As one of the Concord men described the scene, the light infantry's arms were shining in the morning sun. A company of minutemen had marched out to meet them, then turned about-face, and marched back into town—barely two hundred yards ahead of the British. For a time, the fifes and drums of the two armies almost seemed to accompany each other. According to the eyewitness, the Concord patriots stood their ground near the meetinghouse, then gave way as the British light infantry approached. The minutemen retreated to a safer slope beyond the burying ground. After a brief caucus among themselves, they retreated farther, across the Concord River by way of the North Bridge. It was there they were holding their position, waiting for more volunteers to arrive from neighboring towns. The man reporting these events was one of several who had been sent to direct arriving patriots to the North Bridge.

As Jacob approached the hillock, just a few hundred yards above the bridge, he came upon a force of minutemen nearly four hundred strong under the command of Major Buttrick. Opposite them, on the town side of the bridge, was a detachment of fewer than a hundred British soldiers. Barely eight hundred yards sepa-rated the two armies.

Jacob collapsed wearily to the ground among David Brown's unit, next to a farmer from Lincoln who identified himself as Elias Todd. By the looks of the bearded farmer, he and Jacob were roughly the same age. While the two armies stared at each other, Todd took it upon himself to inform Jacob of the unit he'd just joined. Jacob learned that the commander's house was no more than a stone's throw away. In fact, they would pass it when they marched down to the bridge. According to Todd, Brown earlier told his unit how his feebleminded uncle had spent the morning drawing cider for the redcoats. The house was now deserted.

"What of news from the town?" Jacob asked.

"Oughta know in a bit. My boy's there right now, scoutin' around," Todd said. "He's nine. Good age for sneakin' around. Last we heard, the redcoats were goin' door-to-door. Won't find much. Most everythin's been moved already."

As he was speaking, a brown-eyed, barefooted lad ran up to them. His breeches were heavily patched and covered with dirt, his shirt torn and stained. The boy had a smattering of freckles and a full head of unruly chestnut hair. When the lad spoke, Jacob couldn't understand a word he was saying; it was as if the boy's alphabet consisted of only vowels.

Elias Todd held up a hand. "Slow down!" he said in a very pronounced way. The boy took a deep breath and started again. Even at this less excited pace, Jacob couldn't understand a word. When he finished, the boy's father smiled, rumpled his son's hair, and dragged him playfully to the ground, draping his arm around the boy's neck. To Jacob, he said: "This here's Bo. He's my boy."

"Pleased to meet you, Bo."

The boy looked at him with eyes that were neither friendly nor fearful. Sort of a neutral look, as if the two of them lived in different worlds and Bo was barely aware of Jacob's presence.

"Bo here is deaf," Elias Todd explained. "His mother caught the measles just before birthin' him. Took her life, his hearing." To Bo: "But we get along good enough, don't we, Bo?" The boy's eyes came alive, revealing more than devotion to his father; they flashed with intelligence. With the boy's neck in the crook of his arm, Elias Todd pulled his son's head against his chest and rubbed the top of the boy's head again. Bo fought back playfully.

"Bo. It's an unusual name," Jacob said.

Todd laughed. "His name's Jedediah." Todd laughed again when Jacob gave him the puzzled expression he had obviously fished for. He explained: "That's what his momma wanted to name him. 'Course, she didn't know the boy would be deaf. I tried—Lord knows how I tried—to teach the boy to say Jedediah. Workin' in the fields though, I most often just called him boy. He took to that."

The boy grinned and patted his chest with an open palm. "Bo," he said.

There was a pause. Both men checked the North Bridge. The redcoats were as idle as they were.

"Bo," his father said, looking directly into the boy's eyes. "This here is Jacob." Without turning away from his son, Elias reached back and patted Jacob's leg. "Ja-cob," he said again. "You say it. Ja-cob."

With furrowed brow, Bo Todd stared at his father's lips. First, imitating his father's lip movements, then adding sound. "Ja-be," he said. "Ja-be."

After several more attempts, Elias shrugged. "That's as close as he'll get. Can't hear the *c.*"

"Close enough," Jacob said, grinning.

Elias and Jacob looked down once more at the redcoats on the bridge, who returned their gaze. Elias let out a long sigh.

"What did Bo tell you about the town?" Jacob asked.

"British are throwing things in the millpond. Barrels. A couple of cannon. Some shot. That kind of thing. Trifles. Most everythin's been moved. They sent a detachment headed up the way …" Todd wrenched sideways and pointed over his shoulder, "to the Barrett place. Won't find nothin' there either."

"WRIGHT! GET BACK HERE! THAT'S AN ORDER!"

A tall man, looking every bit the well-bred Englishman, strode past Jacob toward the bridge. He stopped long enough to hand his musket to someone, then continued down the path.

"DON'T BE A FOOL, WRIGHT!"

"That's Captain Miles yellin'," Elias whispered to Jacob. With a grin, he added, "Won't do him no good." Pointing to the tall Englishman, he explained, "That there's Ezra Wright. A proper Englishman, he is. Droll fella, but a mighty fine singer. And stubborn."

Wright turned around without stopping. Walking backward he yelled to Miles, "I'm just going to talk to them!"

All eyes from both sides focused intently on the gangly Wright as he reached the colonial edge of the bridge. The British captain came midway across the bridge and held his position. The two conversed for several minutes.

Then Ezra Wright walked back up the hill, retrieved his musket, and said he was going home. Nothing was going to happen today, he insisted. Jacob and the other minutemen watched him disappear over the hill's summit.

Not long afterward, a cry from among the colonial troops sent a huge ripple through the ranks as all four hundred minutemen jumped to their feet. Their attention was drawn to the center of town. A single column of black smoke rose over the roofs. The swell of murmuring escalated into shouts and curses. It took the combined effort of all the commanders to restore order among the agitated patriots.

Joseph Hosmer, a lieutenant and well-known speechmaker, jumped onto a rock. "I have often heard it said," he shouted loud enough for all to hear, "that the British have boasted that they could march through our country, laying waste our hamlets and villages, and we would not oppose them. And I begin to think it is true!" Pointing dramatically to the rising smoke, he turned to one of the commanders. "Will you let them burn down the town?"

A brief council was held. The decision was unanimous. They resolved to march into the middle of town to defend their homes or die in the attempt. The colonials were arranged in a double file. Jacob and Elias Todd paired up, shoulder to shoulder. Actually, they formed a threesome, with the unarmed Bo standing next to his father, carrying his father's powder horn and shot.

Isaac Davis's Acton company was in the front line. Behind them was David Brown's unit, followed by Captain Miles's unit. Before marching, Major Buttrick strictly ordered them not to fire until fired upon, then to fire as fast as they could.

To the fife strains of "The White Cockade," their double column proceeded down the path to the North Bridge, with all the solemnity of men walking to church. As they marched past the deserted Brown home, Jacob saw his commanding officer look longingly at his property. On this warm spring day, the grain in the fields already stood tall and green. The apple trees were beginning to blossom. This was his home. This was what he was fighting for.

When the captain of the British troops saw them coming, he was flustered. He kept peering anxiously over the heads of his men, looking to the town for reinforcements. To his men, he barked orders. The redcoats hastily tried to form ranks, but found it difficult to do so in their narrow confines. So they bunched together. Several of the soldiers began tearing up the planking on the bridge. The colonials were now sixty yards from the other end.

The British fired a warning volley. Elias Todd directed his son to run for cover on the side of the road. The redcoats reloaded. They were outnumbered, and the colonials continued marching straight at them. Jacob could see clearly the faces of the light infantrymen. Some of them were mere boys. They were scared.

A skittish redcoat soldier-boy completed his reloading. In his nervousness, he dropped his powder horn. Powder spilled on his feet and the ground. He was oblivious to it. With shaking hands he raised his musket. Frightened eyes stared down the barrel. The end swayed violently back and forth. Sweat poured down the sides of his face. He licked his lips nervously.

A single shot sounded.

Instantly, a crash of volley fire from the British side followed. Two colonial men fell dead.

Major Buttrick leaped into the air, shouting, "Fire, fellow soldiers, fire! For God's sake, fire!" Instantly, the fire and smoke of a return volley erupted from the colonial side of the bridge. Three redcoats were killed instantly—eight or ten others were wounded. Jacob raised his musket, took aim, and fired.

Next to him, Elias Todd fired at almost the same moment. While Jacob fumbled for his powder horn, Elias simply held out his musket to his side. Bo bolted from his cover. With nimble hands, the deaf boy reloaded his father's musket and had it back in his father's hands before Jacob was halfway through the reloading process. All the time, Elias Todd stood there like a statue, never taking his eyes off the enemy. While Jacob was still priming his musket, Elias Todd fired a second round.

On the far side of the bridge, the redcoats swarmed chaotically. Despite the attempts of their captain to keep them together, they broke ranks and ran, not stopping until they reached the safety of the middle of the town with its superior numbers of British soldiers.

The makeshift colonial army pressed across the bridge toward the town. The Battle of Concord had lasted less than two minutes.

The colonial militia diverted its pursuit, taking up positions behind a stone wall. From here, they watched the British regulars in the center of town.

They noted several things. First, the buildings of Concord were not on fire. The liberty pole had been destroyed and burned, and there was a pile of burned debris, but the town was still intact. Second, they noticed the British regulars acting very indecisively. For more than an hour the redcoats continued their pillaging of the town; then they would be called to ranks as if to march; then they were dismissed and they returned to their pillaging. This happened several times.

Finally, at noon, after four hours in Concord, the British troops formed ranks and marched out of town on the same road by which they entered. This time, however, there was no fife or drum, their exit lacking the flourish of their entrance. They marched mutely. The grenadiers kept to the road, surrounding the walking wounded. Those who were more seriously wounded rode on horseback. The light infantry protected the flanks, marching in the fields on the left and right of the columns.

As he was watching the British begin their return trip to Boston, Jacob noticed a flurry of activity down the stone wall line. Word was being passed from soldier to soldier. No sooner had each soldier passed the word, then he broke from cover and ran toward the open field, the high ground above the Concord road.

The word reached Elias Todd, who passed it along to him. "Meriam's Corner! Let's go!" Jacob passed the message, then scrambled over the wall following the farmer and his deaf son. They ran through fields, jumped over fences, and crossed brooks. They were heading for Meriam's Corner to ambush the retreating British troops.

8

Jacob Morgan leaned his back against a sturdy tree. His head fell against the trunk, and his chest heaved up and down, greedy for air. Above him he saw the underside of branches, new spring leaves, and a clear afternoon sky. It was hard for him to believe all of this was happening in a single day—the express rider Revere, the massacre at Lexington, parting ways with Adams, the battle at Concord's North Bridge. And it was barely afternoon! Next to him, doubled over, also fighting for air—his hands supporting him on a low stone wall—was Elias Todd. Bo lay flat on the ground, face up, his arms stretched over his head. The boy looked like he was surrendering to fatigue. That made Jacob feel a little better. If the nine-year-old boy was out of breath, Jacob need not feel shame over his breathless condition.

They had run about a mile, fast enough to get there ahead of the redcoats. Along the way additional minutemen had joined them, from Reading and Billerica to the north, and a force of East Sudbury men from the south. The colonials now numbered more than eleven hundred men.

The point of their convergence, Meriam's Corner, was a place where the ridge overlooking the road gradually died away. It was here the road narrowed to a small bridge crossing a brook. A perfect place for an ambush. The flanking light infantrymen would be forced to close ranks with the rest of the British columns in order to cross. The minutemen hid behind houses, barns, hills, and trees. Jacob, Elias, and Bo had positioned themselves on the last of the ridge overlooking the target area. They lay in wait in silence. This time there would be no British fife and drum to warn them of approaching troops.

"Here come the lobster-backs, old man!" Elias whispered, poking Jacob playfully in the ribs.

Jacob reached for his musket. It was loaded and primed. He leaned a shoulder against the tree, pointing his musket down toward the small bridge. Elias and Bo Todd sat with their backs against the wall, keeping their heads low. Neither of them showed any signs of anxiety, nothing like the churning Jacob felt in his stomach. The carnage on the North Bridge together with the running had drained him of his earlier excitement, leaving a burning feeling in his gut. Lack of sleep and hunger no doubt contributed to the feeling, but it was more than that. For years, and up until a few hours ago, his feelings against the British had been driven by a sense of moral rightness and patriotic zeal. But now, after witnessing the slaughter on the Lexington common and the wholesale pillaging of Concord, his motivation had changed. The force driving him now was not so lofty. He was driven by anger—a controlled inferno deep inside that would not be quenched until the last British soldier had been forced from American soil. They had no right doing the things they were doing. It was time to match force with force, to kill or be killed.

The first of the redcoats crossed the bridge. Jacob squinted his left eye, and with the right he stared down the length of the musket barrel. He lowered the far end of the barrel until it rested on the chest of a light infantryman who was just stepping off the bridge. He squeezed the trigger. BLAM! The butt of the musket kicked his shoulder. Smoke swirled overhead. The British soldier clutched his neck and fell dead.

All around him, from behind every bush, wall, barn, and house, came similar sounds with puffs of smoke. British soldiers fell in great numbers. The bridge and dirt road were littered with their red uniforms and stained red by their blood.

"One less redcoat!" Elias shouted. He was standing with one foot resting on the top of the stone wall. As before, Elias handed his musket to Bo, who reloaded it while his father stood tall, never taking his eyes off the enemy. Moments later, Bo slapped the reloaded musket into his father's hand. With deliberate, steady movements, the bearded Elias Todd leveled his weapon and fired again. "Two less redcoats!" he shouted.

At the bridge British officers shouted furiously. While still more soldiers collapsed around them, the troops formed firing lines.

"Get down!" Jacob yelled at Elias.

Elias extended his musket for reloading. "Bo's quick," he yelled back. "Plenty of time for one more shot."

Jacob fired his second shot as Bo was handing a third round to his father. Elias Todd picked a target and raised his musket. Jacob pulled back behind the tree.

The thunder of the British volley and the crack of Elias's shot were simultaneous. Jacob was reaching in his bag for another cartridge, when he heard the most awful wail he'd ever heard in his life.

Elias Todd lay spread-eagle on the ground, a gaping black and red bullet hole in his cheek. Bo was at his father's side, his head on the man's chest, wailing and crying out to him with words that had no consonants. His father, the only man able to understand him, could hear him no longer.

A shout from the bridge pulled Jacob's attention back to the enemy. A detachment of light infantry was charging up the slope toward them. All around them minutemen quit their posts and ran into a heavily wooded area.

Ducking low, Jacob sprang toward Bo. Dropping his musket in the grass, he grabbed Bo's arm and yelled, "Soldiers! Soldiers coming!"

The boy refused to look at him, burying his face in his father's chest.

Jacob grabbed the boy again, this time with a stronger grip. "We have to go! Soldiers!" With his other arm he pointed over the wall. He wasn't getting through to the boy. Dropping to his knees, Jacob gripped Bo by both shoulders.

Bo fought back, wanting nothing more than to lay on his father's chest.

Jacob worked his hands up to the boy's head, grabbing both sides, forcing Bo to look at him. "Redcoats!" he yelled. "Redcoats are coming!" He motioned toward the wall with his head.

The boy seemed to understand. He stopped struggling. Jacob loosened his hold on the boy's head momentarily as Bo looked toward the wall.

Snapping the boy's head back, Jacob yelled, "Come with me!"

Bo nodded.

The instant Jacob released his grip, Bo bolted for the wall. Coming at them from the other side was a panting redcoat. When he saw Bo pop up from behind the wall, the soldier stopped and raised his musket.

"Bo! Get down!" Jacob yelled. It was instinct. He didn't stop to think that the boy couldn't hear him. He reached for his own musket, then remembered it wasn't loaded. No time to load it now. Elias's musket was spent too. Jacob looked helplessly at the redcoat.

Maybe it was Bo's age that stymied the soldier, or the fact that he had no weapon, but for some reason he hesitated. It was long enough for Bo to snatch up a rock. The deaf boy hurled it with all his might at the soldier's head. The soldier ducked to one side and the rock sailed past him, but the sudden movement caused him to slip and lose his balance. His arms flailed as he fought to keep upright. It was an unsuccessful effort. With the musket still in one hand, he threw his arms in front of him to brace his fall. When the musket hit the ground, it fired. The stone wall in front of Bo exploded with a spray of rock chips.

Jacob lunged for the boy.

Bo wasn't backing off. He reached for another rock.

Jacob reached him just as Bo let loose the stone. The redcoat saw the rock coming and hid his face in the dirt. The rock hit him in the back with a thud. Jacob circled his arm around Bo's middle, lifted him off the ground, and carried him away from the wall. But after just a few steps, the boy squirmed free and ran toward the wall again.

"Bo! Get back here!" Jacob yelled after him. No response. *What did he expect? The boy was deaf!* Jacob ran after him again.

Bo dropped to his father's side. He retrieved his father's musket, cartridges, and powder and ran back toward Jacob.

Just then, the redcoat's head emerged from behind the wall. Jacob raised his unloaded musket at the soldier. "Got ya covered, Bo!" he screamed.

The redcoat ducked for safety behind the wall.

With Bo at his side, Jacob turned to run. Tree cover was a good thirty or forty yards away. They'd never make it. Jacob expected to feel a lead ball exploding in his back at any moment. He glanced over his shoulder. The redcoat was standing. His musket was aimed at Jacob.

A volley of shot erupted from the trees, peppering the wall in front of the redcoat with shot. One ball found its mark, hitting the redcoat in the shoulder, spinning him around. The redcoat disappeared behind the wall. He never got off his shot.

Jacob and Bo reached the cover of trees to the cheers of half a dozen minutemen.

The fighting on the way back to Lexington grew fiercer and bloodier as Colonel Smith's British troops traveled the six-mile gauntlet between the towns. As the road wound its way up and down hills and over brooks, the redcoats found themselves forced into one indefensible position after another. Outnumbered by an elusive, ever-increasing enemy, the beleaguered British used up their ammunition in aimless shooting. Trained in open-field volley warfare, they didn't aim at specific targets, but merely in the direction that their commander pointed his sword. Their activity had little effect.

The closer the British troops got to Lexington, the harder it was for their commanders to maintain order among them. The only thing stopping scores of them from breaking ranks and running for their lives was the presence of their own officers in the front lines with bayonets fixed on them.

Their fortunes changed upon reaching Lexington around two o'clock in the afternoon. Reinforcements in the form of Lord Percy's nine-hundred-man armored First Brigade finally caught up with them. Lord Percy had been dispatched from Boston in response to Colonel Smith's request earlier that morning. Upon seeing the First Brigade at Lexington common, the retreating troops fled behind the brigade lines to safety, then collapsed to the ground, lying prone, like dogs with protruding tongues.

Upon hearing of the colonials' Indian-style warfare, Lord Percy devised a plan to get the troops back to Boston with minimal loss. His plan inflicted the heaviest damage of the day upon

the patriots. He began by using his artillery. Percy sent a few
warning cannon shots against some overly zealous pursuing minutemen. Although the cannon caused little injury, the firepower
was nonetheless impressive. For the colonials, the sobering shot
came when a cannonball cut through one side of the meetinghouse and came out the other.

After giving Colonel Smith's troops time to rest, Lord Percy
then proceeded to clear a safe corridor in which to escort them
back to Boston. He sent men from house to house along the way,
ordering them to kill anyone in the houses from which sniper fire
came. If necessary, his men were authorized to burn down
houses. Whenever the minutemen showed signs of pressing too
close to his troops, Lord Percy checked them with cannon fire.

The house was deserted when Jacob and Bo entered it. Its
close proximity to the road made it an ideal sniper's post. From a
second-story bedroom window—a child's bedroom, with unmade
bed and a rag doll on the floor—Jacob steadied his musket on the
sill and squeezed the trigger. Below him, another British soldier
fell face forward in the dirt. Without turning around, Jacob
handed the musket to Bo, who was seated on the floor behind
him. In return, the boy handed him the second musket and Jacob
took aim again; Bo was so quick at reloading that, between the
two muskets, Jacob barely had to pause between shots.

Jacob deliberately kept from turning around for several reasons. For one, Bo was used to working in this manner. Just like
he had for his father, the boy placed the readied muskets perfectly in Jacob's hands without any need for him to turn around.
Plus, this way Jacob could keep a ready eye open for redcoats
approaching the house; he and Bo had already been flushed out
of two locations by grenadiers. But the foremost reason Jacob
kept from turning around was the boy. Tears had streaked tracks

down the boy's dirty cheeks, which, every time Jacob saw them, primed his own tear ducts. But there was something else, something that disturbed Jacob. There was a frantic, determined look in the boy's eyes. His breathing was labored. His jaw worked from side to side, teeth grinding. All the while, Bo Todd loaded muskets, swifter than ever before. He was fighting a personal war now. This was his way of getting revenge against the men who killed his father. Jacob couldn't help but think this boy should be running free, barefoot through grassy fields. He was too young to hate, too young to kill.

Jacob's last shot caught the attention of two grenadiers. He pulled back just as one of them sent a musket ball his direction. It splintered the wooden frame, spraying the side of his face with bits of wood.

The look on Bo's face was sheer terror. "Jabe!" he cried. It was clear he thought he'd lost Jacob too.

"I'm all right!" Jacob cried. He crawled over to Bo. "They're coming!"

Bo reached out and touched Jacob's face. His hand came away with blood on it. Jacob reached up and examined it with his own fingers. Splinters. He could feel them under the skin. No time to take care of them now. They had bigger problems.

"I'll be all right," he mouthed to Bo. "Let's go!"

They gathered the muskets, powder horns, and cartridge boxes up in their arms and ran out of the room and down the stairs. The two grenadiers who had spotted Jacob would be approaching from the front of the house, the same side as the upstairs window, so Jacob grabbed Bo's arm and pulled him toward the back.

There was a door in the kitchen that led outside. It stood halfway open. Through the opening Jacob could see two more grenadiers charging toward the house. He stopped so suddenly,

Bo ran into him from behind. Jacob pointed to the back door and shook his head furiously, indicating to Bo that it wasn't safe to go out the door.

Jacob heard the front door crash open with such force it sounded as if it came completely off its hinges. *Two soldiers in the front, two in the back. Which way to go?* They were going to have to try to get past one group or the other.

He reached for Bo, but Bo wasn't there! The boy wasn't anywhere in the room.

"Jabe!" Bo called softly. "Jabe!"

The sound came from the kitchen fireplace. It was a huge brick fireplace, more than eight feet in width, typical for that day. The embers had long since burned out; with the early events in Lexington, the family probably never got a breakfast fire started. A small foot dangled from inside the chimney; then it disappeared out of sight.

Jacob could hear one set of heavy footfalls going up the stairway, but only one. That meant the other soldier was still on the ground floor. And two more would come crashing through the back door at any moment.

He ducked into the fireplace and extended his musket upward into the darkness. It was pulled out of his hand. All he could see above him was Bo's bottom. He was wedged in the chimney with his back against one wall and his feet against the other. *But was it wide enough for an adult?* Careful not to kick the ashes, he pressed his back against the bricks with his arms and pulled one leg up.

The back door crashed open. Boots pounded against the wooden floor.

Jacob pulled up his other leg, slipped, and almost had to lower it to keep from tumbling into the ashes. His back and neck scraped against the rough brick. Grimacing and pushing with all his might, he managed to scoot up a little bit. His knees pressed against his face, and his back and legs muscles felt like they would cramp, but he managed to hold himself in place.

For ten minutes the four soldiers searched upstairs and downstairs, slamming closet doors and cabinets, breaking glass, and cursing. One of them swore that there was no way the sniper could have escaped. Another shouted back at him that there was no place else he could have hidden. The first soldier cursed again and knocked over something heavy.

"Burn it to the ground!" he shouted.

Everything fell quiet. Then, minutes later, one of them said, "All right! Let's go!"

There was a thundering of boots—then all was silent. Although Jacob's back was raw and his muscles screamed in pain, he didn't want to come out of hiding too early. It might be a trap. Moments later, he could smell smoke. Not long after that, he could hear the fire, growing stronger in intensity by the minute.

Both he and Bo began to cough as smoke found its way into the fireplace and up the chimney, which, after all, was what the chimney was built for.

"Jabe!" Bo whimpered.

Jacob inched down until one leg found freedom; then, straining his tired arms, he steadied himself to lower the other leg. Before it was completely free, however, Jacob's arms gave out, and he slammed into the ashes below. Jacob scrambled to the hearth, then the floor. The entire kitchen was in flames. Covering his mouth with his shirt, he looked anxiously to the fireplace. A musket dropped, then another. Jacob retrieved them. A foot appeared. Then there was a plop and Bo fell into the ashes. If it weren't for the danger of the fire around them, Jacob would have found Bo's arrival humorous. It looked like the fireplace had just given birth to a man-child.

Assured that Bo was relatively unhurt, Jacob peered out the back door that gaped open at an awkward angle. The heat from the fire was intense, but he didn't want to leave a house fire only to be greeted by musket fire. He poked his head out. Nothing. It was clear.

With muskets in one hand, he grabbed Bo by the other, and the two of them ran and coughed their way to safety.

It was dark by the time they reached the old Morgan house on the Charles River. Jacob didn't want to risk returning to Boston without first knowing how the redcoats would respond to the day's events. He determined the family residence, which housed select Harvard students, was the safest choice. His reception there couldn't have been more grand.

When word flashed through the upstairs bedrooms that a participant to the day's events was in the study, there was a stampede down the stairs. Their imaginations already primed with a thousand and one rumors, they were more than anxious to hear from an eyewitness. Food and drink were ordered for Jacob and Bo. While they devoured it, the Harvard students crowded in around them, occupying every chair and square inch of floor space. The collegians fired question after question at Jacob until he finally had to wave them off, begging for a moment to eat.

Jacob sat in a stuffed chair. Bo sat between his feet, huddled against his legs. With wide eyes and darting glances at the animated Harvard students, he gnawed on a cold chicken leg. Esau was there, which was no surprise to Jacob. He stood solemnly in the doorway, leaning against the doorjamb with his arms folded. When Jacob's twin first appeared, Bo's mouth gaped open as his eyes bounced from brother to brother.

Setting his plate aside served as a signal to the students to fire another volley of questions, not unlike a colonel's saber-signal to his troops. Jacob fended off the questions with an upraised hand. He took one more gulp of ale, which greatly soothed his parched throat, and said, "I'll tell you everything I saw today, then answer any questions you have." That being agreeable to the men, with muskets and powder horns and cartridge cases strewn at his feet, Jacob began with the early arrival of Paul Revere at Lexington and described the day's events leading to his arrival at the house. By the time he had finished, Bo was asleep against his leg. With his stomach full, the long day's history was beginning to weigh heavy upon Jacob, too. For a couple of hours he fought off his drowsiness to answer questions. Finally, he insisted they hold any further questions until morning.

For Jacob Morgan, the capper of the day was the sour look on his brother's face when Esau's students crowded around, eager to shake the hand of a hero of the revolution.

9

Jared Morgan never made it to England. His ship had sailed three-fourths of the way across the Atlantic when they were hailed by another English ship just ten days out of London. Captains of friendly ships rarely passed up an opportunity to dine with each other at sea, so arrangements were made for dinner aboard the America-bound ship.

On such occasions it was customary for the captain of each ship to invite prominent passengers to attend the dinner with them. Over the years this practice had become something of a competition between captains, similar to a card game, only instead of comparing high cards in one's hand, they compared influential passengers on one's ship. Usually, ships out of England won this game handily when playing with their colonial counterparts. After all, English captains had a deeper reservoir of wealth and royalty from which to draw. But with trouble in the colonies, fewer and fewer people of substance were making the trip to America. And Jared's captain, with his wealthy Boston merchant and world sailor combined in one passenger, felt confident he would win this one. He was disappointed. For when they entered the captain's cabin, seated next to his beaming competitor was the world-renowned Benjamin Franklin.

Jared was as surprised as anyone. During the dinner, Jared was asked what business he had in England. His reply was forthright. "I no longer have business in England," he said, "since my business is presently aboard this ship in the person of Dr. Franklin." Jared declined to divulge anything further, other than to ask if Franklin had received a letter recently from Dr. Cooper, to which Franklin replied he had not. Astutely sensing Jared's desire for privacy, Franklin invited him to his cabin following the dinner.

Franklin's cabin was a cramped one, but the fact that he had a private space at all was a testimony to his importance. As soon as the cabin door was closed, Jared proceeded straight to business. He introduced himself and summarized the meeting with Adams, Hancock, and Cooper that had sent him across the Atlantic in search of Franklin.

"Ah! So they sent you to spy on me," Franklin said.

Jared's face and mumbling protestations prompted a huge belly laugh from Franklin. "I assure you, sir, I never would have …" Jared stammered.

Franklin waved him off. "Master Morgan," he said, holding his ample belly, "forgive me. I meant no offense. Your reputation precedes you. I know you to be a man of highest integrity."

Jared was flattered into silence.

Franklin continued: "Believe me, sir, I have the utmost respect for you. If even the smallest bit of what I have heard is true, I know this about you—you are no man's puppet." Franklin pulled out a chair for Jared to sit on while he perched on the edge of his bunk. With his hands clasped in front of him, leaning forward, his arms resting on his legs, and a boyish look of excitement on his face, he said, "There is one thing, however … I told myself I'd ask you this if ever we came face-to-face." He paused, measuring Jared's response before continuing.

Jared's nod gave Franklin the go-ahead he was looking for.

"Rumor has it—and forgive me for being blunt, I mean no offense—that before you became a merchant, you were," he hesitated, "a pirate."

Jared's expression remained unchanged.

"According to this rumor, you were Smilin' Jack Tar, the notorious pirate aboard the *Dove*. A swashbuckler of great skill and courage who refused to—how should I put this?—skewer his opponents. Might you and this Smilin' Jack Tar be one in the same man?"

Jared had heard the rumors. And this wasn't the first time he'd been confronted with his past. His response had always been to dismiss the rumors as speculations without substance. On this night, however, Jared's standard reply seemed inadequate. Maybe it was the roll of the ship that stirred his sailor blood to take a risk, or possibly it was the presence of the respected elder statesman opposite him who himself had been the subject of many bizarre rumors; whatever the reason, Jared chose not to respond in his customary way.

"If I were that man," Jared said, "would you esteem me less?"

"Esteem you less?" Franklin boomed in astonishment. "Quite the contrary, my dear sir!" A twinkle glittered in his eye when he spoke next. "In my humble opinion, Master Morgan, truly great men are part saint and part rogue. I believe Smilin' Jack Tar is such a man."

For the balance of the evening Smilin' Jack Tar relived his experiences aboard the pirate ship *Dove*, regaling his host with one sea story after another.

Jared's captain was doubly defeated that night on the high

seas. Not only did he lose the contest for the most elite passenger, but he lost his passenger as well. Before the ships set sail in opposite directions, Jared was aboard the ship that was headed for America. The transfer was made at Jared's request and Franklin's insistence. So it was that, ten days shy of his original destination, Jared reversed course and headed back to the colonies—Philadelphia, specifically—with Benjamin Franklin.

The chance encounter seemed as much a windfall for Franklin as it was for Jared. The two men idled away the hours swapping stories—Franklin wove yarns of English and American politics and personalities, while Jared told tales of his travels to China and India. During the course of the journey, Franklin outlined his plan for uniting the colonies and England. The heart of his idea was a union of the colonies, self-governing and self-regulating, yet united to the mother country by ties of blood and friendship. He called it a commonwealth of nations. And, he claimed, if he was able to convince the colonies and mother country of his plan's merits, the resulting union would surely be the most impressive political alliance in all the world.

Jared was impressed, not only by Franklin's brilliant mind, but also by his passion. The statesman spoke of the union as if it were an accomplished fact. He painted such a vivid picture, Jared could envision himself and his family living in the world described. He felt honored that Franklin would take him into his confidence since they'd known each other such a short time. And by the time they docked, Jared was more than eager to assist Franklin in convincing the colonial leaders of the plan's merits.

However, Franklin's plan died a stillborn death. No sooner had they reached Philadelphia when they learned of the conflicts at Concord and Lexington. While they had been isolated at sea, dreaming of an Anglo-utopia, colonial militias and British troops had been butchering each other. Franklin and Jared had been unaware that the Americans and British had turned a page in history without consulting them.

That initial conflict was merely a token of what was to come. Since that day the rapidly organizing colonial army and the British redcoats had clashed again, this time on Breed's Hill. And Boston—along with Jared's beloved Anne—was a city under siege. There would be no grand commonwealth. The two countries were locked in war.

With the outbreak of hostilities, the shortage of supplies in Boston as a result of the closure of the harbor two years earlier grew dramatically worse. Anne and Mercy Morgan found themselves living in a city of turmoil. As supplies of coffee, sugar, and other goods grew shorter, lines to purchase them grew longer, prices steeper, and tempers hotter.

The parlor of the Morgan house on Beacon Street was abuzz with chatter, the clinking of teacups, and the hum of spinning wheels. Surrounded by the accoutrements of Jared Morgan's financial success—a spidery crystal chandelier overhead, an immense scenic carpet below, plaster carvings on the ceiling, and rich brocades at the windows—sat a myriad of women with cloth, scissors, thread, yarn, needles, and patterns all around them. Two spinning wheels whirled busily in the background. The women were there at Anne's invitation, making shirts and socks for the men of the Continental Army.

While men left their farms and businesses to enlist in the army, women went to the fields, operated printing presses, and conducted business—whatever was necessary to feed the family and make a living. In addition, many of them spent extra hours making provisions for the army. Some collected money for soldiers' equipment or relief; others opened their homes to care for the sick or wounded. Many donated their pewter plates, pans, and dishes to be melted down and used for musket balls. One woman organized her neighbors in a two-day bread-baking frenzy. When the colonial soldiers marched by her home, stretched out on long tables was enough bread and cheese and cider to feed the entire troop. Anne Morgan organized a shirt-and-socks manufacturing society at her home. Teams of women rotated in shifts, each one contributing as she was able. The distinctive mark of this sewing society was the sewing of the date on the items. Since the present year was already half over, they'd begun placing the next year's date on the shirts and socks—1776.

For her part, Anne organized the women's efforts; fed them as they worked; read to them from the Bible; and, when pressed, read her poetry aloud. In this way the women who donated their time felt well rewarded for their efforts. Not only did they have the comfort of knowing they were assisting in the war effort, but the time at Anne Morgan's house was personally refreshing. While they sewed shirts, Anne knit their souls together. She led them to share personal news and prayer requests; updates on the war effort were reported; possible locations for scarce market items were identified; and, in general, Anne provided an atmosphere that was morally and emotionally uplifting.

Priscilla Morgan Gibbs—Jared's older sister and business partner—was one of the regular workers. In addition to her book-keeping duties for the family's company, she was co-owner of The Good Woman Tavern in Boston, along with her husband, Peter. Still, she made time to participate at least twice a week in the work at Anne's house. Priscilla had always been a woman of economy, disdaining sentimentality. But at the first meeting of Anne's sewing society, Priscilla was reduced to tears when Anne explained that she got the idea for the society from Deborah's Daughters.

Deborah's Daughters had been Priscilla Morgan's youthful

attempt to supplement the church's teaching with women's Bible studies. Her effort was rewarded by town officials and church leadership with a day's stint in the pillory. Anne was one of the original members of the group. She remembered with fondness how Priscilla's group encouraged her early efforts at poetry before it was abruptly disbanded.

"The way I see it," Anne said to the women at the first meeting of her society, "as long as we keep a needle in our hands, the menfolk won't concern themselves with us."

It wasn't uncommon for them to read personal letters aloud. Anne led the way in this; her own openness encouraged other women to share news of their loved ones. Some of the letters were heart wrenching; others were good news, which prompted joy. The balance of the letters provided a much-needed perspective. While a woman might shed tears of sorrow over a letter one week, her next week's letter could very well evoke tears of happiness.

"I have good news to share with you today, ladies," Anne said, unfolding a letter. "It's from my Jared and it's wonderful news. You see, he's supposed to be in … well, let me just read it to you." Her face aglow with delight, she read:

> May 7, 1775
> Philadelphia, Pennsylvania

My dearest Anne,

Yes, you read correctly—Philadelphia. I'm not in England. Except for God's grace, the trip to England could have been utterly worthless. Had everything gone as planned, I would have arrived in London only to learn that Dr. Franklin had sailed for the colonies two weeks previous. But God is good, because the only way I can explain it is by saying that His hands guided the two ships together in the Atlantic Ocean. Let me hasten to say, Dr. Franklin is a delightful man. Our mutual respect for each other has made us good friends.

At his request, I will assist him for the summer while the

Continental Congress meets. I wish I could tell you about some of the extraordinary things that are happening here, and of the men I have met—representatives from every colony! When I return home, I may be at liberty to tell you more.

My dear, dear Anne. What can I say that would adequately convey my longing for you? At least—thanks be to God—the time of our separation will not be nearly as long as originally thought. I hope to be home by September. You will never know how much I love you, for words are inadequate.

Faithfully yours,
Jared

Anne lowered the letter, smiling sheepishly. "As most of you know, Jared has been away for most of our marriage. The hazards of being a ship captain's wife. And when he told me he was going on this trip to England, I was furious with him for leaving me again. Now, as you can see, it was foolish of me. God has indeed been good to us by bringing my Jared back to America." She straightened in her chair. "All right, who will be next?"

Priscilla was a regular contributor to the meetings. She offered to read a letter from a friend—Abigail Adams, wife of John Adams. Reading from Abigail's letter, Priscilla said:

I told John that we are in no wise dispirited here. We possess a spirit that will not be conquered. If our men are all drawn off and we should be attacked, you would find a race of Amazons in America. And that if the men surrender to the British, they would find an army of women to oppose them. Then I reminded him that the Saracens were killed by their women when the men turned tail and ran from the foe!

Priscilla lowered the letter and laughed. She howled every time she read it. "And knowing Abigail as I do," Priscilla added, "she means every word of it!"

At that moment Mercy entered the room. Everyone fell silent; the only sound, the gentle whir of the two spinning wheels. In a ballroom setting where men and women were dressed in their finest and gaiety and mirth was standard fare, Mercy was the undisputed queen of the night; however, in this setting, where women dressed plainly and work was standard fare, Mercy was a foreigner in a strange land.

Priscilla, especially, went from grinning to grim the moment Mercy crossed the threshold. It was no secret that Priscilla didn't like the girl. They were opposites. While Mercy attracted the opposite sex with her beauty; Priscilla, at Mercy's age, scared them off with her daunting intelligence. Mercy was tall with black hair; Priscilla was short with red hair. Mercy loved attention, parties, and attention; Priscilla loved books, theology, and intellectual discussions. While Mercy lived for the moment, Priscilla was a visionary of the way things should be. Consequently, Priscilla avoided being in the same room with Mercy whenever possible. It was better for family harmony that way. The longer her exposure to Mercy, the harder it was for Priscilla to subdue her skewering wit. The widespread silence in the sewing room told Priscilla she wasn't the only woman in Boston who found it difficult to be civilized around Anne's daughter-in-law.

"You wanted to see me?" Mercy walked over to Anne. Her dress was bright, replete with ribbons and bows. A stark contrast to the working frocks of the other women in the room. Her stomach bulged slightly, the first noticeable indication of her condition.

"Yes, dear. I need your help," Anne said.

Mercy glanced helplessly around the room at the bolts of cloth, thread, and miscellaneous scraps of fabric. "I'm *afraid* I wouldn't be much help," Mercy giggled self-consciously. "My father was a *tailor*, but I never was much good at sewing."

"Do you bake, girl?" An elderly woman seated next to Anne peered over her spectacles to ask the question.

Mercy shook her head. "Mother is a *wonderful* cook, but I just never ..."

"Does she clean?" a mother of ten with hard features asked.

Mercy's forehead took on furrows, the look of the condemned at an inquisition. Anne answered for her. "We are blessed to have servants for most of the cleaning." To Mercy: "What I need for you, dear, is to go to King Street. I heard that a merchant there has a shipment of coffee. I'd like you to purchase some for us."

Mercy's response was a blank look at her mother-in-law.

"You can stand in lines, can't you?" Priscilla asked.

Giggles and twitters erupted in every part of the room.

Her head unbowed, Mercy said, "It will be my *pleasure* to get the coffee. If you would see to it that the carriage is brought around to the front, I'll be out there momentarily."

Mercy wasn't making this any easier for Anne. "As you know, horses are at a premium. Ours are being used at the docks today. I'm sorry, but you'll have to walk. It's really not that far."

Priscilla fought back a laugh. "You *can* ..."

She was cut off by a glare from Anne.

Enough was said to get the idea across. Laughing erupted again.

"I'll be back shortly." Ignoring the ladies' amused faces, Mercy went upstairs, got her purse and hat, and went to get the coffee.

Anne's tip on the coffee merchant must have been the best-known tip in the city. By the time Mercy arrived, it looked like half the female population of Boston was there. Mercy stared at the long line that hugged the businesses on the right side of the street. She considered turning around and going right back home, but no matter how long the line was, the ladies in the parlor would laugh at her for not waiting. So, with lower lip extended, she took her place at the end of the line.

She stood there for over a half hour, and the line did not move. In that time she'd read every sign on the street, had watched the street traffic—mostly women and British soldiers— with indifference, had listened to the women in front of her talk about the dangers and unpleasantries of extracting their children's teeth, and had thought of every distracting thought she could think of. But she hadn't taken a single step forward.

"Excuse me." She tapped the shoulder of the woman in front of her who was describing how a black tooth in her son's mouth wouldn't budge after several hours of work on him, gouging and banging and prying. The lady turned around, annoyed at having her story interrupted. "*Excuse* me," Mercy repeated, "how long have you been standing in line?"

The mother, who had several gaps in her own teeth, looked Mercy up and down, took an immediate dislike to the quality of her clothes, and said, "A fair time longer than you, princess." The woman turned to continue her tooth story.

"Um … excuse me again. Could you be more specific? How *much* longer?"

"Quarter hour!" the woman nearly shouted. "What's it to you?"

"Nothing. *Really*, nothing. Thank you."

Mercy stepped into the street and looked up the line. No change. A half hour and no change at all. *Really! This is ridiculous!* she said to herself. Hitching up her skirt, she marched forward. Midway up the line she stopped and asked another woman how long she'd been waiting.

Two hours.

Farther up the line she asked again.

Two and three-quarter hours.

The women at the head of the line had been waiting over three hours to buy coffee. The door they stood in front of was closed. To the woman standing first in line Mercy asked, "Are you sure this is the right place? The merchant at this location is selling coffee today?"

"That's what he said," came the reply.

"He told you this *himself*, over three hours ago?"

She nodded.

"What's taking him so *long?*"

"How should I know?" the lady in line said. "I'm not his partner! Just get back in line."

Mercy looked down the line, then stepped up to the door. Doubling her hand into a fist she pounded on the door. "Open up!" she shouted. "Open this door, *right now!*" She waited for a response. There was none. She pounded again. "Open up! I'm not going to stop until you open ..."

The door flew open.

A stooped man with a crooked nose and sparse gray hair could be heard cursing before the door latch sounded. With the opening of the door, the curses were louder. But the moment he caught sight of Mercy, he ceased midcurse.

"My, my, what have we here?" he said with flowery tone.

Behind him, casually seated around a table, were two boys. Mercy guessed them to be fourteen or fifteen. One had his feet propped up on the table. They were eating. A third chair was empty, but there was bread and fish at the setting.

The stooped man at the door reached out and took Mercy by the arm. "Come in," he said, "and tell me what I might do for you."

Mercy jerked her arm away from his grasp. "You can sell us some coffee; *that's* what you can do!"

He looked down the line of women. All the way down they were edging into the street to see what was transpiring at the door. "Best you come in," the crooked nose wrinkled at Mercy, "so's we can negotiate privately."

"No. We'll negotiate here, if you *don't* mind."

"But I do mind, lass. Here's your chance. Come in and we'll negotiate, or you'll get nothing at all."

Mercy stepped back in a rage. With hands on her hips, she yelled, "How *dare* you! These women have been waiting over three hours. Are you going to sell them coffee or not!"

The line of women added their voice to Mercy's, demanding that the merchant sell them coffee.

The coffee merchant's lips puckered with rage. Stepping into the street, he shouted curses upon everyone in the line. Then he said, "There will be *no* coffee today! If you want coffee, come back tomorrow! And you can expect to pay five times the going price!"

Not waiting for a reaction, he jumped over the threshold and slammed the door behind him.

The whole street broke out in shouts and curses at Mercy, blaming her for the merchant's actions and the price increase. Seeing the mob of women gathering around her, their faces distorted with anger, shouting, screaming, spitting, shaking their fists, Mercy's first reaction was fear for her life. Some women were inches from her. Hands shoved from in front and behind.

At that moment, deep inside Mercy Reed Morgan, something sparked and caught fire. She didn't know quite how to describe it, but it was as if she had a dormant attribute inside of her that just sprang to life.

"Listen to me! Listen to me!" She raised her hands over her head, shouting over and over the same three words, "LISTEN ... TO ... ME!" It took several moments, but finally the uproar around her died down.

"You're angry!" she shouted.

Her words sparked another outburst that was as difficult as the first to quell.

"You have every *right* to be angry!" she said. "But your anger is misplaced. You're angry with him, but you're taking it out on me!"

Another outburst.

"Being angry with me does you no good!"

Someone shouted back, "I don't know about the rest of them, but it makes me feel better!"

The comment brought some laughter and more shouts.

"Let me ask you this," Mercy shouted back. "Do you want to *feel* better, or do you want *coffee?*"

Several shouted back, "How can we have coffee if he won't sell it to us?"

"Do you know what he's been doing while you've been standing in line all this time? When he opened the door, I saw what he'd been doing! Do you know what he was doing?"

A chorus of voices called for an answer.

"He was sitting at a table with his feet propped up, casually eating lunch! While your children are unattended, while your work at home goes undone, while you stand here wasting precious time, he's eating a casual lunch!"

A growing discontent began to spread across the crowd as indicated by shouts and boos and a few catcalls.

"Is *his* work more important than yours? Is *his* time more valuable than yours? What gives *him* the right to make you stand in line for hours while *he* has a leisurely lunch? And, while we're at it, what gives *him* the right to, on a whim, raise the price of coffee to five times the going price? He's hoarding coffee and gouging prices while *you* stand in line for the privilege of buying it from him!"

The rumbling among the women was getting ugly.

"What are we going to do about it?" Mercy yelled at the crowd.

"Tell us! Tell us!"

A triumphant grin, one that had a touch of mischief in it,

appeared on Mercy's face. "We're going to buy us some coffee," she said. "But first, we must get the attention of the merchant. Does anyone around here know how to open a door?"

The merchant's door didn't stand a chance against a mob of angry women. It was down in quick order and women streamed into the merchant's office. The two young boys quickly escaped. The merchant wasn't as fortunate. Hands that had been strengthened by taking over the men's chores pinned the merchant to the wall. Sweat beaded up around his sparse gray hairs and trickled down his forehead and crooked nose.

Mercy spoke to him in firm tones. "We're here to buy coffee at the going rate. Would you happen to have any for sale?"

The merchant cursed at her and struggled to free himself. "You can't make me sell my coffee to you!" he muttered.

"I don't think that's the answer these ladies want to hear," Mercy said. "Now do you want to tell them that?" He just glared at her. Turning to the crowd, she yelled, "He says he doesn't want to sell coffee to you ladies. I wonder what we might do to *persuade* him."

The mob of women pressed upon him. Their less-than-friendly attitude and strength of numbers convinced him to try another tack.

"It's not here!" he shouted. "The coffee isn't here!"

"Do you mean to tell me that you had these ladies standing outside in the street for over three hours and you don't have any coffee?"

The man was almost crucified then and there.

"Wait! Wait! Wait! I have it! It's just not here! It's in a warehouse!"

"Take us there!" Mercy ordered.

The coffee merchant was loaded into a cart the women had found in the alley. A parade of furious, determined females surrounded it as they marched toward the wharf. Upon reaching the warehouse, they found it locked. When Mercy asked for the key, the coffee merchant refused to give it to her. Whereupon five or six strong women helped him find the key and nearly stripped him bare in the process.

The warehouse was opened, and the women turned their attention to finding the coffee and distributing it. Sacks were hauled, scales were found, and tables were moved into place to transact business. Mercy was so caught up with the project, she hefted a sack of coffee over her shoulder to carry it to the scales.

A kindly woman took the sack from her, patted Mercy's midriff, and said, "Best consider the little one, dear. Besides, someone needs to run this business. You got us started. Why don't you finish it?"

While the women weighed and sold the coffee, the merchant escaped. Mercy oversaw every transaction and handled the money. At the sight of women doing warehouse work, a large crowd of men gathered about and watched the whole thing. And in short order, everyone who came to buy coffee was satisfied. As the last of the women purchased coffee, the merchant returned with the authorities. He ranted and raved for several minutes, accusing the women of kidnapping him, beating him, and stealing his coffee. When Mercy was asked for an explanation, she told the authorities that the man was guilty of hoarding coffee and gouging consumers; in short, he brought it all upon himself. As for stealing the man's coffee, Mercy handed over the money along with a list of every transaction with weight and price paid. "A fair price for coffee, wouldn't you agree?"

Upon reviewing the sheet, the authorities did agree with her. The coffee merchant was held for further questioning.

As Mercy left the warehouse to return home, a band of men who had watched the whole thing applauded her. "If you were *truly* gentlemen," she said, "you would have assisted us rather than stood there *gawking.*"

※

Mercy Reed Morgan walked home triumphantly. When she entered the house, the sewing society was just breaking up for the day.

"Oh my," Anne cried upon seeing her, "Mercy dear, what happened to you?"

"I went to get coffee," Mercy answered.

"Well, dear child, you look a sight! Your face is smudged with dirt, and look at your shoulder and arm, they're filthy! You look like you've been working in a warehouse."

All the ladies of the sewing circle, including Priscilla, had gathered around her.

"It took a little more effort than I thought it would to get the coffee," she said, handing a bag of coffee beans to Anne, "but I was able to get some. At a *good* price, too."

Mercy worked her way through the ladies and started up the stairs.

Priscilla leaned toward Anne and whispered, "Maybe all this time we've been wrong about Mercy."

Midway up the stairway, Mercy stopped and turned back. "Anne, I'm going to lie down for a while. Will you see that I'm not disturbed? But please call me for dinner. I'm *famished.*"

As Mercy continued up the stairs, Priscilla added, "Then again, maybe not."

※

Esau Morgan stood in a Cambridge field, facing the recruiting officer. Along with the other newly-appointed officers to the Continental Army, he raised his hand and repeated this pledge:

"I, Esau Morgan, do declare that I owe no allegiance or obedience to George the Third, King of Great Britain; and I renounce, refuse, and abjure any allegiance or obedience to him; and I do swear that I will to the utmost of my power, support, maintain, and defend the Twelve Confederated Colonies of America against the said King George the Third, his heirs, and successors, and his or their abettors, assistants, and adherents, and will serve in the Continental Army as an officer, with fidelity, according to the best of my skill and understanding."

Esau's change of heart came after the events of April 19. For weeks following, he argued futilely with the Harvard students who lived at the Morgan house. To the last one of them, they had become rabid revolutionaries. He could thank his brother's late-night appearance and war stories for that. At first Esau dismissed their behavior as immature hero worship and a general lack of good sense. He soon discovered, though, that following the events at Lexington and Concord, a revolutionary fever was sweeping the colonies, a fever that stripped even some of the finest minds at Harvard—learned men who had been staunch loyalists—of all rationality.

On a Sunday afternoon, following the morning church service—another tirade against the king and Parliament, replete with Old Testament Bible passages declaring that God's people should be forever free, and this from an elderly minister who had always been a good friend of England—Esau strolled along the Charles River in front of the Morgan's pillared house. Sitting in the cool shade of a tree to the sound of the quiet lapping of the river against the shore, he reasoned over this troubling matter. He concluded:

First, that moving to England alone, without Mercy, held no allure for him. But if he remained in America and something should happen to Jacob, things might still work out between them.

Second, that the situation between England and the colonies

must now inevitably be settled by force. Although the Continental Congress had sent an Olive Branch Petition to the king, he held no high hopes that it would be accepted; for at the same time they rejected a plan for reconciliation by Lord North, appointed a Virginia plantation owner by the name of George Washington as chief of the colonial forces, and adopted a resolution titled "A Declaration of the Causes and Necessities of Taking Up Arms."

Third, that the thought of colonial victory over Britain was absurd, but if the resistance was strong enough, it just might force Great Britain to the negotiation table.

And fourth, that he had to choose a side. Being on neither side or both sides placed him in danger from both sides. In this, his father was right. The future of the Morgans was in America. As was Mercy.

For no other reason than to force Britain's hand to make an equitable settlement with her American colonies, Esau Morgan decided to join the Continental Army. At least that's what he told people who knew him. Because of his education and maturity, he was appointed an officer under the command of Colonel Benedict Arnold.

10

In the summer of 1775 when George Washington arrived at Cambridge to assume command of the Continental Army, a position for which he accepted no pay, he found nearly seventeen thousand men living in the most unsoldierly conditions. Their shantytown consisted either of huts made of sod or tents made from miscellaneous planks or fence rails covered with linen or sailcloth. Most of the men had only one set of clothing, the clothing they wore when they left home—usually homespun-wool breeches, linen shirts, and leather vests. They carried the family firelock, usually a weapon pieced together from the parts of several different muskets. And they worried daily about food for their families back home.

With no trained sergeants and few trained officers, discipline and order were nonexistent. The new commander was shocked to learn that British and American officers talked regularly to each other across lines. Stories of cowardice and insubordination at the battle on Breed's Hill were common.

Washington's first order of business was to turn this shantytown into an organized army. He insisted on precise discipline, forbade

cursing, swearing, and drunkenness. He required punctual attendance at daily worship, neatness among enlisted men and officers,
and the best possible sanitation. Severe penalties were imposed on
infractions, especially theft and straggling away from camp. Each
day, the men were lined up to witness floggings of wrongdoers, from
the commonplace thirty-nine lashes to as many as five hundred.

Such was the general's routine until he had purged from the
camps all officers and men he considered unfit for service. In
addition, men were put to work throwing up defenses, digging
trenches and earthen works, hauling timbers, and planting
pointed trees at the enemy.

Esau walked through the camp to meet Colonel Arnold, his
commanding officer. It was a day of firsts for him; this was the
first time he would meet Colonel Arnold and the other officers of
his company, and it was the first time for him to walk through
camp wearing the items that designated his rank as captain.
Because the army was still in its infancy, there were no standard
uniforms, but he had been given a red silk sash, a small sword
with belt and scabbard, and a silver epaulet which he wore on his
right shoulder. He had to admit to himself that he was enjoying
the salutes of the enlisted men more than he should. Those carrying arms halted and brought their weapons to shoulder; those not
carrying arms were required to halt, face the officer, and remove
their hats in a sweeping motion.

"Jabe! Jabe!"

Esau remembered Bo from the night at the house following the
battle at Concord. He was pulling at Jacob's sleeve and pointing at
Esau. Jacob was walking the opposite direction with two other soldiers who, upon seeing a captain, halted and removed their hats in
salute. Their eyes popped open wide when they realized they were
saluting an officer who looked exactly like their friend. Jacob,

likewise, reached for his hat and then, seeing who it was, dropped his arm to his side. His astonishment turned to rage.

"You traitorous dog!" he shouted. "What are you doing here? How dare you wear the markings of an officer of the Continental Army! Why I ..." He moved menacingly toward Esau.

"SOLDIER! STAND AT ATTENTION!"

The voice came from behind Esau. Instantly, Jacob snapped to attention, then saluted. Esau whirled around and, recognizing who it was, followed his brother's lead.

General George Washington sat tall on his horse, his back straight, his shoulders square. Riding next to him was a colonel Esau didn't recognize, but he was strong in appearance, had a high forehead, a prominent chin, and piercing gray eyes. It was the colonel who spoke. The scowl on Washington's face indicated he was in full agreement with his colonel.

To Jacob, the colonel said, "I suppose you think you have a good reason for attacking an officer." Then, before Jacob could respond, the colonel recognized that the two men were identical twins. "Ah! I see! Brothers." The colonel turned to Washington. "Striking similarity, isn't it, sir? One an officer, the other an enlisted man. That explains it."

"Sir," Jacob said, "it doesn't explain enough."

"Tell me quickly," said the colonel. "And it better be reason enough to convince me to order thirty-nine stripes for you."

"He's a traitor, sir," Jacob said. "I believe him to be a spy. He has never espoused the revolutionary cause, but has been outspoken in his support of England."

The eyes of the general and the colonel shifted to Esau. "Is this true?" the colonel asked.

"Sir, my conversion to the revolutionary cause has been a recent one," Esau replied. "It's true I formerly supported the king, but no longer."

The colonel studied Esau's face. His gray eyes were cold and penetrating. "Have you taken the officers' oath?" he asked.

"Yes, sir."

For the first time Washington spoke. He addressed his question to Jacob. "Do you have any evidence that your brother has aided or abetted the enemy?"

"No, sir."

Washington nodded. "Soldier, I don't think any of us made an easy transition from being loyal Englishmen to becoming loyal Americans. Some made it earlier and easier than others. But by his oath your brother has indicated the transition was made. Unless there is evidence to prove otherwise, this man is an officer of the Continental Army and deserves the respect of his rank."

The colonel to Esau: "Captain, what's your name?"

"Morgan, sir."

"Esau Morgan?"

"Yes, sir."

"You're one of my aides, aren't you? I'm Colonel Arnold. I trust you're on your way to the officers meeting?"

"Yes, sir."

"Take care of this matter, Captain. Thirty-nine lashes for insubordination."

General Washington and Colonel Arnold rode off.

Esau was left alone with the three soldiers and Bo. After a long, uneasy silence, he said, "I'm willing to forget this, Jacob. I won't process the papers for your punishment."

"I don't want any favors from you, sir," Jacob replied, refusing to look at Esau. "Are we free to go now, sir?"

"Have you heard from Mother or Father?"

No answer.

"You haven't been back to the house since April, have you?"

Still no answer.

"I was surprised to see you here. Somehow, I figured you would have sneaked back to Boston to check up on Mercy, considering the condition she's in."

Jacob's eyes leveled on his brother. "What condition?"

He didn't know! Mercy hadn't told him! The thought made Esau almost giddy. His grin spread so wide, he thought it wouldn't stop.

"What condition?" Jacob shouted. The rage on his face was so pronounced, it frightened Bo. "Officer or not, I'll tear you apart if you don't tell me!"

"She's with child," Esau said.

"Why would she tell you and not me?"

"You'll have to ask her."

Jacob nodded and started after Esau. "I know why...."

His two friends grabbed Jacob by the arms to restrain him. It took both of them exerting all their strength to hold him back. Even Bo helped by holding Jacob's legs.

"You're the father, aren't you?" Jacob shouted. "Admit it! You're the father!"

"I suggest you take your friend away from here before he gets himself court-martialed or worse," Esau said to the soldiers holding back Jacob.

Captain Morgan turned and walked away.

Later that day Jacob turned himself in for discipline. Thirty-nine lashes, he told them. He was told he was lucky. With no paperwork, there was no discipline. Not good enough, Jacob insisted. He was insubordinate and deserved to be punished. They looked at him like he was crazy and told him to go back to his unit. So Jacob Morgan cursed the officer in charge and was given thirty-nine lashes.

Esau emerged from the officers meeting rubbing his eyes. He was going to Quebec. Colonel Benedict Arnold had come to

Cambridge expressly to convince General Washington that Quebec could be taken, that it could be taken before winter, and that he was the only man who could lead the expedition successfully.

"Morgan!"

Esau turned and found himself standing face-to-face with his commanding officer.

"Did you take care of that matter this afternoon?" Colonel Arnold inquired.

"Yes, sir, I took care of it."

"A point of curiosity, Morgan. How is it that you are a captain and your brother is an infantry soldier?"

"Jacob never was one for learning. While I graduated from Harvard and Oxford, he worked on the docks. We both have the same amount of militia training. My education made the difference."

"As it should," Colonel Arnold replied. "One more thing...."

"Yes, sir?"

"Is there any truth to your brother's accusation? Are you a loyalty risk?"

"No, sir."

For the second time Esau felt the cold examination of Arnold's eyes. Fifteen seconds passed. Then thirty. Then forty-five. "Our lives depend on each other, Morgan," the colonel finally said. "If I find you're a risk to my command, I'll shoot you myself. Do I make myself clear?"

"Yes, sir."

N

This was a mistake. Esau Morgan had been an officer in the Continental Army for less than a week when he came to this conclusion. *How could I have been so foolish? People don't change. Neither side will ever accept me. The revolutionaries won't ever forgive me for being a loyalist, and the British won't ever trust me because I'm a colonial.*

Storming into his tent, he furiously grabbed his clothing and began packing. It was afternoon on Friday, September 15. In a couple of hours he would be riding out with Colonel Benedict Arnold and the rest of the staff on an ambitious military strike. He'd just returned from the final staff meeting in which the plan of attack was reviewed. The plan itself was simple; pulling it off was hazardous. The target was Quebec. Arnold had been part of the force that had captured Fort Ticonderoga several months earlier. He was convinced that Quebec could be captured as well. The general belief was that, given the choice, the Canadians would willingly ally themselves with the colonials. After all, they were mostly Frenchmen who had come under English control as part of Great Britain's prize for winning the French and Indian War. The idea behind the invasion was not to capture more territory or even to invite the Canadians to join a colonial confederation, but to eliminate an invasion threat by the British from the north. In this, capturing Quebec was essential.

Colonel Arnold was confident he could capture the city with his force alone. He was overruled. General Washington placed the mission under the command of General Schuyler, who was currently in charge of the forces in Lake Champlain. It was determined Schuyler's force would proceed to Quebec by river while Arnold's forces would march through Maine. The forces would then come together to attack the city.

Arnold's route consisted of three stages. First, his army would march overland to Newburyport; second, they would sail to Maine and up the Kennebec River as far north as the river would allow; third, at Gardinerstown, they would appropriate two hundred shallow-draft bateaux specially built for them and move up the river, cross a half-dozen portages through a chain of ponds, and travel down the Chaudiere River, which emptied into the St. Lawrence opposite Quebec. It was the final staff review of this plan that earned Esau his commanding officer's ire.

The only detailed report of the terrain they would be traveling was the 1760 journal and map of John Montresor, a young military engineer who had been at the British siege of Quebec. Montresor's journal and map had been reproduced for Arnold and each of his divisional commanders by Samuel Goodrich, a surveyor and mapmaker for the Plymouth Company.

When Esau heard who was reproducing the maps, he questioned the wisdom of the person assigning the contract to Goodrich. Arnold told him to explain.

"I know Samuel Goodrich," Esau said. "He's done work for my family's business. We own several ships and have purchased maps and charts from the Plymouth Company."

"Are you saying they are not reliable?"

"They have always produced maps of the highest quality for us."

"Then what's your point, Morgan?"

"My point is this, sir. I know Goodrich and I know the Plymouth Company. They are strong loyalists. It wouldn't be the first time a British mapmaker purposely misstated routes or distances."

"I'm aware of the practice," Arnold shot back. "Are you saying these maps are not accurate?"

"I'm not saying that they are inaccurate, I'm only stating what I know. Our survival is at stake. Can we trust that these maps are accurate?"

A wry grin spread across Arnold's face. "Morgan, when was the last time you talked with Goodrich or anyone in that company?"

Esau's eyes rolled upward as he tried to remember. "Two, maybe three years ago," he said at last.

"Two, maybe three years ago, were you a loyalist, Morgan?"

Arnold's point was felt. Esau didn't feel a verbal response was necessary.

"We're a month behind already," Arnold said. "Unless you have more than suspicions, Morgan...."

"No, sir."

The meeting continued and concluded without Esau Morgan saying another word. As the officers and staff filed out of headquarters, Colonel Arnold grabbed Esau by the arm.

"That had better not have been an attempt to delay this mission unduly, Morgan," Arnold said.

The more Esau thought about the maps and Colonel Arnold's remarks, the angrier he got. He took out his anger on the things in his tent. As he packed, he threw things, kicked things, and yelled at inanimate objects. With boots, woolen trousers, jacket, blanket, tomahawk, gun, bayonet, and hat packed, he stomped out to join the others.

As the flap of his tent fell in place behind him, he frantically pushed aside an unwelcome thought. *He was overreacting. He knew it. His tantrum over the map incident was a smoke screen to hide the real source of his concern. Fear. Fear of warfare, to be sure, but more immediate than that. Fear of being inadequate for his position. He was a scholar, not a mountain man. What was he doing leading men into the wilderness a month or so before the onset of winter? Yes, he was more educated, but his education was in accounting, not wilderness survival! And when they reached Quebec, what then? How could a man who had limited experience with a musket lead men into battle?*

He hated everything about this turn of events in his life and in his country. The more he thought about it, the more upset he became. So he stopped thinking about it. He thought of Mercy instead and how his life would have been different if she had agreed to his proposal to go to England. He could see the two of them standing at the railing of a ship, the bow gently rising and falling with the rhythm of the waves, the sun dipping itself into the waters on the horizon. Mercy's face would be lit by the orange sunset, her hair swept back, her smile would be warm and filled with love for him ... for him ... only for him.

Transporting the troops from Newburyport to the Kennebec River, a distance of ninety miles, was considered to be the most dangerous stage of the mission. The week before Arnold and his men arrived, the British patrols had already taken a number of ships and their crews captive to Boston. Upon seeing the clandestine fleet that Arnold's wealthy friend Nathaniel Tracy had managed to accumulate, many of the staff officers thought they looked like little more than dirty fishing boats. Esau knew better. There were eleven ships total, fast sloops and topsail schooners. As Colonel Arnold approached the ships to review them, Esau had already decided that no matter what the colonel thought of them, he wasn't going to offer an opinion. Even if Arnold asked him directly, Esau decided he would be noncommittal.

Arnold praised the work of his friend and astutely recognized the vessels' value for this mission. During the review Esau learned that Arnold was a seasoned sailor, having sailed frequently aboard his own merchant ships to the Caribbean, and once to Quebec. Arnold selected the three fastest ships and sent them out to scout for British patrols. It wasn't an easy decision. They had already been delayed a month by army red tape—Washington wouldn't let Arnold leave until General Schuyler had approved of the plan—and sending out scout ships would only delay them longer. Arnold figured they could make up the time on the march.

It was at Newburyport that Esau first had his leadership challenged. One of the stipulations General Washington made in granting approval for the expedition through Maine was that the inhabitants and natives would be treated kindly. While most of the troops made preparation to sail and loaded provisions aboard the ships, other less industrious soldiers spent their Saturday looting the houses of known loyalists. The leader of their band was one of Esau's men, Abner Stryker, a big-shouldered, slovenly man, with dark, deep-set black eyes.

When Stryker and his men were caught and taken to Arnold, the colonel assigned his aide, Captain Esau Morgan, to preside over the matter.

Esau began by asking the looters if they knew of the order regarding friendly treatment of the inhabitants. Stryker, serving as their spokesman, acknowledged having heard the order. When Esau pressed him for an explanation, Stryker reasoned he did not consider them inhabitants, but British spies. Besides, he continued, he didn't consider loyalists Americans any more than he considered Esau an officer of the Continental Army, for no lobster-back lover like Esau could ever command true Americans.

Stryker's venom had no effect on Esau; common exposure to it had hardened him. However, Esau was troubled by the effect it had on the others within hearing distance, including the guards who were holding Stryker. It was the first time many of them had heard of Esau's former sympathies.

Esau questioned Stryker further. *How had he come to the conclusion that Esau was a British sympathizer?* Stryker related that he was employed by the Morgans as a Boston dockworker and that it was common knowledge on the wharf that Jared Morgan had two sons—one a patriot and the other a redcoat lover.

His face expressionless, Esau let Stryker have his say. Then, loud enough for all who heard Stryker to also hear him, he explained that he had once hoped for peaceful coexistence between England and America, that he no longer thought that possible, and that his sympathies and life were fully committed to America. He ordered Stryker and his men confined to ship to prevent any further occurrences of looting. While the sneer on Stryker's lips told Esau the former dockworker was unconvinced regarding his captain's loyalties, a quick review of the other faces around Esau told him that most of the men were willing to give him the benefit of the doubt.

Esau filed his report on Stryker and sent it to Arnold. The colonel neither approved nor disapproved of the way Esau handled the situation. However, Arnold ordered a full review of the troops the next day, including any soldiers currently being disciplined.

On Sunday, September 17, a clear, warm day, the troops were assembled one mile west of town on the south bank of the Merrimack River. Colonel Arnold sat proud and high in the saddle as his men paraded before him, their colors flying and drums beating. A large, cheering crowd assembled along the route.

From the review the troops were marched in double file to a church service. The Presbyterian meetinghouse that hosted them was a tall, white, high-spired building that towered over the ships that jammed the wharf around it. Inside, the soldiers stacked their arms all over the aisles and the townspeople crowded the galleries. As Esau was settling into his place with the rest of the officers in the front row, he caught a glimpse of someone staring at him. There, a few rows back, was Abner Stryker, his eyes black and menacing.

Chaplain Spring, handpicked by Arnold for this expedition, preached the sermon. Spring was a six-foot-tall, deep-voiced arch-conservative and a student of Dr. John Witherspoon of Princeton. He chose for his text Exodus 33:15, the account of Moses' plea to

God after he ascended Mount Sinai a second time to receive God's commandments for His people. Moses' one request of God, as recorded in the sermon text, was this: *If Thy spirit go not with us, carry us not up hence.*

In unaccustomed fashion, the thundering Spring preached without notes. His words were a stream of eloquence as he discoursed on the marvelous and daring expedition on which the soldiers were to set forth. A profound silence fell upon the people.

Immediately following the sermon, Chaplain Spring admitted that he was thrilled to have the chance to preach over the grave of the great evangelist George Whitefield, who brought the Great Awakening to New England thirty-five years earlier. Whitefield's gravesite was a surprisingly personal bit of information for Esau. His father had experienced a conversion experience after hearing Whitefield preach in Boston. Jared Morgan spoke of it often. These many years later, the elder Morgan's eyes would mist as he recalled the experience.

Someone requested a visit to the tomb. The sexton was hunted up, the key procured, and Arnold and a number of the officers—Esau among them—descended into the tomb. Swords and boots clattered on the stone stairway. It had been six years previous that the evangelist had been laid to rest in this dark vault. As the officers gathered around, the sexton was persuaded to remove the lid from the coffin. Inside, the remains of the evangelist had nearly all turned to dust. Some portions of the graveclothes remained; the collar and the wristbands were the best preserved. With the sexton's permission, some of the graveclothes were taken and carefully cut into little pieces and divided among the officers. Esau Morgan carefully tucked away his piece. The next time he saw his father, God willing, he would present the cloth to him with his love.

That night, Arnold and his officers feasted at the mansion of Nathaniel Tracy. The dinner, following the sermon earlier and the unexpected historical treasure that would make such a wonderful gift for his father, lifted Esau's spirits. The food and wine were of the highest quality, the linen was shining white, and the silverware gleamed as good silverware was designed to do. For Esau, it was a reminder of everything he wanted in life. The only disappointing thing about the evening was that it had to end. Come daybreak, Arnold's men would head for the wilderness.

11

Early Monday morning Arnold's scout vessels returned with their reports. The coast was clear of British patrols. The troops were loaded onto the ships, and by 7:00 a.m. Colonel Benedict Arnold's expeditionary force set sail for the Kennebec River one hundred miles up the Atlantic. Arnold's flagship, the *Broad Bay*, led the way. Less than twenty-four hours later the fleet successfully nosed its way into the river and dropped anchor.

The original estimate was that this transport up the coast would be the riskiest and most dangerous part of Arnold's plan. Though it was accomplished with relative ease, it wasn't without incident. To begin with, not all the ships cleared the Newburyport sandbar. The schooner *Swallow*, overloaded with 250 men and supplies, ran hard aground upon the bar. Agonizing hours passed while rowboats unsuccessfully attempted to free the ship. Meanwhile, the remainder of the fleet bobbed out in the ocean like ducks on a pond waiting for a British hunter to spot them. Finally, Arnold ordered some of the men aboard the *Swallow* transferred to other ships. Likewise, some of the supplies were redistributed. But still the

Swallow would not budge. Reluctantly, Arnold left the ship behind.

Then, farther up the coast, the *Conway* and the *Abigail* lost their way due to heavy rain and fog and overshot the mouth of the Kennebec River. Another sloop, the *Hannah*, ran aground, but was soon able to work herself free. Eventually, all three of the separated ships caught up with the fleet at the mouth of the Kennebec. The mood aboard the ships was joyous. The men felt assured their mission was marked for success now that the most dangerous part was behind them.

Esau leaned on the wooden railing of the *Abigail* and surveyed the land surrounding him. It was rocky and pine covered. A low fog and mist drifted lazily upon the sea, encircled the rocks on land, then tumbled back down onto the river. Noise aboard the ships flushed the land of bird life. Clouds of ducks filled the air, along with cormorants and Canada geese, flying away in their familiar "V" formation. Even in the diffused light the maple trees lining the river's edge splashed the scene before him with clusters of red leaves. After six hours rest, the expedition was on the move again. The ships worked their way up the Kennebec River three miles shy of Gardinerstown where the troops would disembark and continue upriver in small bateaux.

Colonel Arnold had ordered the construction of two hundred small river craft before leaving Cambridge. Major Reuben Colburn's shipyard at Gardinerstown had been given the contract. When Esau first saw the bateaux lining the shore, it appeared that Colburn had dutifully fulfilled the contract made two short weeks previous. But upon closer inspection, Arnold's men discovered that the boats had been badly built. Constructed with heavy, wet green pine, the planks were already beginning to show signs of shrinking and cracking. Beneath the pine were even heavier oak frames. Arnold tried to lift one of them. He couldn't. On the average, they weighed nearly four hundred pounds apiece. How would the men ever be able to carry them on their shoulders for miles over steep cliffs?

Neither were the bateaux uniform in size. Arnold had ordered them to be twenty-five feet long. Some were as small as eighteen feet, not nearly large enough to carry six men, their gear, and guns.

Arnold was steaming, but he didn't waste time arguing with Colburn. He ordered twenty new bateaux built, and the best of those already built he ordered caulked and repaired to make them usable. The expedition would be delayed again.

For three days Colonel Arnold set up headquarters aboard the *Broad Bay.* Separated from his men at Gardinerstown by several miles, he used the relative peace to issue a series of orders, evaluate their lengthening timetable, and write a report to General Washington. One hundred men were sent upriver to Fort Western using the acceptable bateaux. Other troops were sent forty-five miles by dirt road to Fort Halifax where they were to pick up rations. Arnold informed his commander-in-chief that his troops were equipped with rations for forty-five days but still believed they could reach Quebec in twenty days. One final bit of administration overseen by Arnold while aboard the *Broad Bay* was military court hearings. Three Connecticut men were charged with insubordination, a sergeant was publicly stripped of his rank, a thief was drummed out of camp in disgrace, and several men were caught looting Tory houses in and around Gardinerstown. One of the men was Abner Stryker.

"Captain Morgan, this is the second time this man has been brought up on looting charges?" Colonel Arnold asked the question seated behind a desk that had been brought on deck and placed in front of the mainmast for the court proceedings. Esau stood in front of the desk, Stryker at his side, his hands bound.

"Yes, sir. He was disciplined at Newburyport on identical charges."

"Colonel Arnold, sir," Stryker said, "you're not going to listen to this Tory pig, are you?"

"Hold your tongue, soldier!" Arnold shouted.

Stryker started to say something else, but the piercing gray eyes of Benedict Arnold made him think better of it.

"Captain Morgan," Arnold continued, "what punishment was Stryker given in Newburyport?"

"He was confined to ship, sir."

Arnold wrote something in the margin of the written charge against Stryker.

"And what punishment do you think he should be given for this second offense?"

Esau had hoped he wouldn't be asked that question. Arnold was testing him. Too strict a sentence would indicate that his loyalist leanings overshadowed good judgment; too lenient a sentence would mark him as a bad officer.

"I believe Stryker should be returned to Cambridge and reassigned to another unit, sir," Esau said with calm voice, one that covered over his nervousness.

Colonel Arnold folded his hands atop the paperwork and leaned forward slightly. "And do you think this is a just sentence, Captain?"

"Yes, sir, for two reasons. First, this is Stryker's second offense. At his first disciplinary action he acknowledged he was fully aware of the standing order to treat the inhabitants and natives in a friendly manner. This is the second time he has willfully disregarded that order because of personal bias. Second, such action demonstrates a pattern of insubordination, in that he has proven he will obey orders only if he agrees with them. Considering the mission that lies ahead of us, it is imperative that every man receive his orders without question and carry them out without bias. By returning him to Cambridge, Stryker will be given the opportunity to learn from his failures in this unit yet still have the chance to make a positive contribution in another unit."

Benedict Arnold sat back in the chair and studied his captain aide. Esau felt like he was on trial and the judge was about to issue the verdict.

"Very good, Captain," Colonel Arnold said, "maintain discipline, yet demonstrate compassion. So ordered. Stryker will be returned to Cambridge."

A string of curses erupted next to Esau. "This man is a traitor, sir! A known Tory spy! I worked for his family in Boston. You'd listen to a man who isn't fit to clean your outhouse?" He turned and spit at Esau, wetting his shoulder.

Arnold exploded from his chair, his face livid. "Not another word, soldier!" he yelled. "I've already ordered one man's death today. Do you want me to make it two?" To the guards: "Take this man away!"

The sentence of death Arnold referred to was that of a Maine woodsman. In a drunken brawl, he'd shot a Norwich Town musketman. Later that day, Arnold led the woodsman to a gallows and had a noose placed around his neck. Then, at the last instant, he ordered the woodsman sent to General Washington with a letter recommending the woodsman's life be spared.

"Morgan."

"Yes, sir?"

Arnold approached him following the aborted hanging. "I want you to take the prisoners to Cambridge. You will be supplied with all the necessary papers."

"Colonel," Esau hesitated, then said, "I'd rather not."

"Are you disobeying an order, Captain?"

"No, sir. If you order me to go, I'll go. But I would prefer to stay with the expedition."

"Why? It's clear you're not a woodsman, nor are you a soldier. Exactly what was your profession in Boston?"

"I kept the books for my father's merchant business."

Arnold looked at him suspiciously. "Then why insist on continuing this expedition into the wilderness when you could go back to Cambridge? What possible motive could you have?"

"I want to prove something to you, sir."

"Explain."

"You still are not convinced of my loyalty. And I believe that's why you chose me to take these prisoners back to Cambridge."

Arnold didn't respond.

"And if I leave you now, that doubt will remain. The only chance I have of convincing you of my loyalty is by continuing with the expedition."

Arnold answered instantly. "You'll leave in the morning, Captain. Pick up your papers aboard the *Broad Bay* tonight. You sail at 7:00 a.m."

Looking into those hard gray eyes, Esau said, "Yes, sir."

The next morning Esau reported to the *Conway*. The prisoners were already aboard. Moments before they were to sail, Harold Deane, another of Colonel Arnold's aides, appeared. There was a change of orders. Deane would be replacing Esau, who was to report to his designated bateau immediately. The troops were heading upriver. Esau was never given a reason for the change of orders.

The heavy-laden bateaux were paddled, poled, and often times pushed up the Kennebec River. At Skowhegan, nearly fifty miles from the coast, the expedition passed the last settlement and proceeded into the wilderness. Few Englishmen had ever gone beyond this point, and only one had recorded his journey. Montresor's maps would be their guide for the remainder of the trek. It was a crystal-clear afternoon. On both shores beech, maple, ash, elm, and oak trees dropped their leaves into the river. The trees were nearly bare and there was a chill in the air. It was October 2. Ahead of them lay hundreds of miles of trackless forests, swamps, wild rivers, and lakes. And already Arnold's mission was in trouble, afflicted by a series of occurrences that threatened to doom the expedition.

The clumsy, overweight bateaux were a major hindrance. Battered by rocks and rapids, the boats were leaking and, in some cases, falling apart due to poor craftsmanship. They were so sluggish that much of the time the men had to wade in the water and push them along. The unstable bateaux also frequently overturned, dumping bear-skin-covered supplies into the river, drenching equipment and supplies. During times of portage, it took four men to lift a single bateau. The wet weight dug deeply into their shoulders, making their footing slippery and cutting drastically the amount of ground that could be covered in a day.

The night of October 2, the temperature plunged. Weary and drenched from fighting rapids, the men fell asleep in their wet uniforms only to find them frozen solid by morning. The frost and cold increased their fatigue considerably.

On October 3, the bateau carrying the majority of the company's food supply was inspected. The two officers in charge of the supplies were irate. They showed Colonel Arnold their carelessly nailed, badly caulked floorboards. Some of the seams were too wide to be fixed by caulking. Barrels, blankets, and other supplies were soaked. Arnold ordered one of the barrels carrying salted fish to be opened. The salt had washed off; the fish had rotted; writhing maggots covered what was left. The rest of the supplies were in no better shape. Precious amounts of salt beef, cod, peas, cornmeal, and flour had to be thrown away. Eight days were lost in making the necessary repairs before they could continue.

Following Montresor's map, they reached the portage Montresor called The Great Carrying Place. It was a twelve-mile series of portages between the Kennebec River and the Dead River, made easier by three large ponds where the boats could be refloated. Tired and thirsty after paddling all day, many of the men drank from the pond's brackish water. Over a hundred men fell sick with dysentery, and a hospital had to be set up to care for them. It took five days to cross The Great Carrying Place.

On October 15, having pulled their bateaux to the snow-covered summit of Mount Bigelow, it looked like the expedition's fortunes were changing for the better. Below them was a valley that looked as level as a bowling green. Descending the mountain, they soon discovered that their vision of easy travel was a mirage. The greenery was a bog—a nightmare of grass-covered roots, mud, and moss—a fourteen-mile obstacle course that they traversed in a driving rainstorm.

Upon reaching the Dead River at four o'clock in the morning, the soldiers set up camp and spent a restless night. They were later awakened to a roar of rushing water. The severe storm caused a flood to cascade down the mountain. In three days, the water rose twelve feet, obscuring any visible landmarks along the swollen river. There was so much floating debris cluttering the river, seven more bateaux overturned. Food, guns, gunpowder, and clothing were lost.

The following day was spent in rescue operations, plucking men from the raging water and carrying them safely ashore. The total distance the army marched that day was half a mile. That night when they set up camp, the men dubbed the place Camp Disaster.

N

On the night of October 23, Colonel Benedict Arnold, with cloak wrapped over his soggy uniform, knelt on one knee in front of a huge sputtering fire made of wet wood. He had summoned an emergency meeting of his officers and staff. The subject of the meeting: to continue with the mission or go back?

Esau sat Indian-style on the ground, tightly wrapped in a blanket that was as soaked as his clothes. His teeth chattered involuntarily; likewise, shivers shook his frame. Along with the other officers, his attention was at times diverted by a coughing fit. The smoke from the fire aggravated his cough and stung his eyes. The firelight and smoke against a black background of night gave the whole scene a heightened sense of drama.

Point by point, Colonel Arnold explained the situation, punctuating his points by jabbing his left palm with his right index finger. If they were going to turn back, it had to be now. There was enough food left for them to reach the Kennebec River. They were down to near-starvation rations. All the game had been driven off by the noise of the army or by the severe storm. Add to that the frustration of the terribly underestimated distances on the Montresor maps. He looked directly at Esau as he said this.

"In my haste to embark on this mission, I failed to heed the advice of one of my aides who warned me of possible misrepresentations on the maps," he said. "Believe me, I won't ignore his advice again." He gave a slight nod in Esau's direction.

Enumerating the positive things they could be thankful for, Arnold noted that the army was still in reasonably good health; with rationing, the remaining supplies should last until they reached the French settlements along the Chaudiere River; and the cold would bring an end to the rains and make marching and hauling supplies easier. Arnold made it clear that he still believed they could reach their goal, then he called for questions. There were only a few. Then, Colonel Arnold stood up and called for a response from his men.

A thin, shivering Esau Morgan stood. His life of silk and plenty in Boston seemed a distant memory. He'd always had goals and dreams. None of them had been based on physical stamina and wilderness survival. He wouldn't have chosen this course for his life, but now that he was here, he wanted to complete what was started.

"I can speak only for myself," he said. "Given these circumstances, that's what it comes down to, doesn't it? Each one of us has to decide for ourselves whether or not we can go on. We've already been through a lot of hardship, and whichever direction we take, we're all in for more of the same. Well, I want my hardship to count for something. If I'm going to have to endure it, I want it to count for success, not failure. And that's exactly how I see it if we go back now. We will have endured all of this only to admit to our families, our fellow countrymen, and ourselves that we failed. The rest of you can turn back if you want. I'm going to Quebec."

One by one Colonel Benedict Arnold's officers voiced their assent to the plan. They would proceed. In keeping with the decision, Arnold ordered the sick and wounded given a four-day supply of food. They would return to Fort Halifax where they could be cared for. The remainder of the supplies were ordered to be equally divided among the troops. A special detachment of fifty soldiers was sent ahead with all due speed to procure supplies and clear the way for the main army. The rest of the men were to begin reloading their bateaux to move out.

On the morning of October 25, the men awoke in tents sagging from heavy snowfall the night before. Colonel Roger Enos held a secret meeting of his division much like Arnold had done with his officers and staff. However, Colonel Enos's meeting came to the opposite conclusion of the earlier meeting. At first the vote was even, but Enos's officers urged him to break the tie with his own vote. So it was decided they would immediately return and not rush into such imminent danger. In charge of resupplying several of the other divisions, Colonel Enos ignored Arnold's command to redistribute the supplies equally. Enos gave Colonel Christopher Greene's division only a portion of what it was supposed to receive; he kept all the weapons and all the medical supplies and led his division back toward Cambridge.

When word spread that Enos's division had defected with nearly one-third of the army and half of its supplies, the remaining troops were disheartened. It seemed clear that Enos had condemned them all to death.

Without adequate maps to guide them, Arnold's force trudged day after day through the swampy, four-foot-deep headwaters of the Chaudiere River. Some marched in their uniforms; others took off their clothes and put them with their weapons overhead to keep them dry. The supply of food was exhausted. They ate roots and bark off trees. Some made broth from boiling shoes and cartridge boxes. Others ate candles. A number of men fell in the swamps and never got up, or sat at the base of a tree and died.

Esau remembered propping himself against a tree to rest. His head was light. He was weak from thirst and hunger. Through the trees there was a rustling. Possibly game, but he didn't know if he had the strength to hunt it. Possibly Indians, and he hoped they were friendly because he certainly didn't have the strength to fight them. His eyes drifted closed. When he opened them again, he didn't see anything. Again, his eyes drifted closed. Something nudged the side of his face. There was a strong, earthy smell. Then another nudge. He fought to open his eyes. Inches from his face was a huge animal of some kind, short brown-and-white fur, brown eyes. It was right in his face. He had to move aside, away from it, to get a good look. A cow! He jumped to his feet. There were cows all around him! The supplies from the advance party had finally reached them. Esau was so happy he kissed the cow.

At 10:30 p.m., Friday, November 3, Arnold's army reached Sartigan, the first French settlement on the Chaudiere River. They stumbled like drunk men, steadying themselves against trees, falling to the ground, and grasping bushes to help themselves up. The snow was stained with the blood from their bare feet. A trip they thought they could make in twenty days took fifty-one days to complete. Forty percent of the men who started out didn't make it. They either died or deserted.

Esau reeled back and forth across the path leading to the settlement and collapsed on the ground once inside the perimeter. He had to be helped to a large cabin, which served as a barracks. He was beyond exhaustion, beyond hunger and thirst; all he wanted to do was sleep. He closed his eyes, and for the first time in weeks, he did so not wondering whether or not he would awake again. He would survive. He was sure of that now. He would survive.

12

On December 2, 1775, Colonel Benedict Arnold's emaciated corps was reinforced by General Richard Montgomery as the two forces met at Pointe aux Trembles above Quebec. The combined army was small. To Arnold's 650 men, Montgomery added another four hundred, all that he dared bring with him from Montreal. General Schuyler was not among them. His health, which had always been delicate, broke down at St. John's, so the command fell to Montgomery, the son of a baronet and onetime member of Parliament.

Arnold had no trouble placing himself under Montgomery's command. In a matter of weeks, the two were closer than brothers. Both were chafing for action, and both were committed to the immediate fall of Quebec despite decreasing odds of success. Montgomery recommended Arnold be promoted to general for his successful crossing of the province; meanwhile, Arnold lionized Montgomery's military strategy, praising his every proposal.

Even so, it would take more than mutual admiration to capture Quebec. Because of Arnold's delay in reaching the cliffed city, the element of surprise had been lost, and Quebec in turn had greatly bolstered its defenses. Reports from spies indicated that the defenders outnumbered the attackers two to one. Add to that the fact that the invading army's numbers had significantly dwindled, and most of Arnold's men's enlistment ran out at the end of December. They had to move quickly.

Their plan was to attack the fort from two sides. Montgomery would strike from the west, close to the river. His force would ascend the cliff by way of the narrow road, formerly a goat path used by Britain's General Wolfe sixteen years earlier during the French and Indian War. Although Wolfe died in the attack, the British troops captured the city.

While Montgomery attacked from the west, Arnold would approach from the east at a point known as Sault au Matelot. The two forces would meet in the Lower Town and combine to drive up the twisting slope that led to the heart of the Upper Town. The men would wear hemlock sprigs in their hat brims to distinguish them from the enemy. The attack would come on the first snowy night when clouds blocked the moonlight.

On Christmas evening, Montgomery reviewed his troops in a meadow beside the St. Charles River. In honor of the occasion, he distributed an extra ration of rum to the men and informed them that his Christmas present to them was that they could keep whatever they plundered from the city when it fell. The cheer from the colonials could be heard inside the walled city.

On December 27, a snowstorm blew in. At two o'clock in the morning, the men were mustered out of bed for attack. But before they could get into position, the night cleared. Colonel Arnold's men had only a few more days before their enlistment expired. Unless the weather worsened soon, they would be free to return to their homes, and the expedition against Quebec would fail for lack of participants.

December 31, 1775. The wind shifted to the northwest. Clouds gathered. Snow began to fall. At eight o'clock in the evening, sergeants made their rounds among the men, telling them to be ready at midnight.

At two o'clock Arnold's officers began reporting in. He listened as his secretary checked off the muster roll by lantern light. At four o'clock he joined the advance force of thirty men who were prepared to storm the walls. Captain Esau Morgan was at his side. At that same time General Montgomery strapped on his short sword and led his troops through the driving snow to the base of the cliff. Hugging the side of the cliff for over two miles, his men stumbled through the blinding snow.

Upon reaching a barricade of wooden spikes that ran from the foot of the cliff to the river's edge, Montgomery stepped aside and ordered his carpenters to cut an opening with saws. As each spike was severed, Montgomery himself pulled them down. When the opening was large enough, he stepped through, his officers following him. About a hundred feet ahead there was another barricade. To the right was a two-story log house. It was dark and, through the heavy snow, looked unoccupied. He ran toward the second barricade, his officers trailing behind.

Three enormous booms sounded almost simultaneously. Fire and smoke belched from the second story of the blockhouse. A shower of lead balls slammed into Montgomery, hitting him in both thighs, the groin, and his jaw. He was killed instantly. Fourteen of his officers fell with him. The remainder of his force fled in retreat down the precipitous pathway along the base of the cliff. With the death of Montgomery, the west-side attack was defeated in a matter of seconds. There would be no second force to meet up with Arnold in the Lower Town.

※

An explosion of wood from a musket ball just above his head caused Esau to pull back around the corner of a warehouse. His heart jolted from the near hit. His eyes went wide with shock, then closed slowly as he breathed out a sigh.

Arnold laughed. "That was close, Morgan! Good thing you kept your head down."

Unlike his commanding officer, Esau wasn't enjoying his first taste of battle. Running between buildings from cover to cover in the dark hours of the morning, blinded by snow and pummeled by musket balls, was not his idea of a good time.

Their objective was the Palace Gate. In order to reach it they had to run along the foot of a hill between widely spaced warehouses up a slope that led to the walls. In the open stretches between the warehouses, they were subject to a flurry of musket fire from the ramparts above. It was pointless to fire back. The best they could do was run and pray.

Running hard on the heels of Arnold, Esau bolted down the Rue St. Paul. The street narrowed with houses lining both sides. The snow was deep. Footing was precarious. Headway was dangerously slow.

At the head of his column, Arnold rushed toward a log barricade. The plan had been to eliminate the barricade with cannon fire. But the cannon had slipped off the road into a snowbank. Reaching the barricade, Esau followed his commander's example by shoving his musket through the slits and firing at those inside at point-blank range. The sound of his musket echoed within. He could hear the dying and wounded on the other side of the log wall.

"Over the wall!" Arnold yelled. "Over the wall!" His arm was whirling like a windmill, encouraging his men to follow him over the barricade.

Suddenly, British militia opened fire from houses on both sides of the street. All around him Esau could hear the thud of musket balls as they hit the wooden barricade, and the ricochet sound as they sliced through the snow and hit the cobblestones.

"Over the wall, Morgan!" Arnold shouted at him, then turned back a few steps, waving at the soldiers to keep advancing despite the hail of musket balls around them.

Esau found a foothold and boosted himself up. Just as he was about to throw his leg over the top, he looked back. Colonel Arnold was facing the wall again, taking one, two, three determined steps that would propel him halfway up the wooden barricade. But he never made it. With the third step his right leg failed him. He fell hard into the snow. A growing circle of red formed beside his leg.

Seeing his commanding officer on the ground, Esau leaped from the wall and ran to his side. By the time he reached Arnold, the colonel had pushed himself up and was standing on his remaining good leg, resisting any effort to be pulled to safety. As one volley after another whistled by him, he shouted to his men, "Hurry on! Hurry on, boys!"

Finally, Esau was able to convince Arnold to seek haven at the side of the road. Leaning against a wall, Arnold continued to encourage his men forward by waving his sword and shouting at them. When Eleazar Oswald came by, Arnold ordered him to move to the front and take command. Blood was seeping over the top of his boot now, staining his white leggings. Still he refused to allow himself to be taken to the general hospital until most of the men had passed.

With Chaplain Spring's assistance, Esau helped carry Colonel Arnold through the gunfire and between the warehouses to safety and medical care.

The east-side force faired little better than its western counterpart. Every field officer except two was either killed, wounded, or captured. Four hundred and twenty-six Americans—virtually all of the Kennebec group—had been taken prisoner. When

Arnold was informed that Montgomery's force had been routed and that Montgomery was dead, he wept.

Even though the threat of a British counterattack was great, Arnold refused to retreat from the hospital. He ordered the hospital wounded to be armed with pistols and swords should the British come. Esau Morgan sat by his commander's bedside, weapon ready, for four days as Benedict Arnold slipped in and out of consciousness.

"Go get something to eat."

The sound of Arnold's voice startled Esau, who had been dozing in the chair beside his colonel's bed.

"Not hungry," he replied. He rubbed his eyes, then jerked to catch the pistol that was slipping from his lap.

"Help me sit up," Arnold ordered.

Esau placed the weapon on his vacated chair as he pulled Arnold forward, then worked his way behind his colonel and, hugging the man's torso, gently scooted him into a sitting position. Arnold grunted in pain as his leg wrinkled the bedsheets.

"Wasn't even a whole musket ball," Arnold groused.

Esau had already overheard Dr. Senter explain the wound to Arnold's second-in-command, but he let the colonel tell him again anyway.

"It hit something—a rock, stone—before hitting me. Sheared a third of it away, flattening the thing before entering me. Just above my boot." Arnold pulled back the sheet and looked at the bandage as if to confirm that it was still there. He lowered the sheet. "Did the doctor say how long before I would be out of here?"

"I overheard him say four to six weeks."

Arnold cursed. "Too long. Give me a week, then we'll attack again."

"You're fortunate you still have your leg," Esau said. "They discussed amputation. Most were in favor of it. Dr. Senter wouldn't let them."

Arnold took this bit of information soberly. Apparently he hadn't heard it before. "Good man, Senter," he said. Then he chuckled. "He's probably enjoying himself."

"I don't follow."

"He has some real doctoring to do. Tending wounds. Surgery. That sort of thing. A far cry from The Great Carrying Place when all he had was a hundred moaning men with diarrhea."

Esau shared a laugh with his commander.

Arnold studied Esau for a few moments, examining him from his tousled hair and unshaved jaw to his muddy boots. "You're not at all the person I thought you to be," he said.

"Forgive me for saying so, sir, but it's about time you realized that."

Arnold nodded as he laughed. "Prejudice," he said. "Pure prejudice. I use to harass Tories who looked a lot like you. It didn't help that your twin brother was standing there as a comparison. He looked rugged and muscular, while you were soft, thick around the middle, and your hands looked like they had never known a callus." Arnold sized him up again. "It's amazing what a little hike through the Maine wilderness can do for a man."

Esau held out his hands, palms up. He hadn't thought about it until Arnold pointed it out to him, but his hands looked like they belonged to Jacob. They were rough and calloused. And, of course, by nearly starving to death, he had lost the thickness around his midsection.

Arnold lay his head back and stared at the ceiling. He was in a talking mood. "My original dislike for you has roots far deeper than the current political crisis. You reminded me of myself when

I was a lad. I didn't like myself then. I was a coward." He lifted his head and looked at Esau. "Does that surprise you?"

"Having followed you through the wilderness and having seen you stand your ground in a hailstorm of musket balls while wounded, I'd have to say, yes, that surprises me."

Arnold grinned widely, obviously enjoying Esau's response. "I was!" he insisted. "Up until fifteen I was a coward and I hated myself. So I began doing stupid stunts to prove to myself I had courage." His eyes were focused on the ceiling again, reliving scenes of his childhood in his mind. "Once, on a dare, I jumped onto the revolving blades of a waterwheel. I held on for dear life, scared to death, as I was dragged into the water, under the wheel, and up the other side." He paused until another image formed in his mind. "I also used to take running jumps over loaded wagons on main street—to impress the other boys and girls. Ah …!" He sat upright and looked at Esau to tell this one. "Once, on Thanksgiving Day in Norwich, the whole town gathered for a baked-bean dinner. I got a couple of other fellows together and we stole barrels of tar from the waterfront. Then, while everyone was enjoying their meal, we set them on fire atop Bean Hill. It was a marvelous display!" He laughed. "But, of course, the town constable didn't think so. He came charging up the hill after us. While the other fellows ran, I fended off the approaching constable, swinging my coat like a limp sword, screaming and ranting like I was mad!"

Esau chuckled at the scene. "Did you get away?"

"No, I was eventually subdued. I didn't have a chance. The constable must have weighed at least three hundred pounds! All he had to do was sit on me!"

Again the two were laughing, which struck Esau as odd. These were the same kinds of pranks for which Jacob was famous. It was this kind of immature behavior that Esau had always despised in his brother, yet the telling of these rowdy tales by Benedict Arnold was breeding warm feelings of affection in him for his commander.

There was a short interlude as Arnold closed his eyes and rested. When he spoke again, it became clear he had traversed several years during the interlude.

"Are you married, Morgan?" he asked.

"No, sir, never have been."

Arnold's eyebrows shot up. "Not interested in marriage?"

"Oh, I'm interested," Esau said. "It's just that the lady of my affections is unavailable."

Now Arnold demonstrated keen interest. "She's already married?"

Esau nodded. "To my brother."

"You rascal!" Arnold guffawed so loud, several nuns at the hospital made their way into the room to see what was happening. He waved them away, assuring them all was fine. In a quieter voice, he said, "That explains the hatred I saw in your brother's eyes. Come on, Morgan, tell me the whole story."

Esau related how he'd been outmaneuvered for the hand of the fair Mercy Reed Morgan and how he'd always thought that her childless condition was a sign of God's disapproval of the marriage. He didn't tell Arnold about his proposal to Mercy that they run away to England; nor did he mention that Mercy was currently with child.

Arnold's response to the tale was to fold his arms behind his head and state in a philosophical tone, "Relationships with women are never simple, are they?"

"Are you married, sir?"

"Was. I'm a widower. She died last June while I was on Lake Champlain with General Schuyler. She was thirty years old. Died of unknown causes. Her name was Peggy."

"I'm sorry, sir."

The transition from Esau's female relationships to his own propelled Arnold into the past again. His eyes darted from side to side as he relived scenes that only he could see. Finally, he said, "She was the daughter of a high sheriff of New Haven County. She used to worry all the time about my business dealings. The slightest setback and she would think the business was about to fail."

"What type of business was it?"

"Apothecary. My sign on Chapel Street read, 'B. Arnold Druggist, Bookseller, etc. From London. *Sibi Totique.*'"

Esau translated the Latin aloud, "For himself and for everybody."

"I was always proud of that motto," Arnold said, smiling. "My store was the only one of its kind in New Haven. I sold herbs and medicines, cosmetics from London, necklaces, earrings, buttons, pictures, prints, stationery, paper hangings for rooms, even medical books and surgical instruments. I had a small fleet of ships upon which I sailed regularly." His thoughts returned to Peggy with that recollection. "I was gone for long periods of time, even before we were married. I would write her at every post. Rarely did she ever return the favor. I used to plead with her for an occasional line. Once, in Barbados, I delayed sailing for two days, on a hunch that I would receive a letter from her. The thought of spending two months at sea without having heard from her was unbearable." Arnold closed his eyes and sighed heavily. "When we could wait no longer, we sailed. Which was just as well. Peggy hadn't mailed a letter."

Esau thought it best not to respond. Everything he could think of to say sounded trite and patronizing in his mind. It would probably sound even worse when formed into words. He waited in silence for a minute. Then two. The rhythmic breathing of his commanding officer indicated Arnold had fallen asleep. Esau's chair creaked as he rose and walked outside for some fresh air. The memories of Mercy and the shared anguish over his commander's strained relationship with his late wife made Esau's heart feel heavy.

Arnold refused to leave the general vicinity of Quebec until January 4 when he consented to be transported by sleigh to Montgomery's old headquarters at Holland House in Sainte Foy, behind the main American lines. By recruiting Canadian soldiers and by bald-faced bluff, he managed to keep Quebec under siege until April 1 when Brigadier General David Wooster arrived to relieve him.

The day after Wooster arrived, Arnold reinjured his leg. During an alarm, he rushed to mount his horse. The horse lost its balance and landed on his leg. For ten days he couldn't move. During that time he assigned Esau Morgan to be his personal aide. Following his recovery, Arnold was transferred to Montreal to assume command there.

April 29 was a day of surprise for both Benedict Arnold and Esau Morgan.

"Father! What are you doing here?"

A smug-looking Jared Morgan stood in the doorway of Esau's room. As the personal aide to Arnold, Esau had a private room in the mansion of Thomas Walker, a wealthy merchant friend of Arnold's. Esau had been sitting at a small wooden table, scratching out a requisition from his commander when his father made his sudden appearance.

"I'd heard that Benedict Arnold's men were accustomed to hardship," Jared said looking around the room at the paintings, the covered bed, and expansive silk rug. "I see I'll have to return to Philadelphia and set the record straight." Sparkling eyes and a poorly concealed smirk betrayed his threat for the prank that it was.

Esau Morgan met his father in the middle of the room and embraced him.

"It's good to see you. Here, have a seat." He dragged two chairs in front of the fireplace. Although the spring weather had warmed the days, the nights still required a fire to keep the room comfortable.

"So, what are you doing in Montreal?"

"I'm here with a delegation from Congress—Franklin, Samuel Chase, and Charles Carroll. We were sent with gold to resupply your troops, a printing press to issue propaganda in French, assess the military condition, and do what we can to promote cooperation with Canada."

"I thought you were in England."

"Never made it there. Jumped ship mid-Atlantic to join up with Franklin who was returning home. I've been in Philadelphia since. Your mother's not too pleased with me for that. As she mentioned rather pointedly in her last letter, it matters not that I'm nearby in Philadelphia. I'm just as absent as I would be if I were in India. I've tried to get her to join me in Philadelphia, but she never has been much for travel. Besides, she's organized an army of women to sew items of clothing for the soldiers. They use our house nearly every day of the week save the Sabbath. Her conscience would never let her stop doing that just so she could spend her evenings with me."

"That sounds like Mother. How is she?"

"Last I heard, your mother's fine. So is Mercy." Jared saved his son from having to risk asking directly about Mercy. In solemn tones he added, "She lost her baby."

The news struck Esau with double impact. On the one hand, he was concerned for Mercy's health; on the other hand, his theory that tied God's blessing to Mercy's inability to bear children breathed new life.

"Is she all right?" he asked.

"Physically, the doctor says she's fine. Emotionally, your mother says Mercy hasn't quite recovered."

"Does Jacob know?"

"Word was sent to him. I assume he received it."

An uneasy silence lay between them like a massive, invisible stone. Esau couldn't decide whether to scale it by taking his father into his confidence or to let it sit there until his father changed the subject. His indecision lasted long enough for his father to make the decision for him.

"So, how are you doing? You look thin."

Esau pulled at his clothes that hung loosely on him. "I lost some weight in the wilderness. But I'm doing fine."

"You look better—stronger—than I've ever seen you. Army life seems to be good for you. Although I must admit I'm surprised you enlisted."

"After Lexington and Concord, I had no other choice if I was going to continue living in America."

"Well, you've certainly won the hearts of the members of Congress, and all the colonies I might add. Your Benedict Arnold is a hero. It doesn't matter that Quebec remains under British control. The spirit of your march through the wilderness and courageous attack against superior odds have excited the colonies like never before."

Esau basked in his father's words. Coming from a man with his father's adventurous credentials, there was no higher praise than this.

"You heard he was promoted, didn't you? To brigadier general."

Esau nodded.

"Had you heard about Enos and his men?"

"No, what happened to them?"

Jared crossed one leg over the other and grabbed the upper

knee with interlaced hands. "They reached Cambridge safely and well fed after deserting you in Maine. Washington had them all arrested."

This brought a huge grin from Esau.

"Enos was brought up on charges, but the court-martial failed to convict him. He claimed he left to ensure the success of the expedition. That if his men had stayed with the main force, all would have died of starvation."

Esau's face reddened in anger. "Of all the …"

Jared cut him off. "The man could have said anything. The panel for the court-martial was packed with his friends. All of his officers were there to testify for him, while you and the remainder of the expedition were in Quebec. After the trial he was reassigned, but his soldiers would have nothing to do with him. Naturally, they regarded him as a traitor for quitting his command without leave. Eight days later he resigned his commission. Last I heard, he was linked up with the Virginia militia."

It seemed to Esau that a measure of justice was done in spite of the courts. "What's next for you?" he asked his father.

"If I have my way, back to Boston. Congress has authorized privateering. We can put our ships to good use. Franklin has taken a liking to me. He's indicated he would like me to return with him to Philadelphia. There's strong talk about declaring colonial independence from England."

Esau's mouth fell open.

"It surprises me too," Jared continued. "King George refused to receive the Olive Branch Petition, then promptly proclaimed the colonies to be in open rebellion. Attitudes have hardened on both sides. I fear there's no turning back now. It looks like our choices are limited to two: fight for independence and pray for victory or be conquered and pray for mercy."

His father's assessment of the political landscape disturbed

Esau. In his mind he could see men like Sam Adams and John Hancock gleefully rejoicing that they had succeeded in their devious scheme to split the colonies from their parent. He didn't know which disturbed him more—the news itself or the thought of Adams succeeding.

"What's next for you?" His father's words pulled him back into the conversation.

"I'm with Colonel, I mean, Brigadier General Arnold. Wherever he goes, I go."

Jared Morgan took a long look at Esau. "I know this hasn't been an easy transition for you, politically or physically. But I want you to know I'm proud of you, son."

Esau basked in his father's praise for but a moment, then he bolted toward his pack and retrieved his Bible.

"I have something for you," he said with a self-satisfied grin.

He took a piece of aged cloth from between the pages of his Bible and handed it to his father.

"What's this?" Jared asked, examining it carefully.

"It's a portion of a wristband."

"A very old one at that," Jared said. "Who did it belong to?"

"Someone you knew; more accurately, someone you once saw. He played a significant role in your life." Esau was clearly wanting to draw out this presentation to his father, to enjoy the moment for as long as he could. To his delight, his secretive method had hooked his father's curiosity.

"All right," Jared said, going along with the game, "where did you get it?"

"Newburyport."

"Newburyport?" A furrow formed on Jared's brow. "Newburyport ... what's at Newburyport?"

"I attended a church service there before we departed for Quebec."

"A church service...." The clue was tantalizing, but not very helpful.

"At a Presbyterian church."

Jared shook his head. No help there.

"There was a tomb underneath the pulpit."

A light was beginning to dawn. With a delightfully surprised look, Jared said, "Whitefield's tomb!"

Esau nodded.

Suddenly, the piece of cloth in Jared's hands took on holy proportions. "This is from Whitefield's tomb?" His voice was breathy, reverent.

"The sexton allowed all of the officers to take a piece. Knowing that you were saved during Whitefield's preaching, I thought you might like to have it."

Jared's eyes grew misty as he looked from the cloth to his son and back to the cloth. "I'll treasure it all my life," he said. "Thank you, Esau. Thank you." He stood and embraced his son.

It was a spiritual moment for both men. Gone were politics and war and controversy and differences as the small swatch of cloth from George Whitefield's graveclothes reminded them both of far greater things—faith and family love.

Benedict Arnold was just as surprised as Esau at the appearance of the commissioners from Philadelphia. Their presence meant that he had made some headway with all the letters he'd sent requesting supplies and additional support. The elderly Franklin, who had just turned seventy, surprised Arnold with his plan to protect American interests from British naval incursions. He had instigated the building of several huge *chevaux de frise*, a submerged line of pointed timbers designed to impale enemy ships, to be strategically placed on all major river arteries. Arnold enthusiastically envisioned the same kind of device across the St.

Lawrence River. With Franklin's support, Arnold also got the commissioners to approve his plans to build forts at two important posts on the St. Lawrence.

That night, Arnold threw a party for the commissioners at his Montreal headquarters mansion. He was in high spirits. And why shouldn't he be? Some of America's finest citizens were in attendance. At the head of the list was Benjamin Franklin, America's most celebrated celebrity; Charles Carroll of Maryland was one of the wealthiest men in all the colonies; and the irascible Samuel Chase, a rich Maryland merchant, was a friend of Arnold's from his previous stay in Montreal and one of his most vocal supporters in the Congress. Also attending the party were Major General John Thomas, who was on his way to Quebec, and Boston merchant Jared Morgan, friend of Franklin and father to Esau Morgan, Arnold's personal aide.

The evening was impressive, even by the high standards of the wealthy guests. It began with a reception. Wine was served while people crowded the room, meeting each other and paying compliments. Then the guests were ushered into another room where a number of French ladies were awaiting them. After tea and a time of chatting, they dined on a most elegant supper, which was followed by a program of singing by the ladies.

For Esau, it brought back memories of similar balls in Boston and Philadelphia. After Maine and Quebec, it was certainly a grand time for him. However, he couldn't stop thinking that something was missing. The party would be ever so much more lively if Mercy were there.

13

Anne's horse raced wildly under a flat gray sky. What had begun as a leisurely spring afternoon in the fields outside Boston had turned into a heart-wrenching battle for her life. She'd lost control of her horse, normally a gentle creature. Not today. Today the mare ran as though possessed, swerving erratically from one side of the road to the other, her eyes rolled back in her head—red streaked, frightened, furious, horrifyingly fixed on her rider.

Jump! Jump! Anne kept saying to herself. But she could not let go of the reins, they were wrapped tightly around her hand, binding her destiny to that of the wild horse. The ground beneath rushed by, jagged with rocks and debris.

The horse dragged her rider toward a bridge made of rough, black timbers. It was out of place; it hadn't been there before. The clouds overhead matched the dark color of the bridge, hovering menacingly, ominously over it. Anne must not cross that bridge. She didn't know why; she only knew she must not cross it.

She screamed the horse's name over and over, pulling back with all her might, digging into the stirrups with her legs to no effect. The horse continued headlong toward the bridge.

Just then she noticed a clump of trees with men lying under it. They seemed to appear from nowhere. She screamed to them for help. They didn't hear her. She screamed again. No response. As she drew closer, she understood why. They were all dead, covered from knees to head with their greatcoats.

Miraculously, her horse slowed. The mare wandered toward the tree as if pulled there like a magnet, then stopped, her sides heaving mightily from the gallop. The heavy sound of the horse's breathing gave an eerie rhythm to the scene before them.

A boy stood among the dead men. Chestnut hair. He stood proper, erect. A silver chalice was cradled in one hand. "Master needs water," he said in a distinguished English accent while looking straight at Anne. "Master is thirsty." The boy reached down to the still form at his feet. His free hand fumbled with the greatcoat.

On the greatcoat were initials—J. M. Embroidered in red. J. M. Jacob Morgan! Anne had embroidered those initials on that cloak!

Anne tried to look away, but she couldn't. The boy pulled aside the greatcoat. Beneath it was the blackish pallor of a dead man. It was Jacob! The boy lowered the chalice to Jacob's face. Unresponsive lips refused the water; it streamed down Jacob's gray, hollow cheeks.

Anne screamed. Instantly, her horse bolted toward the bridge. Thunder cracked, a loud close sound. No, not thunder, cannon fire. The horse reached the black bridge just as she saw the line of redcoat cannons on the other side. The hollow clop of her horse's hoofs was interrupted with the louder crash of cannon balls hitting the bridge. The railing beside her exploded with one hit; another ripped a huge gash in boards in front of her. Her horse reared as the bridge rocked crazily to one side. Another hit. Wood and splinters flew everywhere. The boards below the horse gave way. The beast stumbled, her feet falling between the planks.

Anne tried to release the reins. They held her tight. She was falling. Falling with the horse through the planks, falling into the river. Jagged rocks rushing upward. She screamed and screamed and screamed.

"ANNE! ANNE! It's me, Mercy! Anne! Anne!"

Mercy's full black hair fell forward on both sides of her face. Her eyes were wide and wet with tears. She swallowed once. Twice.

"Anne! You're frightening me!" Mercy cried.

Her hands extended downward, gripping Anne's shoulders tightly, shaking harder and harder until Anne's head was bouncing on the pillow.

"I'm all right," Anne said. But her voice betrayed her. The hoarse whisper that came out was not convincing.

Mercy's lower lip trembled. She held it still by biting it.

Anne cleared her throat. "Mercy, I'm all right." Her voice was stronger this time.

Mercy's eyes closed. She raised her head heavenward, and as she did, her hair rushed back on both sides of her face, like the tide going out. The porcelain face that appeared was covered with relief.

"Was it that same dream?" Mercy asked.

Anne nodded. The dream had recurred several times a week for more than a month now. Anne had told Mercy about it, all except for the part about Jacob. When she came to that part, she merely said the dead man under the greatcoat was a soldier.

"Do you want me to make you some tea?" Mercy stood over her, fully in control of herself, hands on hips. Her stance reminded Anne that Mercy was thin again. There were no traces of her pregnancy. On more than one night through the ill-fated pregnancy, and after, Anne had comforted Mercy late at night with a cup of hot tea. The two would sit in the drawing room, sip

their tea, and Anne would read Scripture aloud. Anne smiled at
the thought that Mercy had come to accept this as standard procedure when they were alone and troubled.

"I'd like that," Anne said warmly.

The two women bundled up in blankets in chairs arranged
around a small table, sipping their tea. Anne's open Bible rested
on the table between them. A solitary lamp shared the table. Its
circular glow provided them a cozy cave of light in the darkened
room.

"I feel like *I* should be reading to you from the Bible," Mercy
said. "Like you always do for me. But I wouldn't know what to
read."

"Try Second Corinthians, chapter one," Anne said.

A puzzled look peered over Mercy's teacup.

"It's in the New Testament. About three-quarters of the way
through the Bible."

With an awkward grin, Mercy set down her teacup and picked
up the Bible. She flipped pages near the back of the book. Anne
patiently let her find 2 Corinthians without further help. While
Mercy turned page after page Anne noticed how much Mercy had
changed in appearance. The previous year had taken its toll.
Mercy looked older, in some ways more mature, but in other ways
harder, lines that revealed a growing cynicism. Her eyes brightened, indicating she found 2 Corinthians.

"Begin with verse three," Anne said.

Mercy looked up at Anne, then back down at the Bible. She
raised it closer to her eyes and read aloud: "Blessed be God, even
the Father of our Lord Jesus Christ, the Father of mercies, and the
God of all comfort; Who comforteth us in all our tribulation, that
we may be able to comfort them which are in any trouble, by the
comfort wherewith we ourselves are comforted of God."

She looked up from the page, astonished. "You chose these

verses for me, didn't you?" Returning to the page, her finger pointing to certain words, she said, *"we ... comfort them ...* by the comfort wherewith we ourselves are comforted." A look of discovery shined in her eyes. "In the past, you have comforted me, now it's my turn to comfort you!"

"And the source of all comfort is God," Anne added.

"That's what is so amazing about you," Mercy said. "You know right where to look in the Bible for verses like this. I wish I could do that."

"It's no mystery," Anne replied. "The more time you spend with something, the more familiar you become with it. Anyone can do it."

"I still think you're a special woman," Mercy said. "With Jacob gone, and all the wartime shortages ... and losing my baby," a sad hand gently stroked her tummy, "you have always been here to comfort me. I love you for that, Anne. I really do."

The next day, before the troubling aftereffects of Anne's nightmare had time to wear off, a letter was delivered from Jacob that propelled Mercy upstairs in a hysterical fit of wailing. The letter accused her of adultery with Esau. He said it was fortunate the baby was never born, otherwise he would always wonder whose child it was.

While Mercy wept uncontrollably facedown on her bed, Anne sat on the edge. With one hand she rubbed Mercy's back, her other hand held Jacob's letter as she read it for herself.

"Oh no, Jacob, no," she said softly as she read and wept.

BAM! BAM! BAM! BAM! BAM!

Downstairs someone was pounding on the door.

The hand holding the letter dropped to the bed. Anne looked up. "Lord, what now?" she said in exasperation. She waited for a servant to answer the door.

BAM! BAM! BAM! BAM! BAM!

Because of the war, they had only one house servant left. *He must be outside*, Anne concluded. She patted Mercy on the back. "I'll be right back, dear," she said.

Halfway down the stairs she met Priscilla charging up. Behind her the front door stood wide open. Priscilla was out of breath.

"What regiment is Jacob in?" she asked.

Anne knew the answer, but the suddenness of the question and Priscilla's breathless presence chased it from her mind.

"Is it the Massachusetts Sixth?"

"Um ... that sounds right."

"Weston is his commander, right?"

"Colonel Weston, yes. I'm sure of that. He reports to Colonel Weston."

Priscilla laid a hand on Anne's forearm. "We've got trouble."

A sniffing Mercy sat up in her bed. Priscilla sat on one side, Anne on the other, as Priscilla told them what she had heard. A drunken stage driver arrived bearing a letter from Peter, who was with Washington's troops near New York. They had known the driver for years. He was a disreputable sort whose services or confidences could be bought by either side. Normally, Peter wouldn't have trusted the man to carry his letter. Priscilla concluded that Peter used him this time because no one else was available.

The driver came crashing into The Good Woman Tavern with Peter's letter in his hand. He demanded a drink before delivering it, then collapsed on the floor. Priscilla and a helper hoisted him into a chair and proceeded to pour coffee down him. Meanwhile the driver rambled on about a British trap. "Won't the good ol' boys of Massa ... Massach ... Massa—of Boston be surprised when they cross the river?"

To speed things along, Priscilla summarized his story from

there. The stage driver mentioned Colonel Weston, "Boston boys" several times, Oxkirk something, and Milford, the small valley near Milford. Mercy's face drained of what little color it normally had.

"Milford," she said in a detached tone. She grabbed Jacob's letter, which was still on the bed, and began scanning it.

"Yes, Milford," Anne said, remembering what she had just read.

"What?" Priscilla squealed. "Is Jacob at Milford?"

Mercy read aloud from the letter, "... heading for New York ..." she scanned further "... Ox Creek Bridge, just south of Milford"! Her hand dropped with a thud to the bed. "O Lord, help us," she cried.

Anne looked at her with a stunned expression. Unwanted images clamored for attention. A horse out of control. A cluster of trees. Lifeless bodies covered with greatcoats. She squeezed shut her eyes, trying to force the images from her mind. Yet one word stubbornly refused her every effort to oust it. Unforgivingly, it pounded inside her head. *Bridge ... bridge ... bridge.*

"If we're stopped by British patrols, I won't lie to them," Anne said.

"Even if it means our lives? Or the life of your son?" Mercy couldn't believe what Anne was saying.

"I won't lie," Anne insisted. "We'll have to trust God to get us through somehow."

Anne and Mercy traveled the road from Boston to Milford. The farther they strayed from Boston, the riskier the journey was for them. It was a crazy idea. And uncharacteristically, it was Anne's crazy idea.

Priscilla, Mercy, and Anne were all in agreement that Jacob's regiment had to be warned. But while Priscilla and Mercy argued that they could find someone to relay the information for them, Anne insisted that she had to do it. The unlikely team of Priscilla and Mercy could do nothing to dissuade her. So Priscilla, never one to back away from a challenge, offered to go with her. Mercy pointed out that Priscilla was needed at the tavern. If any more vital information was forthcoming from the stage driver or another source, it would most likely surface at the tavern. If it did, Priscilla could send someone after them. Mercy said she would accompany Anne. It was Anne herself who cast the deciding vote. Mercy was right. Priscilla was needed at the tavern. And it made sense that God would protect a mother and wife in their attempt to protect the man they both loved. Priscilla agreed. She was persuaded by Anne's words, which were spoken more confidently than they were felt by the one speaking them.

While the horses trotted at a brisk pace, Mercy leaned toward Anne. "Under that tree up ahead. Two soldiers. Looks like British uniforms."

Anne peered ahead. Although partially cloaked by the tree's shade, they did indeed look like two mounted British officers. "I won't lie to them," Anne said.

"You won't have to!" Mercy hissed. "Let me do the talking!"

The British officers spurred their horses toward the women, blocking the road. The older one was short and stocky with a square, no-nonsense jaw and hard eyes; the other officer looked like he was barely into his twenties. He was tall and gangly with large ears and a disproportionately large mouth that curled upward in a perpetual grin.

"That's far enough, ladies," the older one commanded. "Do you mind telling me where you're going?"

Looking him directly in the eye, Anne said, "We'd rather not, sir."

This brought an immediate scowl.

"What she means," Mercy interjected quickly, "is that we doubt our trifling business is of any interest to a busy man like you."

"Hughes," the stocky officer said to the taller one, "check their things."

A long leg swung over the back of his horse as Hughes dismounted. He approached Mercy first. She gave him one of her renowned dazzling smiles, which prompted a wide, goofy grin in return. "There's nothing to find, I assure you," she said to the one in command.

"If it's all the same to you, we'll check for ourselves."

Mercy smiled and shrugged. "Whatever you say, General."

"Lieutenant."

"Forgive me, I don't know all those braids and buttons and things. You just look like a general to me."

The lieutenant smiled appreciatively while Hughes moved from Mercy's horse to Anne. Moments later he reported that he found nothing of consequence and from their lack of provisions they couldn't have come far.

"For your sake, I'm hoping you are both loyal subjects of King George," said the lieutenant.

"I am subject to no man, sir," Anne stated flatly. "My allegiance belongs wholly to my master, the Lord Jesus Christ."

The lieutenant was taken aback, then bristled at her response. His big-eared partner crossed himself.

"I did not ask your religious affiliation," the lieutenant snapped. "My orders are to detain all travelers who cannot prove their loyalty to the king. I ask you again, madam, are you loyal to King George?"

"Boston!" Mercy cried out. "That's where I've seen the general before," she said pointing at him, but speaking to Anne. "He was that gallant young officer I told you about who attended the governor's ball several years ago."

The lieutenant was shaking his head. "I've never been to the governor's ball."

Anne said, "Mercy, I don't remember you telling me ..."

"Mercy?" the lieutenant said. "Mercy Reed? I thought you looked familiar!" His grin looked uncharacteristically out of place on his square jaw; so much so, it almost looked like it hurt him to smile. But he did so anyway. "I was stationed in Philadelphia when you attended your first ball! When you made your entrance, I thought you were the most beautiful creature I'd ever seen." The lieutenant was gushing. "It took me most of the night, but I was determined to have at least part of a dance with you. It was after midnight, but finally I did. I danced with you! You probably don't remember me...."

Mercy clasped her hands to her chest. "Oh yes! I remember everything about that night. It was the most *wonderful* night of my life."

"Excuse me, Lieutenant," Anne said, "but we really must be on our way. Will you let us pass?"

Still looking at Mercy, he said with a nervous chuckle, "You wouldn't be warning your husband of some troop movements or anything like that, would you?"

"With God as my witness," Anne said, "we are not warning my husband about any troop movements or anything like that."

"All right," he said, his eyes still glued on Mercy. "You may pass."

"But, sir," Hughes said, "our orders are to turn everyone back."

"Shut up, Hughes," the lieutenant replied. "What are they going to do? They're only women!"

Anne and Mercy rode in silence until the two British officers were out of sight. Then, with closed eyes, Anne said, "Praise God Almighty!" To Mercy: "And may He forgive you for lying."

"What do you mean?"

"You lied. You didn't remember that man, did you?"

"I never said I did. He said, 'You probably don't remember me,' and I agreed with him. I didn't remember him!"

Anne laughed and shook her head. "I stand corrected."

The sky grew overcast as they continued their journey. It was flat gray. Anne's mare grew uncharacteristically skittish. Anne kept a close rein on her, the leather wrapped tightly around her right hand. It was starting. The sky. The horse. The reins. This was her nightmare, only she wasn't sleeping this time.

"Are you feeling all right?" A look of concern covered Mercy's face.

Anne nodded. "How much farther?"

"I think it's just over that rise." Mercy pointed to a small hill about a quarter mile distant.

Thunder cracked in that direction. No. Not thunder. Cannon fire. Anne's horse flinched and jumped.

At the crest of the ridge they stopped. Below them, a regiment spread out before them on their side of the river. A solitary black bridge crossed it. On the far side was a larger valley. Bodies of soldiers spotted the greenery. About twenty of them.

Mercy looked at Anne. From the cruel twist of Anne's mouth and the lack of color in her cheeks, she could tell something was wrong. "What is it?" she asked. She followed Anne's line of vision to a cluster of trees just to the right of the bridge. Still forms were littered around its base. She remembered.

"Your dream!" Mercy exclaimed. "That's why you insisted on coming." She stared back at the cluster of trees and the full realization hit her, the truth of Anne's dream that had been kept from her. "Jacob!" she said, her voice quivering. "The dead man in your dream. It was Jacob, wasn't it?"

Instead of answering, Anne jabbed her heels into the mare.

The horse responded instantly, propelling both of them down the hill toward the bridge. The wind raced through her hair and clothes; beneath her, the dirt road was a blur. It was all Anne could do to keep from falling off as the cluster of trees loomed larger and larger the closer she got to it.

She passed soldiers standing outside their tents, beside the road, standing in formation, all of them staring after her like she was insane. Anne urged the mare until they were almost upon the cluster of trees. She pulled the reins back. The mare slowed. Just then a boy with chestnut hair came up the rise from the river. He carried a pewter cup, dripping with water.

Anne dropped the reins and jumped down from the horse. She moved toward the tree as though she were under a spell, not wanting to go, but unable to stop herself. Greatcoats covered the faces and torsos of the men lying at the tree's base. The only thing that distinguished them from piles of clothes was the way their legs and shoes stuck out from beneath the edges of the cloaks. In the middle, just like in her dream, there was a greatcoat with initials. J. M. Embroidered in red. Her handiwork. The one she made for Jacob.

A whimpering prayer escaped her lips as she drew closer. She bent over the greatcoat with Jacob's initials. With trembling hands, she reached down and pulled back the cloak.

"Oh no!" she cried.

The man under the cloak had blonde hair. It wasn't Jacob!

"Mother? Mother! Whatever are you doing here?"

Anne whirled around. Jacob stood a few feet from her, holding a pewter cup. The boy with the chestnut hair stood silently beside him.

"Jacob! O Jacob!"

Jacob turned just as Mercy leaped into his arms, her momentum nearly knocking him over. His exclamation of surprise was interrupted by her kisses covering his mouth. A fair number of amused men gathered around them. Bo wore a puzzled but comical expression on his face. Jacob broke away. "What is going on here?"

Anne was by his side, clutching both of them. "We have to talk, son. It's urgent. Is your commanding officer nearby?"

Anne and Mercy Morgan recounted the information about the British trap to Jacob and his commanding officer, Colonel Weston, in the colonel's tent. From him, they learned that just before their arrival, the colonial troops had gained a victory over a smaller British regiment that fled into the hills. Their confidence bolstered from that engagement, they were just about to move across the bridge in pursuit of the fleeing British.

"Could it be a trap, sir?" Jacob asked.

Weston stroked his mouth and several days of stubble on his cheeks. "If I were going to set a trap in this valley, I'd send a small force into the valley as a lure, positioning the main force behind the hills. If the enemy took the bait, they'd cross the bridge in pursuit, like we're about to do. As soon as they were across, I'd knock out the bridge, cutting off their retreat."

"The bridge!" Anne cried. "Yes! They plan to destroy the bridge! With cannons."

Colonel Weston looked hard at her. "This is part of the information you heard? They plan to knock out the bridge with cannons?"

"I didn't hear it," Anne said. She paused.

"Well?" Weston said. "How do you know about the bridge?"

"I dreamed it."

Thin eyebrows arched high over the colonel's eyes. It was clear that Anne's mention of the dream clouded her credibility in the colonel's mind.

"I can assure you, Colonel, my mother is not an empty-headed woman given to supernatural nonsense such as spooks and apparitions. She is a godly woman with a keen mind."

Anne reached over and patted the back of Jacob's hand. "Thank you, dear."

The colonel looked from one to the other, cleared his throat, and said, "As I was saying … I'd knock out the bridge to cut off their retreat, pound the …" he stopped himself, looked at the women and rephrased his thought, "pound them mercilessly, then send my troops down to mop up." He mentally reviewed his strategy. "Yes, it could work that way. It could be a trap."

"What do you suggest, sir?"

"Morgan, send out two scouts. Have them circle to the right and left. Tell them to look for signs of troops behind the hills. I want them back with a report in two hours. Understood?"

"Yes, sir." Jacob exited the tent smartly, leaving the colonel alone with Anne and Mercy.

The colonel looked at one, then the other, shifting his weight from foot to foot. Grabbing his cap, he reached for the tent flap. There was no verbal thanks. The colonel merely nodded at the ladies, then disappeared. Jacob returned momentarily and ushered the ladies out.

Anne turned to her son. "I thank God you're all right." She described her dream to him, his eyes growing wider as she told it. Afterward, he shook his head.

"Zeke Taylor," he said. "That's the name of the man under my greatcoat. A poor farmer from Connecticut. Didn't have one of his own. Caught a musket ball in his chest this morning. Zeke just looked out of place there, him being the only one not covered and all."

There was a moment of silence between them for the dead soldier.

"I'm sure you and Mercy want to be alone for a while," Anne said. "I'll just walk over here and ..."

"Mother, wait just a minute." He called to Bo, who was standing a short distance away, evidently waiting for him. Looking straight at the boy, he said distinctly, "Bo, this is my mother. She's ridden a long way. Would you take her to get something to drink?" Briefly, he told his mother about Bo's father, the man's death at Meriam's Corner, and Bo's limited hearing and speech.

Smiling, Anne said, "I've already met him." Laughing at Jacob's puzzled expression, she explained, "In my dream. Funny, though. In my dream he spoke the King's English!"

Bo grinned. He liked that. Reaching for Anne's hand, he led her toward the cooking area where there were several fires, boiling pots, pans, and cups. Anne and Bo got better acquainted while Jacob and Mercy found a place where they could be alone.

※

Two hours later when the scouts returned, massive British troop placements were confirmed. Not only were the hills laden with troops, but with heavy artillery as well. A war council was called to determine an alternative strategy and route to New York.

Jacob Morgan was one of the last to hear the report; he was with Mercy in his tent. The flaps were closed, but it was no secret what was taking place on the other side of the canvas. If there had been a war in the valley that day, with a full complement of cannon, it would not have been as loud as the shouting in Jacob's tent. Anne needed no directions to her son's quarters. Not only did the sound of voices guide her, but the entire side of camp faced the direction of Jacob's tent. Soldiers of every description had positioned themselves on camp stools, logs, the ground, whatever they could find to sit on, with cups and mugs in their hands, and focused intently on the drama being played out before them. Jacob accused his wife of unfaithfulness; Mercy retorted that she had every opportunity to be unfaithful but hadn't been, only now she wished she had. He threatened to bring charges of adultery against her in church; she said if she knew he felt that way, she would have never come to the camp, content to let him die in the valley across the bridge. Outside the tent there were occasional nudges, nods, and winks as the soldiers rooted for one side or the other.

Anne motioned for her young companion, Bo, to wait for her while she approached the tent. Mercifully, Bo couldn't hear what was going on, and Anne didn't want him to witness it. She didn't bother to announce herself. She lifted the flap and entered. The interior fell silent the moment they saw her. The faces of both Mercy and Jacob expressed surprise, then shame, at her sudden appearance. Mercy's face was wet, her eyes puffed horribly. Jacob was red all over; his jaw was tense, his hands clenched.

Softly, Anne said, "You have entertained the troops long enough. Mercy, we need to get back home. I'll wait for you outside while you say good-bye to your husband."

There was a groan of disappointment from the audience as she emerged from the tent. She ignored it. Kneeling down before her new friend, she placed her hands on Bo's shoulders and told him how happy she was that Jacob had someone to protect him. Bo grinned appreciatively.

The first half of the return journey to Boston was covered with a heavy cloak of silence. Anne was the first to break the stillness.

"You and Jacob said some horrible things to each other back there."

Mercy lowered her head and daubed her nose with a handkerchief, but didn't respond.

"Did you mean them?"

They rode a few feet farther in silence. Anne waited.

"No. Of course, we didn't mean them. At least I didn't. But I was angry. He hurt me and I wanted to hurt him back."

Still Anne said nothing.

"I did the right thing!" Mercy complained. "But he doesn't believe me! Sometimes he makes me wish I'd done the wrong thing just so he'd have good cause to be angry!"

"Really?"

Mercy's head snapped up, her eyes narrowed. "I can't believe what you are inferring!"

Anne rode calmly for a short distance. Then she said, "Esau is still in love with you."

Another stretch of silence.

"It's no secret," Anne added. "If I see the way he looks at you, Jacob probably has too."

"I can't control another person's feelings for me." Mercy was getting defensive.

"Is that what you told Esau during your garden rendezvous?"

"Who have you been talking to? Why, I would never ..."

"I saw you myself ... from my bedroom window."

Mercy's expression was that of a cornered mouse, looking for a way of escape.

Anne pulled her horse to a stop; Mercy did likewise. Anne said, "How can I convince you that all I want is the best for you and my sons? I know Esau; as long as he is convinced there is a sliver of hope for the two of you, he will never let you go. And I know Jacob; he will feel threatened until he is convinced Esau is no longer a possible suitor. Only you can settle the matter, and your marriage has no chance of happiness until you do."

"But Esau is so sweet. I don't want to hurt him."

"You must hurt him."

Mercy was incredulous. "How can you say that? You're his mother!"

Anne's eyes grew moist. "Unless you hurt him—break your relationship unconditionally, tell him you don't love him and never will—he will continue to love you. If he loves you, he will never allow himself to love another woman. Don't you see? By holding on to him, you destroy any chance he has of finding happiness in love."

Anne's tone grew sharper as she pressed her point. "How long has it been, Mercy? Over ten years! You have been married ten years. Has Esau's devotion to you diminished one ounce in that time? Has he shown interest in any other women? Ten years of his life have passed in mourning for what might have been! You have to cut him loose! He's too stubborn, too competitive, too pig-headed to let you go himself. If you have any feelings for him at all, you have to be the strong one and hurt him!"

Tears came to Mercy's already red and puffy eyes. "I never thought of it that way. I didn't realize I was hurting him. It's just that I enjoy having him around. He's been my counterweight to Jacob. I could always depend on him for a kind word and a smile when I needed it." She closed her eyes, the next few sentences coming through sobs. "That's awful of me, isn't it? I've ruined ten years of a good man's life for selfish reasons."

This troubling thought, added to the accumulated frustrations of the day, proved to be too much for Mercy. Sobs tumbled from her uncontrollably, shaking her torso with such intensity that Anne feared she might fall off the horse. Helping Mercy down, Anne led her to a nearby oak tree situated next to a small pond. Whitewashed farmhouses and barns lay sparsely scattered in the distance. They were about two hours out of Boston.

After getting Mercy situated, Anne led the horses to the pond, then found a small patch of grass upon which to sit under the tree.

"How do you do it?" Mercy asked.

"Do what, dear?"

"You're gentle, kind, and you're loved by everyone. How do you do it?"

"I don't do it."

A handkerchief rimmed the bottom edge of each eye. "I understand. It comes naturally for you."

Anne laughed. "Good heavens, no!" She stretched forward to make physical contact with Mercy's hand. "I'm not laughing at you, dear," she said, "just at the thought that relationships come easy for me."

"Then what did you mean when you said you didn't do it?"

"Well, I'm going to sound like one of those evangelists, but I don't do it. Jesus Christ does it through me."

Mercy didn't look away at Anne's statement, so she continued. "From the Bible, Philippians 2:3–4." She closed her eyes and quoted from memory. "'Let nothing be done through strife or vainglory; but in lowliness of mind let each esteem others better than themselves. Look not every man on his own things, but every man also on the things of others.'" Her eyes opened. "I've found this to be the secret of relationships. The more you try to draw attention to yourself to get people to like you, the fewer friends you gain; but the more you concern yourself with their interests and needs, the more people will want to be your friend."

Mercy thought about what Anne said. "I can see how that has worked for you. I've found that the more unattainable you are— to men especially—the more they desire you."

"So by making yourself unattainable, whose interests are you serving? Yours or theirs?"

"Mine." Mercy tucked her handkerchief away. "Still, you said you didn't do it. What did you mean by that?"

"Simply this. I'm a selfish, conceited woman."

It was Mercy's turn to laugh. "You are not! You're the least selfish person I know."

Anne shook her head. "It's the truth. If it weren't for my Lord, the Anne Morgan that you have come to know wouldn't exist. He has changed me. He taught me how to love unselfishly by filling me with His love."

Mercy sniffed and straightened her dress around her. "I could never be like you."

"And there's no reason why anyone would want you to be! The world doesn't need another Anne Morgan. But your husband needs a wife who loves him wholeheartedly; and Esau needs a woman of courage to tell him that she could never love him in any way other than as a sister-in-law; and Mercy Reed Morgan needs to be able to wake up each morning knowing that she is loved, assured that her destiny is in God's hands."

Rubbing her hands, Mercy said, "Is that possible?"

Anne moved to her side, throwing her arms around her. "Oh yes, dear! Everything is possible with God!"

Under an oak tree beside a small pond on the road to Boston, Anne and Mercy Morgan prayed to God.

A large crowd had gathered around the Old State House as a weary Anne and Mercy Morgan rode into town. The street was so crowded, there was no room for their horses to pass through. Mercy suggested an alternative route, but Anne's curiosity was a stronger influence on her than fatigue. She dismounted and asked an elderly man standing with his wife at the edge of the crowd what the excitement was all about.

"A delegation from Philadelphia," he said, "just arrived and …

wait ..." Several figures emerged onto the balcony of the state house. "Listen for yourself," the man said, pointing to the men on the balcony.

The crowd hushed. One of the men standing on the balcony produced a piece of parchment and began reading. His voice was as clear as a clarion bell:

> When, in the course of human events, it becomes necessary for one people to dissolve the political bands which have connected them with another, and to assume, among the powers of the earth, the separate and equal station to which the laws of nature and of nature's God entitle them, a decent respect to the opinions of mankind requires that they should declare the causes which impel them to separation.
>
> We hold these truths to be self-evident, that all men are created equal, that they are endowed by their Creator with certain unalienable rights, that among these are life, liberty, and the pursuit of happiness. That, to secure these rights, governments are instituted among men, deriving their just powers from the consent of the governed. That, whenever any form of government becomes destructive of these ends, it is the right of the people to alter or to abolish it, and to institute new government, laying its foundation on such principles, and organizing its powers in such form, as to them shall seem most likely to effect their safety and happiness....

Anne Morgan stood at the edge of the crowd, sensing the importance of this day. History was being made. The world was no longer the same as it was yesterday, but then, neither was God's kingdom. The emotion of her thoughts caused her to tremble. What a day this had been! On the same day, God's kingdom had been increased by one person, her own Mercy, and the number of nations in the world had also been increased by one, the United States of America.

14

February 7, 1777
Passy, France

My dearest Anne,

This is my third letter to you since I arrived in Paris, December 21, 1776. I fear my previous letters have not reached you. The report I have received is that the ship bearing them was captured by the British. The standard procedure in such an event is for the captain to dispose of all correspondence from commissioners by throwing it overboard before capture to keep vital information from falling into the hands of the British. I'll assume this is what has happened to my previous epistles and will pen this letter as if it is the first.

Our crossing aboard the 16-gun sloop *Reprisal* was a fast but rough passage. Lambert Wickes was the captain, an able seaman. If you recall, we met him at one of those fancy Philadelphia balls four, or was it five, years ago. He's a good man. His orders for this voyage were to avoid all other ships, to run if pursued, and to fight only if there was no other recourse. It goes without saying that if Franklin were detained by a British ship, he—and those accompanying him—would surely find themselves wearing nooses in London.

As you might expect, the turbulent sea had no ill effects on me. However, Dr. Franklin was more than glad when we reached shore.

The fowl on board proved too tough for him to eat, so he had to sustain himself with salt beef. The limited diet caused him to break out in boils on his back, legs, and arms. They weren't grievous enough to keep him from his scientific interests though. He took soundings, measured the water's temperature, and estimated the portion of the journey spent in the Gulf Stream. His "old friend," he called it.

We sighted land on December 3—Belle Isle off the Britanny coast. The following day we anchored in Quiberon Bay. We were supposed to continue on to Nantes, but the wind changed and after four days Wickes negotiated with a fishing boat to take us ashore at Aunoy.

The overland journey to Paris went without incident. One night we traveled well into the evening. When Dr. Franklin commented on the scarce number of travelers on the road, our driver amused himself by stopping near a wood we were to pass through to tell us that a gang of eighteen robbers infested it, and that a short two weeks previous the gang robbed and murdered some travelers on this very spot. Franklin bid him to cease his stories and continue his driving.

Our first few weeks in Paris we stayed at the Hotel d'Hambourg which proved to be inconvenient due to the number of interruptions from people offering goods, services, etc. So we moved a short mile to Passy. For the most part, it is a little town with small cottages and narrow streets hidden among woods and vineyards. We reside at the Hotel de Valentinois as the guests of M. Chaumont. Anne, I wish you could see it. It has spacious grounds, multileveled terraces, and a chain of pavilions overlooking the River Seine. In the distance you can see the spires of Paris.

My darling Anne, it is my most fervent prayer that my separation from you will not be a lengthy one. My soul aches every time I remember the last days we spent together. It was insensitive of me to say the things I did. You don't know how difficult it is to argue with someone who wants nothing more than to be with the one she loves. What can I say in my defense? When we were younger, my lengthy absences were rationalized by the thought that we were building a life for ourselves. If that were still the issue, I would gladly exchange our ships, our warehouses, our wealth for the chance to spend the remainder of my days with you. Who would have known that in our later years I would be

called away for a purpose which is far greater than material things?
Anne, I'm too old to be a soldier. I'm not a politician. I am confounded
that there seems to be little I can do in defense of our newborn country. My darling, I wish I could make you understand. It's not that I don't
want to be with you. I had to come to France because, for some reason, Dr. Franklin feels I can be of use to him here. And if by assisting
him, we are able to secure funds, supplies, ammunition, and ships that
will aid the success of our military forces, then with God's help this is
what I must do!

It is difficult for me to comprehend all that has happened in the
past few decades. Who would have thought that American colonists
would be in France as friends? Why, just a few short years ago G.
Washington was fighting the French and Indians in our western
regions, and now the French are sending guns and powder to him for
the American cause! Surely, God has His hand in this; and I must be
part of it.

Anne, please forgive me for being a brute when I saw you last. My
greatest fear is that by some unfortunate occurrence I will not live long
enough to make it up to you. I trust God will not allow this to happen.
Our lives are in His hands. I also pray that you receive this letter
quickly. I eagerly await your reply. May it be filled with your forgive-
ness. My love for you is boundless.

I am forever your husband,
Jared

Jared's epistolary endearments were motivated more by reason than emotion. It wasn't that he didn't feel these things for
Anne, but his feelings were clouded by his anger. He was still
upset with her for putting him on the defensive about the Paris
trip. The letter was his attempt at marital diplomacy; its objective
was to open a dialogue toward reconciliation. A revival of feelings
would follow. At least, that was his hope.

He entrusted the dispatch of his letter to Dr. Edward
Bancroft, a good friend of Franklin's from his colonial agent
days in England. Bancroft packed Jared's letter with a batch of
correspondence from the other American commissioners.

Then, secretly, he diverted the package from an American-bound ship to a British man-of-war. Jared's letter never reached Anne.

※

Jared followed Franklin into an elegant salon. The elderly commissioner was escorted by their hostess, Madame Brillon. She was a stunning woman in her early thirties who, Jared had heard from several sources, was an excellent musician. Her complexion was flawless and pale, her hair piled high and adorned with feathers as was the custom, and her gown had a fitted bodice with a low neckline. A frilled ribbon adorned her neck.

Monsieur Brillon, twenty-four years his wife's senior, showed no outward sign of displeasure over the lavish endearments his wife bestowed upon Franklin or the overt affection with which Franklin reciprocated. Such public displays of affection left Jared feeling uncomfortable, but Franklin thrived on it, as did the ladies of Paris. Wherever the renowned American went, the ladies flocked around him to greet him; he, in turn, would kiss each of them on the neck. Following one particularly busy evening of kissing for Franklin, the elderly commissioner explained his kisses to Jared.

"Somebody in Paris gave it out that I loved ladies," he said, "and then everybody began presenting me their ladies, or the ladies presented themselves, to be embraced; that is, to have their necks kissed. For as to kissing of lips or cheeks it is not the mode here—the first is reckoned rude, and the other may rub off the paint. The French ladies have however one thousand ways of rendering themselves agreeable."

At the Brillon's salon, well-dressed servants bowed deeply as huge folding doors opened at their approach. A colorful assembly awaited them, all of them eager to greet Franklin. After extending their cordial (to Jared) and affectionate (to Franklin) salutations, the guests went about their partying, some waltzing, others in small groups conversing happily in a language that Jared Morgan didn't begin to understand.

The dinner was more of the same, only seated, and with various courses of food and wine. Two kinds of fish were served, thick slices of cold meat, and several puddings and pastries. The atmosphere was festive and free, Jared noting especially that the women were wholly uninhibited in their behavior, following the example of their hostess. Several times Madame Brillon threw an arm carelessly around Dr. Franklin's neck during the course of dinner conversation; and afterward, she sat on his lap while Franklin entertained everyone with his best dinner stories, which he communicated as best he could with his barely adequate French.

The only stiffness in the gathering seemed to reside in a single person—Monsieur Jared Morgan. His silk suit felt confining and stuffy, but that was nothing compared to the discomfort of wearing a powdered wig. He had always detested wigs, and when Franklin purposefully refused to wear his while in France—to create the impression of a rugged colonial—Jared prematurely rejoiced that he would not have to wear one. His celebration was short lived. If everyone went wigless, the other commissioners argued, they would appear as nothing more than a band of rustics emerging from the wilderness. It was all right for Franklin to go wigless; it merely heightened his brilliant-but-eccentric image, which would work to their advantage. As for the rest of them, they would wear wigs. So, for the good of their mission, but not without much private grumbling, Jared agreed to wear his powdered wig.

Adding to his discomfort at the Brillon's party was the fact that he understood none of the French conversation. The few guests attending the party who spoke English were usually limited to idiotic phrases like, "Long live George Washington," to which Jared would grin and nod his head overenthusiastically. He felt like a buffoon.

Resting comfortably in a stuffed chair, balancing the gorgeous Madame Brillon on his lap, Franklin held up a hand to calm the laughter from one story so he could begin another. Jared unobtrusively worked his way away from the guests, through an unpopulated room, which had a piano and several portraits of, presumably, previous generations of Brillons, and into an exquisitely manicured garden. Shutting the door behind him, he stepped into greenery and silence. It sounded wonderful.

In front of him stretched a labyrinth of walkways bordered by trees, bushes, and flowers. A quaint well was situated under a tree, a swing dangled from a hefty limb on the other side. Although he couldn't see a brook or stream, he could hear the faint sound of water trickling nearby. From the salon inside came the muted sounds of a burst of raucous laughter. Another Franklin anecdote had scored a success.

Jared smiled and sighed as he meandered down the walkway. He thought how different he was from Franklin. While the elder statesmen was at his best in a crowded room, Jared preferred more intimate gatherings—definitely quieter places, like the middle of the ocean on a calm night, or here in this …

"Pardon moi, monsieur."

He hadn't heard anyone come out the door behind him, yet upon turning around he found himself face-to-face with a charming Frenchwoman. From her attire, she was a woman of wealth. Her powdered wig and ringlets were flawlessly coifed, her gown was white, heavily ribboned, and full with a square-cut neckline and puffed three-quarter sleeves. A fan stylishly covered her face, all except her eyes, of course, which were sparkling blue. There was a hint of amusement in them.

"I'm sorry." Jared's arms flailed helplessly at his sides. "I don't speak French."

"I know," she replied in English with a thick accent.

"You speak English?"

"*Un petit peu.*" She measured a small distance between her thumb and forefinger. "A little bit."

"Is there something I can do for you?"

"Keep me company?"

Jared blushed. "I'm afraid I wouldn't be much company. Dr. Franklin is the one who is best at that."

The Frenchwoman turned halfway around and looked back at the chateau, assuming a position between Franklin on the inside and Jared on the outside.

"He is marvelous, *n'est-ce pas?*" she said.

"There is not another like him."

Her eyes lowered modestly. "May I make a confession, Monsieur Morgan? I followed you out here."

"Why? Have I done something wrong?"

From behind the fan, her laughter was airy, not forced. "Indeed, no," she said. "It's just that I wanted to get a closer look at Dr. Franklin's *plagiaire*—how do you say in English—pirate!"

Jared wasn't pleased to hear the word associated with him. "Is that what Dr. Franklin is saying about me?"

"Monsieur, *s'il vous plait,* do not take offense. It is merely a rumor. But in our social circle, a pirate—especially one as gallant as you—would be a treat. Without our rumors and scandals and affairs, our lives would be so dull. As for Dr. Franklin, he speaks very kindly of you."

"Then I will take no offense, madam."

Eyes that sparkled like blue diamonds peered over the fan. "But you still have not answered my question, monsieur. Are you this infamous Smiling Jacques Tar everyone is talking about?"

"I am a humble merchant, madam," Jared said. "Nothing more."

She looked at him askance, measuring the truth of his response. "I can see you are a man who treasures his privacy."

"As are you, madam, for I don't even know your name."

She extended a hand: "*Je m'appelle* Rosalie LaFontaine."

Jared politely kissed her hand.

"What? No kiss on the neck like Dr. Franklin?"

Jared blushed. He began to stammer a disjointed response about his feelings on that matter, when Madame LaFontaine's giggling indicated she was teasing him.

"I hope you don't think me too bold," she said, "but would you mind greatly if I lowered my fan. I'm not young anymore and my arm is aching."

She held the fan in place until he gave his consent. The face that emerged from behind the fan was that of a beautiful, mature woman. Her nose was delicate, as were her lips. The only thing Jared found displeasing in her appearance was the amount of face paint she used. Her cheeks, especially, showed a touch too much color.

"I loathe the pretense of these parties," she exclaimed.

"Then you wouldn't mind if I took off this blasted wig?"

Her laughter carried across the garden, striking a youthful chord in Jared's heart, one that hadn't been struck since his courting days with Anne.

Jared leaned against a tree. The grass beneath him was cool, as was his head now that he had removed the wig. Madame LaFontaine insisted, then complimented him on how much more handsome he looked with it off. She swung herself lazily on the rope swing nearby as they discussed the eccentricities of the much-celebrated Dr. Franklin.

"You're not like the others," Madame LaFontaine said. "I get the impression that the other commissioners don't like Dr. Franklin."

"It's not that they don't like him," Jared replied. "They object to his work schedule. He refuses to meet with them before breakfast, a time they insist is most convenient to read over letters, deliberate, and determine the proper responses. He breakfasts so late that when he is finished there is already a crowd of carriages lined up on the street with people who have come to meet him—philosophers, statesmen, academicians, economists, and a variety of scientists, not to mention those who simply want to talk to him socially. I'm surprised at how many women and children come just to meet him. For his part, he takes great pleasure in greeting them all. Another thing the commissioners object to is that he is invited to dinner every day and rarely declines an invitation."

"Do you think he would come if I invited him to my house?"

Jared suppressed a smile. The way Madame LaFontaine asked the question, she sounded like a little girl pleading for a favor. "Like I said, he rarely refuses an invitation."

"Would you encourage him to accept my invitation?"

A coy smile accompanied her request. Self-consciously, Jared glanced quickly away. "I really don't think that will be necessary," he said. "I'm certain he will accept." Quickly returning to the original topic of discussion, he continued, "Another thing that irks the other commissioners ..."

"*Pardonnez moi* ... irks?"

"Disturbs."

Madame LaFontaine nodded in understanding. "*Merci.*"

"... that disturbs the other commissioners is that Dr. Franklin rarely studies his French, other than using it during social occasions. And I have heard them complain that when they leave something for his signature, it rarely gets returned in less than two or three days."

"It sounds like Dr. Franklin is negligent in his duties. Is he?"

Jared smiled. "Indeed, Dr. Franklin spends a good deal of time socializing, playing cards, backgammon, checkers, and chess—in fact, sometimes I think that's why he brought me along with him. To play chess. We're pretty well matched."

This brought an approving smile from Madame LaFontaine. "I'm sure your assets to Dr. Franklin and your country go far beyond your abilities to play chess."

Jared shrugged off her compliment.

"Does Dr. Franklin's daily schedule annoy you?" she asked.

He hesitated before replying. "This whole process annoys me. But then, I'm not a statesman, nor a diplomat. I trust Dr. Franklin and his abilities to get things done. This past year I've watched him work with the Congress. He has a keen mind. He can play the mediator when needed and can press his point effectively when needed. The problem I have is with me, not him. I'm just not one who does well in social settings. I need to be doing something. Even on long voyages, there was something that needed to be done every day aboard ship—caulking, tarring, or mending rope, repairing sails, etc. I have never been one to spend long hours sitting around and chatting."

"A man of action. I can see that in you," said Madame LaFontaine.

"It's different for Dr. Franklin," Jared continued. "He has the art of living in the best fashion for himself and for others, making the most effective use of his tools and resources. He eats, sleeps, and works as he sees fit to meet his needs. And regardless of what others say about him, he handles a tremendous amount of business."

Jared stared with unfocused eyes into the distance as he

thought about the man who had become such a strong force in his life. Madame LaFontaine allowed him his thoughts. The only sound was the creaking of the rope against the tree branch as she swung.

"We were playing chess aboard the *Reprisal* on the way here," Jared said, his gaze still far off. "Dr. Franklin was telling me about his objectives here in France. He said it was his intention to procure ..."

Madame LaFontaine interrupted him. "Procure ... I don't know the meaning of this word."

"Procure. To get, to take possession of something."

"I understand now. Go on."

It took Jared a moment to remember what he was saying. "Oh yes, to procure what advantages he could for our country, by endeavoring to please the French court, and to prevent anything being said by our countrymen that may have a contrary effect."

"Push me!" Madame LaFontaine pleaded.

Her sudden change of topic took Jared off guard.

"Please!"

He moved behind her and shoved gently.

"Higher!" she yelled.

He pushed harder.

"Higher!"

Jared had estimated Madame LaFontaine to be in her late fifties, yet swinging back and forth she was giggling like a young girl. Her youthfulness seemed to strip away years and years of adult concerns, seriousness, and responsibilities. Jared felt young again. Carefree.

"Tell me about yourself, Monsieur Morgan," Madame LaFontaine yelled while at the top of an arch.

"Not much to tell."

"Married?"

"Yes."

"Children?"

"Two. Twin boys."

"Really?"

"Identical."

"Are both of them in the army?"

"One is under the command of Brigadier General Arnold, the other is under General Washington's command."

"Arnold and Washington! How impressive."

"I'm proud of them. How about you? Married? Children?"

"Widowed," she said catching his eye as she swung back toward him. "We were unable to have children."

"What did your husband do?"

"Architect. He worked for the king."

"Interesting!"

"He enjoyed his work. Died in a fall from a scaffold."

"I'm sorry."

"He died nearly twenty years ago."

"And you never remarried?"

"Not much to pick from in my social circle. A lot of artist types. They talk a lot, rarely do anything worthwhile. Pampered. Spoiled. I'm better off without them."

Jared stepped off to one side and watched Madame LaFontaine swing as her momentum decreased naturally. "If I'm not being too personal—you are obviously financially secure, you have no husband—may I ask how you spend your days?"

Madame LaFontaine laughed at the question. "Too personal? Hardly, my dear Monsieur Morgan. Indeed, my husband earned us a good deal of money. I'm a patron of the arts. I sponsor promising students and other worthy causes."

"Other causes?"

"Political causes, Monsieur Morgan. Like your America. Many of us in France believe the best thing we can do to fight our old enemy, England, is to support your American war. Your revolution works to our advantage. And we wouldn't want the fire of your revolution to go out for lack of fuel."

"Is that why you want to talk to Dr. Franklin?"

"That, and other reasons."

Jared didn't ask what other reasons she was talking about. Dragging her feet lightly on the ground, Madame LaFontaine brought the swing slowly to a stop. She released the rope and placed her hands demurely in her lap.

"By inviting Dr. Franklin over for dinner," she said, "I'll get to see you again."

※

Jared stayed up late that night in his room at the Hotel de Valentinois in Passy. He wrote a long letter to Anne. Then one to Esau and another to Jacob. Then he wrote to Priscilla, asking her question after question about the status of the business.

He never had been one to write letters before. In the past his practice had been to communicate to everyone through Anne, thus limiting his correspondence to a single letter. However, this night was different. His desk was piled high with letters, long letters; he wrote well into the night, long after everyone else had retired; he wrote because he was frightened. He was frightened by his inability to keep his thoughts from wandering back to the Brillon's garden, and the swing, and Madame LaFontaine. Unless he consciously forced himself to think of other things, he found himself remembering her smile, her laughter, her carefree attitude. These thoughts made his heart beat like a lovesick youth, and he didn't want to feel like a youth. He wanted to feel old. Old and married.

Yet try as he might, as he dozed off to sleep, in that place

between waking and sleeping, he saw Rosalie LaFontaine swinging on the swing, lighthearted and beautiful.

N

Thousands of miles away in Boston, Anne Morgan sat at her
writing desk, unable to write, unable to sleep. Words eluded her.
She had tried writing a poem. Her imagination was dry and bar-
ren. Taking a poem she'd been working on previously, she thought
she'd polish the phrases. But each change only made the poem
worse. The only way to save it was to put it away before she
destroyed it completely.

On a fresh sheet of paper she wrote a letter to Jared. The
words began haltingly, then flowed, then poured faster than she
could record them. One page. Two. Four. Laying her pen aside,
she read what she had written, then tore the pages apart and
threw them away. She didn't want to admit to herself that the
words in the letter came from her. They were sharp, accusatory,
dispensers of guilt. The letter was a mirror to her soul, and she
despised what she saw.

The last words she had spoken to Jared were angry words.
She hated him for leaving her again and going to Paris; she hated
herself for feeling as she did. It was just that she had been patient
all her life. She had sacrificed; she had been understanding about
his long absences; she had been supportive in everything he did,
knowing that her time would come, a time when the two of them
could spend the rest of their lives together. *Well, her time had
come, and where was Jared? Sailing to England, or in
Philadelphia, or Canada, and now Paris. In the last year he had
been home less than a week. It wasn't fair.*

Anne Morgan extinguished the candle on her desk. She felt
her way through the darkness to the bed, huddled under the covers, and wept, hoping that sleep would relieve her of her misery.
But sleep let her suffer for several hours. Then, finally, it took

pity on her and numbed her anguish with a black, dreamless slumber.

N

"How do you know I'm not a spy?"

Rosalie LaFontaine held her teacup daintily as she asked the question. A bemused Franklin sat on the other side of the table. Jared Morgan completed the party of three. They were on Madame LaFontaine's stone patio. An impressive three-story mansion sat solidly on one side of them, and the largest expanse of grass Jared had ever seen lay on the other. To the right was a wooded area that occasionally stole Jared's attention from the course of the conversation. Twice deer—several doe and a buck—had ventured boldly from the wood, surveying the landscape and sniffing the wind. Both times Franklin's cutting laughter sent them scurrying back into the safety of the forest.

"A spy, madam?" Franklin laughed. "Well, if you are a spy, it would indeed be my pleasure to be deceived by one as comely as you. For I daresay, my pride would never permit me to return to America if I had been *outwitted* by a spy; but if I had been *seduced* by one of your beauty, my pride would remain intact, and my colleagues would be quick to forgive an old man like me."

Madame LaFontaine delighted in Franklin's wit. Still, she pressed her point. "But, sir, do you not fear that you are being overcasual regarding English spies in France?"

"My dear madam, would you have me adopt a false name and write letters in invisible ink like my colleague Silas Deane? He has left me at a disadvantage by taking the only good spy name available—Jones. I would be forced to use an inferior substitute, like Smith."

It was clear Franklin was not about to take the matter of spies seriously, at least at this informal meeting. Entering into the spirit of frivolity, Madame LaFontaine said, "The way I heard it, he announced that in the presence of English-speaking people, he would speak only French. To which our Foreign Minister Vergennes quipped, "'He must be the most silent man in France, for I defy him to say six consecutive words in French!'"

Franklin pounded the table in laughter with the flat of his hand, rattling the teacups.

"Is Monsieur Lee as secretive as Monsieur Deane?" she asked.

"Without doubt, Arthur Lee is the most aggressive member of our commission," Franklin replied. "His hostility toward me is one of long standing. He greatly desired my London post as an agent to Massachusetts and finds it difficult to work with me again. However, I am determined that any problems we might have personally will not interfere with the greater good of securing aid from France in our fight for independence."

"And how would you respond if I told you I knew as a fact that Monsieur Lee currently employs six clerks who are English spies?"

"I would say, madam, that if Monsieur Lee cares at all what the British think of him, he had better be careful with his words."

"Do you take none of this spy business seriously?" asked a smiling Madame LaFontaine.

"As it is impossible to discover in every case the falsity of pretended friends who would know our affairs, and more so to prevent being watched by spies when interested people may think proper to place them for that purpose, I have long observed one rule which prevents any inconvenience from such practices. It is simply this: to be concerned in no affairs that I should blush to have made public and to do nothing but what spies may see and welcome. When a man's actions are just and honorable, the more they are known, the more his reputation is increased and established. If I were sure, therefore, that my *valet de place* was a spy, as probably he is, I think I should not discharge him for that, if in other respects I like him."

"And you, Monsieur Morgan, do you feel as cavalier as Dr. Franklin about these things?"

The warmth with which she addressed Jared distracted him momentarily. "I have learned in all things politic," he said, "to trust the sage advice of my friend Dr. Franklin."

Both Madame LaFontaine and Franklin smiled broadly at his response.

"And you claim you are not a diplomat!" she said. "Why, Monsieur Morgan, you are sounding more like one all the time."

"Dear lady," Franklin exclaimed, "I see no reason to insult this good man."

The three of them shared a laugh, during which Madame LaFontaine gazed fondly at Jared, a look that did not escape Jared or Franklin.

Following tea, Madame LaFontaine offered to show the two men around her chateau and grounds. Upon entering the library, Dr. Franklin excused himself from the remainder of the tour. He suffered from gout, which made walking difficult for him. However, he insisted Jared and Madame LaFontaine continue without him. Jared objected that perhaps it would be best to take Dr. Franklin home. Franklin assured him he would be fine, especially since he was surrounded by so many interesting-looking books. Whereupon Madame LaFontaine took Jared by the arm and led him into the hallway. Glancing back into the library, Jared caught a wink from Franklin.

For the remainder of the evening, Rosalie LaFontaine was the perfect hostess, polite and warm, but not overly friendly. Jared left her mansion feeling ashamed at himself for presuming that she might hold any affection for him other than that of a friend. He concluded that he had misinterpreted common French flirtation for something more serious. This realization left his male pride slightly bruised, but his predominant feeling was one of relief.

With the enthusiastic support of Pierre Augustin Caron de Beaumarchais, the playwright of such popular comedies as *The Barber of Seville* and *The Marriage of Figaro*, the American commissioners were successful in drafting an agreement of assistance with the French government. A fictitious private concern was organized, by the name Roderique Hortalez et Compagnie, through which military supplies were shipped to America. The first consignment contained 8,750 pairs of shoes, 3,600 blankets, 4,000 dozen pairs of stockings, 164 brass cannon, 153 carriages, 41,000 balls, 37,000 light muskets, 373,000 flints, 514,000 musket balls, nearly 20,000 pounds of lead, 161,000 pounds of powder, plus mortar bombs, more than 11,000 grenades, and 4,000 tents. Madame Rosalie LaFontaine was one of the largest financial contributors to this shipment.

In addition to the supplies, Paris authorities secretly permitted American privateers to fit out in French ports as they preyed on England's commerce. This request was not readily granted at first. In many eyes the difference between privateer and pirate was microscopic. It was American merchant Jared Morgan who successfully convinced French officials of the advantages of letting the American privateers sell their booty in protected ports.

By the first months of 1778, it was estimated in London that the privateers had cost Britain 1,800,633 English pounds. Five hundred and fifty-nine British vessels had been captured. As part of the agreement, after each capture, Franklin had agreed to study the papers, judge the legality of the action, and then write to the admiralty of the French port to which the ship had been brought. This task he assigned to Jared. For the first time, Jared Morgan felt he was contributing something worthwhile to the American cause for independence.

15

Six ragged continental soldiers huddled against the cold inside a tent. The depth of the snow outside had dramatically climbed the sharp angle of the tent's sides overnight. It was two feet deep. The hazy light from an overcast sky barely penetrated the canvas. A lantern was needed inside to conduct the proceedings.

The six soldiers were in a circle on their knees. They were bundled in blankets, their breeches torn and shredded, most of them were shoeless. A burly sergeant presided over the gathering. Holding seven halfpennies in his hand, his head lowered, he stared through bloodshot eyes with a challenging glare at the soldier opposite him. The baby-faced soldier likewise held seven halfpennies. On the count of three both men tossed their halfpennies into the air. Before they hit, the sergeant shouted, "Tails!"

In rapid succession, the pennies plunked softly in the dirt. Everyone in the circle leaned forward and counted, some silently, some aloud.

"Ten tails, four heads!"

"Ha!" the sergeant yelled in triumph, gathering all the halfpennies that showed tails.

The losing soldier cursed and picked up his four measly half-pennies. "How does Vernet do it? Will someone explain it to me? How does he do it?"

The winning sergeant belly-laughed. "Clean livin' and lotsa prayin', that's the secret to winnin' at toss-up, son."

A round of groans and eye-rolling and curses circulated among the gamblers. This made the sergeant laugh all the louder.

Just then the tent flap flew open. Without exception, every man in the circle jammed halfpennies into pockets and looked innocently toward the opening. A skinny young regular with a pockmarked faced shoved his head through the opening.

The sergeant cursed at him. "Lower the flap, Riggs! Ain't you got no brains at all?"

Riggs' Adam's apple bobbed up and down excitedly. He glanced quickly outside the tent, then back inside. "Vernet, the dummy's comin'! He's almost here. Want me to fetch 'im?"

A wide grin spread across Sergeant Vernet's heavily stubbled, bulky cheeks. "Please show Master Dummy into my parlor," he said with mock formality. His mean-spirited satire got him the laughs from the men in the circle he'd hoped it would.

Moments later the flap lifted again. The skinny regular pulled a reluctant Bo by the arm.

"I said Sergeant Vernet wants to see ya!" he yelled loudly at Bo. "He's a sergeant, you has to come."

A shivering Bo entered the tent, wearing a worried look on his face. Six grinning soldiers greeted him with exaggerated friendliness. They made room for him in the circle opposite Sergeant Vernet and pulled him to the ground. Bo was as ragged as the rest of them, only he wasn't wearing a blanket. Pieces of raw cowhide were strapped around his feet for shoes. White flakes of snow spangled his chestnut hair.

"I am Sergeant Vernet," said the leader of the soldiers. He, too, spoke in a loud voice, slowly and deliberately.

Bo stared at the sergeant's chapped lips as he spoke.

"You are a civilian, aren't you?" Vernet asked.

Squinting eyes indicated Bo didn't understand the question.

Vernet rolled his eyes. "Dummy," he muttered under his breath.

Bo understood that word, even though it was muttered. He frowned.

Vernet tried again. "You," he pointed to Bo, "soldier?" He fired an invisible musket.

Bo shook his head no.

"I know," Vernet said loudly. "That means I have to give you a civilian test."

Another shake of the head.

"Yes. Me sergeant. You civilian. All civilians must take a test to stay. Otherwise you have to go back to your home." Leaning toward the soldier on his right, he added in a whisper, "Or the cuckoo farm."

Several of the soldiers heard the side comment and laughed.

"Bo go now!" The ragged boy tried to stand. The soldiers on each side of him pulled him back to the ground. The sergeant was irate.

"You sit, boy, until I say you can go!" A beefy finger jabbed angrily at the place where Bo was sitting. From his forehead to his stubbled chin, the sergeant's face was blazing red.

Bo's bottom hit the ground with a thud.

"How much money you got?" he thundered.

Bo shrugged, pretending not to understand, though he did.

"Search his pockets," the sergeant ordered.

They found two halfpennies.

"Put them in his hand."

The moment the halfpennies were back in Bo's hand, he tried

to slip them into his pocket again. The two soldiers stopped him.

"Like this, dummy!" The sergeant held two halfpennies in his hand, palm open. "Like this, like this!"

Bo followed his example.

"Now this is what we'll do. Watch! One, two, three!" With each count, his hand moved upward as though conducting a waltz. With the third count the sergeant's halfpennies flew upward, then fell to the ground. "See? Now you do it! One …" the sergeant reached out and helped Bo move his hand. On three the coins popped out of the boy's hand and onto the ground. A cheer went around the circle.

"Now together." The sergeant retrieved his coins. Bo followed his example.

"Together. All right?" He bounced his hand several times until Bo bounced his hand in rhythm with the sergeant. "Good! Now, one, two, three!"

As the coins tumbled in the air, the sergeant shouted, "Tails!" Four soft thuds were followed by a chorus of screeching laughter and catcalls. All four halfpennies had landed heads up.

The sergeant's hands flew up, his face a portrait of fury. The other soldiers fell quickly to silence. Slowly, Vernet lowered his hands and said to Bo in mock sympathy, "I'm so sorry. This is bad, very bad." He pointed to the four coins. "Look! All heads. You lose!" He picked up the coins and pocketed them.

"Bo's! Bo's!" The deaf boy reached for his coins.

The sergeant slapped his hands away, shaking his head. "You lose!" he shouted. "Four heads are the worst you can have! You have to go home. You can't stay with the soldiers anymore. You failed the test. Go home!"

Bo shook his head. "No home. Jabe! No home!" His eyes brimmed with fear.

"Jabe? What's a Jabe?" someone asked.

"Who knows?" the sergeant sneered. "Probably a pet mule or something." To Bo: "Do you want to stay? Do you want to stay with soldiers?"

Bo nodded enthusiastically. A tear fell down his cheek.

"You can stay, if you give me something. You have to give me something!"

The eyes of some of the soldiers in the circle brightened. They understood now what the sergeant was after. The halfpennies were nothing in a camp where food was scarce and clothing inadequate. The eyes of those with no shoes fell to the raw cowhide strapped to the boy's feet. Men who must march in the snow without shoes would be willing to pay a small fortune for those two strips of cowhide, as high as ten dollars in gold coin.

"You can stay if you give me the cowhide." The sergeant pointed to Bo's feet.

Bo hesitated.

"Give me the cowhide, or you have to go home!"

Slowly, Bo unstrapped the coverings from his feet and handed them to the sergeant. Within seconds he was ushered out of the tent. Bo's toes curled under as he stepped into the makeshift road of frozen mud and snow. He couldn't hear the laughter and shouting coming from the tent behind him.

As the last days of 1777 trudged by, the delegates to Congress packed up their things and left for their homes. It had been an unsettling year for them. British General Howe had sent them fleeing from Philadelphia in September, when he took over the city. The Congress moved first to Lancaster, then to York. Now that winter was setting in, they adjourned to their homes and their families. The soldiers of the Continental Army were not so lucky.

From Whitemarsh, Washington's army of eleven thousand

men crossed the Schuylkill River on a cold, rainy, and snowy night upon a bridge of wagons set end-to-end and joined together by boards and planks. They settled temporarily at a place called "the gulf," so named because of the great chasm between the hills. It was here they celebrated a day of Thanksgiving as decreed by Congress. Having had nothing to eat for two or three days previous, each soldier was given an eighth of a pint of rice, a tablespoon of vinegar, and a sermon upon which they were to feast.

The sermon text was from Luke's gospel, the portion of the account that records the teaching of John the Baptist. *And the soldiers likewise demanded of him, saying, And what shall we do? And he said unto them, Do violence to no man, neither accuse any falsely.* Afterward, those soldiers who had been raised on the Bible took it upon themselves to circulate the remainder of the verse that had gone unspoken during the sermon: *And be content with your wages.*

From the gulf they marched upriver until they reached the point where Valley Creek joined the Schuylkill. At the junction to the east the ground rose swiftly to a 250-foot crest, then straightened out onto a rolling plateau nearly two miles long. Here they would winter. It was an easily defended position should Howe get any ideas about attacking. However, resources were scarce. Some of the men would be forced to travel the full two-mile length of the valley carrying wooden buckets to get water. An old forge on the ravinelike creek gave the place its name—Valley Forge.

Jacob Morgan pulled his blanket tightly around his shoulders with a groan. The last thing he wanted to do was give up his place on the log next to the fire. He and four other men on sentry duty shared a fire, rotating turns as they guarded the perimeter of the camp. The regular who alternated duty with Jacob danced nearby, telling Jacob to hurry. Since Cambridge, Jacob had advanced to corporal and then to sergeant, exchanging his green epaulet for red. However, at the moment his epaulet was hidden under a blanket, and the impatient regular was nearly frozen. No time to insist on respect for rank. With a sigh, Jacob pushed himself up off the log. The dancing soldier slid in behind him, eagerly holding out stiff hands toward the fire as Jacob shuffled down the snow-packed trail along the camp's perimeter.

He felt miserable. He was weak, his joints ached, and his head felt like it was filled with liquid that sloshed from side to side, throwing him off balance whenever he tilted it one way or the other. A cough grated his already-raw throat. He moaned as he walked.

Reaching the outer limit of his post, he propped his musket against a tree and buried his hands under the blanket close to his body. He leaned around the tree to check on the enemy. Not too far distant, a single British soldier huddled close to his own fire. He'd been there for as long as Jacob had been on duty. They kept an eye on each other. Nothing more.

Pulling back, Jacob leaned against the tree. He shivered and took a short breath; too much of the frigid air would chill his insides and send him into a coughing fit; as he exhaled, white vapor billowed before his face.

A thick cloud blanket stretched over him from horizon to horizon; light was dispersed equally through the heavy layer, making it difficult to tell precisely what time of day it was. Late afternoon, that's all he knew for sure. All around him, everything was covered with soft white and equally soft shadows. Jacob used to like the snow. After his first winter as a soldier he despised it; there was no English word strong enough to describe how much he hated it.

As he wiped a dripping nose, his thoughts drifted to Boston and home. He imagined Mercy and his mother in the parlor sitting in front of a robust fire. His mother would be reading aloud, some of her poetry or possibly from the Bible. He envisioned Mercy's head resting back in the chair, her eyes closed, listening to the words.

The crack of a limb brought him instantly back to the present. Instinctively, he reached for his musket and looked toward the redcoat sentry. He'd heard it too. Crouched by the fire, his arm reached for something on the ground, presumably his firearm. Their eyes locked on each other. Satisfied the sound came from neither of them, they both searched the surrounding terrain. Nothing. Everything was white and cold and still.

Jacob's arm relaxed, returning to its warm place under the blanket next to his chest. The sudden movement had brought pain to his arm and back and legs, reminding him of his aching muscles that stretched from one aching joint to another. It was a combination of pains that plagued him. His muscles were sore not only from his sickness, but also from constructing wooden huts.

Upon arriving at Valley Forge, the army immediately set to work building huts suitable to winter in. Until the huts were constructed, everyone, including General Washington himself, lived in tents. A man by the name of Isaac Potts had offered the general his fieldstone house for the winter. Word had it that Washington delayed accepting the man's offer until after the wooden huts were completed.

The officers' huts were of individual design and construction. They boasted two doors and fireplaces, one at each end, and were more spacious than the soldiers' huts. Groups of six men formed a "mess" to cook and eat together. Two of these groups lodged in each of the soldiers' huts. Each soldiers' hut had a single door and fireplace, usually a stone hearth and a wooden chimney. The structure was made with notched logs. Mud was plastered between the logs to keep out the cold, but the sealed timbers also kept in the smoke and odors; no windows would be cut out until spring. The floors were dirt and bunks were to be added later.

Jacob chuckled as he remembered the previous day's work, when he and Bo caulked their hut with mud. Bo thought it great fun to play in the mud; Jacob found it tedious until he remembered that his ancestor Drew Morgan, the first Morgan of his family's line to come to America, built a house in the early Massachusetts colony with tree limbs, thatch, and mud. He wondered what his ancestor's reaction would be if he knew that almost 150 years later Morgans were still stuffing mud between timbers for housing.

Thinking of houses, his mind drifted back to Boston and Mercy and the Morgan's mansion on Beacon Street. He thought of snuggling with Mercy under the covers with clean sheets. Warm. Comfortable. Mercy in his arms …

Another twig snapped. This one louder, closer. Jacob snatched his musket and dropped to his knees in one motion. The barrel of the musket level to the ground, he moved it cautiously back and forth, his eyes darting to and fro three, maybe four times as quickly as the musket. About fifty feet away, a bush rustled.

"Halt!" Jacob's musket pointed at the bush.

"O Lord, save me! Don't shoot! Please, don't shoot!"

Hands appeared first, followed by a thin, tattered form. The boy couldn't have been more than eighteen years old. His face was filthy, his hair dirty and matted; he wore a baggy coat with holes in it; his breeches had patches on patches; his feet were bare.

"Come here," Jacob said. "Closer to me. What's your name?"

The boy's eyes had a wild look about them. They darted in the direction of the camp, to Jacob, then a quick glance behind him to a wooded area.

"Don't think of running," Jacob warned. "I'd have to shoot you."

The boy's eyes grew wide, then settled on Jacob. "You wouldn't really shoot me, would you? I'm a Yankee. You wouldn't shoot a Yankee, would you?"

"Only if I had to," Jacob replied. "What are you doing out here?"

"Getting water! My sergeant sent me to get water!"

"Then where's your bucket?"

The boy looked helplessly around him at the ground. "I ... I must have lost it."

"What's your sergeant's name, boy?"

The boy licked his lips, his eyes becoming even more anxious.

"I asked you your sergeant's name!"

The boy refused to respond.

Jacob looked down the barrel of his musket at the boy. He was thin as a scarecrow, shivering cold, and frightened nearly to death. "You're a deserter, aren't you, boy?"

The boy stood there and shivered.

Sweat broke out on Jacob's forehead. His head felt feverish. His throat was already raw; yelling only made it worse. He was tired and aching. He didn't need this. Not now anyway.

"Look," Jacob said, "if you're in trouble with your sergeant, or something like that, maybe I can help you work things out with him. Running away won't do any good."

"It's not that at all," the boy said.

"Then talk to me! You can begin by telling me your name."

The boy blinked a few times. "Can I put my hands down?"

"If you tell me your name, you can put your hands down."

The boy seemed to contemplate whether or not the price was too high for lowering his hands. "Silas Brooks. My name's Silas Brooks. Can I ..."

"Yes, you can lower your hands. Now tell me, Silas, why are you deserting?"

Thin, scrawny arms and bony hands wrapped themselves around his chest. A few more blinks produced tears. Silas wiped them away and wiped his nose while his hand was out. "I wanna go home," he whimpered. "I've had enough of war. I wanna see my momma. I just wanna go home." Silas began to sob.

Jacob lowered his musket. "I want to go home too," he said. "But deserting isn't the way to do it. What do you think your momma will say to her son who ran away from his responsibilities? Do you think she can be proud of a boy who is a deserter?"

Silas Brooks sobbed and sniffed and wiped his face with his arms.

"Come back with me to camp," Jacob said softly. "We're going through some difficult times right now, but we can make it. We're Yankees, you and me. We're tough. Then, when your enlistment's up, you can go home to your momma a war hero, and she'll be proud of you. You want your momma to be proud of you, don't you, Silas?"

The boy looked up at him. His eyes were no longer darting back and forth. He was thinking about what Jacob was saying.

Jacob held out an arm to him. "Come on, come back with me right now."

Scrawny Silas Brooks emerged from behind the bush. The snow crunched under his bare feet, leaving footprints stained with blood. Jacob checked the British sentry. The redcoat was on his feet, his musket at the ready, following the events on the American side.

As an indication to the British sentry of his intentions to protect the boy, Jacob moved from behind the tree a few steps closer to Silas, his arm reaching toward him, ready to take him under his wing like a mother hen. As he did this, he thought of Bo. For more than a year, Jacob had been Bo's substitute father, an arrangement that had been good for both of them. Before now, Jacob hadn't realized he had paternal instincts, but they were surfacing. First with Bo, now with Silas.

With head lowered, Silas Brooks reached Jacob's side. The only thought on Jacob's mind was to get the boy safely back to camp. Then, without warning, bony hands lashed out at Jacob, attaching themselves to his chest; they shoved him with astonishing strength. Jacob, caught off balance, slammed against the tree and tumbled to the ground; his musket thumped into a snowdrift nearby. Like a jackrabbit, Silas bounded away through the snow.

Jacob scrambled to his knees and retrieved his musket. He raised the piece into firing position; his target, the back of a fleeing Silas Brooks. Jacob's finger curled around the trigger. The boy was thin, but still close enough to make an easy target. Jacob took a breath and aimed down the barrel.

He couldn't do it. He relaxed and the barrel of the musket drooped.

Just then, Silas made a mistake. He darted to his left through a hedge that had served as an unofficial boundary line between the two armies. Jacob's head jerked toward the British sentry. His musket was raised at Silas.

"Halt! Halt, I say!" the British sentry yelled.

Silas kept running.

"Stop! Don't shoot him!" Jacob yelled. "He has no weapon!"

The British sentry glanced over at Jacob, then repositioned his sights on Silas.

"No!" Jacob yelled.

The British sentry wasn't listening.

Silas continued to run.

BLAM!

At the sound of the musket, Silas Brooks jerked, but he didn't fall. Frozen in his tracks, he turned slowly around, his hands held high. The look on his face was one of deadly fear and surprise. He wasn't hit and he couldn't understand why.

A puff of smoke rose into the tree limbs above Jacob Morgan. The British sentry lay facedown on the ground. For several seconds Silas stared at Jacob—and Jacob at him. Then the boy was gone, running again. Running home to his momma.

Relieved of sentry duty, Jacob trudged wearily back to camp with the other men. All he wanted to do was to collapse onto his cot and sleep. There had been no immediate response to the shooting incident. No one came. No one challenged him. He reported the incident to the others. They grumbled about it. Once the dead redcoat was discovered, things would be tense along the line. Possible skirmishes. Snipers. As if they didn't already have enough to worry about just to keep warm.

They passed another sentry on the road leading into camp. He had no shoes, so he stood on his hat so that something would be between him and the frozen ground. Jacob was immediately grateful for his shoes. They had holes in the sides, and the soles were so thin he could feel the smallest rock when he stepped on it, but they were better than no shoes at all. And Bo had cowhide fashioned into makeshift moccasins. It had cost Jacob five dollars in gold coins for the drafty footwear, but at least the boy's feet were covered.

He spied Bo in the distance at about the same time Bo spotted him. The boy ran toward him excitedly as he always did when Jacob came off sentry duty. The boy's display of affection stoked the warm fatherly feelings inside Jacob. Then he noticed Bo's bare feet.

"Where are your moccasins?" Jacob shouted.

"Jabe! Jabe! Bo stay!" the boy shouted excitedly.

It didn't take long for the story to come out. With communication between the deaf boy and his surrogate father faltering at best, Jacob still heard enough to choose a course of action. His anger pushed aside all feelings of sickness. With Bo leading the way, they went to the gambling tent. After a few graphic threats from Jacob, the sole remaining occupant, one of the original circle of gamblers, told him he was too late. The cowhide moccasins had already been sold. No amount of threats could get him to divulge the name of the seller, but he readily identified the man who bought them. On to tent two.

At tent two, a kindly looking man with a long, peppered beard started when Jacob threw open the tent flaps. The bearded fellow was wearing Bo's moccasins. At first Jacob demanded he return them, then softened his request when it became evident that the man wanted nothing more than warm feet. He had not been part of the deception directly and knew nothing of Bo. When told the story behind the sale, he was as incensed as Jacob. Still, he refused to relinquish the moccasins until he got his money back. And he knew where to find the culprit behind the whole affair. "Vernet!" he muttered threateningly.

Jacob knew of the man, enough to be able to recognize the sergeant on sight, but he had never had dealings with him directly. Jacob, Bo, and the bearded soldier marched through the mud and snow in search of Sergeant Vernet. They found him standing outside his tent.

With two against one, Jacob and the bearded soldier verbally launched into Vernet. Their initial onslaught confused him. Then he saw Bo and summed things up quickly.

"Not my fault," he said. "You shouldn't let the boy gamble like that. We played toss-up; he lost. Simple as that. He bet the shoes; I won."

"That's not the way I heard it," Jacob said.

"That's not the way I heard it either," echoed the bearded one. "I want my money back!"

Vernet refused. "It's a done deal! Besides, I don't know why you two are getting so worked up over a dummy."

Of all the things Vernet could have said, that was his worst choice. Jacob lit into him, fists flying, knocking Vernet into the icy mud. The two sergeants rolled and punched and gouged, knocking over a tent, overturning a cart carrying mud for a nearby hut, and gaining the attention of a good number of bored soldiers who circled around them.

※

From behind his desk, General Washington read the report and studied the two muddy sergeants who stood at attention in front of him. His nose was straight, long and strong, accentuated by a large forehead; tired eyes rested on each side; his lips were pursed in disgust. From the inside of the walled markee tent, Jacob thought it seemed much smaller than it looked from outside. An ink stand and two quill pens were set before Washington on a small, cloth-covered table. Behind the general and to his left was his bunk.

Jacob found it difficult to stand without weaving from side to side. His success in fighting back the symptoms of his illness was temporary. The illness rallied and counterattacked with reinforcements. His head pounded so badly, he thought it would explode; his nose was a veritable fountain; and it took every bit of energy he had to keep from shivering conspicuously.

Washington had listened carefully to the accounts of both men, neither story resembling the other. Before punishment was pronounced, Washington restored the property situation to its previous status. He directed that the moccasins be returned to Bo and the gold coins to the bearded soldier.

There was one constant in the stories told by the two sergeants, and it wasn't good for Vernet. Gambling was outlawed in camp. A string of orders had been issued on the subject, and Washington was eager to enforce them. He sent Vernet out of the tent under guard so that he could deliberate the appropriate punishment.

To Jacob he said, "I see by your record this is the second time you have been disciplined. The first was in Cambridge for insubordination to an officer."

"Yes, sir."

A glimmer of recognition appeared in the general's eyes. "Twins, wasn't it? You have a twin brother."

"Yes, sir."

Washington nodded as he remembered the incident at Cambridge when Jacob refused to salute Esau. "You had a boy with you then, if I recall. Is he the deaf boy whose moccasins figure into this skirmish today?"

"Yes, sir."

"Your son?"

"No, sir. His father was killed following the fighting at Concord."

"So he's no relation at all to you?"

"No, sir."

"Then why is he still with you?"

"He has no one to look after him. His mother died shortly after he was born. We've been together since Meriam's Corner, sir. We take care of each other."

"And you were taking care of him by punching Sergeant Vernet?"

"It wasn't a wise thing to do, but yes, sir."

"Quite right. It wasn't wise, Sergeant!" Washington's tone was hard and loud. "According to these papers, Sergeant, you have been recommended for promotion. However, I find it difficult to promote a man who has yet to learn respect for authority, commissioned or noncommissioned. Your promotion is hereby rescinded."

Washington reached for a pen and recorded something on the paper before him. Within the same minute Jacob learned of his promotion and lost it.

"Is that all, sir?"

Without looking up, Washington said, "I'll dismiss you when I'm ready, Sergeant."

"Yes, sir."

Jacob was losing the battle against his shivers. If he didn't lie down soon, he'd fall over. While the general shuffled a couple of papers and scratched another comment, Jacob decided that it would be best if he report sick tomorrow. He was in no shape to do any soldiering.

"On another matter," Washington said at last. "I want you to muster your squad on that open field on the west side of the camp. You will report to Baron Friedrich von Steuben. He's a fine Prussian officer who, God willing, will teach you discipline. You and your men be there at six o'clock in the morning, sharp. Do you understand?"

"Yes, sir," Jacob wheezed.

16

"Nein! Nein! Nein! Nein! Nein"

Friedrich von Steuben's large nose bobbed up and down inches away from Jacob's nose; German curses flew freely. Von Steuben yanked the musket from Jacob and took a step backward.

"Like this!" Steely eyes drilled into Jacob; it was von Steuben's way of making sure someone was paying attention. With a thick German accent, sometimes mixing German and English words in the same sentence, von Steuben barked the commands as he performed each step: "ONE. Half-cock the firelock! TWO. Get the cartridge!" He reached into a cartridge box, grabbed a paper cartridge, bit the top off, then placed his thumb over the opening to hold in the powder. "THREE. Prime!" He shook some of the powder from the cartridge into the pan. "FOUR. Shut pan! FIVE. Charge with cartridge!" He placed the cartridge in the musket's barrel. "SIX. Draw the ramrod! SEVEN. Ram down the cartridge! EIGHT. Return the ramrod!" He immediately brought the musket to shoulder attention. "NINE. Shoulder firelock! TEN. Poise firelock!" Holding the musket vertically with both hands, he raised his hands until they were in front of his face. "ELEVEN. Cock fire-lock! TWELVE. Take aim!" He jammed the musket's butt against his shoulder. "THIRTEEN. Fire!" With exaggerated motion, he pretended to pull the trigger. "BOOM!" he shouted. He lowered the musket to the first position and said, "Ready to load again!"

The Prussian officer threw the musket at Jacob. "You do it!" He counted out the steps for Jacob. "One! Two! Three!" He paused. *"Nein! Nein! Nein! Nein! Nein!"* Curses saturated the air.

For three days Jacob and eleven other men in his squad had been drilled by von Steuben. There had been a lot of teeth-grinding, but they were beginning to grow accustomed to this bombastic newcomer. Von Steuben was a demanding perfectionist. And when he became frustrated over the soldiers' slowness in learning, it wasn't uncommon for him to swear in his native tongue. Other times he would swear in French, still other times it would be in a mixture of French and German. Once, when he ran out of foreign words to swear, he called for an aide to swear for him in English. It didn't take Jacob and the other soldiers long to learn that von Steuben wasn't going to be satisfied until every soldier loaded his musket the same way—von Steuben's way.

By the time the soldiers mustered at six o'clock in the morning for this training, von Steuben had already been up for three hours. He would have already read for a spell, smoked a pipeful of tobacco, then had a cup of strong coffee. This routine, performed the same way every day without variance, was the beginning of his busy, well-ordered day. The Prussian officer had been recruited to drill the continental soldiers using a simplified manual of arms and to teach them field maneuvers until the army of patchwork militias functioned under unified commands. From sunrise to sunset, he worked with one small group of soldiers after another in what was being called "The school of the soldier." He would then send these small groups back to their commands to spread his teachings until whole brigades and divisions were doing things in identical fashion.

Of the twelve men in Jacob's group, he was one of the slowest to learn von Steuben's manual of arms procedure, which by consequence made him the recipient of von Steuben's verbal wrath. Two things accounted for Jacob's slowness. First, since much of the fighting to date had been Indian-style—from behind trees and walls and fences—he had depended upon Bo to load for him. So naturally, on the first day of soldier school Jacob had brought Bo with him, thinking the boy might learn something from the Prussian expert. But von Steuben refused to let the boy stay. From now on, the Continental Army would fight like an army, in ranks. A little boy would only get in the way, so the Prussian instructor chased Bo off the field. The second thing that slowed Jacob down was his head cold, which had showed no signs of letting up. The illness made it difficult for Jacob to concentrate; several times he caught himself staring vacantly off into the distance for no reason. Then he'd realize he was two or three steps behind everyone else in the loading procedure. And once behind, it was impossible for him to catch up.

"Nein! Nein! Nein! Nein! Nein!" von Steuben screamed. "Your grandmother could do this quicker than you! Everyone look at Morgan! That's wrong! Wrong! WRONG!"

Grabbing Jacob by the arm, von Steuben pulled him in front of everyone else.

"I count," he said. "You load," he pounded Jacob on the chest. "They tell you when you're wrong. Ready. ONE. Half-cock the firelock! TWO. Get the cartridge! THREE...."

Reaching for the cartridge, Jacob's eye caught the letters ET on the flap. Elias Todd. This was Bo's father's cartridge case. His mind drifted to the stone wall near Meriam's Corner; Elias Todd lay on the ground, face up; Bo was stretched over him....

"Nein! Nein! Nein! Nein! Nein!"

Von Steuben's huge nose bobbed inches away from his.

Bo had been instructed to stay away from the vicinity of the officers' huts. It wasn't that Jacob didn't trust him; it was just that Jacob knew how trouble often had a way of finding unsuspecting boys, and if trouble found Bo, Jacob didn't want a commissioned officer attached to the other end of it. But Bo had run out of other areas in the camp to explore, and Jacob was at soldier school, so he wandered into officer country.

The weather had broken and it was a rare sunny day. Most of the road that wound through the huts was still frozen over, but some spots had melted into muddy holes and ruts. With his hands in his pockets, Bo followed the road. As was normal for a deaf boy, a panorama of silent activity stretched in front of him.

Bo saw six horses tied up in front of one hut. A large man, his face glistening with sweat, walked to one of the horses, lifted a rear foot, and studied it. Then he pulled a glowing orange piece of metal from a fire with big tongs, placed it on a pointed anvil, and hit it with a hammer. Each time the hammer kissed the orange metal, yellowish white sparks exploded from it noiselessly.

Passing another hut, Bo was startled when out of the corner of his eye he saw a door fly open. A monster of a man backed out, his arm repeatedly pointing at something inside. Following him out, another large man, this one walking forward, used similar gestures to the backward-walking man. Just then, Bo got a better look at the man backing out of the house. It was Vernet. Hiding his head with a hand, Bo pressed on down the road, wanting to get away before Vernet saw him.

When he thought it was safe, Bo took a quick peek behind him. Vernet's back was to him, and he was walking the opposite way down the road. Bo breathed easier and began exploring again.

Beside the next hut a woman was hanging out laundry. Her lips moved flowingly as she pinned clothing to a line. At times her brow furrowed while her lips slowed, moving more dramatically; then a huge smile broke out, one with lots of white teeth, and her lips and tongue performed a merry jig.

Although women in army camps were not plentiful, neither was it uncommon for them to be there. It wasn't unusual for wives to accompany their husbands when they enlisted. The women of the camp usually found themselves cooking, washing, and mending. Occasionally, when the need arose, they fought alongside the men.

Bo was mesmerized by the singing woman. He had slowed his walk to watch her, ready to look away and resume his usual pace should she spy him. Presently, a side of the hut that had been blocked to him came into view. Seated in the sun beside the log hut was a boy about his age. In his hands the boy held two light-colored wooden sticks. With them, he hit the top of a canister. Bo had seen similar canisters carried by boys in the British army on the day they marched down the road to Concord. Those British boys also hit their canisters with sticks. Intrigued, Bo was drawn to the boy and his canister.

As Bo approached, the boy stopped what he was doing. He smiled. His lips moved. Bo recognized one word, "name."

"Bo," Bo said, patting himself on the chest.

The boy's lips moved again. "My name …" was all Bo could make out; the boy's lips barely moved as he talked. The look of confusion on Bo's face prompted the boy to repeat his introduction. This time, Bo caught it.

"Zach," Bo said, pointing to the boy on the ground, mimicking his lip movements. The boy smiled and nodded his head.

A shadow loomed beside Bo, causing him to start. A friendly face appeared; it was the woman hanging up the laundry. Her yellow hair was pinned up on top of her head; kindly sky-blue eyes looked him over; full lips mouthed, "What did you say your name was?"

"Bo."

"Your name is Bo?" This time her lips pronounced the words more crisply. Not waiting for a reply, she looked first at one of Bo's ears, then the other.

"Bo," Bo repeated.

The boy on the ground, his mouth open, stared up curiously at his mother and Bo.

The woman's lips moved again. "You can't hear me, can you?" she mouthed, shaking her head.

Bo touched his ears with his fingers and shook his head no.

The woman's head turned away from Bo toward Zach. The back of her head seemed to do a little dance, indicating to Bo that she was saying something to Zach. The longer her head danced, the wider Zach's mouth and eyes opened.

Then the boy's mouth moved, "You can't hear me?"

Bo touched his ears again and shook his head.

The boy hit the canister with the sticks. "Can you hear that?"

Bo shook his head.

The golden-haired woman took Bo by the hands and placed them on the side of the canister. She said something to Zach, and he responded by hitting the canister with the sticks. Bo jerked his hands away. It felt like a thousand ants were crawling on them. The woman smiled kindly and rubbed his hands, showing Bo there was nothing on them. She placed her hands on the side of the canister. Bo followed her example. Zach hit the canister again; Bo felt the ants again. Another check of his hands revealed nothing there. Eagerly, he placed his hands again.

"Mo'," he said.

The golden-haired woman smiled broadly and nodded to Zach who beat the drum again. Bo's eyes grew wide with excitement.

That night, and for many nights following, Bo went around beating things with sticks—canteens, wooden boxes, cooking utensils—always placing his free hand on the object to feel the vibration. Cooking pots seemed to give him the greatest satisfaction. Jacob had no idea what he was doing or who taught him about vibrations; but of one thing he was sure, it was getting on his nerves. It was a rare occasion for any soldier to be in his hut alone, and on this particular night there was no one else in the hut except Jacob and Bo, and Jacob intended on taking full advantage of the occasion by relaxing on his cot.

"Bo! Stop that!"

Jacob had reclined with a towel over his head. After a full day of von Steuben's curses, all he wanted was silence. Bo didn't hear him. The boy's back was to him. He was banging on a cast-iron kettle with a wooden spoon, his head moving in rhythm with the beat. Jacob reached over his shoulder and grabbed the spoon from his hand. Bo whirled around. He held out his hand for the spoon. Jacob shook his head.

"No! Too loud."

Jacob's explanation didn't satisfy the boy. Bo grunted and stretched out his hand again.

"It hurts my head," Jacob said.

Bo's eyes grew angry. He jumped to his feet and rushed out of the hut, leaving the door open. Jacob followed after him as far as the door. He watched as Bo plucked a stick from the ground and was tapping things with it as he passed by—the sides of huts, trees, wagons. Jacob felt badly for Bo; soldier school had kept him busy, and he and Bo hadn't had much time alone together. But tonight, Jacob's head felt like it was splitting open, and there was no way he could tolerate Bo's banging.

Jacob closed the door and lay back down on his cot. He repositioned the towel over his eyes and took several deep breaths to calm himself. The room was mercifully silent. His mind drifted, tiptoeing to the edge of sleep, then backing away. Yet even though there was no sound in the room, the rhythm of Bo's pot-beating was still in Jacob's head. *Odd*, he thought. *The rhythm was similar to that of a military command, the drumbeat of a call to march.*

❖

Relief came in several waves to the troops at Valley Forge. Supplies increased with the appointment of Nathanael Greene as quartermaster. Greene scoured the countryside and found uncovered caches of abandoned and forgotten supplies. He shipped this windfall immediately to the plateau at Valley Forge. The second wave of relief came in the form of a providentially early running of shad up the Schuylkill River. Upon seeing the crowded fins in the river, men jumped into the river with pitchforks, shovels, baskets, and broken branches—anything they could find to scoop the fish onto the river bank. Tons of fresh fish were eaten, tons more were salted away in barrels. The third form of relief came in the form of spring and warmer weather. The melting snow and patches of green grass seemed a portent of good things to come. General Washington's men had survived; but more than that, they were stronger for the experience—more determined, better trained. Washington's army had limped into Valley Forge licking its wounds; now it was ready to emerge like a lion on the prowl.

On May 5, 1778, while the sun splashed the valley with spring light, a new order was circulated from the commander-in-chief and recorded by all orderlies. Read aloud to the troops, this is what it said: "General After Orders. Six o'clock p.m.—It having pleased the Almighty Ruler of the Universe propitiously to defend the cause of the United States of America and finally by raising us up a powerful friend, among the princes of the Earth...." A staggering announcement followed this prelude. France had officially declared herself an ally of the United States of America. This meant that French funds and supplies would no longer have to be smuggled in by subterfuge; they would be available in generous quantities. The French army and navy were to cooperate whole-heartedly with the American effort against the English.

Jacob couldn't help but smile broadly and think of his father who, as far as he knew, was still in France. He looked forward to the day when he could sit down with his father and hear the real story behind this timely announcement.

Naturally, the French announcement had an impact on British plans. One direct consequence was the abandonment of Philadelphia. Sir Henry Clinton had been sent to replace General Howe, and no sooner had Clinton settled into Philadelphia than he received orders to relocate his base of operations to New York. That meant a long march by the redcoats, one that would string them out over a great distance, with a rested and eager Continental Army poised to strike along their exposed flank.

The sound of drums echoed through the camp. A general call to arms. Jacob and the men of his hut jumped in response. Moments later, they stood in the warm morning sun, armed and formed neatly into ranks. Moments later, Lafayette, the marquis from France who served without pay and distinguished himself in the battle of Brandywine Creek in which he was wounded, rode briskly by, inspecting the men. Washington had placed him in charge of the upcoming expedition. Rumor had it that General Charles Lee, the senior general, had declined the assignment.

Now they had to move quickly before the British escaped. While the American generals debated how best to attack General Clinton, the British had successfully moved past the American forces. The plan now was to close in behind them and attack them from the rear. To the tune of "Yankee Doodle," the drums and fifes got the army started. They stepped out smartly, impressing themselves with the unity of their movements—a tribute to von Steuben's winter drills.

Bo marched at Jacob's side in the light infantry unit, as he had always done. When von Steuben saw the boy in the ranks, he spurred his horse toward Jacob's unit, shouting profanely. In his typical, bombastic manner he ordered Jacob to send the boy back to camp. Bo's reaction was near hysteria. Clinging to Jacob's legs, the boy wailed and wailed; it was not a tantrum—the sounds coming from him were fear driven. Jacob had to break rank. While unit after unit passed them by, he reasoned with and cajoled Bo to return to camp. As Jacob talked, the boy kept looking up imploringly to von Steuben, who hovered over them atop his mount. Staring back at him was the grim, granite visage of a Prussian officer. Bo finally conceded.

As Jacob ran to catch up with his unit, von Steuben rode beside him. "The boy is too young for war," he said in disjointed English. "In a tight maneuver, someone might trip over him." Then, he galloped away.

Jacob glanced over his shoulder in Bo's direction. The boy hadn't moved. His head and shoulders and arms drooped as though the heat of the sun were melting him. Jacob knew how he felt. This was the first time since Concord he had gone into battle without Bo at his side. As Jacob stepped into rank, a worm of anxiety began snaking its way through his insides.

At Englishtown, New Jersey, the American troops prepared themselves for attack. The youthful Lafayette had them primed and ready for action. Just as the assault was about to commence, General Charles Lee stormed into the American camp, reclaiming command from the Frenchman. He had changed his mind; he wanted charge of the expedition now and had successfully argued his case to Washington. The troops were dismissed to their tents.

For the rest of the afternoon and all that night, while Lee reevaluated strategy, the soldiers listened mournfully as in the distance they could hear the rumble of the redcoats' heavy wagons moving north and out of reach beyond Monmouth Court House.

The dawn of June 28 gave promise of a scorching day. No new orders were forthcoming from Lee, even though reports drifted in that the British were rapidly falling back. Then word came from General Washington. Lee was ordered to attack immediately; Washington was sending the remainder of the army to his support.

※

The sound of fife and drums brought Jacob to his feet. He emerged from the shade of his tent, squinting against the stifling sun. His unit moved smartly into action. Leaving the road, they marched through low hills and around swampy ravines. Other American troops could be seen scattered across the terrain, now behind a hill, now in sight again. Just as Jacob thought they'd cleared a swamp or hill and would attack, they would be ordered to reverse themselves and take another route. Other units showed similar movements, one minute advancing, the next retiring.

Lafayette appeared, riding across the front, urging the units onward. As he neared Jacob's unit, the Frenchman was stopped by one of General Lee's aides with a message.

"Commanding General Lee gives his regards and this message," said the aide. "Sir, you do not know British soldiers. We cannot stand against them." Lafayette was ordered to cease commanding the army to advance. With a curse, the Frenchman urged his horse in the direction of General Lee's headquarters. The aide followed leisurely behind him. Jacob's unit was brought to a dead halt. They stood baking in the sun, awaiting orders.

To their right, they could hear an occasional volley of shots and some cannon fire, but it was quite distant. However, the sound of combat, though distant, had its effect on them. Even though a hill cut off their view, they couldn't help but take occasional long glances in the direction of the battle. Jacob stood as relaxed as he could and surveyed the scene in front of him, wondering if his unit would see any action today. They stood at the edge of a long field. On this side, the field was bordered by small hills and swampy ravines; on the far side, a thin forest marked the edge. To his left he could see two other American units having emerged completely onto the field; a third unit was partially hidden by a hill. In front of the two forward units was their company drummer, a fairly small boy. His drum was nearly half his height. Another boy stood next to him. Chestnut hair. Ragged clothes ... Bo!

Jacob's heart nearly failed him. Bo was standing alongside the drummer boy in the front of the entire American army! Jacob's pulse raced; his eyes darted back and forth as he tried to decide what to do. He wanted to run into the field and pull the boy back to his position, but von Steuben's training had ingrained itself. He couldn't break rank. *Should he yell? No again, same reason. How could he get a message to Bo? Even if he could get the boy a message, what would he tell him? Go home? Bo had already disobeyed that one. Come here? He might do that. But what if von Steuben came by and saw Bo in the ranks again?* Suffering with indecision, Jacob shifted in place from one foot to the other. *No need to do anything rash,* he reasoned. *Everything is quiet. From all indications, nothing is going to happen today anyway.*

BOOM! A thundering smoke belched from the forest at the far side of the field, followed by a frightening salvo of cannon fire. BOOM! BOOM! BOOM!

Dirt erupted all along the front ranks, rising high above the earth, then plummeting back down to whence it came through great clouds of smoke. Another roar of a different kind followed close behind, also coming from the forest. Horses' hoofs, the blast of cavalry bugles, and the cries of soldiers. The American response sounded; orders were pounded out on the drums. Fall back. Retreat.

In panic, most of the men in Jacob's unit broke ranks and fled in disorderly retreat. Jacob held his ground, trying to catch a glimpse of Bo through the smoke. Of the two front units, one fled in panic, the same as Jacob's unit. The other turned smartly and began an orderly retreat. Jacob still could not see Bo and the drummer. The smoke was thickest where he had seen them last.

Jacob ran down the small decline toward the field. In the distance, British cavalry rushed to meet him. As Jacob ran, the smoke began to clear. Forms began to take recognizable shapes. Jacob bit his lip; the shapes were not vertical, but close to the ground. Jacob ran harder. As he ran, he fixed his bayonet to the end of his musket. The heat rising from the field was oppressive; he could feel it through the soles of his shoes: a thick, humid heat that made it difficult to breathe. Jacob's lungs burned for lack of oxygen as he took short, hurried breaths.

Reaching the edge of the field, he checked the speed and progress of the onrushing cavalry—full gallop, closing fast. He looked to the boys—there was some stirring, but they seemed unaware of the closing British cavalry. He was too far; the cavalry was coming too fast. He didn't know if he was going to reach them in time.

He ran faster, urging his complaining lungs and legs onward. The British cavalry had reached the middle of the field. Their sabers were drawn. The sun's bright rays reflected on the shiny blades, casting bolts of light that pierced the dissipating smoke.

Jacob could see the boys clearly now. Bo was alive! The boy sat on the ground, holding the drummer boy in his lap, propped against his chest. The drummer boy's head was bloodied and hung to one side in an awkward, lifeless manner. Bo was weeping uncontrollably. Holding the drummer boy's limp arm, he tried to place a drumstick in the boy's hand. Then he'd let go. The stick and hand fell silently to the ground. Bo pulled the arm up and tried again with the same result.

"Drum, Zach! Drum!" he cried repeatedly.

"Bo! Get down!" Jacob waved frantically, hoping to get the deaf boy's attention.

The cavalry had almost reached Bo and the drummer boy. Jacob's joints screamed in pain from the furious pounding they were taking as he ran across the hard ground; he ignored them and increased his effort. He had to reach Bo before the British did. His toes dug into the dirt field, every step pushing off with as much energy as he could muster.

Just a few yards away now.

Jacob could see the mustached face of the cavalry rider bearing down on Bo. His sparkling sword was raised high over his head; his eyes were fixed on the two boys. The cavalry soldier next to the mustached one had dark eyes that were fixed on Jacob. Now even Bo was aware of the approaching cavalry; the pounding of the horses' hoofs must have given their presence away. The deaf boy turned in horror to see them crashing down upon him.

At the last moment, Jacob dropped his musket and leaped for the boys. He flew several feet, knocking them flat on the ground and landing on top of them. The unmoving drummer boy lay between him and Bo. Bo let out a whimpering cry as his back and head slammed against the dirt. An instant later, Jacob heard a saber swoosh over him, inches away. Thundering hoofs rushed past them on both sides.

A volley of musket fire sounded from the American side. There were several thuds as some of the British soldiers took direct hits and fell to the ground. Bo struggled against the weight on top of him, clawing and kicking.

"Bo! It's me! Jacob!" He lifted up slightly to give the boy a look at his face.

"Jabe!" Bo cried, recognition setting off a renewed flow of tears. "Hep Zach, Jabe! Hep Zach!"

Jacob placed a reassuring hand on the side of Bo's face, then hurriedly checked over his shoulder on the cavalry. *Would they come back?* Between a jumble of horses' legs Jacob could see an American force with bayonets drawn, rushing toward the line of cavalry. The Frenchman Lafayette led them with his saber drawn. The British cavalry wheeled around and headed back toward the forest, and again Jacob and Bo separated them from their intended destination. Scattered American shots peppered them from behind. Jacob covered the two boys with his body as the redcoats galloped past them a second time. Jacob had seen this tactic before. They weren't running away, merely regrouping. They would be back.

Quickly, he rolled off the two boys and examined the drummer. There was no sign of life. He had an ugly gash on his forehead, and a large red spot spread across his midsection. He wasn't breathing.

"Zach! Zach!" Bo cried. He shook his friend's shoulder, trying to wake him.

Jacob cradled Bo's head in his hands. He established eye contact and yelled, "He's dead, Bo! There's nothing we can do!"

Behind Bo, in the distance, Jacob could see the British cavalry moving into formation for another charge.

"Let's go!" he yelled at Bo. Jacob grabbed Bo's hand to help him up. Bo's unexpected resistance nearly pulled Jacob back to the ground. "What are you doing?" he screamed at Bo. "Look! They're coming again!"

"Zach!" Bo tried to lift the dead drummer.

"Leave him!"

"No!"

Bo held Zach under the arms and was dragging the boy toward American lines.

As the British cavalry sounded another charge, Jacob scooped up the drummer boy in his arms. Bo retrieved the drum, the drumsticks, and Jacob's musket. They ran toward American lines with British horses close behind them and American muskets pointed at them.

Jacob didn't know if he could make it. The heat had taken a lot out of him. The dead boy in his arms was a bulky burden, which slowed him considerably. Bo had passed him, the drum slapping against his legs as he ran. In front of them, Jacob saw Lafayette reach down with his sword, tapping two light infantrymen on the shoulders. Having gained their attention, he said something to them and pointed toward Jacob with his saber. They nodded and raised their muskets. It looked like they were aiming straight at him!

The pounding of hoofs grew louder. The drummer boy's head rocked back and forth, his legs dangled over Jacob's arm, and he seemed to grow heavier with each step. Jacob urged his legs to keep going, but they were no longer listening to him. The horses behind him were so close, he could hear them snorting angrily.

A volley of shot from the American side boomed like a thunder-crack. Smoke swirled over the heads of every soldier on the front line except two, the two men who had received instructions from Lafayette. While the other soldiers reloaded, these two kept their muskets trained on Jacob. He managed a quick glance over his shoulder. Two British cavalry soldiers were almost on top of him, their sabers high and threatening.

Two more cracks, two more puffs of smoke. Two riderless horses sped past Jacob, their riders flying through the air, hitting the ground with sickening thuds. An astonished Jacob saw Lafayette congratulating the two soldiers closest to him for their marksmanship.

Jacob and Bo made it safely behind the line of American soldiers. For Zach, the drummer boy, it was too late.

※

Jacob draped a comforting arm around a sobbing Bo as the two sat in the dirt beside the road to Englishtown. Zach's drum and drumsticks lay next to Bo, Jacob's musket next to him. A steady stream of men passed in front of them, some in near panic, others in orderly fashion, as they continued their retreat from the British. Zach's body had already been taken by a friend of the family who witnessed the incident. At first, Bo wouldn't let the good Samaritan take Zach's body. Not until Jacob convinced him that Zach's mother would want to hold him one more time did Bo release his friend.

With no shade nearby, the sun beat down on them mercilessly. Jacob was hot and wet and exhausted and parched. The dust kicked up by the passing soldiers didn't help much.

"Monsieur!"

The voice came from above Jacob. He had to squint against the bright sky to see who was addressing him. When he did, he leaped to his feet. It was the Marquis de Lafayette.

"The boy, the one you were carrying, is he all right?"

Jacob shook his head. "No, sir. He's dead."

A genuine sorrow spread across Lafayette's features. Jacob had never been this close to the marquis before. The man looked so young. Yet he had an unmistakably noble air about him. "Was he your son?"

"No, sir."

"Then this one must be your son. Is he hurt?" Lafayette was speaking of Bo.

"He has no wounds, sir. He grieves for his friend." Jacob let the reference to kinship with Bo go uncorrected, partly because he felt it unnecessary under the circumstance, partly because he had come to think of Bo as his son and the verbal association sounded good to him.

"You were a brave man today, *monsieur.*"

Jacob shook his head. "Thank you for saying so, sir. But being chased across a field by British cavalry is hardly a brave act. However, I do want to thank you for fending off those two horsemen. For a moment there, I didn't think I would make it."

"Do not be so modest about your efforts, *monsieur.* The bravery was how you got into that field in the first place. Not many men would run headlong into the face of a British cavalry charge."

The two men's attention was drawn from their conversation to the speedy approach of a horseman coming from Englishtown. A huge dust cloud trailed in the horseman's wake. The rider wore a sweat-stained blue- and buff-colored uniform. He sat tall in the saddle and didn't pull up until he was within feet of Jacob and Lafayette.

"General Washington!"

Both Lafayette and Jacob saluted the general whose face was crimson red and dripping with sweat.

"Who ordered this retreat?" he thundered.

"General Lee, sir," Lafayette replied. "He does not believe we can stand against the British soldiers."

Through clenched teeth, Washington demanded, "And where might I find General Lee?" Each word was clipped short, almost as if the general would lose control if he let more than one of them leave his mouth at a time.

Lafayette gave directions to General Lee's headquarters in Englishtown.

"General Lafayette," Washington ordered, "spread the word. As of this moment, I am assuming command of this battle. If you happen to see General Lee before me, place him under arrest! And do what you can to get these soldiers turned around. They're heading the wrong way!"

Washington looked down at Bo and the drum next to him.

"Drummer boy," he said. "Sound the call to arms!"

"Excuse me, General Washington," Jacob said. "Bo isn't the drummer boy. He can't play the drums. He can't even hear you. He's deaf. You see, the drummer boy was killed earlier today and we're just ..."

A sharp, crisp call to arms sounded behind Jacob, cutting him off midsentence. Behind him, with Zach Miller's drum strapped on, Bo stood tall, beating out a call to arms. A look of fierce determination resided in his unfocused eyes; his jaw was set firmly; his lower lip trembled. But his hands and wrists moved confidently, sounding an unmistakable message. All around them soldiers stopped and looked in their direction.

Washington called out to them. "You heard correctly!" he shouted at them. "Form ranks! As soon as I get back we're going to assist the redcoats on their way, and we're not going to let them stop until they're back in England! Prepare for attack!"

All around them, men cheered. Like disturbed ants on a hill, they scurried about to find their units. Washington reined his horse around; then, over his shoulder, he said, "Talented son you have there, Sergeant."

"Yes, sir!" Jacob replied.

Lafayette appointed Jacob to command a unit of light infantry. Bo was appointed the drummer. Lafayette passed orders to

Jacob, and Jacob mouthed them to Bo, who beat them with authority. To one side, von Steuben watched his troops proudly from his vantage point on a hill as Lafayette and Washington rallied the men to action. For the first time since Lexington and Concord, the separate states' militia coordinated like a united army.

As the day wore on under a scorching sun, with the battle surging in favor of one side, then the other, casualties mounted. Many men collapsed, not from wounds, but from intense thirst, succumbing to the heat. As evening neared, both armies were exhausted.

※

Jacob and Bo lay under a tree as shadows stretched long and approaching twilight brought with it a hint of a breeze. Jacob nursed a cup of cold water, an oasis in a wooden mug. Bo lay beside him, faceup on the grass, intently following the antics of a nervous bird as it hopped from limb to limb above him. Jacob reached over and playfully slapped Bo on the stomach. Bo curled up like a bug.

"You didn't tell me you could play the drum!" Jacob said.

Bo snatched a drumstick and, without getting up, reached overhead and rhythmically tapped the tree trunk.

Jacob nodded. "I remember. The wooden spoon and the pot. I can still remember that headache too. Still, I don't understand. Beating a pot with a spoon and playing the drum are two different things."

Bo shrugged. He couldn't see the difference.

"You learned while I was in soldier school, didn't you? Zach taught you."

The mention of Zach's name brought a sober expression to the boy's face. He nodded.

"I'm sure Zach was a good friend."

Bo focused again on the bird in the tree, fighting back tears.

Jacob gave him a few undisturbed moments to remember his friend. Then he tapped Bo on the shoulder good-naturedly to establish contact again. With a chuckle, he said, "I'll never forget today. Here I was explaining to General Washington that you didn't know how to play the drum while you, behind my back, sound the call to arms! I was so dumbfounded, I almost dropped my teeth!"

The visual image of Jacob dropping his teeth set Bo to laughing. He laughed and laughed until tears streamed freely down his face.

The frenzied pounding of horses' hoofs leaped over the hill, followed by the horses themselves and their riders—Washington and Lafayette.

"Morgan!" Washington bellowed his name.

Jacob jumped to his feet, as did Bo.

"Report on the condition of your men."

"Exhausted, but we're in good shape."

"Can they fight?"

"At your order, sir."

"I need an accurate assessment of your men, Morgan. The British are retreating and I want to attack, but the men are exhausted. I'm looking for troops who still have enough in them to chase redcoats. It's no reflection on your leadership or the loyalty of your men. Can they do it?"

"Give the word, sir, and Bo will call them to arms."

A warm look in his eyes and a half smile indicated General Washington was pleased with Jacob's response. Leaning toward Bo, he said directly, "Son, sound the call to arms."

Soon afterward, Jacob stood at the base of a small hill that separated him from the field upon which so much fighting had taken place that day. As he awaited the order to advance, he gripped and regripped the sword with which he commanded his men. Bo stood beside him, calmly, almost serenely, his eyes forward, his jaw firm. The boy's lack of fear was total, almost unnerving. *How could one so young face a battle with such bravery?* But then, considering all he'd been through—never knowing his mother, living alone and poor with his father, being deaf; he'd survived the skirmishes at Lexington and Concord, witnessed the death of his pa, been chased and shot at by redcoats, outlasted a winter at Valley Forge, and most recently, stood next to a boyhood friend when the blast of a cannon shell ended his life. Jacob compared that to his own boyhood—both a mother and a father, a secure and wealthy family, school, boyhood pranks. That was the way a boy's life was supposed to be, not like Bo's.

The signal was given to advance. Jacob Morgan led his unit up the side of the hill and halted just shy of the crest. He waited for the signal to proceed. Another glance at Bo. The boy's expression had not changed. Calm. Determined.

An overwhelming feeling came over Jacob. He wanted to take the boy away from the battle right now, to grab him by the hand and drag him to safety, to take him to Boston and deliver him to the house on Beacon Street where the boy would be safe, where he could live a normal boy's life.

The second signal was given. Bo made eye contact with Jacob. Jacob nodded. The drum sounded. Slashing his sword forward in the air, Jacob Morgan urged his men over the hill into battle.

Although the day was late, the ground was still hot. The field was littered with guns, and bodies, and equipment. Jacob stepped over one dead redcoat as he and his men pursued a company of them across the field. For the most part, the colonials had bright red backs to shoot at as the British retreated. A few of the enemy turned and fired parting shots.

Shouting at the top of his voice, Jacob encouraged his weary unit to press forward. They were halfway across the field now, and Jacob was again beginning to feel his age. His legs begged him to rest; his lungs burned; and his arms felt so tired, so weary. But the last of the redcoats were disappearing into the woods. They had succeeded in taking the field. Just a little farther.

Jacob never saw the redcoat, nor the puff of smoke. He felt something slam into his side just above his left hip, like the kick of a horse. It was an odd feeling, a sudden flash of pain that spun him around. Geography sped before him—forest, field, hills, forest again, then the ground close up, then the sky. Without lifting his head, he reached for the wound. It was warm and wet, and when he touched it, it blazed. Then the fire began to dim, as did everything else around him.

He felt calm. Just like Bo had looked earlier. Calm. Unafraid.

Just then, Bo's face appeared over him. His expression was much different now. Horrified. Frightened. Tears spilled from his eyes rapidly. The boy was trying to say something, but no words were coming out.

This wasn't the way it was supposed to be. Different. It was going to be different for Bo, better. Not this.

Jacob tried to lift a hand to reassure Bo that everything would be all right. He would take Bo away from all this. Take him to Boston. Safe there. Love there. But try as he might, Jacob couldn't lift his hand. Nor could he speak. There would be no assurances. Not today. *Funny*, Jacob thought, *how quickly the sun was setting tonight.*

17

Philadelphians lined the streets to cheer the parade of the Massachusetts Continentals as the American forces secured the city following the British pullout. Immediately behind the troops, riding in a coach-and-four and receiving the loudest accolades, was the newly appointed military governor, Major General Benedict Arnold. His aides and servants, including Esau Morgan, accompanied him.

For Esau, the celebration of the moment was tempered by the city's devastated condition. Whole neighborhoods of houses had been burned or dismantled for firewood; virtually every wooden fence had been consumed. The British had toppled the gravestones in the Presbyterian church to use it as a field to exercise their horses. Churches were stripped bare of their pews, pulpits, and galleries to warm the soldiers' barracks. Building interiors had been ruined by moisture and littered with trash. All the furnishings of Independence Hall had been burned to warm five companies of British artillery that had been quartered there. The city's squares and commons had been churned to mud and littered with debris. The streets were jammed with broken-down carts and wagons; carcasses of horses lay exposed next to them. About the only section of the city unscathed by the British occupation was the brick townhouses of the Quakers and loyalists.

Block after block, Esau found himself grimacing at the condition of Mercy's hometown. It was a scarred replica of the city he remembered in the days when he came courting. He'd have to be sure to check on Mercy's parents. The mental image of walking up the front steps of Mercy's old house prompted a nostalgic tide to rise inside him.

Arnold and his staff settled into the Penn mansion at Sixth and Market Streets. Though they were the city's liberators, the mood among the staff was far from festive, due largely to the projected emotions of their leader. Arnold had been appointed to the position by General Washington, who insisted he needed a fighting man in the position should the British decide to return. And though Arnold accepted the high-level position, he did so because it was the only one forthcoming. Arnold didn't want a rear-level position—he wanted another field command. The fact that he hadn't been able to ride a horse since the Battle of Saratoga was, to him, a minor inconvenience.

While the Battle of Saratoga was an unqualified victory for the American forces, it was a tainted victory for the ambitious Benedict Arnold. Though he had no command of his own that day, he led an assault against British General Burgoyne that threw the redcoats back upon Bemis Heights. Shortly thereafter, Burgoyne called for terms of surrender. It was this convincing victory that persuaded the French to declare themselves an ally of the united colonies. And once again, Arnold was a military hero; also, once again, during the course of the battle, he was wounded in the left leg.

A Hessian's bullet shattered Arnold's left femur. Ordinarily, the leg would have been amputated. Arnold vehemently resisted, saying he'd rather be dead than crippled. For two days and nights, he fought to keep his leg. The news of Burgoyne's surrender seemed to help him recover faster, and the doctors no longer pressed for amputation. As in Quebec, Esau remained by his side during his hospital recovery.

Their task in Philadelphia was to provide tranquillity and order among the city's varied population—radical Whigs (anti-Washington and pro-Washington alike), a large population of loyalists, and pacifist Quakers. Arnold and staff found themselves in the midst of a murderous four-way political cross fire for control of the nation's capital. Everything he did was criticized and challenged, especially his insistence on inviting loyalist women to revolutionary social events.

"What the general has chosen to wear is his business, madam. Now, if you will excuse me."

Esau strode purposefully across the room even though he had no purpose in crossing the room other than to place distance between himself and one of General Arnold's outspoken critics, a woman in her late fifties who had taken it upon herself to register her disgust with Esau over the military governor's powdered wig. It had been Esau's misfortune to be introduced as one of the governor's aides within her hearing.

The room he crossed was the elaborately decorated ballroom of Penn mansion. The music swelled as he skirted those who were dancing. It was August 25 and the occasion for celebration was King Louis XVI's birthday. Military governor Arnold was officially the host of the French ministry in Philadelphia, a position he took seriously. He organized the ball to promote diplomatic goodwill, inviting all of the city's leading citizens regardless of their political backgrounds. The woman who had just complained to Esau did so because in her estimation, the governor, by his dress, was favoring the loyalists over the Whigs.

Fashion had become a revolutionary issue. Continentals had rejected powdered wigs for men and preferred instead short-cropped, unpowdered hair. Likewise, the continental ladies abandoned the enormous headdresses of white hair, which they associated with the shameful mistresses of British officers, for a more natural, what they called easy, manner of hairdress. Gentlemen's hats went from the tall conical hats, which resembled Hessian helmets, to the preferred tricorne. Even shoe buckles came under fire. The silver could better be used to serve a soldier as a tankard or coffeepot, it was thought. When the military governor, a man who loved high fashion, refused to yield to the simplified revolutionary dress, he sparked the ire of many of his opponents.

For Esau, there were more important things to spend one's time on than arguing fashion or defending his superior's right to choose his own fashion. In fact, he didn't want to be at the ball at all. It reminded him too much of Mercy.

It was here in Philadelphia that she had made her first social appearance. It was here that she gained her reputation as the delightfully charming and stunningly beautiful daughter of a common Philadelphia tailor. It was in settings such as this one that Mercy was most at home, captivating every person who came near her. It was in a setting similar to this one that he had first seen her, desired her, fell in love with her. This French-oriented ball was too much for him. It brought back too many memories.

He tried to put her out of his mind. She had not written to him in over two years. Letters from his mother occasionally spoke of her, but not in ways he wanted to hear. She was well; bearing up under the distressing shortages of supplies; showed uncanny abilities in obtaining items that were particularly scarce; had some kind of spiritual experience following a risky trip to Jacob's unit.

According to his mother, Mercy was a changed woman, more mature, more spiritual. Esau found it hard to imagine Mercy as spiritual. She was a sprite, a nymph, a pixie—not a saint. But then, Esau reasoned, his mother always saw people as she wanted them to be rather than how they were.

The absence of music brought Esau's attention back to the ballroom. Conversations softened, no longer having to compete with the music. Then the orchestra began again; it was just a momentary pause while a couple members of the orchestra shuffled seats.

Esau gazed longingly toward the open door. Better to leave this place and bury himself in paperwork than to wallow in memories and work himself into a masterful depression. He glanced toward the front of the ballroom. A pair of feminine eyes caught his. They were young and sparkling, situated under a mountain of white hair that was spangled with French bows. A dainty finger shook at him; an equally dainty head forbid him to do what he was thinking. Both belonged to Peggy Shippen. It was as if she had read his mind. Esau smiled sheepishly and turned back into the room.

Eighteen-year-old Peggy Shippen was a younger version of Mercy Reed. Considered by many—mostly men—to be the most beautiful woman in Philadelphia, she was the daughter of Judge Edward Shippen, a wealthy Philadelphian who wished to remain neutral in the revolutionary conflict. Consequently, the radical Whigs regarded him as a loyalist and traitor when he cooperated with the British during the occupation; and though he now cooperated with the Continental Army and military governor Arnold, their opinion of him remained unchanged. The fact that the governor didn't rebuff him only served to sour their opinion of him as well.

However, Benedict Arnold's interest in the Shippen family was not political; it was purely romantic. The comely young daughter of Judge Shippen had captured his heart, and although Arnold was twice her age, he entertained thoughts of courting her.

It was Peggy who had insisted Esau not leave the party. Earlier, she caught him going out the door, grabbed hold of his arm with a delicate hand, and gently dragged him back into the ballroom. Although she gave no reason, she made him promise he would stay. One look at her playful eyes and he agreed.

This was the second time Esau had encountered the young Philadelphia beauty. Their initial encounter came during the July Fourth celebration a little more than a month earlier, the second such celebration in the nation's brief history. At that party Esau learned that the Shippens and Reeds had been friends for years. According to Peggy, some of her earliest memories were the stories women still told of the incomparable Mercy Reed and the festive Philadelphia balls of a happier day. And when she learned that he was Mercy's brother-in-law, she said she just had to meet him.

Peggy meant well. And Esau liked her, but she knew nothing of the heartbreak of his relationship with Mercy. Peggy was too young to know how her smile, her gaiety, together with this setting, this city, tore him apart with thoughts of what should have been. But now, even he was coming to realize that he and Mercy would never be together in the way he so desperately wanted them to be. He chuckled bitterly. It only took years of being separated from her, over two years of no direct contact with her, and the saltiness of Philadelphia society in his wounded heart to bring him to that conclusion.

Again the music stopped, and Esau decided that, promise or no promise, he had to leave. The French king's birthday party would have to get along without him. More than anything else, he needed time to be alone, to grieve.

A majestic chord sounded.

"Madams et monsieurs!" a portly announcer hailed with a particularly bad imitation of a French accent. "It gives me great pleasure to introduce the long-absent belle of Philadelphia, Mercy Reed Morgan!"

Peggy Shippen led the applause, clapping happily, obviously pleased by Esau's reaction.

The orchestra swelled to a crescendo, followed by a light and lively tune.

Entering through massive double doors with the party attendees parting before her like the sea parted before Moses, Mercy glided gracefully into the room. It was as if time had gone backward one giant leap and Mercy was making her first public appearance in Philadelphia. She was stunning, the epitome of French high fashion. She wore a tall wig of white hair adorned with tiny pink bows; her gown was white with more pink bows and a square-cut neckline.

Esau was reminded of the first time he saw her. It was here in Philadelphia, years and years ago. Just as it was then, so it was now—the eyes of everyone in the room were upon her. There was one difference. An important one. Then, her eyes moved about the room from guest to guest; tonight, they fixed on him.

She moved directly to him and held out her hand. "Surprised?"

The thin smile on her lips, so characteristic of her, together with her familiar perfume acted on Esau like a narcotic.

"Astounded," he replied. His voice portrayed a calm that had no emotional foundation. Moments earlier, there had been an emotional void; all feelings for Mercy were gone forever, or so he thought. Then, the instant he saw her enter the ballroom, all those absent emotions and a thousand more flooded back into the void, swirling around and around inside of him.

"Aren't you going to ask me to dance?"

Esau took Mercy by the hand and led her into the middle of the room. The other guests watched as he held out his arms and Mercy stepped into them. The music began and they danced. After a few moments another couple joined them, then another, and another. Esau was completely unaware that anyone else was in the room.

"*Do* forgive me for surprising you like this," Mercy said. "It was Peggy's idea. She's *such* a sweet dear. She thought the reunion of two family members would be *wonderfully* romantic."

"I agree with her."

Mercy blushed. For some reason this disturbed Esau. It took him a moment to realize why. He had seen Mercy blush hundreds of times before, but only when it was to her advantage. This blush was different. It was genuine.

"You'll have to forgive Peggy," Mercy said. "She's young. She has *undoubtedly* heard rumors about you, Jacob, and me, but I don't think she meant anything by this other than a reunion of family. I apologize if this is uncomfortable for you."

Again Esau was taken aback. *Mercy apologizing for someone else's discomfort? This was so unlike her!* The Mercy he knew made the most of a man's uneasiness; that's what gave her an advantage over men. Esau looked hard at the woman in his arms. *Who was she?* She looked the same and smelled the same, she even danced the same, yet this Mercy was different from his Mercy.

"No need to apologize," Esau said casually. "In fact, I'm in her debt because it brought you here to Philadelphia."

"It was your mother's idea, really."

"Oh?"

"She suggested I come to Philadelphia to make sure my parents were all right. I hadn't heard from them since the British occupied the city. So we *prayed* about it. Then, we learned that General Arnold was appointed military governor, and it seemed that my coming here was God ordained, since we knew *you* would be here to protect me."

This wasn't Mercy's vocabulary. *We prayed about it. It seemed that my coming here was God ordained.* These were his mother's words, not Mercy's. Esau tried not to make too much of it. After a moment's thought he concluded it was only natural Mercy would have picked up words from his mother. The two women had been through a lot together, having spent day after day with each other for the last few years. Naturally, they would start talking like each other.

"Come!" Mercy took him by the hand. "Mother and Father are anxious to see you again."

Although Esau had intended on calling on the Reeds, his duties had prevented him from actually doing it. They were well and in good spirits, of course, since Mercy was back in Philadelphia. Next they joined Peggy and General Arnold. Esau introduced Mercy to the general. His gray eyes had a glint of foreknowledge of her, having heard about her from Esau while recuperating in Quebec. For much of the evening the four of them sat and talked. Although Arnold couldn't dance, he kept them entertained with his lively wit and stories. Occasionally Mercy and Peggy were taken from them by officers who had enough brass in them to approach the general. The women were always promptly returned at the end of the dance with a multitude of thanks. And no officer asked for more than one dance.

There was one sober moment when Peggy asked Mercy about her husband. Mercy explained that a Boston shoemaker, a friend of Jared's, had stopped by the house to report that he had seen Jacob get hit during the Battle of Monmouth. *"Actually,* he thought it was Esau," Mercy said. "But when he described the location of the battle we knew that he was mistaken and that it was Jacob." The shoemaker reported that Jacob was dead. "We haven't received any official word yet," Mercy concluded. She reached over and touched Esau's hand. "I'm sorry you had to hear the news this way," she said. "I'd hoped to be able to tell you privately."

Esau stared absently across the ballroom. Somehow he'd always thought he'd feel more than he was feeling at the moment upon receiving this kind of news. Of course, he didn't expect to feel deep sorrow after the antagonistic life he and Jacob had shared; nor did he feel elation. Only a demented person would feel happy over someone's death. It was more like the kind of feeling you get after you have finished reading a long book. You turn the last page, close the cover, and feel a sense of completion. That's how Esau felt when he heard of Jacob's death. While the book of Jacob's life was closed, Esau's would begin a new chapter.

"Are you all right?" Mercy asked. She held his hand with both of hers now. They were warm and soft and soothing.

The beginning of a new chapter, Esau thought.

Arnold's gray eyes conveyed a knowing look to Esau. He understood. After all these years of waiting, Esau's dreams of Mercy were about to come true.

The night passed too quickly. Every moment of it, Esau drank in Mercy's smiles and laughter like a thirsty man on a desert island. On the one hand, he was already in heaven; on the other hand, he couldn't wait to get Mercy alone.

Esau was forced to wait nearly a week before seeing Mercy again. Throughout the week his brother's death was constantly on his mind. It seemed strange to him that for the first time since they were born, there was only one face on the earth that looked like his. Never again would people mistake him for his brother, or vice versa. For Esau it felt almost eerie to be one of a kind.

The military governor's office kept Esau and the rest of Arnold's staff occupied deploying troops around the city, carrying out arrests by order of Congress, supervising prisons, and gathering intelligence on British troop movements in the forests and mountains of New Jersey.

A growing concern, one that Arnold officially assigned to Esau, was the increasing strength of anti-Arnold sentiment in Philadelphia by radical Whigs. For Esau it was Boston's Adams and Hancock all over again, only with different names and faces. Dealing daily with these irate troublemakers nearly made Esau long for the good old days in the Maine forest when they were starving to death. At least then the issues of the day were significant—survival; find food or starve; build a shelter for warmth or freeze to death. In Philadelphia the hotly debated issues were should the governor have issued a pass to a known loyalist, did the governor use public wagons to transport private goods, and had the governor imposed degrading services on militiamen?

At the heart of these complaints was Arnold's closeness to the Society Hill section of town, specifically Fourth Street, and even more specifically, Judge Shippen's house. Arnold's unofficial assignment to Esau was to do what he could through Mercy and her family to persuade the judge to let Arnold court Peggy.

Judge Edward Shippen, a lawyer and merchant, was a gray-haired, heavy-jowled man with sad eyes and a large nose. Having inherited his wealth, he was a man who preferred to maintain his estate rather than work to increase it. He was cautious and conservative in his business dealings, and so it came as no surprise that he would be that way with his family. He was cool to military governor Arnold's initial correspondence seeking permission to court his daughter. In the letter, Arnold stated that he expected no dowry since he had enough money. He only wanted Peggy and her father's permission to court her. Judge Shippen didn't say yes, but he didn't say no either. The judge told Arnold he would have to wait while he wrote to his father to seek advice.

Meanwhile, Esau was to promote Arnold's cause through the Reed family, something he was more than willing to do.

※

"How long will you be staying?"

Esau and Mercy strolled arm in arm down Fourth Street. They had spent the last hour paying a social call on the Shippens, speaking highly of Governor Arnold whenever possible. At every mention of his name, Peggy's wide-set, blue-gray eyes would light up. Though she appeared to be shy, she was intelligent and educated, able to converse at length about literature, business, or politics. She was better educated than most women of her day—adept not only at needlework, drawing, dancing, and music, but also in reading and writing. Her writing style had a clarity that put most learned men to shame. Esau was quite fond of her because she reminded him of Mercy when she was younger and because he knew that Peggy would make Arnold a good wife. Mercy and Peggy seemed to be drawn from the same ball of yarn; their affinity for one another went to the very soul, and they loved each other like sisters.

"I may stay through the winter, depending on Momma's health," Mercy said distractedly. Her attention was focused on a section of burned-out buildings. "When I was little, I used to walk with my mother to that building to buy bread. It was the first place my mother let me walk to alone. I remember carrying the loaf home in two arms, thinking I was an adult." She smiled at the memory. "I think I was seven."

"I wish I could have seen you as a little girl," Esau said.

"Oh *no* you don't!" Mercy cried. "I was scrawny and awkward and ugly. No girl should be seen at that age."

Esau laughed. "My guess is that you were as cute then as you are beautiful now."

Mercy's eyes lowered. "You shouldn't say things like that."

"You used to like it when I told you how beautiful you are."

"Things change, Esau. Philadelphia isn't the same city it was when I left it; I'm not the same woman I was when you left Boston."

"I can see that," Esau replied. "You're more mature. It's becoming."

Mercy fished for a handkerchief and dabbed her eyes with it. "You're not making this easy for me, are you?" she said.

"Making what easy for you?"

They had reached the Reeds' house. Mercy led Esau behind the house to a small garden. Compared to the Morgan's garden on Beacon Street it was miniature. Still, it had a cozy small stone bench, a plot of green grass, and a patch of flowers. Mercy sat on one half of the bench, offering the other to Esau.

"Do you remember when I told you it was your mother's idea that I come to Philadelphia?"

Esau nodded. "To make sure your parents had survived the British occupation."

"That was only part of the reason. You are the other part."

Mercy inhaled deeply as she worried her handkerchief in her lap. Although her less-than-encouraging tone and actions kindled a sense of foreboding in him, Esau allowed her the time she needed to formulate her thoughts.

"Your mother thinks—and I agree with her—that until I release you, you will never give yourself permission to love another woman."

Esau smiled knowingly and gazed at her out of the tops of his eyes, the same way he would if he were listening to a child. "Is that all?" he said.

Mercy stiffened. "What do you mean, 'Is that all?'"

"I mean, is that all that's bothering you? Because if it is, the problem is easily solved." Esau put his hands on top of hers. "I don't want to be released by you. I don't want to love another woman. I love *you*. I have since the moment I first set eyes on you, and I will until the day I die."

Mercy pulled her hands away. Her eyes closed. "O Lord, forgive me!" she cried. "I should have done this such a long time ago." To Esau: "What must I do to make you understand? I can't return your love!"

Esau was perplexed. Someone had changed the rules and forgotten to tell him. Previously, it was simple—Mercy's way of encouraging him was to put him off, he would persist, and she would reward him with one of her famous heart-satisfying smiles or a touch of her hand or a peck on the cheek. *He had done everything right tonight, hadn't he?* She put him off and he came back. But instead of a reward, he got tears. *What did she want from him? What could he say to her that would earn him that soul-stirring look on her face to which he was addicted?*

"I understand you can't return my love right now," he said. "You need time to mourn for Jacob. You're a widow now. But, my dearest, don't you see? This is God's way of putting things right! After all these years of waiting, our time has finally come. The way is clear for us to love each other openly. For us to marry!"

God's way of putting things right. Mercy visibly reacted to the words as if they had taken on solid form and hit her in the chest. Her eyes glazed over. A reservoir of tears built up on her lower lids, pushing one, then another over the edge.

Esau continued softly: "Mercy, dear, I know this is painful for you, but don't you see? How could I possibly leave you now that you are all alone?"

Mercy's shoulders slumped forward and shook softy with

sobs. Esau stretched a tentative hand in her direction and placed it on her shoulder. She didn't move away. He ached to take her in his arms and comfort her, but he restrained himself. It was a painful time for both of them; painful but necessary, he concluded. They had to break from the past before they could proceed with their future.

Mercy's sobs grew softer. Intertwining her fingers, she raised her hands until they touched her nose and lips. "Dear God, show me the way," she prayed as she wept. "Give me wisdom. Give me the words to say."

Of all the things Mercy could have done at this moment, this was the last thing Esau would have expected of her. He removed his hand from her shoulder as if he suddenly discovered he was touching a stranger. His face was a portrait of disbelief.

Mercy's shoulders straightened, her head raised, and her eyes cleared. She dabbed her nose and inhaled deeply. That which came into her was more than just air; Mercy was filled with a strength and confidence Esau had never witnessed in her before.

"Esau, please listen to me," she said softly, firmly. "I love you. I always will. But I don't love you the way you would like me to. You're family. You're my husband's brother, and I love you with that kind of family love."

"Mercy, Jacob is dead!"

"Until I receive some kind of official notice to that effect, I must continue to believe that Jacob is alive. He is my husband—I can do no less. As for you and me, we will never be any more than we are now—related by family."

"I can't accept that," Esau shouted. "I understand your need to be sure Jacob is really dead. I'm willing to wait for that notification. But I cannot, I will not believe that you no longer love me."

Mercy rose calmly from the bench. She stood tall, her hands

clasped comfortably in front. It was a posture with which Esau was familiar. Standing that way in the garden twilight, Mercy reminded him of his mother. Her voice was clear as she spoke. "You don't understand," she said. "Whether or not Jacob is alive is not the issue. God has made it clear to me that I have been wrong to allow you to think there can be anything between us. Even if Jacob is dead, I could not marry you. God will not let me. It is not a matter of availability; it is a matter of obedience to God."

Mercy thanked Esau politely for walking her home, said goodnight, and went into the house.

Reluctantly, Esau conceded that Mercy was right about one thing—the world was changing. From what he saw, it was going from bad to worse and nothing was able to stop it.

Formal charges were brought against Arnold for his actions as military governor of Philadelphia. To Esau's chagrin, once again radical elements, with their relentless litany of hate, were destroying something good. This time, they would not be satisfied until a good man, a revolutionary hero, was destroyed.

Arnold appealed for a quick trial and judgment so that the matter could be laid to rest. Each time a court-martial was convened to address the charges, it was dismissed for more pressing wartime matters. Month after month passed with the cloud of impropriety overshadowing everything Arnold attempted to do. Meanwhile, his critics grew even more vocal with their dissatisfaction.

He requested reassignment. Since he could still not ride a horse, he proposed a joint naval expedition with the French to seize key ports in Bermuda and Barbados. Although Washington and Congress expressed interest, nothing came of it. Discouraged, he then considered leaving the military. Several friends in the New York legislature had proposed that the state give Arnold one of two confiscated loyalist manors for his services in defense of their state during the Canadian campaigns. Arnold expressed interest.

He prepared to travel to New York to meet with the delegation and look over the land. The thought of founding a new settlement on the New York frontier appealed to him.

Hours after he crossed the Delaware River, the Philadelphia radical Whigs, outraged that Arnold might escape their formal charges, rushed to print eight charges against him to be read and distributed publicly. To put teeth to their charges, they proclaimed that until Arnold was removed from office by court-martial, they would no longer pay any of the army's costs and would call out the local militia only in the most urgent and pressing necessity. Furthermore, they announced that the militia would no longer do Arnold's staff's bidding.

The uproar that ensued was so great, Arnold was forced to return not only to defend himself, but also to maintain order. Again, he pressed Washington for a quick trial or a dismissal of the charges, since the unanswered charges were ruining his reputation.

When the radical Whigs got wind of Arnold's agony over the delay, they proceeded to extend his suffering. Because they mistrusted a military tribunal judging one of their own in the first place, they wrote a threatening letter to Washington stating that unless the army judged Arnold's misuse of wagons a serious offense, the state would never again use its wagons to transport Washington's army. They knew that Washington was preparing a major offense that would depend upon their Conestoga wagons. Then they demanded an indefinite postponement of the trial while they gathered evidence and witnesses.

Washington bowed to their pressure and postponed the trial indefinitely, leaving Arnold shaken.

※

"The governor would like to speak to you."

An aide verbally passed the message to Esau without stopping at his desk. Laying down his quill, Esau rubbed his eyes. It was only midmorning and already he was tired. He attributed his early fatigue to the depressing atmosphere that permeated the Penn mansion. Benedict Arnold's surly mood was contagious, and it was transmitted freely to the staff. Esau mentally braced himself for more of the same as he entered Arnold's room.

The military governor sat behind a small desk, his hands clasped contentedly over his midsection. He wore a grin that could only be described as silly, a mouth formation Esau had never seen on him before.

"Have a seat, Esau." Arnold gestured to a wooden chair. "When I first met you, as you already know, I didn't like you," he said with a smile. "In the Maine wilderness, when I learned you had been correct about the maps, I respected you, but still didn't like you. I just couldn't shake that first impression I had about you being a loyalist. Then, in Quebec, in the hospital, when we talked, and you told me about Mercy and your brother and your family, I warmed to you. Then again in Saratoga, and when I first saw Mercy at the French birthday ball, I began to understand you and even admire you."

He sat forward in his chair, his hands clasped on his desk.

"And now, for what you have done for me—I can't find the words to thank you."

Esau beamed. "Judge Shippen has given his consent!"

Arnold nodded.

"Congratulations, sir!"

During the winter months, Mercy and Esau played match-makers with Peggy Shippen and Benedict Arnold. Mercy and Peggy had become close, Mercy acting as her big sister and adviser in matters of courting. Although Judge Shippen's father expressed reservations over a number of things laid to the charge of General Arnold, the judge gave in to his daughter's threats of becoming ill should the indecision in the household be continued.

Esau served as an envoy between the ladies and his superior. It was painful for him—watching two people fall in love while the person he loved most dearly was so close, yet still out of reach. Following the episode in the garden, Mercy maintained a proper distance from him, never letting him proceed beyond the bounds of proper affections between relations. For the time being, Esau assented to the restrictions. At least Mercy was near; having her in Philadelphia was better than her being in Boston. However, Esau had not abandoned all initiative. At his fervent request, Major General Arnold had written to Washington's staff to confirm Jacob's status once for all. Esau eagerly awaited the report.

"When is the wedding?" Esau asked Arnold.

"April. Judge Shippen's loyalist leanings and my current controversy prevent us from having a proper wedding, the kind of wedding Peggy deserves. Instead, it will be a private affair with a few family members and close friends. Peggy and I want you and Mercy to be there."

"It will be my pleasure to attend." Esau's expressed sentiment was genuine. The pressures of the office and the constant barrage of criticism by Arnold's enemies had exacted a toll on the general. It had soured Esau as well. If this was an indication of the kind of justice and order the colonies preferred over the established order of society England provided them, he wanted nothing to do with it. The storm of Arnold's controversy had given new life to Esau's dream of a future in England. He had no desire to remain in a land where a minority band of rabble-rousers could manipulate the Congress, the army, and influential leaders to their narrow-minded end.

※

On April 8, 1779, Major General Arnold's carriage rode down Fourth Street, stopping outside the Shippen house. Esau rode with him, assisting the still-limping general from the carriage and up the house steps. Arnold wore the blue uniform as befitting his rank. His sister Hannah and his sons were also in attendance, as was one other aide, Major Clarkson. Throughout the brief ceremony, Arnold leaned on Clarkson's arm, still unable to stand for any length of time on his left leg.

The bride was beyond beautiful. Her initial presence so stunned the general, it brought tears to the veteran soldier's eyes. During the ceremony, Mercy stood beside Esau, her arm linked in his. He took it as an unspoken admission that in her heart she knew that someday they, too, would stand before a minister and get married.

For three days following the wedding, General and Mrs. Arnold greeted scores of guests at the Shippen home. Then they traveled the short mile to Penn mansion where they set up house-keeping.

※

Esau walked briskly from Penn mansion to the Reeds' house. He wasn't sure how much time he had left. Winter was over and so was the Arnold's wedding. Although she hadn't set a date, Esau knew that Mercy would soon be making plans to return to Boston, and he didn't want to waste a single opportunity to be with her. He'd hoped that the status of Jacob would have been resolved before she returned to Boston, but records and documents moved at a snail's pace in the Continental Army, and there still was no word.

He turned onto the Reeds' street, and their house came into view. His heart accelerated slightly, like it always did whenever he anticipated a meeting with Mercy. *What kind of power did that woman have over him to affect him this way after so many years?*

From the other end of the street, a horse appeared bearing two riders, the one behind shorter than the one holding the reins.

Esau stopped stone still. The horse continued to the Reeds' house, then halted. The mirror image of Esau Morgan dismounted followed by a young boy.

"Jacob!"

Mercy's hysterical scream came from the house. The front door banged open as she flew down the stairs and walkway and into the arms of her husband.

"O Jacob! Jacob! You're alive, thank God, you're alive!"

Mercy was swallowed up in Jacob's arms as they embraced and kissed and cried together. The boy stood nearby, happily watching the reunion.

"And Bo! You've grown, haven't you? You're a young man now!"

Mercy broke away from her husband and smothered the boy in a hug that embarrassed him. Then she returned to Jacob's arms.

"Thank you, God," she said over and over. "I never want to let you go. Never. Never."

With Mercy sandwiched between them, the trio disappeared into the Reeds' house.

Esau didn't move. There was no telling how long he stood there, without moving, barely breathing, reliving over and over the scene that had just been played out before him.

Hugs for Jacob. Hugs for the boy.

But no hugs for Esau.

Never ... never.

It was over. Mercy was forever lost to him.

He felt cold, empty, inanimate, like a stone. And like a stone he stood there, feeling nothing. Nothing at all.

18

Benedict Arnold's first contact with the British was through his wife's former suitor, Major John Andre. Peggy Shippen Arnold had managed to keep in contact with the British officer since the days of the occupation. Had the British remained in Philadelphia, Peggy might well have become Mrs. John Andre instead of Mrs. Benedict Arnold.

A pleasant, good-natured, and talented young man, Andre was not your typical army major. He wrote poetry, sketched, and played a major part in Philadelphia's social scene during the occupation, including hand printing party invitations and personally designing the gowns and hairdos the ladies wore. When the British pulled out, many Philadelphians—including Peggy Shippen—were sad to see him go.

When there was no letup in the attacks against her husband following their wedding, Peggy wrote to her friend Andre, who had been promoted to the position of chief of the British secret service. She expressed her husband's dissatisfaction with the baseness and ingratitude of the American people. Andre sensed an espionage coup in the making. With General Clinton's approval, he immediately took the initiative to establish negotiations with General Benedict Arnold through his wife, Peggy.

After initial contact was established, Arnold insisted negotiations continue without further involving his wife. Andre suggested a courier, but Arnold wanted someone he knew he could trust, someone who was as disenchanted as himself, someone who would be willing to cross over to the English side, paving the way for him and Peggy. He thought of his aide, Esau Morgan.

"John Anderson?"

"Drew Matthews?"

The two men approached each other cautiously. They were both on foot, holding the reins of their horses in one hand. Clouds blocked the moon's light, making the forest dark and dangerous. A torrential rain poured down on top of them with such force they had to shout to communicate.

Esau glanced nervously behind the man calling himself John Anderson. He couldn't see far, but it looked like the operative had come alone. Anderson, likewise, scanned the terrain behind Esau. The two men used code names to identify themselves. Esau chose the name Drew Matthews. Drew was the first Morgan to come to America; Matthews was Drew's wife's maiden name. John Anderson was none other than John Andre of the British secret service. They met beside the creek at Pine's Bridge, east of the Hudson River.

"You brought the letter?" Andre shouted.

Esau responded by reaching into a pouch.

Before he could produce the letter, the thunder of horses' hoofs and wagon wheels could be heard on the road. Each man looked at the other in horror, thinking that the other had betrayed him. Esau shook his head. They weren't his men. Andre responded in similar fashion.

"Under the bridge! Quickly!" Andre shouted.

There was a generous portion of exposed bank under the bridge on both sides of the river. Andre and Esau hunkered down under the wooden bridge, their horses side by side, standing in the stream, but also under the bridge. The pounding of hoofs against wooden planks was deafening. Twenty or thirty horses and half a dozen wagons must have crossed before the sound mercifully stopped. Between the darkness and the rain and the limited visibility from their sheltered position, they never did know whether the soldiers crossing over them were American or British.

Shoulder to shoulder, their faces a matter of inches from each other, Andre turned to Esau and said, "I'm certain we can do better than this. On my way here, I saw a barn about a quarter mile up the road. The house next to it was burned to the ground. The barn looked deserted. We could get out of this rain and build a fire."

The thought of it being a trap crossed Esau's mind; he was new to espionage, and he suspected everything. But he was soaked to the bone and figured if Andre had wanted to trap him, he could have already done it. So with a nod, he followed Major John Andre to shelter.

A fire crackled happily between them. Esau's eyes burned and watered from a combination of the bright light against the dark reaches of the barn and the smoke from the wet wood. Layers of clothing littered the ground around them, drying out. Esau found the man sitting across from him as likable and entertaining as Peggy Arnold described him. He was a small man in his late twenties with hair that hung in curls near his ears, dark eyebrows, a thick nose, and small, boyish lips. At the moment, they were reminiscing about prior Philadelphia festivities, and Andre was describing the Mischianza, a full day and night celebration organized as a farewell party for General Howe. It was the most lavish entertainment Philadelphia had ever known.

"It began with a water pageant." Andre used his hands and arms freely as he talked. "Officers and their ladies rowed upriver in decorated barges, with bands playing and flags waving. They disembarked at the Walnut Grove where we had reconstructed a jousting field. With all the splendor of medieval times, we had seven Knights of the Blended Rose do battle with seven Knights of the Burning Mountain. It was a bloodless battle, of course, all in fun. Elegant ladies dressed in Turkish costumes were everywhere!"

Esau couldn't help but be amused at Andre who was getting carried away in his retelling of the festive event.

"Following the joust there were dancing and gambling and eating and drinking. The bars were decorated in modern elegance, the gambling room was in the style of ancient Egypt. The evening banquet was exquisite—four hundred thirty guests! After which there was more dancing and drinking and gambling. All of it crowned with the final event at four o'clock in the morning—fireworks!" Andre's arms simulated a multitude of explosions above his head. "That, my dear Master Morgan, is the way life is meant to be lived—fun, carefree, exciting. Unlike ..." he reached down and picked up his soggy uniform jacket, "this dreary battle activity."

Esau chuckled. "You sound very much like someone else I know. She is most at home at parties."

"You're speaking of Mercy?"

The startled look on Esau's face prompted John Andre to explain.

"Peggy told me about her; she thinks Mercy is the greatest woman alive. She also told me about you and Mercy ... not much,

I don't think she knows much … just that you would like your relationship to be more than it is."

There was an openness about John Andre that made Esau feel at ease, enough at ease to tell him briefly of his history with Mercy Reed Morgan. It seemed an insignificant revelation when compared to the fact that he was meeting secretly with a British agent.

"I had someone like Mercy in my life," Andre said. His face sobered and his voice took on a serious, reflective tone. "Her name was Honora. Absolutely no brains, but what she lacked intellectually, she made up a thousand times over in beauty. How I pined over her! I wrote her love letters that were pages long, sonnets with caricatures in the margins! I even had an advocate in her sister, Anna, who was just the opposite of Honora, brains but no looks at all. Anna and I used to exchange letters devising ways I could capture the heart of Honora. But the beautiful Honora was attracted only to the one thing I did not have— wealth. Nor did I have prospects for it. And when I spoke of bolting from my dreary desk-merchant position …"

"You worked for a merchant?" Esau interrupted him.

"My father was a merchant. I balanced his ledgers."

"Mine too!" Esau replied.

"I hated it!" Andre said. "I used to draw pictures in the margins of the ledgers. It used to infuriate my father."

"Well, that's one way in which we're different. I enjoy ledgers and records."

Andre shuddered. "You can have them. The arts interest me— poetry, drama and theater, art. But they don't pay well, so Honora jilted me. So I turned to military service. For me, it was better than bills and accounts, debits and credits."

"Peggy showed me some of your sketches of her. You're quite good."

Andre shrugged off the compliment. "Adequate maybe, not exceptional."

"Oh, before I forget …" Esau reached for the pouch carrying the letter from Arnold.

Upon receiving the letter, Andre unfolded the pages.

"It's in code," Esau said.

"A sensible precaution."

Andre refolded the pages, then slapped an open palm with them.

"Your general is quite insistent that he be compensated adequately for his defection," Andre said.

Esau understood the comment to be in regards to previous correspondence. "He is a man of wealth," Esau responded, "all of which he will forfeit by going over to the British side."

"Temporarily lost, at best," Andre said. "Once the rebellion is crushed, he will have all of it returned to him. His insistence of huge quantities of money up front suggests he doesn't think the British can defeat the colonials."

"I've known Arnold for many years now. He's aggressive. That's what makes him a good general. He'll press for everything he can get now and reevaluate his strategy as needed."

"An accurate assessment," Andre said, smiling. "And what about you, Esau? What do you want?"

"I'm not in the position to ask for anything. I'm not a person of consequence in this war, nor can I deliver anything worthwhile to assist the king's efforts."

Andre placed Arnold's letter in a leather bag. "We have dealt with other men who have a lot less to offer," he said, "yet they don't hesitate to ask for things in return for their loyalty to the king. What does Esau Morgan want in exchange for his loyalty to King George?"

"My loyalty is not for sale," Esau said. "I give it of my own free will."

He still hadn't answered the question. Andre waited for him to do so.

"All I have ever wanted is a land where I can live in freedom and peace, where I can earn enough money to live decently, raise a family, and enjoy life. When I went to England for school, I thought my dream was only a couple of years away. Upon my return I was to marry Mercy Reed, become the accountant for the family business, and raise a family of loyal English subjects in thriving Boston colony. My dream died a stillborn death. My hope is that by going back to England I can start again, dream a new dream, even though I'm getting on in years."

"You have the soul of a poet, Esau Morgan. We're alike in that way, you and I. Unhappily, people like us rarely find what we're looking for. Sometimes I wish I were more like your General Arnold. He grabs for everything he can get and doesn't waste his time dreaming of what might be. When this war is over, men like him will own everything, while you and I will have nothing, except our dreams."

※

Benedict Arnold was finally brought to trial for the charges leveled against him by the radical Whigs of Philadelphia. He refuted every charge in speeches of inordinate length, his voice often shaking with fury and indignation. On three of the five remaining charges he was acquitted; on a fourth it was determined he could have acted more prudently; and on the fifth—the most minor charge—he was judged guilty, but without criminal intent. He was sentenced to receive a reprimand from his commander-in-chief. In his letter of reprimand, General Washington tempered it with praise for Arnold's previous service.

But Arnold was in no mood for reconciliation. His good name had been tarnished. The reprimand was proof enough that soldiers were helpless against the villainies of politicians. More than ever he was determined to advance through promotion, if not in the American army, then in the British. While continuing to negotiate with John Andre of the British secret service, he also sought advancement to active duty as an American general.

Following the winter of 1779 and into the spring of 1780 there was a general sense of melancholy among the American troops. In many cases it manifested itself in rudeness to officers, vocal discontent, and, in some cases, mutiny.

"What's wrong, Esau? You're unusually quiet tonight."

The youthful Peggy Arnold had placed her fork on her plate and folded her hands in her lap, giving the Arnolds' sole dinner guest her complete attention. A slight bulge appeared as her hands flattened her dress against her midsection. Peggy was with child.

Esau glanced up from his plate to respond. For an instant his mouth hung open; the words he intended to utter never left his mouth, halted in their tracks by the stunning beauty of Peggy Shippen Arnold. In that instant he looked up, he saw, not a young Mrs. Arnold, but a young Mercy Reed. Her captivating eyes. Fresh pale complexion. Delicate mouth. All these reminded him of Mercy.

"Um … uh," he closed his mouth and lowered his eyes to his plate. "Excuse me, I just thought of something else midsentence. It distracted me. Forgive me. Um … no, nothing's wrong. I'm all right. Maybe a little tired from last night's ride, that's all."

"Andre gave you a response?" General Arnold asked the question, then forked a piece of turkey into his mouth, chewing vigorously while he awaited an answer.

"Yes, sir. It's in my coat pocket."

Arnold nodded and forked in another bite.

"How is John Andre?" Peggy said. "Oh, how I wish I could see him again. Does he ever say he thinks of me?"

Esau shot a quick glance at the general. A scowl indicated he was not pleased with Peggy's inquiry regarding a former suitor. "Major Andre has fond memories of his time in Philadelphia." It was a diplomatic response, one that he hoped would satisfy Mrs. Arnold without offending the general.

"Did Andre tell you ..."

The general interrupted his wife. Still giving attention to his plate, he said, "Summarize their position. Are they willing to give me what I want?"

Negotiations between Arnold and the British had come down to one compound question—how much money did the general want to defect, what could he deliver for that amount, and was it worth it? Esau had always known there was a mercenary side to Benedict Arnold, but he seldom had to deal directly with him on money matters. The general's military leadership abilities were inspiring, as was his undying determination to succeed. In Esau's mind, these were the qualities that made him a great man. To listen to the man haggle over money and complain that no one appreciated his true worth made him smaller, almost petty.

"The British think you're asking too much and delivering too little."

"Did you tell Andre I can give them West Point?"

"I did."

"And what did he say?"

"He said you can't give something you don't have."

General Arnold threw his napkin on the table and rose from his seat. "I'll get it. You just watch me. After all I've done for this country, Washington owes me something. He'll give me West Point."

"Yes, sir."

Esau hoped Arnold would be content to let the matter drop

there, but apparently his sullen facial expression bothered the general.

"You disagree with that decision?"

General Arnold stood at the head of the table, his hands on his hips. Peggy joined her husband in staring at Esau, with a genuine look of interest in his response.

"No, sir," Esau said. "If I have learned anything over the years of our association, it is to trust your tactical strategies."

Apparently, he was still not convincing. Arnold pulled out a side chair from the table and sat close to Esau.

"You have been a trusted aide for me, Esau. More than that, you have helped me through two painful convalescences, and you were instrumental during my courtship with Peggy. Now you are risking your life going back and forth across the lines in my correspondence with Andre. If something is bothering you, I want to hear it."

Esau slowly took his napkin from his lap and placed it next to his plate. As he did, he searched for the right words to say that would adequately express how he felt without at the same time indicting his dinner host and superior officer and friend. "For me," he said, "the decision to go over to the British side was a long time in coming. That's where my loyalties lie; they always have. The only reason I joined the Continental Army was that I was convinced a show of force would bring Parliament to the bargaining table. I fully expected that the resulting dialogue would create an American parliament in which we would be self-governing, yet maintain our world ties with England." With a chuckle, he added, "I'm not much of a political prognosticator, am I?"

"No one could have foreseen the direction we've taken as a country," Arnold replied.

"All I have ever wanted is to be a good Englishman, to live quietly in some little town with a wife who loves me, to raise children, to dabble in the arts and social life—in short, to enjoy the security and fruit of the English empire." His voice softened, almost to a whisper. "I always thought that picture included Mercy. I guess I was wrong about that too."

Peggy spoke up. "I think it's a lovely picture, Esau. And I'm sure you'll find a good woman who will love you the way you deserve to be loved."

She meant well, but Esau found no comfort in her words. "Anyway," he continued, "I don't see that there is a life for me in America. My future is in England. I simply want to cross over. I don't want to hurt anybody in the process."

"And you think that's what I'm doing by offering to deliver West Point to the British—hurting people?"

"That's your decision, sir. I couldn't do it."

To Esau's surprise, Arnold didn't get angry at his candid response. The general clasped his hands together and leaned forward, resting his elbows on his knees.

"As far as military armament and manpower, West Point has little significance," he said. "However, strategically, it is the key to the Hudson River and that whole territory, especially when you take into account Washington's proposed plans. Turning over West Point to the British will do two things. First, it will swing geographical advantage to favor the British; and second, when word is spread that I have sided with the British, many—I daresay tens of thousands of men and women who are tired and discouraged by this whole war—will be persuaded to raise their voices and stop all this nonsense. Then, we can lick our wounds and turn to the serious business of repairing broken ties with our fellow Englishmen again. And those of us who had a part in securing the unity of our nation will be revered and rewarded. In short, Esau, I do this not to hurt people, but to bring about a speedy end to this war so our people can heal."

"I only pray that it will come about quickly, sir."

"As do I," said Arnold.

In his explanation Esau noticed the general refrained from mentioning anything about the money he was demanding from the British. He chose to let the omission pass without comment.

"Events are turning to our favor," Andre said.

"So it would seem," Esau responded.

The two men sat comfortably in the New York woods, their backs against trees. The sun had gone down, and the coolness of the trees was finally gaining a victory over the hot summer air. Patches of sky that peeked through the foliage above them were beginning to turn dark.

"The surrender of Charleston in May was significant," Andre commented. "With Cornwallis now in charge of southern operations, we'll see some more victories. What's the status of Washington's troops?"

"They're discouraged. Another mutiny last May."

Andre nodded solemnly. "And General Arnold? I suppose he wants more money."

"It's in his letter. His price has doubled to twenty thousand pounds."

Andre whistled when he heard the sum.

"Do you think Clinton will pay it?" Esau asked.

"He wants West Point. He'll meet Arnold's price."

Esau shook his head. "That's a lot of money."

John Andre sat forward, embracing his knee with his arms. "This means your part in these negotiations is coming to an end. When are you going to come over?"

Esau shrugged. "Soon."

"Why not tonight? I could put you up in my house until you get a place of your own. I'd enjoy being able to talk to you in places other than under bridges during rainstorms, in old abandoned barns, or so deep in the wilderness even the squirrels could get lost."

Esau smiled. The offer was tempting. He'd found a friend in John Andre. "I'd like to, but I can't," he said. "There's still something I have to do."

"Something I need to know about?"

Esau shook his head. "It's personal. Before I can come over for good, I have to go back to Boston one more time."

Beacon Street was free of traffic as Esau rode quietly toward the Morgan family's Boston home. It was a warm, late summer evening in New England. The street lamps were already lit, their round glow illuminating the cobblestone street, the orderly trees interspersed between the lamps, and the steep walkways that led to well-lit, fashionable houses. The Maine expedition, not to mention his recent frequent forest treks, had given Esau a greater appreciation of civilization, be it Boston or Philadelphia. But of all the streets of all the civilized nations in the world, this one held a special place in his heart. This was home.

He rode to within sight of the house where he was born and raised, then pulled his horse to a stop. Staying under the shadow of a large tree, he gazed at the house for nearly a quarter of an hour, allowing memories and emotions to wash over him. The house itself was bathed in the white light of a full moon. Sitting atop a hill, overlooking sparkling Boston Bay, it had become a symbol of the Morgan family history in New England—prominent, solid, financially and socially secure. A brief sigh escaped Esau's lips as he directed his horse back down the street in the same direction from which he'd just come. He wasn't leaving yet, but for what he was about to do, he wouldn't be using the front door.

Esau clung to the shadows of the hedges behind the Morgan house. Half of the walkway and one side of the hedges were ablaze with the moon's white light, making the opposite side black by contrast. Esau was counting on the blackness to conceal him from straying eyes that might appear unexpectedly in the windows of the house. As he worked his way through the maze of hedges, he noticed his mother's room was dark. Mercy's room was lit. He waited, hoping to catch a glimpse of her. His wait went unrewarded. After several wasted minutes, he proceeded.

Moving from shadow to shadow, he worked his way toward the side of the house, the side with Mercy's bedroom window. He had to race across a moonlit grassy area several yards wide to get from the hedge to the house itself. He was immediately below Mercy's upstairs window. The stone walls were still warm from baking in the summer sun. Farther down the side of the house, a light spilled out a window and onto the grass. The parlor. It was the window nearest his mother's reading chair, the chair she was sitting in the day she caught him running from Mercy's room. Esau inched his way toward the front of the house.

He froze. The clop-clop-clop of a carriage echoed down Beacon Street. Esau crouched low, still against the side of the house. From the house's elevated vantage point, even in a crouching position, all he saw was the hat of the driver and the top of the carriage as it moved unhurriedly down the street. He waited until the carriage was well past the house before he continued.

The parlor window stretched open wide. Tiptoeing near it, he listened for sounds coming from inside. He heard none. Maybe the room was empty, maybe not. It was best not to assume anything. Getting down on all fours, Esau crawled under the window, making every effort to be as quiet as he could. As he passed under the window, he thought he heard a sigh and the rustle of a page, but he wasn't sure. Once past the window, he stood again and completed his journey to the front of the house. At this end of the parlor large, multipaned, arching windows overlooked Boston Bay, affording a breathtaking view from inside. These high-arching windows couldn't be opened and the curtains were rarely pulled. This would be his portal to the room. Unless someone was deliberately staring out the window at the bay, he should be able to get a glimpse inside without being seen himself. He crouched low and edged his way past the curtains. He poked his head around them, ready to pull back suddenly should anybody be looking in his direction.

Anne Morgan was sitting in her usual chair beside the window under which Esau had just crawled. Her back was partially turned toward him as she bent over her open Bible resting on the table in front of her. A finger pointed to her place as she read. Even with the limited light, Esau could see that his mother had aged since he saw her last. There was more gray in her hair, and she bent closer to the Bible as she read. Being this close to his mother, spying on her, sent a chill through him. *Yet how many times had he seen her in this same position? How many times, as a young lad, had he interrupted his mother's Bible reading with a question or request or a complaint about Jacob?* It seemed fitting that this was how he would see his mother tonight, since it could possibly be the last time he would ever see her.

A rush of emotion urged him to march into the room and tell his mother good-bye properly. He fought it with reasoning. This way was best. He'd gone over it a hundred times. His mother wouldn't understand what he had to do. She would try to talk him out of it. It was better this way. Someday, maybe, he could make her understand, make them all understand. But not tonight.

"I went to your room looking for you, but you weren't there. I should have known you'd be down here reading your Bible." Mercy entered the parlor and walked straight to Anne.

The sight of Mercy sent another surge of emotion over Esau, this one of tidal-wave proportions. He gritted his teeth against its onslaught. *Would he ever be able to look at this woman and not feel this way?* He ached inside with a love that could never be requited.

The two women chatted briefly. Esau could hear every word. "They're almost ready," Mercy said. Then she asked Anne to remind her to take some blankets to Mrs. Wickersham who would see that they were delivered to the Massachusetts militia. "Mrs. Wickersham thinks that if we start collecting them now, the troops will have them by winter. You know how army supply is."

Another figure entered the room—taller, male.

"I think that does it, ladies. I'm packed."

Jacob!

Esau's brother strode self-assuredly through the doorway into the parlor and went straight to Mercy, putting his arm around her waist. She raised her head and kissed him on the chin. A chestnut-haired boy straggled into the room behind him, the same boy Esau saw with him in front of the Reeds' house in Philadelphia.

What was Jacob doing here? With his brother's unexpected entrance, all of Esau's emotions of love instantly vanished, dissipated by a storehouse of anger and hatred and envy.

Anne rose from her chair and raised her arms for a hug. Jacob stepped into them and warmly embraced his mother. "Be sure to thank General Washington for me. It was thoughtful of him to allow you to come home for a few days."

Jacob smiled down at her. "He said it was the least the army could do considering the suffering they'd put you through for letting you believe for so long I'd been killed."

Anne insisted on a second hug. "I just thank God you're all right."

While they hugged a second time, Esau glanced at Mercy. She stood nearby with tears in her eyes as she watched mother and son. The boy ... *the boy was looking straight at Esau!*

Esau jerked his head back. His heart pounded uncontrollably. *Had the boy actually seen him? Or was he just looking out the window?*

"Jabe? Jabe?"

Esau could hear the sound of the boy's voice coming from inside. Frantically, Esau looked for a place to hide. He dove down the grassy embankment that fell away from the house and down to the street. He rolled across the grass to the base of a towering hedge that separated the Morgan property from their neighbors. He rolled and rolled until he hit the trunks of the hedges. Outstretched leafy limbs barely covered him. He positioned himself on his belly. From his hiding place, he could barely see over the grassy ridge. Jacob and the boy were standing at the parlor window looking out. Jacob shielded his eyes from the light in the room, pressing his face against the glass.

"No one's out there, Bo," he said. Jacob turned back into the room. "Probably just a reflection."

While Jacob walked away, the boy continued to peer outside. Esau pressed himself as far under the hedge as he could.

Just then, the clop-clop-clop sound of another carriage came up the street. It stopped in front of the Morgan house, and the driver bounded up the steps two at a time to the front door. A moment later Jacob, Mercy, Anne, and the boy emerged from the house, following the driver down the steps toward the carriage. The driver carried a small trunk. Jacob walked between Mercy and Anne, holding their hands, and the boy trailed, still scanning the front of the house.

At the carriage, the three Morgan adults turned to one another to say their good-byes. The driver loaded the trunk, then took his place in the driver's seat. The boy gave up his search and hopped into the carriage.

No better time than this, Esau said to himself.

While Jacob explained to the women that the carriage would take him as far as Roxbury where he and the boy would pick up a horse for the remainder of their journey, Esau crawled out from under the hedge and, staying low, made his way back up the slope. Once clear from their line of sight, he ran down the side of the house and let himself in the back door.

The hallway was dark. With his hands extended in front of him, Esau felt his way through the house. His boots clomped softly on the wooden floors. Most of the rooms in the house were completely dark. Rounding a corner, he could see the light coming from the parlor. When he reached his father's study, he quickly went inside. Feeling a little safer behind the closed door, he waited for a few moments until his eyes adjusted to the dark.

The room was just as he remembered it. The Chinese emperor above the fireplace mantel watched silently as Esau crossed the room to get what he came for. Laying open on a small round table was the Morgan family Bible. He laid his hand upon it reverently. It was without doubt the most treasured heirloom of the Morgan family, the symbol of their Christian faith. Esau Morgan's plan was to take it with him back to England where he felt it now belonged; from the beginning, it had been an Englishman's Bible, and he was going to make sure it would always remain an Englishman's Bible. Esau closed the book, lifted it from the table like it was the Ten Commandments themselves, and pressed it to his chest.

At the door of the study he heard female voices inside the house. He pressed his ear against the study door; it was not sufficient for him to make out what they were saying, so he cracked the door ever so slightly, hoping it didn't creak. He was fortunate. It made not a sound.

Mercy asked if Anne was coming directly upstairs. Anne said she would be up shortly; she wanted to read a while longer. Presently, Esau heard footsteps on the stairs, then all was quiet again.

He waited several moments, then pulled open the study door. It creaked. He stopped and listened. No response. No one was coming. This time he pulled up on the latch in an attempt to relieve the old hinges from the weight of the door. It worked. The door swung open noiselessly. A moment later, he was in the hallway. A few quick steps and he could be out the back door and on his way, his mission a success. But he couldn't resist the urge to take one last look at his mother.

With painstaking care, he tiptoed to the parlor doorway. Anne Morgan was on her knees, her elbows resting on the chair in which she had previously been sitting, her dress arranged neatly around her on the floor. She was praying.

His first impulse was not to intrude on his mother's private communion with God. Yet as she prayed softly, but aloud, he stayed and listened.

Anne Morgan prayed for a safe journey for Jacob and Bo; then she asked God to watch over them and be their shield in battle. Next, she prayed for Mercy, "Jacob's faithful wife and my dear sister in the Lord," that she would continue to be strong in her faith and that God would reward her and Jacob with children. Then she prayed for Esau.

"Lord, how I long to see him," she prayed, "to throw my arms around him and hold him close like I was able to do with Jacob tonight. Dear Lord, keep him safe by the power of Your mighty hand and bring him home to me. And please, Lord, fulfill his life by sending him a Christian woman who will love him. He's been alone so long and he has such a great capacity to love. Send him someone to love, someone who will love him in return. O Lord, give him Your wisdom and patience during this time of crisis."

While Anne continued praying, now for her husband in France, Esau Morgan moved quietly away from the door. Heading quickly down the hall, he stepped into the garden and out the back to his waiting horse. Gripping the Morgan family Bible tightly under his arm, he rode quickly down Beacon Street. He tried not to think what his mother and father's reaction would be when they learned that their son had defected to the British and when they discovered that the family Bible was missing.

19

Following the American victory at Saratoga, the fortunes of the American diplomats in France improved considerably. While the French sent an official ambassador to Congress, Congress gave its senior diplomat, Franklin, the title of minister plenipotentiary, fully authorizing him to transact business on behalf of the United States of America.

Several diplomatic milestones had already been passed, most notably an official audience with Louis XVI, king of France, and the treaty of alliance between the French and American nations. According to the provisions of the treaty both nations pledged themselves to fight until American independence was assured; both nations agreed that neither of them would conclude a truce or peace with Great Britain without the formal consent of the other; and both promised to protect each other's possessions in America from the present time and forever against all powers.

"Virtually the whole world is on our side." Franklin gestured emphatically from the couch in his suite in Passy. His foot was elevated to ease the pain of his gout. His audience at the moment consisted of a single person. "The fall of Charleston is merely a temporary setback," Franklin insisted.

Jared sat straight backed in a chair opposite him. It was late at night and he had brought America's minister plenipotentiary home early from a party at the Brillon's house. A flare-up in Franklin's foot cut the evening short, at least shorter than usual. During the carriage ride home and into the house, Franklin had continued expounding the argument he'd begun in the Brillon's parlor, the argument being that American independence was assured if the United States and her allies would hold their course and remain patient.

"Look at the declared belligerents lined up against England...." He counted them off on his fingers. "The United States, France, Spain, and Holland. Now then, add to that the members of the Armed Neutrality Treaty: Russia, Denmark-Norway, Sweden, the Holy Roman Empire, Prussia, Portugal, and the two Sicilies. Virtually the entire trading world is lined up against Great Britain!"

"You're preaching to a convert," Jared replied with a grin.

Franklin threw back his head and laughed. "Well, it's such a convincing argument, I just wanted to hear myself say it out loud."

"Madame Brillon did seem to be making too much of the British victory at Charleston."

"My point exactly!" Franklin boomed.

Jared rose. "Well, if you'll excuse me, sir, I'll be turning in."

"Sit ... sit." Franklin motioned him back into his chair. "Keep me company for a while longer. I fear this blasted foot is going to keep me awake most of the night."

Jared was tired and wanted to get to bed, but he dutifully sat back down. For a moment or two, a topic of conversation eluded them. The two men stared vacantly in different directions.

"Received a letter from the Netherlands today," Franklin said after a bit. "John Adams has settled in there. Estimates it will take a year or two to negotiate a commercial treaty with them. But it will be worth it, if he can do it. The Dutch are the bankers of Europe, you know."

"So I've heard."

Another long silence. Franklin chuckled. "Adams described his situation by saying he was a man in the midst of the ocean negotiating for his life among a school of sharks."

Jared laughed with him. Then the room fell quiet again.

"Have you heard from Anne recently?" Franklin asked.

"Three letters came about a month ago."

"How are things in Boston?"

"Anne says there is no end to the shortages, but she and Mercy are surviving."

"And the boys?"

"Last she heard, Jacob's men helped put down a mutiny in Washington's camp."

"At Morristown."

Jared nodded.

"And Esau?"

"According to Anne, there's talk of General Arnold being appointed commander at West Point. If that comes through, I imagine Esau will go with him. The two of them have been close since the Canada campaign."

Franklin rubbed his eyes. A good sign. He was getting tired. "The Morgans have certainly distinguished themselves in this noble effort," he said.

"The boys have. I'm proud of both of them."

"And they should be proud of their father! You've done a good work here, Jared."

"Maybe so. Being so far removed from the actual events,

sometimes it's hard for me to believe the things we hear about are really happening."

"Don't belittle the money you've helped raise for the war effort. We both know that Madame LaFontaine has contributed an incredible amount of money to our cause, and she's done it because of you."

Jared shook his head. "Thank you for the kind words, but I can't see that I've done anything. Sitting around and chatting over tea, attending parties, smiling, bowing … that's not fighting for liberty. For me, heading a ship into a line of British cannons—that's battle. It's hard to compare an afternoon tea with that kind of action."

Franklin grinned mischievously. "Sometimes, my dear friend, being in the company of a beautiful lady and controlling yourself is a far greater battle than ever was fought with guns and ships. Think of it as hazardous duty of a different sort."

"It's clear I'll never win a battle of words with you," Jared replied. "I'll have to content myself with my long string of victories on the chessboard."

"I've been distracted of late," Franklin protested. "Besides, your winning streak isn't all that long."

Franklin was in a jovial mood. So Jared decided the time was right to approach him with a request that had been much on his mind.

"Dr. Franklin," he said, "I have a request of you."

"Speak freely, Jared."

"It's been four years since I've seen Anne. I'd like to go home."

"Four years! Has it been that long?" The elder statesman reflected briefly. "You're right. Imagine that, four years!"

"If it's all the same to you, sir, I think it's time for me to return to Boston."

Franklin took a long look at the man sitting opposite him. "My dear Jared, I have no hold over you. You have always been free to go whenever you please. I'm at a loss to understand why you think you must have my permission."

Jared looked down at the floor for a moment, formulating his thoughts. "When I first agreed to work with you ..."

"If I recall, you were sent to spy on me."

Jared matched Franklin's grin. "When I first agreed to work with you," he began again, "I told myself that the best thing I could do to help the cause of the revolution was to assist you in whatever way possible. At that time, I made a commitment that I would make myself available to you for as long as you could use me."

"A commitment to whom?"

"God. Our country. Myself."

"Go on."

"So, you see, in order for me to fulfill my commitment, I feel I have to hear from you that I'm no longer needed."

Franklin pondered Jared's request and comment. After several moments of thought, he said, "I wish I could grant what you request, Jared. But the truth is, I need you here. There are events unfolding even now that you can help me with. Of course, should you go, I'm sure I can find others to assist me. But if I understand you correctly, you're asking me if I still need you, and the answer is, yes I do. Naturally, you're free to go and with my blessing. I'm sorry if I cannot give you what you want. But knowing you, you want a truthful answer, and that is what I have given you."

Jared pursed his lips. It wasn't the response he'd hoped for. Even still, Franklin left the door open for him to leave should he choose to accept it, "with his blessing." He thought of Anne and Boston and how much he wanted to see them again, to live in his own home, to have a wife again. Then he weighed that against the commitment he'd made four years previous. At the time he'd made the commitment, he didn't realize the task would take so much time. *Had he known, would he have still made the same decision?* It all boiled down to this: be true to his word and fulfill his commitment regardless of the personal cost, or do what he wanted to do.

"You mentioned some unfolding events," Jared said. "What events?"

June 10, 1780
Passy, France

My dearest Anne,

It is late evening—actually, it's early morning, I should have dated this letter the 11th. Anyway, I have just put Dr. Franklin to bed. Of late, his gout has been troubling him greatly, making it difficult for him to walk any distance. But while his legs fail him, his mind (and tongue) are as sharp as ever. We are fortunate to have such a man representing our new country in a land so ancient and filled with tradition.

Although this letter follows quickly after my previous one, for some reason I felt I needed to write you before retiring tonight. I tried to ascertain whether you needed to hear from me or I needed to write to you. What does it matter? When I write, I'm close to you, as close as I can be for now, and that thought alone gives me sufficient cause to take pen in hand.

I always pray that my next letter will bear the announcement that I'm coming home. Sadly, this is not that letter. My prayer remains unanswered. Tomorrow afternoon (pardon me, this afternoon—I still forget how late it is) I set out on a mission for Dr. Franklin, one of great significance. If our hopes for this mission are realized, thousands of people's prayers will be answered. At the moment, that's all I can tell you, other than this—I love you and miss you. Loneliness at sea was never as painful as our current separation. Maybe I'm just getting older. Pray for me as I pray for you.

Your husband,
Jared

Benjamin Franklin's carriage slipped unobtrusively down a narrow lane lined with timeworn poplar trees leading to the French countryside. Nothing uncommon. Franklin was known to take an occasional ride through the nearby hills and fields. Only this time, the carriage would circle back through a patch of woods and enter Paris by way of back roads; only this time, the trip was far from occasional; it could change the course of history; and this time, the carriage wasn't carrying Dr. Franklin, but one Jared Morgan.

Pressing himself against the back of the seat so he could not be seen by passersby, Jared reviewed the instructions he'd received from Franklin. Picking up from their earlier discussion, the American foreign minister promised Jared this would be his final assignment. Once this mission was completed, Jared could consider his commitment fulfilled. The details of the mission itself tempered Jared's mounting joy.

Word had reached Franklin that the British were interested in beginning a dialogue with him, one that would lead to a peace treaty. Several things about the message disturbed the diplomat. One, the source of the communiqué had proven himself untrustworthy in previous dealings; two, their insistence on a specific route to Paris and the location of the meeting place itself—the slum district—begged suspicion regarding the veracity of the communiqué; and three, any separate negotiations with Great Britain could be interpreted as a violation of the American-French treaty, which, if made public, could seriously damage relationships with their ally leading to cutbacks in shipments to America. Still, Franklin thought the potential reward worth the risk. Jared disagreed with him.

The message could be a ploy, Jared argued, to discredit America in the eyes of the French by drawing American diplomats into false negotiations, then publicizing them. Another possibility was kidnapping. Putting America's most famous statesman on trial in London would be a serious blow to American morale.

Franklin agreed; that's why he wanted Jared to go with him, for protection. Though not a young man, Jared was still fit enough to provide a measure of security; but more importantly, his past profession as a pirate had demonstrated his invaluable ability to keep calm under fire. As a counterproposal, Jared offered to go alone. Before Franklin could object, Jared explained the benefits. If it was a ploy, Jared could insist he was acting on his own, and damage to American-French relationships could be minimized. If it was a kidnap attempt, they would succeed in nabbing only a minor character in the scheme of things. And if the attempt at contact was legitimate, hopefully Jared could ascertain that, and the negotiations could proceed from there.

"Or we could scare them off," Franklin had added.

"A possibility."

It took a while, but Jared eventually succeeded in convincing Franklin that he was too valuable to expose himself to danger at this early stage. So Jared set out alone in Franklin's carriage to make initial contact with British agents in Paris.

The carriage rolled from one side to the other as it left the road, deviating from Franklin's usual route. Jared bounced involuntarily on the seat as the carriage crossed an untilled field toward a small patch of forest that was thin enough to be able to see through to the other side. On the far side was another road, this one going to Paris.

The inside of the carriage grew darker as it ducked under the foliage. Jared scanned the area through his square open window. A procession of trees moved across his vision from left to right.

THUMP!

The carriage jerked forward as a great weight hit the roof.

Jared heard a muffled cry, followed by the driver's body flying past his window; he reached for the pistol in his waistband, too late! The door flew open—a man wearing a handkerchief over his nose and mouth jumped in, his pistol pointed at Jared. He hollered "GO," then fell against Jared when the carriage bolted forward, the serious end of his pistol gouging into Jared's chest.

The intruder ended up on the seat next to Jared. He cursed so vehemently, the bottom flap of his mask raised from the wind showing teeth with uneven gaps between them. Jared understood the curses. English with a British accent. Trees whizzed by the window. The carriage bounced crazily, emerged from the trees, rocked violently from side to side, nearly tipping over, as the kidnapper's accomplice steered the carriage onto the road, away from Paris.

"You're not Franklin!" the intruder shouted.

"Strange you should mistake me for him," Jared said. "We look nothing alike."

The British intruder rewarded his humor with a pistol-butt across the mouth. Jared was then bound, gagged, and blindfolded.

As best as Jared could estimate, they continued on for about an hour. There were several changes in direction, right, right, left, right, then left again, across terrain that included at least one stream, several roads in various conditions, and—from the steady rhythm of bumps—a plowed field that had hardened in the sun, he guessed.

The carriage stopped. Jared heard the door fly open.

"What ... why ... that's not Franklin!" another heavily accented British voice stammered.

"They don't even look alike!" the intruder beside him said.

"Why didn't you tell me to stop!" the new voice yelled.

"Why? Would stopping somehow get us Franklin?"

"But ..."

"We had to get away. Could have been an ambush for all we know."

"It wasn't an ambush!" Jared shouted. The gag muffled his words, translating them into incomprehensible sounds.

A fist catapulted into his stomach, doubling him over. Being blindfolded, he never saw the blow coming and didn't realize until now how much a difference a moment of preparation could make.

"He's not Franklin ... kill him!"

"Not so fast. We need to think about this."

"Well, not out here. Bring him inside."

Jared heard the sliding of a wooden latch, then a long creak, the sound of a big door, possibly a barn. He was grabbed by the arm and wrestled into a cold place. The sounds repeated themselves as the big door slammed shut. It was definitely a barn; Jared could tell from the smells. Hands came from nowhere, shoving him off balance. He twisted to his side, hitting the ground with his shoulder, his head banging against dirt and straw. As far as Jared could determine, there were only two of them; at least only two of them were talking.

"I say we kill him! He's no good to us."

"Maybe we can still get Franklin; hold this fellow hostage, threaten to kill him unless Franklin agrees to meet with us."

"We can kill him and still do that! Franklin won't know he's dead."

"I just don't like killing. Nobody said anything about killing. Our job was to nab Franklin. It's not our fault he wasn't in the carriage."

"Well, I don't have any problems with killing ..."

Jared tried to say something. He only swallowed the cloth gag a little bit more in the attempt.

The big door opened and closed.

"What? I'm supposed to stand here and watch you murder somebody? We don't even know who he is!"

Jared tried to yell his name, squirm to sit up, something ... anything....

BLAM!

Jared jumped at the sound of the explosion. Pieces of dirt and rock stung and cut his face.

"Why did you hit my arm? What is it with you?"

"I said I don't want anything to do with killing! I say we go back into town and tell ..."

Apparently the gunman did something to cut off his accomplice, for there was a momentary pause before the man continued, and when he did, his tone was lower.

"... we should get advice before we do anything, that's all I'm saying. Things are different from what he expected."

Reluctantly, the gunman agreed. They dragged Jared to a wooden post of some sort and tied him to it. Then they left him.

His hands were behind him, between him and the post. He couldn't see anything, nor could he shout or talk; about all he could manage was a high-pitched scream, which he tried for a while, then tired of the effort. If they had any brains at all, they certainly wouldn't have left him anywhere near any kind of traffic. His knees were against his chest. He tried to raise himself up, but the ropes uniting his midsection with the post prevented that. He tried to think of his options. They seemed to be limited to one—try to get untied. Until he did that, he could do nothing else.

Adding to his misery was that there was no way to tell how long he had been there, if an hour had passed or two or three, even whether it was night or day. After a while he guessed it was night. He struggled a bit more, grew weary, and dozed off. *But for how long? Was it morning yet?* He couldn't tell. There were no sounds around him. No rooster, no farm animals of any kind.

The cloth in his mouth not only pinned his tongue to his bottom teeth, but also soaked up any and all moisture. He was incredibly thirsty.

Jared tried to work the ropes against the wooden post. As he did, the ropes also worked against his flesh. Soon his wrists were raw, exposed, burning, and wet. If he repositioned his hands too close to the post itself, he was rewarded the sensation of tiny, ragged-edged daggers of wood; the splinters cut deep and lodged under his skin; he could feel them working back and forth. To take his mind off the pain, he consoled himself with the thought that Franklin wasn't in the carriage. At least that was a victory. He thought of Anne and the twins and Mercy. He thought of what he might do when his abductors returned; a hundred and one scenarios played in his mind, most of them ending in his death.

After hours of effort rubbing his face against his shoulder, Jared had managed to work the blindfold up above a corner of his eye, enough so that he could see out of the lower part of his right eye and tell light from dark. According to his calculations, he had been captured three days previous. It was a guess. The pounding in his head, coupled with intense thirst, caused him at times to pass between consciousness and unconsciousness at irregular intervals.

Because his hands were behind him, he had no way of knowing if he was making any progress with the rope or not. He was losing hope of ever getting free. At first, his greatest fear was that the men who kidnapped him would come back and kill him; now his fear was that nobody would ever come back, that he would be unable to get free, that he would die alone in a French barn.

A new idea for escape came to him in a dream; whether it was a dream of sleep or delirium, he didn't know. In the dream he remembered Howard Keefer, a thin-nosed, freckle-faced lad on one of his trips to China. He wasn't much of a sailor; he made only one voyage and said he'd had enough. But Howard had a knack for entertaining his shipmates. He boasted that no one could tie him up so that he could not escape. Such a boast would not go unchallenged aboard ship. Men lined up for a turn to tie up Howard Keefer. And without exception, he always worked himself free. On some of the easier escapes it almost looked like he shrugged off the ropes; the more difficult ones he squirmed his way out. Said he did it by thinking thin. That was it. It was as if Howard Keefer were telling Jared he could escape his bonds simply by thinking thin.

As Jared slipped in and out of his dream states, he wasn't sure if he ever really knew a sailor named Howard Keefer or if the boy was a product of Jared's mind. But instead of trying to fray the ropes, Jared began to try to work his hands free. *Think thin. Think thin.* The words kept repeating in his mind. *Was it his imagination, or did all the rubbing loosen the ropes a bit?* One thing he wasn't imagining was the pain. The sores on his wrists felt like fire. *Think thin. Think thin.*

After a full day's effort, Jared was making progress. Or at least he thought he was. Maybe he was just hoping for progress. He worked his hands back and forth, thinking thin. *No, it wasn't his imagination.* He pulled hard with his right arm. An invisible knife jabbed his wrist. *Dislocated? Broken?* All he knew was that every tug brought even greater pain. But he tried again, fighting the pain, thinking thin.

Then, his right hand slipped out. Once he passed a certain point, that's what it did—it slipped right out. A triumphant moan escaped Jared's parched throat. His shoulder ached so badly, he had to bring his hand forward in stages. He reached for the gag and pulled. Too tight. He tried the blindfold. It came off with relative ease. Though it was twilight—or was it dawn, he wasn't sure—the light assaulted his eyes. He managed to free his other hand. It took both of them to loosen the gag. He worked his mouth and jaw; the jaw was tight; his tongue was so dry it stuck to everything it touched. Soon his legs were free. The rope around his torso was harder to untie than he thought it would be, because the knots were behind the post and it was difficult for him to turn and reach them. Finally, the last rope dropped to the dirt. Jared lay beside it.

He had been right about the time of day. It was twilight because the barn was getting darker. His first thought was water. He looked around. The barn was bare. No tools of any kind. With an enormous effort, he worked himself onto his knees, his hands also supporting him on the ground. Such a simple position, such a major victory. He remained in that position until he felt confident in his ability to maintain it. Then he placed one foot on the ground. With the help of the post that had been his jailer, he pulled himself up. He was wobbly, so he waited. But his strength failed him. He dropped to his knees.

He rested, then tried again. This time he was successful. He stumbled across the barn, pulled on the big barn door, and opened it just wide enough to get out. Stars were beginning to appear in the night sky. Jared spied a well. He groped his way down the side of the barn toward it.

"You there! Hey you!"

A man's voice. Thick British accent.

Jared tried to run. One step and he was on the ground.

Two men hovered over him, lifting him to his feet.

"It's him!"

Jared balled his fist in an attempt to strike. He passed out.

※

Jared Morgan was aboard the *Dove*, standing at the helm,

steering the ship into the wind. There was a storm on the horizon, wave after wave leaped over the starboard side, crashing down upon him. Odd. The sky above was clear. Stars were shining. Then another wave crashed upon him. Not a ship, a well. Someone holding his arms.

"Take it easy, don't drown him!"

A British voice.

Jared fought to get away. Stronger arms held him secure.

"Don't fight us, man. We're here to help you."

Jared didn't believe them. He fought harder.

"Listen to me, listen to me! You were kidnapped four days ago. The kidnappers were after Benjamin Franklin, but got you instead."

Got to get away!

"You were on your way to meet some friends of England. A matter of importance."

Jared eased up, not because he was convinced, but because he had no strength left.

"Your name is Jared Morgan, we've come to rescue you. The lads who did this to you belong to a radical English sect that wants America defeated at any cost. They don't want peace. We uncovered their plot and learned of your predicament. I say again, we're here to help you."

The two men holding him were middle aged. Jared remembered his captors being younger.

"The sooner you stop struggling, the sooner you can have some more water. That's what you want, isn't it? Let us help you."

Jared had never tasted anything as sweet as the water from that French well. He was loaded into a carriage and taken to Paris where, true to their word, the two British men who found him nursed him back to health. Jared spent three days with them before he was well enough to travel. In that time, he learned that they had obtained his location in the barn by torturing his captors. His rescuers were deadly serious about opening up dialogue with Franklin about peace. They gave Jared gifts and assurances, enough to convince him that they were telling the truth.

An initial meeting with Franklin was arranged. Jared oversaw the arrangements, taking every precaution imaginable. The British proved more than cooperative.

Franklin listened to Jared's detailed description of his ordeal like a boy listening to the tales of Sir Lancelot. "I would not have survived that," he said several times. "Well done, Jared. You undoubtedly saved my life and made contact with the British. Outstanding!"

"I only hope the negotiations bear fruit," Jared said.

"They look promising."

Franklin's driver appeared at the door. He had survived the blow to his head and some nasty scrapes and bruises from the fall from his carriage seat, but otherwise was doing well. He motioned that it was time for Franklin to leave. The minister and Jared stood.

"One more thing," Franklin said. "I may have spoken prematurely when I told you this would be your last mission for me. Something has come up and I need you to help me. Please forgive me, Jared. If there were anyone else who could do this, I would certainly enlist him. But in this matter, I trust only you to represent me."

The driver interrupted. They were going to be late unless they left immediately.

"Tomorrow afternoon," Franklin said. "Come tomorrow afternoon and I'll give you the necessary letters and fill you in on the details."

Franklin hobbled toward the door, then stopped.

"Oh, by the way, Madame LaFontaine has invited you to a dinner party tonight. The invitation came during your unexpected absence. Seems she feels we've been neglecting her. Can't have that. Tell her I send my fondest regards."

Jared's first impulse was to refuse. He was tired and sore and—after hearing about another mission—depressed. The last thing he wanted to do tonight was to socialize with a mansion full of Frenchmen.

"Who else will be going?" he called after Franklin.

Too late. Franklin was gone.

Like a gloomy colleague, depression accompanied Jared Morgan in the carriage ride to the LaFontaine mansion that evening. Franklin's news that Jared's return to Boston would be delayed worked on him like a disease, draining him of emotion and energy. His ego wouldn't allow him to admit to himself that Franklin's surprise announcement of another mission was having such a profound negative effect on him. He reasoned his feelings were the result of physical fatigue. It would take time for him to regain his strength. He was tired, that's all. But as his carriage pulled up in front of Madame LaFontaine's, his rationalization did nothing to alleviate his black mood.

To Jared's surprise, the guest list for the dinner party was a short one. It consisted of two names, his own and his hostess'. Rosalie LaFontaine expressed blushing surprise when Jared asked the arrival time of the other guests. She merrily insisted her invitation was clearly worded, offering Jared an avenue of polite refusal should he feel uncomfortable with the arrangement. The question arose: Did Franklin accidentally or intentionally obfuscate her invitation? At this point, with everything ready, Jared felt awkward at the thought of leaving abruptly. He agreed to stay for dinner. Mentally, he determined to make it a short evening.

They dined in candlelight on the stone terrace behind the mansion. It was twilight; the stars overhead, one at a time, made bashful appearances. The rich field of dark green grass added an expansive feeling to the intimate setting while deer and small animals ventured from the misty blue forest like characters stepping from a storybook onto a stage. From the first time Jared sat on the terrace, this place had become his favorite spot in all of France. Tonight, the pastoral panorama soothed him like an enchanting elixir.

While Jared ignored his food, preferring to devour his surroundings while there was still available light, Rosalie LaFontaine happily consumed her dinner until she noticed Jared wasn't eating.

"Is something bothering you?" Madame LaFontaine asked. "You've barely touched your food. I can have something else prepared for you if you prefer."

Jared glanced at his plate. "No, that won't be necessary. This is fine. Thank you, anyway."

She folded her hands and rested her chin on them, studying him a moment. "Are you uncomfortable being alone with me?"

The bluntness of her question took Jared by surprise. The moment they walked onto the terrace, he hadn't thought any more about his being the only guest. In fact, having first been distracted by the abrupt turn of events, then by the captivating dinner setting, Jared had not yet taken a long look at his hostess. He did so now. Light-blue eyes gazed fondly at him, reflecting the flames of the candles. Against dark shadows, the flickering sources of light flattered Madame LaFontaine's lightly powdered cheeks. Natural brown hair, piled high, decorated her delicate white ears with curls. A pale blue ribbon, the same color as her evening gown, accentuated a graceful neck. She was a fairy-tale princess in a storybook setting. Entranced by her elegant, mature beauty, Jared felt the level of his discomfort rise.

"Um … no, um … I'm just tired. Some recent … um, events have left me … well, tired, that's all … just tired. My apologies. I'm

… I'm afraid I'm not very good company tonight."

"The kidnapping ordeal," she said.

"You know about that?"

Madame LaFontaine smiled coyly. "I told you once before, rumors, scandals, and affairs keep our lives in Paris from becoming dull." Reacting to the anxiety on his face, she reached out and touched his arm. "That's all I know about the matter, Jared, and that from Dr. Franklin himself. He said only that there had been a kidnap attempt on his life, and you voluntarily sprung the trap on yourself to save him. He's deeply affected by your willingness to sacrifice yourself … as am I. Were you badly hurt?"

Jared felt relieved. General knowledge of their secret dealings with the British could be disastrous. "My wrist is still sore, but other than that, I'm fine."

"How bad is it? Let me see."

He felt rather foolish, but out of politeness, he rolled up his sleeve. Madame LaFontaine rose from her chair to get a better look.

With motherly hands, she held his arm up to the light. "Jared Morgan! This doesn't look good at all! You still have splinters in you! And this burn, from rope?"

Jared nodded. Then, when he realized she was too busy looking at the wound to see his nod, he said, "Yes. Rope."

Before Jared could stop her, she sent a servant to retrieve a needle and some ointment. While the servant stood nearby, holding the bottle of ointment on a silver tray, Madame LaFontaine plucked at the splinters.

"OW!"

Rosalie LaFontaine shook her head. "Why is it …"

"OW! That hurts!"

"… that men can be so foolhardy and brave at times …"

"OUCH!"

"… yet are little babies when it comes to splinters? Hold still!"

"I can't, it hurts!"

"There, that's the last one." Madame LaFontaine dabbed two fingers in the ointment, then gently rubbed it on Jared's injured wrist. Jared watched the top of her head move from side to side as she applied the ointment, continuing to examine the wound from every possible angle. He was reminded of when he and Chuckers and Will went wolf hunting the night of his father's funeral. Jared came home with a nasty bite on his ankle. He remembered his mother doing this same head-lowered examination to his ankle wound. Now, as then, he felt uneasy with the attention he was getting. Only tonight was worse. Tonight there was a witness. Madame LaFontaine's stiff-and-stern servant sent occasional unsympathetic glances his way.

"That feels much better," Jared lied. "Thank you."

He attempted to retrieve his arm. Rosalie LaFontaine had a secure hold on it.

"I'm not finished! Sit still!" Looking up briefly with her sparkling blue eyes, she added, "I would have guessed you to be a poor patient. You just can't sit still very long."

A couple more dabs and she declared the procedure finished. Jared gratefully got his arm back and immediately returned his sleeve to its proper place. The servant was dismissed.

"Thank you," Madame LaFontaine said.

"Why are you thanking me? I should be thanking you."

"Yes, you should," she said with a giggle. "But I thank you because I no longer get many opportunities to care for a man. I enjoyed it. Shall we go inside?"

Madame LaFontaine led Jared into the library where she had arranged for entertainment. For an audience of two, a violinist and pianist played selections from Bach and Handel and a few pieces from an emerging child prodigy by the name of Wolfgang

Amadeus Mozart. The audience sat apart at arm's length on a sofa. Every element of the evening—the music, the company, the conversation, even the ointment—seemed to combine for a relaxing and entertaining time. The depression Jared arrived with had long since departed without him. He had not felt this at ease since coming to France four years ago. Rosalie LaFontaine was as pleasant to talk to as she was to look at, and Jared completely forgot his mental affirmation to make it a short evening.

After the musicians left, Jared and his hostess talked late into the night—about his travels, about her experiences in the French world of art, politics at home and abroad, their mutual admiration for Benjamin Franklin, and on and on until it was past two o'clock.

"It's too late for you to return to Passy," Madame LaFontaine said. "Please stay the night."

"That's very gracious of you, but I really ..."

She placed her hand on his arm. "Jared, I don't want this evening to end. You are such wonderful company. You may have any room you wish, and in the morning we can take a leisurely stroll through the wooded area—it's so beautiful that time of day with the sun breaking through the trees, the dew covering the foliage, the birds and squirrels foraging for food ... oh, please stay. It would make me so happy."

Whether it was the lateness of the hour, or the emptiness of four lonely years, or the warmth and nearness of a beautiful woman, or a mixture of all these things, Jared agreed to stay the night.

Madame LaFontaine escorted him to an upstairs bedroom decorated with dark woods, tapestries, and a balcony overlooking the field of grass and forest. She kissed him warmly on the cheek and closed the door, leaving him alone in the room.

No sooner had the latch clicked, then Jared wished he hadn't agreed to stay. He walked to the multipaned glass doors that opened out to the balcony. Standing there, he stared out into the night. *This just didn't feel right. It was wrong for him to be here. But what could he do about it now? Should he leave? If he did, what would Madame LaFontaine think of him when she found him gone in the morning? She had been nothing but kind to him; how could he repay her kindness with rude behavior? He never should have agreed to stay.*

For a half hour Jared agonized over what to do. Several possible courses of action played out in his mind, none of them satisfactory. His mind went back years earlier, when he was an inexperienced tar aboard the *Dove*. While the ship was careened on Cat Island to scrape the barnacles from the hull, a number of Jared's shipmates took him to New Providence Island in an effort to initiate him. To their disappointment, he wasn't much for drinking, so they introduced him to the second phase of his initiation—a prostitute. But the thought of going up to the prostitute's room was revolting to him, and Jared bolted from the tavern, leaving his friends and the prostitute behind.

Sitting on the edge of the bed in the French mansion, Jared wondered why he thought of that particular incident right now. The idea of comparing Madame LaFontaine with the New Providence Island prostitute was ludicrous and insulting. Madame LaFontaine was a wonderfully kind woman. *So what made him think of New Providence Island? The feeling in his stomach. It was the same now as it was then. The situations were different, but the feeling was the same. It was a feeling that this was wrong. Wrong.*

Just then Jared thought he heard a tap on the door. *Was it a tap? Or just an unfamiliar sound in an unfamiliar house?* The door cracked open.

"Jared?"

Rosalie LaFontaine stepped demurely into the room. She was stunning in a flowing, sheer, white negligee; her hair was down, draped elegantly over her shoulders. Jared had never seen a more sensuous vision in his life.

"May I come in?"

Jared hung his head and prayed; it was such a deep, agonizing prayer, that it sounded like he was moaning.

"Are you all right? Or do you wish me to leave?"

Rising from the edge of the bed, Jared crossed the room and took Madame LaFontaine's hands in his.

"No, I don't want you to leave," he said. "It is I who must leave."

Light-blue eyes expressed disappointment and hurt. "I thought we experienced something special tonight, or was I mistaken?"

"No, you weren't mistaken. It was a wonderful evening and you are a lovely hostess and—I hope—a dear friend. It's just that I can't stay. It's wrong."

"Is it wrong that two people care for one another?"

"It's wrong for us to take our relationship beyond what it already is. It's unfair to you because someday, maybe soon, I'll leave France and the heartache of our parting will be that much greater. It's unfair to a wonderful woman in Boston to whom I have pledged myself in marriage."

"But you want to stay with me tonight. I have seen it in your eyes all evening."

"You're right. I want to stay."

"Then, why not surrender to your feelings?"

"Madame LaFontaine—Rosalie, I am at a loss to explain my feelings because they are in conflict with what I know to be right. All I can say is that for much of my life I have lived by this maxim: God's ways are always best. It has served me well in the past, and I have to believe it will serve me well now. Please forgive me. I never should have let things go this far."

Madame LaFontaine raised Jared's hands to her lips and kissed them. "No, it is you who must forgive me. Dr. Franklin said you were a religious man. But I am a lonely woman, and I have tempted you to forsake your values simply to ease my loneliness. You must think me evil."

"I think nothing of the kind. Until the day I die, I will never forget tonight and the wonderful evening we spent together."

※

Franklin was sitting behind his desk, scratching on a piece of paper with a quill pen, when Jared entered the room. Without looking up, he motioned Jared to a chair in front of the desk. Jared sat and waited for Franklin to complete his thought. The American emissary sighed heavily, laid aside his quill, then removed his eyeglasses and rubbed his eyes.

"So tell me, Jared, how was your evening with Madame LaFontaine?"

It was a simple question. Jared wondered if Franklin realized the flood of thoughts and emotions the question provoked. He replied simply, "Madame LaFontaine is a gracious hostess and we had a memorable time."

Franklin appraised Jared for a long moment, as though he were trying to find a hidden message in Jared's response. Whether he just gave up after a few moments or merely determined there was no hidden message to be found, he moved on to other business. He picked up a sealed letter from the edge of his desk and held it in front of him.

"As I mentioned yesterday, there is a sensitive matter that requires my immediate attention. Unfortunately, I cannot respond personally. Jared, I trust you to go in my place. During these last four years, I have learned that you have greater diplomatic skills than you give yourself credit for. You will need all those skills for this assignment."

He handed the letter to Jared.

"I want you personally to deliver this correspondence to the address listed and wait for a response."

Jared looked at the letter. It was addressed to Anne Morgan, Boston, Massachusetts.

"On my behalf," Franklin continued with a smirk, "I want you to convey my sincerest thanks to this fine woman for the great sacrifice she has made in our ongoing revolutionary effort. She cannot be commended too highly. Tell her my only regret is that I am not able to deliver the message personally."

"Thank you, sir," Jared said softly, his voice muffled with emotion. "I willingly accept this assignment." Then, with a smirk of his own, he added, "And knowing your reputation with the ladies, may I say that I am most grateful you are unable to deliver this letter personally."

Franklin laughed loud and long.

The day before Jared Morgan left Passy, France, for America, a batch of letters from Anne caught up with him. He sat in his room poring over the epistles, his emotions rising, knowing that he would soon be sailing home and that in a matter of months he would once again be embracing the author of these letters. Having sorted them in order by date, he read the chronology of the revolutionary battles and daily life in Boston as described and interpreted by his wife. By the time he had finished the last letter, he was greatly troubled, troubled enough to overshadow the joy of his return home. In the final letter Anne informed Jared that both Esau and the family Bible had turned up missing and that she had recently received a letter from Esau's commanding officer, General Benedict Arnold, informing her that it was believed Esau had defected to the enemy.

20

Flames vaulted into the night sky, pouring out every window and door in the two-story house. The fire had been at work less than ten minutes, but in that brief time the flames, like jackals stripping a carcass, had consumed everything except the skeletal frame. The resulting blaze was so bright, Esau could see everyone and everything around the circumference of the house as if it were midday. He saw the soldiers in red who set the fire, callously enjoying their handiwork. He saw the family that had been forced from their home—a mother, two boys, and three girls—huddled under a tree. The mother's upturned face was wet and shiny with tears, her cries for God's help muffled by the roar of the inferno. He saw the look on the children's faces as they clung to their hysterical mother— their young faces portraits of horror and hate, broiling hatred for the men in the red coats who had done this to them. And, illuminated by the fire on that September night, he saw the bright red sleeves on his own arms, the sleeves of a British uniform.

The first time he donned the uniform, he felt a twinge of pride. For him, it was a visible reaffirmation of the decision he had made, a decision he should have made years before. Joining the

Continental Army was a mistake, he realized now; believing Mercy would leave Jacob and run away with him to England was a mistake; and not having the courage of his own convictions, but allowing himself to be swayed by his family's opinions, was a mistake. But that was past. He had a new life now, one that began when he put on a red coat.

Of course, the red coat was temporary. His plan was to sail to England and begin a new life, a new destiny really, not only for him but also for all future Morgans. But before he could go, there was unfinished business. His crossing over to the British side was only half the plan; the plan would not be complete until General Benedict Arnold had crossed over to the English side. As soon as that was accomplished, Esau felt he would be free to go. The last time he saw the general, Arnold expressed interest in Esau carrying on as his aide in the British army, but Esau wanted to get to England as quickly as possible and had already decided not to accept the offer, though he hadn't told Arnold yet. So until Arnold was safely on the British side, Esau would wear the coat of red.

The thrill of the new coat, however, soon evaporated in the light of reality. British General Clinton did not trust colonial loyalists. Because he could never be certain who was loyal and who was a spy, he chose not to put confidence in any of them. Instead of incorporating them into the regular forces, they were assigned to raiding parties. In Esau's case, a raiding party of seven who called themselves the Bloody Scouts.

These loosely organized raiders followed no predetermined plan as they went from house to house determining the loyalty of each residence. Those households whose loyalties lie with the revolutionaries were plundered and often burned. Occasionally, in their zeal, the marauders would accidentally destroy the home of a Tory if sufficient proof was not readily forthcoming of loyalty to the crown.

Esau hated his assignment and despised the members of the Bloody Scouts, especially their leader, Jed Odell, a Virginian. Before the start of the hostilities in 1775, Odell—a barrel-chested man with an unkempt salt-and-pepper beard and a wild left eye that stared off to the side—was a renegade and scoundrel, frequently jailed for nefarious activities. When war broke out, his lack of ethics and undisciplined life seemed better suited to raiding than it did to any organized armed effort. That's why he joined the British side, not out of political or philosophical reasons, but because he could plunder with full military authority. And he was good at his job. The Bloody Scouts had a distinguished record as raiders, if you could call it that. It was a distinction Esau failed to appreciate.

If it weren't for the fact that Andre's negotiations with Arnold for the delivery of West Point were proceeding rapidly, Esau would have quit the raiders and the army completely. However, Andre encouraged him to endure the discomfort of his unpleasant assignment for the short duration, so that he would be available for the greater mission with Benedict Arnold. Esau agreed to endure.

So Esau's existence in New York became a life of two extremes. If he wasn't sitting around a campfire with a band of dirty, rowdy, belching raiders following a day of plundering and raiding, he was attending an art exhibit with Andre and the rest of New York high society. It was these times with Andre that made life bearable for Esau. John Andre had become the brother Jacob never had been to him, nor he to Jacob.

Andre and Esau shared a love for the finer things of life, which Andre somehow always seemed to acquire. After all, most people liked Andre. Those who didn't were either jealous of him or felt he was an empty-headed buffoon who was given more credit than he deserved, advancing in rank only because he was a favorite of General Clinton's. In candid private moments, Andre confessed to Esau that the barbs in these remarks were not without effect on him. But he didn't dwell on them long. There were plenty of other things to do besides fret over what people thought of him.

"Sit still!"

Esau rubbed the back of his neck. "I've been sitting still so long, I'm growing stiff. If I don't move, I'll probably freeze in this position!"

He was sitting on a stool beside a window in a New York room Andre had fashioned into a makeshift art studio. The artist, with paper clipped to a thick board, glanced from his subject to the sketch, then back again.

"Anyone ever tell you that you have a strong nose?" Andre said.

"Not that I recall. My father used to say I had a thick head."

Andre laughed, then complained, "Now look what you did! You made me mess up the drawing!" His nose wrinkled in concentration as he worked to correct the flaw.

Esau rose from the stool. "I can't sit here any longer."

"That's why I don't draw men!" Andre complained. "Unlike ladies, they can't sit still long enough for a decent sketch."

"Let me see it."

Esau reached out his hand for the drawing. Andre turned it facedown, securing it in place with a flat hand. "Not until it's finished. Go back to the stool and sit down."

Rotating his head to stretch his neck muscles, Esau moaned. "How much longer will it take?"

"Don't be such a baby. I'll be done shortly."

Esau resumed his place and pose on the stool.

"You know, I've been thinking," Andre said.

"You can do that and draw at the same time?"

"That does it, I'm erasing all your hair!"

Esau bellowed.

A minute or two passed before Andre could continue his thought. "As I was saying … this sounds like a Shakespearean drama, but do you realize how much our lives are interwoven?"

"How do you mean?"

"Just that for the last four or five years our lives have been interweaving in time and geography until recently when they've come together."

"How so?"

"For example, we were both in Canada in the early stages of the conflict. You were in Quebec with Arnold, I was at Fort Chambly."

Esau turned toward Andre in surprise. "I didn't know that."

"Turn back into the light," Andre directed him. "I was part of the group at Fort Chambly that surrendered to Montgomery."

"You were a prisoner of war?"

"For fourteen months in central Pennsylvania. I thought I was going to spend the whole war there sketching the countryside and Quakers. In December of seventy-six, we were exchanged for American prisoners. Then, after the fall of Philadelphia, as you know, I was assigned there."

"Where you orchestrated one of the greatest parties of all time."

Andre grinned widely. "Philadelphia has the loveliest ladies in all America."

"And from what I heard, you almost married one."

"Two."

"Two? You scoundrel!"

"Like I said, Philadelphia has the loveliest ladies! There was Peggy Shippen, who is now Peggy Arnold. Can you imagine her preferring a general over me? Then there was Peggy Chew."

"Another Peggy!"

Andre shrugged. "I must have a weakness for girls named Peggy. Either that, or it's easier that way to keep their names straight when you're courting both of them at the same time!"

Continuing Andre's line of thought, Esau said, "Then I arrived in Philadelphia soon after you pulled out."

"See what I mean? Interwoven. Then, of course, there's this matter with Benedict Arnold."

"Is he close to coming over?"

Andre put a few finishing touches on the sketch. "He wants a meeting. Face-to-face."

Esau's eyebrows shot up. "Really? Why?"

"He wants to see if we're really serious. But that's all right, we feel the same way."

"So you're going to meet him?"

"We're going to meet him."

"We? We as in you and me?"

"Done!" Andre declared the portrait finished. He turned it toward Esau.

Esau cocked his head and studied the sketch. "Looks like my brother."

"Of course it looks like your brother, you're twins!"

"No, I'm serious," Esau said, waving a finger over the sketch. "The eyes are different, closer together, more serious. That's my brother. When are we going to see General Arnold?"

"Do you think of your brother very often?"

"Occasionally."

"How do you think he'll respond to your coming over to the British side?"

Esau grunted. "He'll feel vindicated. He's been calling me a traitor for years."

"Does that bother you?"

"Not as much as it used to, especially considering that the whole nation is fighting over issues we fought about since we were young men. The thing that bothers me is that he ends up with the family—my father and mother and, of course, Mercy."

Andre reexamined his sketch. "Do you want me to tear it up?"

"That's not necessary. Just fix the eyes … and maybe the tip of the nose, and the chin is slightly off, and the hair is all wrong.… Or you can tell me when we meet with Arnold."

"Soon. Maybe a week, maybe two. My understanding is that he's already preparing his side to meet under a flag of truce. But, if you'd like, I can arrange to drag this thing out a little longer, knowing how fond you are of raiding the countryside with Odell."

"You'd better watch what you say, or the next house we raid may be yours."

Esau hung back as he usually did as the Bloody Scouts approached the targeted house. A stately three-story house came into view, white paneled with evergreen shutters and, according to Odell, "plentiful in plunder, the home of a known revolutionary sympathizer. An easy job, and a pleasant one at that," he added. Esau wasn't sure what Odell meant by his last comment, but whatever he meant, if it came from Odell's mind and mouth, it couldn't be good.

While the rest of the raiders remained on their mounts, muskets across their laps, Odell approached the front door and pounded on it, calling for those inside to come out for questioning in the king's name. He then stepped back, his musket pointed at the door.

No one answered his summons.

Odell issued his challenge again, threatening to burn down the house if no one came out. The front door moved a crack, stopped, then slowly eased open. The head of a diminutive young Negro woman poked out. Her eyes were wide with fright.

"Don't hurt me, sir," she yelled. "Please, don't hurt me!"

"I'm gonna skin you and burn you alive unless you get out here right now!" Odell shouted at her.

The Negro woman took small, tentative steps until she was outside, her back against the door. She wore a kerchief over her head and a kitchen apron. The woman's hands gripped one another in fear.

"I have it on good authority that there's just you, a man slave, and the lady of the house livin' here. That right?"

The Negro said nothing; she just trembled.

"Answer me!" Odell shouted. "Is that right?"

"I don't see that that's any of your business!" The steady voice came from the left side of the house. A blonde woman held a musket to her shoulder, its barrel pointed at Odell.

The Negro woman, seeing that attention was taken off her, slipped back inside the house, slammed the door, and locked it. Odell scowled at the door, then turned his attention to the woman with the musket, his whiskery cheeks spread wide in a wicked grin. "My, my, my," he said. "I was told you was a right handsome woman. But I had no idea you looked this good."

For the first time ever, Esau agreed with Odell. The woman was a striking vision even with a musket in her hands. Blonde hair was gathered atop her head, leaving wispy curls for bangs and along the back of her neck. Her skin was fair; she was thin, but not delicate. She, too, wore an apron, but this one was heavier, more like a workshop apron.

"State your business, or get off my property."

"There's no need to hold that musket on me, my dear," Odell said in sugary tones. "We can transact our business without it." He took steps toward the woman.

The woman took aim. "I'll only ask you one more time: State your business, or get off my property!"

Odell stopped. He looked at his men, then at the woman again. "You be careful, now, little lady. One word from me, and you're dead before you can yank that trigger."

It was all bluff. None of the other scouts moved. They were dirty. They were crude and mercenary, but Esau was confident none of them would shoot a lady, even Odell. Esau figured Odell had other things in mind for her.

"Isaac!" the woman cried out.

"Right here, miss!"

Odell swung around. Protruding from an upstairs window, a middle-aged Negro man trained a musket on Odell.

"You so much as twitch, and Isaac will blow your head off," said the woman.

Esau smiled, watching the standoff from a distance. He liked this woman. She was outmaneuvering Odell at every step. Still, she was greatly outnumbered, especially if the scouts were allowed to scatter. Something had to be done before Odell realized that. Esau dismounted and, with musket in hand, moved toward the front line of raiders.

"Look, lady…" Odell put on his reasoning voice. Esau had seen him use it before. Odell never reasoned—it was a delaying tactic. "Our job is to make sure that all the residents in these parts are loyal to king and crown. If you can convince me that you're not a revolutionary sympathizer, I'll order my men to ride away."

"And what would it take to convince you of that?" she asked.

"I'm sure if we go inside and sit down and talk about this, you can find something that will convince me. I'm a reasonable man."

"My husband was Colonel Charles Matteson, a grenadier in the king's army. We both come from loyal English families. Satisfied?"

Odell acted like he wanted to believe her, but just couldn't bring himself to do it. His eyes blinked several times. Each time they reappeared, though, the eye that strayed wildly to the side had a wicked glint in it. "That explains your husband, ma'am, but he's dead and I need to be assured that you are still loyal."

The woman frowned, not happy that Odell knew so much about her personal life. "Colonel Charles Matteson was killed on the return march from Lexington. I have given my husband on behalf of the king's cause. What more proof do you need?"

"I'm satisfied," Esau said to Odell. "How about the rest of you?" He looked to the other scouts for response.

The other scouts stared dumbfoundedly back at him.

"The woman lost her husband!" Esau shouted at them. "That's proof enough, don't you think?"

This time he got a few of them to nod.

"Shut up, Morgan! I'm in charge here!" Odell's murderous eyes accompanied the reprimand. Turning again to the woman, Odell said, "If you are a loyal subject of King George, then you won't mind me taking a look around inside. Since you have nothing to hide, that is."

Odell couldn't be allowed inside the house. Once inside, there would be no stopping him. It wouldn't be the first time Odell had looted and burned a Tory house. Afterward, official apologies were issued explaining that in war unfortunate mistakes sometimes happen. Nothing would be done, though, to restore lost property, not to mention lost lives. Esau looked around for some way to change the odds in the woman's favor. He checked the other raiders. They were tense, waiting on Odell for some kind of signal. Esau evaluated the woman's condition. Unchanged. She was steady, cool. Beautiful. The Negro in the upstairs window still had his musket leveled on ... what was that? The Negro's musket barrel was drooping! The Negro noticed it and quickly reached out and straightened it with his hand! *What was going on here?*

"Odell!" Esau yelled, still distracted by the drooping musket. "There is no doubt this house is loyal to the king. If you do anything to injure life or property here, I'll see that you're brought up on charges!"

"You shut your mouth, Morgan!" Odell shook a threatening fist at him. "I'm in charge here."

"Not anymore." Esau raised his musket at the other raiders, easing his way around so that his back was to the house. "Ma'am, you keep your musket on this man," he pointed to Odell, then glanced at the woman. Fiery eyes met his in response. She didn't trust him any more than she did Odell. Right now that didn't matter, as long as she kept her weapon on Odell. Esau glanced at her musket. His heart sank. There was no powder in the pan! The cock hammer had no flint! He had just allied himself with a man holding a melting musket and woman with a musket that wouldn't fire!

Swallowing hard, he spoke to the raiders. "I'm asking you to turn around and ride away. This is a loyalist house. We're British soldiers, not common criminals! But if you insist on following Odell in this illegal action, at least three of you will die before you even get started."

The Negro in the window understood Esau's meaning. He pointed his musket from Odell to one of the other scouts. Esau had to check. *Good. The Negro's musket barrel didn't droop with the sudden movement.*

"Odell," Esau said, "you will be the first to die. You know how it is, these kinds of mistakes sometimes happen in war."

Odell's eyes were moving side to side. He was thinking and that was never good.

"More than three of you will die," the woman shouted. "Look at the upstairs windows, gentlemen."

The raiders all glanced up. They didn't like what they saw. Protruding from one window, then another, were two more muskets. Esau did a double take. He was closer than the others. One of the window muskets was bent slightly to the right; the other musket's barrel was chipped. Underneath it was white. *What was going on here?*

"Get on your horse, Odell!" Esau shouted. He wanted to get Odell's eyes off the upstairs muskets. "Looks like you picked the wrong house today." He motioned to the renegade leader to mount up.

"Let's go, Odell," one of the scouts said. "Nothing for us here." Some of the other scouts had already turned their horses aside.

Odell angrily rubbed his whiskers, his wild eye quivered. Shaking a finger at Esau, he said through clenched teeth, "You're finished with this unit, Morgan. I'm going to bring so many charges against you, you won't get out of jail for a hundred years." He stomped to his horse, mounted, and, with one last sneer at Esau, rode away. His men followed close behind him.

Not until the horses were out of sight, leaving only a flurry of dust, did Esau close his eyes and sigh deeply. "I can't guarantee that he won't be …"

The woman had her musket trained on him.

"I'll thank you to get off my property now," she said.

Esau rolled his eyes. "Why, of all the ungrateful … and if I refuse?"

"I'll shoot you." She was dead serious.

"With what?" Esau shouted. "A musket that doesn't have any flint? Or are you going to shoot me with the drooping musket or the one that points sideways?"

The woman slowly lowered her musket.

"It's a good thing Odell is stupid, or we'd all be dead!" Esau shouted.

The woman's temper flared. She brushed wisps of fine blonde hair out of her eyes and marched up to Esau. Her jaw was firmly set; sharp, intelligent eyes narrowed angrily. "I didn't ask for your help!" she shouted. "I am perfectly capable of defending my property!"

"I can see that," Esau replied. "Forgive me for almost ruining your flawless strategy. However, next time, I suggest you try using real guns with real powder and shot!"

"Are you quite finished running my life for me? For if you are, I would appreciate it if you would get off my property!" A thin arm pointed the direction for him.

"It would give me no greater pleasure than to leave your property, ma'am."

He secured his musket and mounted his horse. As he spurred the horse down the road, he couldn't keep himself from looking back. The blonde woman stood with hands on hips in front of the house, watching him ride away.

Esau hadn't traveled far when a musket discharged from behind a nearby tree. A ball whizzed past his face. His reaction sent him tumbling from his horse, hitting the ground with a breath-jarring thump. Before he had a chance to recover, Odell and the Bloody Scouts towered over him.

"Well, look what we got, boys," Odell gloated. "We caught ourselves a weasel! Get him on his feet."

Four pairs of hands jerked Esau to an upright position. The grizzled leader of the scouts pressed his face close to Esau's, one eye boring into his, the other glaring off in a totally separate direction. Rancid breath billowed around Esau as Odell spoke.

"This is how the report's gonna read," he said. "We was hot on the trail of a known revolutionary sympathizer. He was a wild one, crazy out of his mind, had this sword he kept slashing around." Odell pulled a large hunting knife from a sheath strapped to his leg. "This crazy man ignored all our warnings. Then along comes Esau Morgan. I yell at him to stay away from the madman. But does Esau Morgan obey his leader? No, of course not!"

Odell became dramatic at this point, taking on the role of a story-teller with heightened voice inflection and facial expressions.

"Poor ol' Esau tries to capture the crazy man all by himself. Well, before we can stop him, the crazy man turns on Esau and slashes at him with his sword, cutting him unmercifully—his arms and legs, his belly, his face. I tries my best to get there to help my fellow scout, but alas I'm too late. Poor Esau, bleeding and in pain, drops his musket."

One of the scouts handed Odell Esau's musket.

"The crazy man picks it up! BAM! Oh! Poor, poor Esau Morgan! Shot in the head! What an awful way to die! Of course, we tried to catch that crazy man, but by the time we recovered from the shock of losing our poor Esau, the crazy man got away!"

Odell grinned a wicked grin.

"So, what do you think of my report?"

Still struggling to catch his breath, Esau gasped, "No one will believe it."

"'Course they will!" Odell cried. "You know how it is, these kinds of things sometimes happen in war." Changing tone he ordered his men, "Tie him to that tree."

Esau was shoved back against a tree. Just as he was regaining his breath, the blow against the tree knocked it out of him again. Instinctively, he tried to bend over to catch his breath. Strong hands shoved him back, shoulders to the tree. Odell approached him, knife drawn.

"I'm going to enjoy this," he jeered.

"HOLD! What's going on here?"

The hoofs of horses announced the presence of a troop of British regulars, the officers riding in front, the regulars marching behind them. A tall, straight-faced lieutenant was the officer who spoke.

"What are you doing to that man?"

Odell's wild eye quivered while he formulated a story in his mind.

"Interrogating him, sir."

"To what end?"

"We have evidence to believe he's aiding the enemy, sir."

"He's aiding the enemy while wearing a British uniform?"

"Yes, sir," Odell replied. "By disobeying my direct orders, a prime suspect traitor escaped. I do firmly believe that this man here was in league with the wretch."

"I see," said the officer.

"That's not true!" Esau yelled.

Odell rammed an elbow into Esau's midsection.

This displeased the lieutenant. "Let the man speak!" he ordered.

"You can't believe a word he says, sir," Odell said. "He's a traitor!"

"I'm fully capable of determining that myself, sir."

It took a full minute for Esau to recover enough to speak. "They intend to kill me, Lieutenant."

"Lying dog!" Odell bellowed.

"Shut your mouth, soldier, and let the man speak, or I'll have you arrested!" The lieutenant motioned to two of his men. With bayonets fixed, they stepped forward and pointed them at Odell.

Esau continued: "It's true, I have been insubordinate."

"See! What did I tell you?" Odell cried.

"But only because this man was about to do injury to a decent woman. This man is using his authority for personal gain and gratification. As a gentleman, I could not stand by any longer and watch him destroy good people's lives."

The lieutenant to Esau: "Do you always question your superiors' orders, soldier?"

"Yes he does, all the time, sir!" Odell said.

"Sir, the woman had done nothing wrong. Her husband, Colonel Matteson, was a grenadier in the army."

"Matteson?" The lieutenant reacted to the name as if slapped by a glove. His eyes targeted Odell. "The white house a short distance back with green shutters?"

The look on the lieutenant's face struck Odell dumb.

Esau answered: "Yes sir, that's the one."

Dismounting, the lieutenant approached Odell. "How dare you, sir!" he said, keeping his rising anger barely under control. "Mrs. Abigail Matteson is one of the finest women I have ever known! She would no more be a traitor to the crown than I would. Do I look like a traitor to you, soldier?"

Odell was quaking by now.

The lieutenant rattled off five names in rapid succession. An equal number of men responded by surrounding the entire Bloody Scout band. "Cut this man loose!" he ordered.

"Consider yourselves all under arrest. If you resist or attempt to run, you will be shot!"

"Sir," Esau said as the ropes fell away, "might I request that Major John Andre be informed of my arrest?"

For a second time the lieutenant visibly responded to a name. He stepped closer to Esau. "For what reason?"

"We are working together on a project. It's important he knows my location at all times."

The lieutenant looked Esau over, unsure what to make of him.

"Get on your horse, soldier."

⁂

His back against a cold stone wall, Esau stretched his feet out in front of him. They crossed over more than halfway to the other side of the cell. *Not what you would consider spacious accom-modations,* he thought. The cell was damp and dark, with a horizontal sliver of an opening high above him. The furnishings consisted of a chamber pot in the corner and the wooden slab upon which he was sitting, which projected from the wall. The wood was unfinished, but rubbed so smoothly from the anxious squirming of the backsides of the prisoners who had preceded him, that there was no chance of splinters. The temperature was cool, but the penetrating chill reached far deeper into him than that of mere physical cold. It seemed to be an eerie commentary on his life since coming over to the British side.

So far, with the exception of the time he spent with Andre, his excursion on the English side had been a miserable one. Certainly not anything like he'd imagined it would be. *But then,* he reminded himself, *he wasn't in England yet. Things would be different once he reached England. Much different.*

"Does your nursemaid know where you are?"

The amused eyes of John Andre peered through a small, square hole in the heavy wooden door. Esau leaped to his feet.

"You looked like a prisoner condemned to death sitting there!" Andre said.

Esau laughed. "The atmosphere of this place has that kind of effect on people. Are you here to visit, or to gloat, or to get me out?"

Andre's eyes grew serious. "Were you really insubordinate to your commander?"

Just then the jailer arrived. Andre stepped aside; there was a rattle of keys and the click of a lock. The door swung open. Andre stood there.

"Well, come on! Or do you want to take up permanent resi-dence in there?"

The chill wore off soon after Esau and Andre arrived at the

major's spacious and luxurious manor. Esau described to him in detail the whole horrible afternoon—Odell's evil intentions, the orchestrated response of a strong-willed woman and her two Negro servants, the drooping musket, her musket in all its disrepair, the success of the bluff and the woman's curious way of thanking Esau for risking his life for her, Odell's reprisal, and the fortunate arrival of a no-nonsense lieutenant. Andre howled with laughter.

And though Esau took pains to balance his description of the woman with all the other facts of the eventful day, there was a certain spark in his eye whenever he spoke of her.

Andre noticed the spark, but said nothing.

21

"Listen to this!"

John Andre sat up from his reclining position on the sofa. He was reading the *Royal Gazette* newspaper. Esau sat in a chair next to a window, looking out at the street and letting the sun warm him. His mind was wandering, occasionally frequenting the memory of a white house with evergreen shutters and its blonde inhabitant.

"There is an art exhibit on the upper end of Queen Street." He looked at a clock on the fireplace mantel. "We can just make it. It says here the exhibit is open from three o'clock to five o'clock this afternoon. Admittance is two shillings."

Esau didn't stir. Sitting in the sun had drained him of energy and initiative. "You go if you want to. I'll stay here."

"Nonsense!" Andre sprung to his feet. "You'll enjoy it."

Esau didn't reply directly; he just moaned.

"Come on!" Andre tossed Esau's hat into his lap. "If it will make you feel better, I'll pay your admittance."

"Major John Andre paying? It's worth going to the exhibit just to see that!"

The streets of New York City on this Saturday afternoon were uncluttered and unhurried, adding to Esau's feeling of laziness. He loved this time of the afternoon, when the shadows were long and the air began to cool. As they neared the upper end of Queen Street, Andre did a double take through an open door at the house whose address was No. 95.

"It can't be!" he exclaimed. To Esau: "Wait right here."

Andre bounded up the steps and disappeared through the doorway. While waiting for him, Esau casually crossed his arms and looked up and down the unfamiliar cobblestone street. He felt out of place here. This wasn't his city and it never would be. An anxious anticipation crept over him, the same feeling that always came whenever he thought of his lack of permanent roots. It would be different once he reached England. He'd find a city in which he could get established—possibly Oxford, maybe even London. And he would establish roots. It would be his city.

"Esau!"

Andre emerged from the house. "You won't believe who is in there! When I saw him pass by the doorway, I thought to myself, 'No! It can't be!' But it is! General Howe is here! I haven't seen him since Philadelphia!"

General Sir William Howe was the first commander of the forces in Philadelphia during the British occupation. He was a handsome man, known for his large dinner parties, enjoyment of fine ladies and French wines, and his love for high-stakes poker. It was for General Howe that the extravagant Mischianza was produced.

"Sorry you had to wait for me," Andre said breathlessly. "But I had to talk to him."

Esau smiled and said, "I'm glad you got to see him again." Then he proceeded down the street.

"Wait!" Andre yelled. "He wants to meet you!"

An astonished Esau turned around. "Me? Why would he want to meet me?"

"Well, I told him about you. About your part in the ..." he leaned close to Esau, "... General Arnold situation. And he wants to meet you."

"Really?"

Andre nodded.

"Let's go," Esau said.

"I'll wait for you here."

Esau stopped. He was puzzled.

"Go on!" Andre urged. "This is your special moment. I don't want to spoil it."

Going up the stairs, Esau entered the house. A door stood open to his left, the figure of General Howe was bent over a desk, quill in hand. Esau stood in the doorway a moment and waited. The general didn't acknowledge him, so Esau quietly walked in.

"Excuse me, sir. I'm Esau Morgan. Did you want to see me?"

The general didn't look up. He seemed paused in thought. Esau waited.

General Howe looked very much like Esau had heard him described. He was a big man, even when seated behind a desk. His hand was poised steadily over his letter. Esau caught himself looking at the paper, drawn to the words. Then he realized what he was doing and quickly averted his eyes. He waited a minute, then two, then three. The general hadn't even recognized that he entered the room yet. Nor had he moved in all the time Esau had been there.

"Excuse me, General. You wanted to see me? Esau Morgan?"

A howl of laughter coming from the doorway startled Esau. Doubled over, holding his belly, was Andre. The only thing that kept him from collapsing on the ground was the doorway itself.

Confused, Esau looked back at the general. The general still had not moved! John Andre was beside himself with laughter, tears rolling down his cheeks, and the general paid no attention to him!

"Wax!" Andre managed to say between howls, pointing at the general. "He's a wax figure!"

Esau couldn't believe it. He looked at the still unmoved General Howe again. It was remarkable! The features, the pigmentation looked real! The hair was real, as was the general's uniform! This whole thing was set up to trick him! The look of realization on Esau's face when he turned back to Andre sent the major into new spasms of laughter.

This time Esau joined him.

"I can't get over it," he said after the laughter died down.

He and Andre hovered over the wax figure, examining it from all angles.

"I know the man," Andre said, "and the first time I saw it, it had me fooled."

"Whoever did this is amazing," Esau said. "Absolutely amazing!"

"Why, thank you, Master Morgan. I'm glad you approve of my work." Standing in the doorway, pushing blonde wisps of hair out of her eyes, was Abigail Matteson, the woman who lived at the white house with the evergreen shutters.

The real waxwork exhibit was held at No. 100 on the upper end of Queen Street. It had an assortment of figures, some historical, some contemporary, some well known, others just studies of ordinary people. All the figures had one thing in common—they were realistic down to the smallest detail.

John Andre and Esau Morgan strolled with the artist through her exhibit.

"I recognized Abigail's house from your description when you told me of the events with the Bloody Scouts," Andre said to

Esau. "And when you described the drooping musket protruding from the window, I almost exploded inside! I knew exactly what Abigail had done! They were wax muskets!"

"Weapons are hard to come by," Abigail said. "A woman has to defend herself. I keep reminding Isaac to keep them in a cool place. That morning, he'd pulled them from under his bed and left them laying on top. He got distracted, and by the time that awful raiding party came later, the sun had moved so that it was hitting the bed. As you might expect, the wax was soft."

Esau to Andre: "Why didn't you tell me you knew Mrs. Matteson?"

"Because the wax muskets inspired me to greatness! Why not trick my good friend Esau Morgan?"

"You ought to be locked up," Esau said.

"I can attest to that!" Abigail added.

Andre and Abigail shared a warm glance. It made Esau wonder what kind of relationship they had. Just then, Andre heard his name called from across the room. A young man and woman stood arm in arm, motioning him to join them. Andre excused himself, leaving Esau and Abigail alone.

"I hope you weren't offended by Andre's trick," she said.

"I'll get even," Esau said smiling. "Do you have a figure of George Washington? I could put it in his bedroom so that it's the first thing he sees when he wakes up."

Abigail laughed. She wrinkled her nose as she did, her blue eyes contributing as much to the smile as her lips.

"How long have you known Andre?" Esau asked.

"A couple of years now. We met shortly after his release as a prisoner of war. And you?"

"Several months. But I feel like I've known him for years."

"Andre is like that."

A moment of awkward silence passed between them. Esau

searched his mind desperately for something to talk about.

"I should apologize to you and thank you," Abigail said.

"Oh?"

She nodded. "The day you saved me from the raiding party. You risked your life for me. I've never thanked you for that."

"As I remember, you pointed an antique musket at me and ordered me off your land."

A look of hurt crossed her face, and Esau wished he hadn't said what he just said.

"At least let me explain," she said. "Of course, at that time, I had no idea who you were, and the thought occurred to me that the whole thing was an elaborate ruse."

Esau chuckled. "You gave Odell too much credit. He doesn't have enough brains to be clever."

"Odell? The man with the strange eye?"

Esau nodded.

"I could tell that right off. You see, I didn't think he was the leader. I thought you were."

"Me?"

Abigail nodded. "The way I had it figured, you set it up to look like you chased the others off, so that I would be grateful to you. Then, once they were gone, you would expect me to relax my guard, maybe even invite you into the house. Then you would— well, let's just say you would have achieved your objective and the others would return."

Esau laughed.

"Well! I fail to see what's so funny, Master Morgan!"

She turned away. Esau caught her by the arm.

"No, you misunderstand." Her eyes were sending warning signals. "Please, I wasn't laughing at you. I was laughing because now you've given *me* too much credit. I could never have come up with a plan as elaborate as that one!"

Abigail warmed, but only slightly. Esau released her arm and Andre returned. She excused herself to attend to other guests at the exhibition, and Esau mentally chastised himself for not handling the conversation better.

※

Back at Andre's manor, the two bachelors resumed their positions and activities, the ones they were engaged in before Andre's trick on Esau. It was a spacious manor they were sharing, in keeping with Andre's style of living. In each occupied city, because he was a general's favorite—first Howe, then Clinton—Andre was early in line to choose from the houses deserted by wealthy revolutionary leaders. In Philadelphia, he had occupied Benjamin Franklin's house and enjoyed dabbling in the famous man's workshop. In New York, he chose the house of a rich newspaper owner whose weekly publication had been vehemently anti-British and was no longer in circulation.

"How did you meet Abigail?"

Andre looked up from the paper he was reading, his blank look indicating a preoccupied mind. "What was that?"

"Abigail. How did you meet her?"

"I first noticed her at social functions. She's invited to all the best ones. Well regarded in elite society circles. I first met her at one of her exhibits."

Esau nodded as if in casual interest. "Is she one of your girls?"

Andre lowered his paper. A wolfish grin appeared. "What do you mean, 'one of my girls'?"

Nonchalantly waving his hand, Esau said, "It's a legitimate question. In Philadelphia there were the two Peggys, and who knows how many others. Is Abigail one of your … well, one of your Peggys?"

Andre's eyes brightened. "Why do you want to know?"

"Just conversation. After all, you and she did play quite a trick on me. I simply want to know who I'm up against."

A warm smile indicated Andre felt his suspicions were confirmed. "Abigail Matteson is no one's girl," he said. "And I doubt if she will ever be anyone's again. She's a strong woman, intelligent, and, as you have seen, extremely talented. She's friendly and warm, but only to a point. I've seen more than one man attempt to advance beyond friendship. She has a strong line of defense against such tactics. As far as I know, no one has succeeded in breaching her barricade."

"Yet she was married—to a grenadier. He was killed near Lexington."

Andre expressed surprise that Esau knew this information.

Esau explained: "She told Odell about him in an attempt to persuade him that she was a loyal Englishwoman."

"She also has two sons," Andre added. "John and Thomas, both of them are in school at Cambridge."

It was Esau's turn to express surprise. Then the more he thought about it, he realized how foolish he was to expect otherwise. Most people his age had children. He was the exception, not the norm.

"From what I've heard of Colonel Matteson, he was a stolid military rationalist—ran his home with the same cold orderliness he used with his men. It wasn't until after he died that Abigail was allowed to pursue her craft, then she was forced to do it out of necessity, to earn enough money to live."

"How can a woman as warm as Abigail marry a man like that?"

"How do you know Abigail is a warm woman?" Andre joked.

"All right, I'm interested in her! Do you mind? She strikes me as a warm sort of a woman."

Andre was enjoying himself at Esau's expense. But he was also pleased for Esau and wanted to see his friend happy. "To you and me, Abigail's marriage seems a mismatch. But who's to say? She evidently saw something in him she liked. Maybe he was just different from what she had known before. You know how it is when you're young and ready to explore the world. Everything that is new and different from what you already know is viewed as better. She came from a traditional Puritan family, he from a long line of deistic rationalists—well, look at the boys' names: John, as in John Locke, and Thomas, as in Thomas Hobbes."

"She told you that?"

Andre nodded. "The colonel named them. And according to Abigail, they are the image of their father. Both have embraced deistic rationalism with a fervor. To them God is distant and reason is supreme."

"Is that what Abigail believes?"

Andre shrugged. "I don't know. She's spoken of her husband's and sons' beliefs, but never of her own."

Esau leaned his head back and stared at the ceiling, taking in all he'd learned of Abigail Matteson.

"Did I tell you I was riding out to her house Tuesday?"

Esau's head shot up. His friend was toying with him.

"Really!" Andre insisted. "I'm sitting for her. She's going to do a wax bust of me."

Straightening in his chair, Esau's mind searched frantically for a way to invite himself along.

"There's no need to beg me," Andre said in jest. "Esau Morgan, would you do me the favor of accompanying me to Abigail Matteson's house on this Tuesday next? I so much would appreciate your company."

"Well … I don't know if I'm free on Tuesday.…"

The modeling was scheduled for afternoon. Although the September days were still warm without much of a morning chill, still the wax was more pliable by the afternoon. The ride to Abigail's house was a scenic reminder of the days not long past when he nearly lost his life. They rode by the tree to which he was tied when Odell was about to cut him. The three-story white house with its green shutters coming into view reminded Esau of the seething fury he saw on Odell's heavily whiskered face; the Bloody Scouts armed with muskets arrayed behind him; the self-confident, beautiful woman protecting her house with a musket that couldn't fire; and, of course, the drooping musket from the upstairs window. If Esau lived more than a hundred years, he would never forget the drooping musket.

Since that fateful day, Esau had been assigned to Andre, and Odell had been brought up on charges. Although the Americans condemned the raiding parties because they served no military objective, the British found them useful for keeping their loyalist soldiers occupied while giving the American troops an elusive problem with which they were forced to commit defensive resources. The British rarely concerned themselves with the conduct of their raiding parties, with some exceptions. Abigail Matteson was one of those exceptions. Odell and his Bloody Scouts crossed the line between tolerance and intolerance with their attempted raid on such a prominent New York socialite who had, time and again, proved her loyalty to the crown. A court-martial put Odell and his Bloody Scouts out of the raiding business and into various terms of incarceration. As for Esau, he assumed his assignment to Andre meant that events regarding Benedict Arnold's betrayal of West Point were soon at hand.

Missy, the Negro kitchen maid who had wrung her hands during Odell's challenge and raced from one upstairs room to another propping wax muskets in the windows, was the first to greet Andre and Esau upon their arrival. She ushered them into Abigail's workshop, telling them that Abigail would be down shortly. She had an extra smile for Esau. He assumed it was her way of thanking him for his part in the rescue.

Abigail Matteson's workshop was spacious but cluttered. Tables lined the walls filled with containers, brushes, a variety of tools unknown to Esau; tarps hid piles of things in the corners of the floor; a small stove with a merry fire was situated against one wall. A chair and a stool were placed conspicuously near a window. A heavy smell of melted wax and turpentine pervaded the room. Walls were decorated with a variety of wax relief works— Esau recognized a relief of the French philosopher Voltaire and another of Adam and Eve being expelled from the garden of Eden. Sculpted pieces in various stages of completion lay scattered about—heads, arms and hands, ears. The disconnected body parts gave the room an eerie feeling, insinuating that there was a secret, foreboding side to the lovely blonde artist.

"Gentlemen."

Abigail Matteson appeared in the workshop doorway, standing as grand as any young maiden had ever stood atop a ballroom stairway while making her first society entrance. It wasn't her clothing or adornment that struck the image in Esau's mind, for her dress was lovely, but plain, and she wore no jewelry. It was her poise, coupled with a heavenly visage of pale skin, blonde hair, and incredibly blue eyes.

She greeted each man cordially, equally, then proceeded with her work. Andre was positioned on the stool near the window, the natural light illuminating his face. Upon realizing there was no chair for Esau, she called to Missy who brought one from the dining room. Abigail positioned the chair herself, placing Esau closer to Andre than to her.

Conversation turned to her recent exhibition on Queen Street as the artist circled her subject, examining his facial features. Esau grew uncomfortable. The longer Abigail hovered around his friend, the more jealous he became, as though something inside him sprung a leak and he was filling up. While Abigail relayed some of the comments she received about her work, both good and bad, Esau imagined how he would feel if her face were circling his, at times mere inches away.

Andre's eyes caught his. The smirk on his friend's face indicated Andre sensed what Esau was thinking. Esau felt his face redden.

"Is that how you want your bust to look?" Abigail snapped. "With that silly grin on your face?"

"No, ma'am," Andre said, straining to remove the silly grin.

Abigail donned an oversized apron. She then removed a large piece of wax from under a tarp that had been setting in the sun on a workbench. Sitting in the chair opposite Andre, she placed the wax in her lap, under the apron, and began working it with her hands.

"Aren't you going to do sketches first?" Andre asked.

"I never do sketches."

"Really?" The artist in him was intrigued. He wanted to watch her work. Abigail reminded him he was the subject and ordered him to hold his pose. "But you're not even looking at the wax!"

That was true. The wax and Abigail's hands were hidden under the apron.

"I know what I'm doing, Master Andre."

That was quite evident by the confidence with which she worked. She rarely took her eyes off Andre while, beneath the apron, hands pushed and gouged and smoothed the wax. At times her forearms strained and she grimaced while working; at other times she worked serenely and talked freely.

"Do you mix anything with the wax?"

This was one artist talking to another. Esau didn't mind. While Abigail studied Andre's face, he studied hers, although he could not be too bold about it, for at times she would glance in his direction, and he had to be careful that she didn't catch him looking at her too often.

"I mix Venice turpentine with the wax," she said.

"And how do you get the flesh color?"

"Flake white and a bit of *cinabrio.*"

"Cinabrio?"

"Vermilion."

Andre nodded in understanding.

"Are you an artist too, Master Morgan?"

The blue eyes focused on Esau. "No, just someone who loves art."

"Oh? What media?"

"I like oils, mainly pastoral scenes. And I'm partial to ceramics. My mother's influence."

"Your mother is a collector of ceramics?"

Esau nodded. "My father was one of the first merchants in Boston to establish a line of trade with China. So we have quite a collection of vases and figurines."

"Really? I'd love to see them!" Then she caught herself. "Boston. That's hardly possible for either of us right now, is it?"

"Not if you didn't mind it being the last thing you ever saw," Andre joked.

"Of course, nothing we have here can compare to the art in England and on the continent," Esau said. "American efforts are rustic at best."

"Oh?"

It was Abigail's offended voice that challenged him, but both she and Andre leveled scowls at him.

"No, I didn't mean it that way," Esau stammered. "Truly, I didn't. Your work is magnificent, Abigail. I mean, I couldn't tell it from the real thing, remember?" He chuckled nervously and didn't seem to be making much progress in pulling himself out of the embarrassing hole that he'd dug and fallen into. "All I meant was that in England and France and Italy they have such a rich heritage of art, I mean with the Renaissance painters and all that ..."

With a deadpan expression, Andre said to Abigail, "I suggest you make the eloquent Master Morgan your next subject. You can show him with his tongue hanging out and tied in a knot!"

If Andre's barbed wit was the only chastening he received for his stupid blunder, Esau would have considered himself lucky, but he wasn't that fortunate. Although Abigail laughed with them at Andre's humor, there was no mistaking the fact that she had a definite glint of disappointment in her eyes.

"I made my comment in jest," Andre said, "but that's not a bad idea. Esau would make a good subject for you, Abigail. Artist to artist, look at that strong nose and chin."

Abigail didn't look. Her attention was concentrated on the current project in her lap, her hands moving in a stroking fashion. "I'm afraid," she said while rubbing, "that my workload is rather heavy right now." She rubbed some more. "There!"

Her pronouncement of the completion of her work brought both men's eyes to her lap. Abigail pulled back her apron to reveal her creation. What had once been an elongated block of wax was now a rough bust of Major John Andre, lifelike from any angle.

For the remainder of the week a portion of each day was spent in Abigail Matteson's wax-modeling studio as she completed the bust of Andre. After the second day, Esau expressed his reluctance to Andre about accompanying him to Abigail's house, since he had no real reason for being there. Andre insisted Esau join him, threatening to order him to come if necessary. It wasn't. Esau was easily persuaded. As for Abigail, she never commented one way or the other about Esau's continued appearances.

Saturday the bust was nearly complete. Andre had brought one of his powdered wigs for the head and an officer's coat to drape over the shoulders. Abigail had added eyebrows and lashes and had painted portions of the face—the lips and cheeks and eyes—to make it even more lifelike. As usual, Andre was sitting on the stool by the window and Abigail sat in a chair. The bust was perched on a rough pedestal as Abigail's steady hands guided a small brush, adding highlights next to the eyes that indicated a hint of wrinkles.

Abigail had sent Missy to the market, so Esau went to the dining room to get a chair. He had to pass through the kitchen and sitting room to reach the dining room. In the sitting room, on sofas and chairs, sat wax figures of people—a British general, a New York merchant, a young woman who looked like a housemaid, and others. Esau's first reaction was to apologize for barging into the room and disturbing them. He quickly looked behind him, expecting to see Andre and Abigail at the doorway, having another bit of humor at his expense. There was no one there, only him and the wax figures.

Esau took a moment to study each of the figures up close. Abigail's work was amazing. Astonishingly real. Other than a slight imperfection at the base of the general's neck, like a patch that had not been completely smoothed over, her work was flawless. Realizing that several minutes had already passed and not wanting to appear to be snooping, Esau hurried into the dining room to get his chair.

He grabbed the dining-room chair closest to the doorway and was about to carry it to the workshop when something stopped him. At the head of the table there was a single setting, uncleared since breakfast. In the chair to the immediate right of the setting was a draped figure. Facial features poked against the covering from underneath, and the portion of an arm was showing where the covering came up short.

Esau glanced behind him to see if he was still alone. No one in sight. Like a burrowing beetle, curiosity wormed its way through his mind. Esau set the chair down and moved to the head of the table. He checked the doorway again. He was alone. Slowly, he reached for the edge of the covering and lifted. The image that emerged from beneath the covering was so startling it knocked him backward into the chair at the table's head.

"Did he get lost?"

Abigail looked up from her work and glanced over her shoulder in the direction of the doorway. "Sometimes I wonder about your friend," she said.

Andre smiled. "He's taken with you."

A look of shock appeared momentarily on Abigail's face, then quickly disappeared, replaced by the concentration of a professional as she set brush to wax again. "I don't have time for that sort of thing," she said.

"Abigail, don't judge Esau by my life. He's a good man, loyal—and I don't mean politically, though he is that too. Perhaps someday he'll tell you why he's never been married. Unlike me, Esau will make some woman very happy for a lifetime, whereas I prefer to make many women happy for a short time."

Abigail chuckled at Andre's self-description. "If I hear of a woman who is looking for a good man, I'll be sure to send her to Esau."

With a shrug, Andre said, "I think the two of you could make each other very happy."

Another glance over her shoulder. "I prefer a man who can successfully navigate through three rooms by himself."

"Maybe we'd better go see what's keeping him," Andre suggested.

Abigail set down her brush and wiped her hands. Then she and Andre went in search of Esau. They found him in the dining room, sitting at the head of the table.

"Oh my!" Abigail cried.

Andre let loose a sidesplitting roar.

Seated at Abigail Matteson's dining table were two identical Esau Morgans.

The crackle and pop of a fire was the only sound in the house other than their hushed voices. They sat on the floor, a backgammon game spread between them.

Abigail tossed the dice. "Doublets!"

Esau groaned.

With victory in sight, Abigail hit two of his blots, bringing to a total of six of Esau's stones resting on the bar.

"Ruthless! Absolutely ruthless!"

Unfazed by his remark, she completed her doublet by bearing off two of her stones.

Esau smiled as Abigail set the stones she removed beside the board, then brushed back stray blonde hairs away from her eyes with the back of her hand. It was a mannerism she used frequently when working with wax, one that he had come to love about her.

"Do you surrender?" she asked.

"What? When I'm so close to victory?"

"Yours is a world of fantasy, Master Morgan, if you think you can win this one."

Esau studied the board. "Double sixes ought to do it," he said.

"If I roll double sixes, I've got an excellent chance of winning. Watch this."

He rattled the dice in his hand, then sent them flying with a flourish. A three and a four. Both points were blocked by Abigail's stones, rendering Esau's turn useless.

Esau held out his hands as if to be bound. "Consider me your prisoner of war. All I ask is that you torture me no longer."

Abigail squinted her eyes in a mean look. "Torture? You don't know what torture is; it has only just begun."

It was a week to the day since the double Esau incident. At first Abigail was furious that Esau had uncovered the wax figure of his own likeness, and she ran from the room. With Andre's urging, Esau went after her. He found her behind the house leaning against a tree, weeping. In soft tones, he told her how flattered he was that she did what she did. When that gained no positive response, he decided to tell her how he felt about her, that from the first day he saw her he was attracted to her, that he thought of her often, and that he re-created her image in his mind a thousand times a day. So if there was anything wrong with what she had done, he was just as guilty; he merely lacked her skills to bring his image to life.

She turned around and faced him, eyes red and swollen.

Esau told her that he didn't know how much longer he was going to be in New York and that he couldn't begin to compete with the wit and charm of the fellow sitting at her dining table, but that if she was willing, he'd gladly replace the figure with a living, breathing model. Or, if she preferred, he would leave.

Abigail Matteson invited him to stay for dinner, and they got along so well together, she invited him to come back the next day and the next. Seven days and seven dinners later, they played backgammon in front of the fire in the parlor on the first chilly evening of September.

"I've been wanting to ask you something, but I hesitate to bring it up," Esau said.

Abigail's guard visibly raised.

"If it's going to hurt our relationship," Esau said, "I don't even want to ask it."

"You have to ask it now." She was serious.

"Tell you what," Esau said, "if you're offended by the question after you hear it, or simply don't want to answer it, put away the backgammon game and we'll pretend I never asked it."

Doubtful eyes questioned whether that was possible. Even so, she nodded in agreement.

"It's about my wax double." He paused.

Her hands remained in her lap.

"Where is it? I haven't seen it since that day in the dining room."

Abigail's face remained neutral. She reached toward the backgammon board and picked up a single stone. Twirling it over and over in her hands, she kept her eyes fixed on it as she spoke. "It's in a place where I can see it."

Esau knew he was on uncertain ground. Still, she hadn't objected to the first question, so he thought he'd try another on the same subject. "If you didn't want me to see ..." he searched for the proper pronoun since the figure was so lifelike, it ... *him?* "If you didn't want me to see him, why did you leave him out?"

"That was unintentional," she said, still speaking to the stone. "Missy was supposed to clear the table and put ..." she smiled, liking Esau's choice of pronouns, "... *him* away."

"One more question?"

Softly, "Yes?"

"How did you do it? I mean, Andre did a sketch of me. I had to sit in front of him for almost two hours and his sketch looked more like my brother than me. And with Andre, you took all that time doing his bust. How is it you could do a likeness of me so perfectly when I never sat for you?"

The backgammon stone twirled faster in her hands. "It wasn't necessary for Andre to come every day last week. I can do a bust after one sitting of about an hour."

"Then why …"

Abigail plopped the stone onto the board. "Do I have to come right out and say it? I told him to come every day because I wanted to see you. After the first day, it wasn't him I was studying, it was you. That's why I could do the wax figure of you from memory. There, are you happy?"

Happy didn't begin to describe how Esau felt. He was soaring.

To hide her embarrassment, Abigail began collecting stones from the board in hurried fashion. Esau reached down and touched the back of her hand. Like a frightened rabbit, the hand froze. Tenderly, Esau's fingers encircled and covered it. Abigail's eyes raised. They leaned over the backgammon board and kissed.

They saw each other every day, right up to the day Esau and Andre traveled to meet Benedict Arnold. Hand in hand they would stroll after dinner around the grounds surrounding Abigail's house, or sit across a backgammon board, or simply sit and talk late into the night.

To encourage their romance, Major John Andre, with the British secret service, assigned Esau to general surveillance in the vicinity of the Matteson house. New York was not without its share of spies, and there was an effective spy ring operating in the area, so the orders could be easily defended if questioned. Unofficially, Andre instructed Esau to concentrate his surveillance activity on Abigail, spending as much time with her as he possibly could.

Andre was not the only one encouraging their romance. Missy and Isaac, Abigail's Negro servants, approached Esau together and told him that Abigail was so much happier now that he was courting her.

※

"Tell me about Mercy."

They were in their favorite place, in front of the fire in the parlor. Esau lay with his head in her lap; she arranged and rearranged his hair with her fingers. At the question, he tensed, prompting a playful chuckle from Abigail.

"There's no need for you to feel threatened," she said warmly, stroking his hair.

"How do you know about Mercy?"

"Major Andre mentioned her, said I should ask you about her sometime. He meant it in a complimentary way."

Slowly the story spilled out—the battle for Mercy's hand and its dubious outcome, then Esau's long-standing hope that someday Mercy would be his wife.

"That's sweet," she said softly.

He looked up at her quizzically. "Sweet? How can you think that's sweet?"

"I'm not saying you were right in everything you did, and you probably should have seen the proverbial handwriting on the wall much sooner than you did. I think it's sweet that you could love a woman for that long without giving up and without having any satisfaction. You didn't, did you? Have satisfaction, I mean?"

"No."

"Do you still love her?"

It had been months since he'd even thought of Mercy; even so, years of emotions could not be wiped away in a few months. He weighed one against the other. "No," he concluded. "No, I don't think I do."

A warm hand swept across his forehead. "I know," she said.

The fire danced and popped.

"Tell me about your husband, the colonel."

"A stern man, good, conscientious, ambitious."

"Did he love you?"

"As much as he was capable of loving."

"Why did you marry him?"

Blonde curls fell forward as she looked down at him and smiled.

"You don't have to tell me."

Looking into the fire, her eyes glazed over as she remembered the past. "He was tall, handsome, a man who was sure of himself. He wasn't afraid to challenge traditional thinking. Back then, to me that was exciting."

"And now?"

"Over the years, I've discovered that the beliefs of my parents aren't as outmoded as I had once thought. Isn't that strange how as you grow older, things you once thought foolish become suddenly profound."

"What belief are they?"

"Were. They're both dead."

"Sorry."

"My parents and ancestors were Puritans, originally settled in Hingham, later moved to Oyster Bay, Long Island."

"Mine settled in Boston."

"I could tell that about you, that you had a strong religious upbringing. That's one of the things that attracted me to you. You have definite religious beliefs and can still be a strong man. There was a time I didn't believe the two could coexist."

"Sometime I'll have to tell you about my ancestor Drew Morgan. Quite a man. He's the one who first came over from Edenford. In fact, it's his legacy that I want to continue when I

return to England. I guess you could say that's my primary motivation for wanting to return there."

Abigail fell silent. She stared into the fire, lost in thought.

For the remainder of the evening she was distant. And when
they said good-night to each other, she turned her head when
Esau leaned forward to kiss her. The kiss landed on her cheek.

22

The air was brisk as Major John Andre and Esau Morgan boarded the barge. The sun was beginning to peek over the horizon. A shiver caused Esau to quake. *The damp air penetrating his clothing or the anticipation of their mission?* He wasn't sure which.

"Steady there." Andre turned to him with an assuring grin.

"A chill," Esau replied matter-of-factly.

The barge slipped into the Hudson River. The two passengers rode in silence, the weight of the day's events heavy on their minds. The plan was a simple one. The barge would take them to the *HMS Vulture*, a British sloop commanded by Captain Andrew Sutherland, patrolling off Tellers Point. There, under a flag of truce, they would confer with Major General Benedict Arnold. The American general would deliver maps of West Point's defenses, and British Major Andre would finalize the details of Arnold's crossover to British lines and his recompense. The two would then return to their respective sides and await the mutually agreed-upon date for the attack on West Point.

Although the meeting was not without risks, it was a relatively safe encounter; otherwise, British General Clinton would never have agreed to let Major Andre go. It wasn't uncommon for officers from opposite sides of the war to confer under a flag of truce regarding administrative duties that were mutually advantageous. It was a convenient cover for Arnold and a suitable stage for treason.

In his final meeting with Andre before departure, General Clinton gave him explicit instructions. First, he was to go as a British officer. Under no circumstances was he to adopt a disguise; for by removing his uniform, he could be considered a spy. Second, Arnold must come to him. Nothing should be allowed to lure Andre behind American lines. Third, if Arnold appeared to be holding back, Andre was to return immediately. A new British squadron had recently arrived, freeing another force for a quick dash to West Point, but there could be no delays. With these things understood between the two men, Major John Andre left to meet Arnold. Esau Morgan accompanied him. It was thought Esau's presence could influence Arnold positively should the general show signs of wavering.

"We're making history today," Andre said from the front of the barge, a twinge of excitement in his voice.

"I know." Esau smiled weakly. The water of the Hudson lapped against the barge as the trees on the shore, drier than normal for this time of year, slipped slowly by them. If all went well, English history texts would record the names of Arnold and Andre as courageous saviors of the empire whose bold vision brought about the downfall of an ill-fated colonial rebellion. Esau's name wouldn't be mentioned. That didn't matter. It was enough that he would be able to tell his children and grandchildren that he was there to witness the historic event.

The thought of heirs prompted his mind to wander to Abigail. It was a curious thing—they were so happy to have found each other, and he was confident she loved him as much as he loved her, yet every time he mentioned future plans, she grew distant. *What is it about the future that causes her to react that way,* he wondered. *Maybe she's hesitant to move to England. Of course! Her whole life and her career are in America. How insensitive of me to assume she could easily leave everything behind.* He determined to talk with her about her feelings about leaving America upon his return. Then the question arose, *What if she is unwilling to leave America?* Would I be willing to stay in America for Abigail? That question would be much easier to answer if his and Andre's mission was successful and the British regained control of the colonies.

They reached Dobbs Ferry by midafternoon where they were to meet the *Vulture.* The plan called for them to wait there should they arrive first, but an anxious Andre ordered the barge to continue upriver since the tide was with them. They rendezvoused with the sloop in Haverstraw Bay, fifteen miles downriver from West Point.

Captain Sutherland greeted them warmly, but once the pleasantries were completed, Andre and Esau discovered that both captain and crew were tighter than an overwound watch.

"We were fired upon," Captain Sutherland said.

"When?"

"This morning. I spied a white flag on shore at an American outpost and sent a boat to investigate. The outpost opened fire on us."

"A serious breach of military courtesy," Andre said.

"It could be more than that," the captain replied. "If you have been found out, it could be a trap."

That explains the captain and crew's reaction, Esau thought. It would take a lot more than a breach of courtesy to shake the officers and crew of a man-of-war, especially men who were hardened by service at such an exposed location.

"It could be a signal from Arnold," Andre said.

"The post is under his command," Captain Sutherland said. "Do you think he's warning us away?"

"Possibly."

"What do you want to do?"

Major Andre stared toward the shore. Then he said, "We'll stay and see if Arnold comes."

The captain responded, "If there's any further sign of trouble, my first concern is the safety of the ship."

"Understood."

For the remainder of that day and into the night, Andre paced the bridge of the ship. There was no sign of Arnold. But there was no further trouble either.

The next morning passed and there was still no contact. By midafternoon, Captain Sutherland was growing increasingly impatient. Andre stalled him by reminding him that Arnold had to show; he had too much to lose. All the British had to do to neutralize him was to allow his correspondence to fall into the hands of the American army and he would be ruined. Arnold needed this meeting to show his good faith.

Sutherland agreed to stay a little longer.

"Do you think the plot's been discovered?" Esau stood beside Andre on deck. He spoke in low tones.

"I don't know," Andre replied, his face and voice showing the strain of the wait. "In our last correspondence, Arnold mentioned it was nearly impossible for him to slip away on some days. Both Washington and Lafayette are in the area. They make regular inspections of the troops and usually stop at West Point for breakfast. He says that the younger officers, Lafayette especially, come by frequently because of Peggy. He says they're all in love with her."

"Who isn't in love with that woman?" Esau asked incredulously.

A wolfish grin appeared, wiping away all traces of tension from Andre's face.

"You have to admit, she is remarkable," he said.

That's more like it, Esau thought. *That's the carefree Andre I know.*

"Sutherland is pressing me to leave."

"You don't want to."

"Not yet, but he outranks me." A pause. "So this is what we're going to do."

As the sun lowered itself behind the American fortifications along the river, Andre went below to his quarters and Esau sought out the captain. He explained that Andre wasn't feeling well—a recurring stomach ailment. Andre requested they delay their departure at least until morning, hoping that he would feel better by then. The captain agreed.

Esau's report wasn't entirely untrue. Before the mission, Andre had suffered a stomach ailment, and his stomach didn't feel well at the moment, but in truth his current discomfort was caused by two days of nervous tension, not sickness.

In the early hours of September 22, a boat with muffled oars was challenged as it drew near the *Vulture*. The man in the boat identified himself as Mr. Smith with a message for John Anderson. This was Andre's code name in all his correspondence with Benedict Arnold.

It was two o'clock in the morning when Andre and Esau were brought on deck. Mr. Smith delivered a letter to Andre. It was in Arnold's handwriting. Andre was to get into the boat. Mr. Smith would take him ashore where he would meet Arnold.

Andre didn't hesitate. "I'll get my coat and hat."

Once below deck, Esau blocked his way. "We've already stretched beyond reason General Clinton's instruction about delays. Going onshore would be a direct violation of his order not to be lured behind American lines."

Andre pushed past him. "You're free to stay onboard if you wish. I'm going."

"Wait!" Esau grabbed his arm. "Didn't you notice? That boat was not flying a white flag of truce. What if it's a trap? Let me go. If it is a trap, then they have a small fish, nothing more. And if Arnold is really onshore, I'll persuade him to come aboard under a flag of truce."

"No. I'm going ashore. No operation goes exactly according to plan, adjustments are always needed in the field. This is a field adjustment, nothing more. Are you with me?"

"I'll get my coat."

Just before the two men climbed aboard the boat, Captain Sutherland offered them civilian greatcoats since they were still in British uniforms and wouldn't be going ashore under a white flag. Major Andre refused. He'd already violated two of General Clinton's instructions regarding the mission; he thought it best not to disobey the third one.

"Who's that?" Smith pointed a shaking finger at Esau. "I'm to bring John Anderson, no one else. I don't like this ..."

"He's with me," Andre interrupted.

"I'm not going anywhere with him!" The man was frightened.

"You have a choice." Andre's eyes hardened, as did his voice. "Either row us both to shore, or get out of the boat and we'll row ourselves."

Mr. Smith glared at Andre and Esau and then, muttering, gripped the oars and began rowing. As the *Vulture* grew distant, its lights reflecting on the river's surface, Esau turned toward land and scanned the shoreline. Hugging the water's edge was a forest of fir trees. What little light the moon afforded was swiftly gobbled up by the trees just a few feet inland.

The short trip was made in silence. Upon reaching shore, Smith shooed them toward the trees. "He's in there."

With Andre in the lead, the two men marched into the trees. The major walked as confidently as if he were striding into history. Esau didn't feel as confident. The trees were dense and they couldn't see far. Leaves crackled underfoot, announcing their presence. There was an occasional groan and pop, not unusual for forests. Tonight, however, the forest sounds seemed ominous.

"HOLD THERE OR BE SHOT!"

Both men pulled up abruptly.

"WHAT IS THIS? WHO ARE YOU?"

The sudden shout caused Esau's heart to pound madly.

"John Anderson," Andre answered, his voice surprisingly calm.

"I know John Anderson," said the voice. "He travels alone."

Esau recognized the voice. "Sir, General Arnold, it's me. Esau Morgan."

"Esau?" The voice was skeptical, then firm. "Both of you step forward, slowly, so I can see you."

Andre waited until Esau was beside him. Together, they walked forward until Major General Benedict Arnold came into view, his hand gripping a pistol.

"Esau! It is you! And in a British uniform. I thought you had more brains than that. You almost got the two of you killed, coming unannounced with Mr. Anderson like that."

"His presence isn't the only unexpected change in plans. Why didn't you meet us aboard the *Vulture?*" asked Andre.

Arnold scowled at the major with his piercing gray eyes.

"General," Esau said, "allow me to introduce Major John Andre."

The pistol lowered. "I couldn't get away until now without arousing suspicion," Arnold replied.

General Arnold meant for the meeting in the woods to be only a preliminary one, it being too cold and inconvenient a place to plan the salvation of the English empire. He brought none of his papers with him and only one spare horse for Andre. To Mr. Smith's chagrin—his real name, not a fake one as Esau had assumed—Esau was given his horse. Smith would secure another horse in Haverstraw and catch up with them. Their destination was Smith's house, just north of Haverstraw.

They were challenged by sentries on the outskirts of Haverstraw, posted there by Arnold himself. Arnold identified himself and they were allowed to pass. It must have looked an odd sight to the sentries to see an American general escorting two British soldiers through the town in the early-morning hours.

Upon reaching their destination, the three of them quickly went to work. Arnold spread out maps of West Point on a large table. He tactically evaluated the fortress, in effect planning the attack against his own command. He pointed out the fort's weaknesses, including those defenses he had artfully weakened in anticipation of a British assault. He drew their attention to a large gap in the fortress wall, made by his order under pretense of preparing the wall for repairs. Arnold seemed particularly pleased with himself as he told them how he had removed one of the links from the iron chain that stretched across the Hudson to prevent unauthorized ship passage. The link was replaced with a temporary one so weak that it would snap when struck by a ship under way.

Following Arnold's presentation of what he was prepared to do and when, Andre negotiated payment. At this point, the general's tone hardened. He demanded ten thousand pounds sterling for his services, the risks they entailed, and his resulting losses in property. Furthermore, he insisted that both he and Peggy be guaranteed safe refuge in New York before the plan was executed. Andre countered that he was authorized to go only as high as six thousand pounds sterling, but that he would use his influence with General Clinton to urge that the sum be increased to ten thousand pounds.

Arnold to Esau: "Can he do it? Will Clinton listen to him?"

"Yes, sir, I believe he can. General Clinton highly values Major Andre's advice."

"Good enough."

It was past four o'clock in the morning, and the sky was growing light. Arnold excused himself to see if Smith, who had safely returned home himself, could arrange breakfast for them. Arnold left the room with his characteristic limp.

"What do you think?" Andre asked Esau. He spoke in hushed tones.

"He can do it. I have no doubt about that."

"What is it that troubles you?"

"He's a different man from the one I knew during the Maine expedition. His wounds and political battles have taken their toll on him. He's hardened, cynical, mercenary. There was a time when I admired him; now I'm not even sure I like him. Did you hear him? It's clear why he's doing this—two reasons, revenge against those who have opposed him and money. In Canada, he had ideals. There is nothing idealistic about him now."

"General Clinton despises him," Andre said. "Says he has no stomach for turncoats."

"Then why work with him?"

Andre chuckled softly. "You are naive, aren't you? Clinton needs the victory. He needs it badly."

The mood was jovial at the breakfast table, though Smith grew increasingly concerned that transporting two British soldiers in broad daylight was a risk he didn't care to take. He refused to row them back to the ship. There was talk of waiting until evening for Andre and Esau's return when they could use the cover of darkness.

BOOM!

A cannon shot shook the dishes on the table.

BOOM! BOOM!

Jumping from the table, Arnold ran outside to see what was happening. Andre and Esau ran to a window. On the far side of the river, at Verplanck's Point, the American post was firing on the *Vulture*. A portion of the deck near the bridge exploded. Wood and splinters showered the deck. There was no fire and it looked like minimal damage. But it was enough. The *Vulture* hauled in its anchor and moved downstream. Soon it was out of sight.

General Arnold stormed back into the house, enraged and cursing.

"Who gave him that gun?" He cursed, then repeated himself. "Who gave him that gun?"

Naturally, he didn't expect an answer from anyone in the room. His eyes jumped back and forth as he thought through the situation. Moments later, still enraged, he explained.

"Twice the commander of that post requested bigger cannons. Twice I refused him, knowing that the guns that size would put your ship at risk. Major Andre, you must believe me. I have no idea where the commander of the fort got that cannon, but I'm going to find out."

Andre believed him. It was inconceivable that Arnold would jeopardize his ten thousand pounds in sterling at this point of the negotiations. But the problem remained. *With the ship gone, how were they going to get back?*

An atmosphere of increasing panic saturated their conversation. Arnold insisted he had to get back to West Point. It was too risky for him to escort two British soldiers to safety. With the water route no longer available to them, their thoughts turned to the roads. Arnold formulated a plan. He would secure American uniforms for Andre and Esau and give them a pass that would get them safely past American sentries.

Andre refused. This was the third of General Clinton's warnings. Under no circumstances was he to assume a disguise. Arnold was adamant. He was the senior officer, and this plan had the best chance of succeeding. He explained that according to military law, once Andre and Esau came behind enemy lines, they technically came under his command and, in effect, were already prisoners of war. Further, he reasoned, it was recognized by all armies that making an attempt to escape is the duty of every officer and, therefore, if they were captured, their punishment would not be as severe as it would if they were caught as spies.

Andre understood the explanation, but he still didn't like it. However, this wasn't the time for a debate and he agreed to Arnold's plan. So the general wrote them a pass, then left hastily to return to West Point. It was left to Smith to secure uniforms for them.

By midafternoon, they were ready to leave. Andre and Esau had exchanged their British uniforms for American uniforms and civilian greatcoats. Andre hid Arnold's maps in his riding boot. Smith outlined the land route that would get them to White Plains. Accompanied by their host, whom Arnold had badgered into escorting them to White Plains, the two men mounted horses bearing the Continental Army brand.

The first part of their ride was without incident. They crossed the Hudson at King's Ferry. Smith talked with the operators of the ferry and several passersby in an amiable way. Esau commented that Andre was unusually quiet. His friend responded with talk of the theater and music and art in a rambling, uneasy manner.

They approached the farthest extent of the American lines. Beyond them lay the middle ground between the two armies and the safety of White Plains. Suddenly an American military unit appeared and they were ordered to halt.

The commanding officer identified himself as Captain Ebenezer Boyd. Andre introduced himself as merchant John Anderson and Esau as his wealthy backer. He handed the captain the pass Arnold had written for them.

Boyd scrutinized the pass.

"General Arnold, huh?" he said, squinting at the pass in the bright light. "You friends with the general?"

"That's right," Andre said.

Boyd looked impressed.

Esau looked over at Smith who was having a hard time sitting still in his saddle. The feeling was shared; only Esau hoped he was able to conceal his nervousness better than Smith. Captain Boyd handed the pass back to Andre.

"A word of warning," he said, taking half a glance over his shoulder, "I can't protect you any farther than this. Beyond this point is dangerous territory, hunting ground for cowboys and skinners."

"Cowboys and skinners?"

"Criminals, deserters from both sides. They take advantage of the absence of lawful authority by preying on homesteads and travelers. Mind you, it's getting dark. It's best not to travel at night. So be careful, and God go with you."

Captain Boyd and his unit rode off.

The close call with the American soldiers was too much for Smith. Although he had agreed to take them all the way to White Plains, at Pine Bridge he left them and returned home. The encounter with Boyd had just the opposite effect on Andre. The uniforms and Arnold's pass worked together effectively. His mood lightened considerably.

"Do you remember this place?" he asked Esau.

Esau looked around and failed to make a connection.

"This is where we first met. Over there a little ways." He

pointed to the edge of the stream. "It was raining. And this is the bridge we hid under when we heard some troops come thundering in our direction."

Esau grinned. He recognized the place now. It looked much different in clear light and from atop the bridge.

"A good omen, I think," Andre said. "The place we met is also the site of the completion of our greatest victory."

"You read too many dramas. Besides, we're not home yet."

"We're as good as home," Andre boasted. "The good Captain Boyd convinced me of that. He even gave us God's blessing."

"What about the skinners? It's getting dark; do you think we should find a place to lodge for the night?"

"Doesn't hurt to be cautious. I remember a farmhouse down over there. Follow me."

At the farm they found a friendly Scotsman willing to give them a room for the night. The room was small with a single four-poster bed. The two bachelors shared the bed, choosing to sleep with their clothes on.

Just as Esau was dozing off, Andre said, "You asleep?"

A sigh. "Not yet."

"Promise me something?"

"What?"

"When we get back to New York, you won't tell anyone about this. It'll ruin my reputation."

Esau got to laughing so hard, it took him another half hour before he could get to sleep.

Dense early-morning fog shrouded the riders as they set off. Andre was eager to make his report to General Clinton, so the two men got an early start.

They had ridden a good distance and were approaching Tarrytown when they came to a tiny stream with an equally tiny bridge. Without warning, three men leaped out at them, two of them grabbing the bits in the horses' mouths while a third held a musket on them. The attackers were all dressed differently, none of them well. A giant of a man, and apparently their leader, wore the red-and-green tunic of a Hessian soldier, which led Andre to believe in the confusion that they had fallen into the hands of a British patrol.

"Gentlemen!" he shouted. "I hope you belong to our party."

The huge man holding his bit said, "What party?"

"Why the lower party, of course, the loyalists of New York City. Thank God, we are once again among friends. I am glad to see you. I am an officer in the British service and have been on business in the country and hope you will not detain us."

Andre pulled out his gold watch and offered it to the man-mountain in return for their immediate release. His captor wasn't impressed.

"Get down," he growled. "We're Americans."

Realizing his mistake, Andre fumbled for Arnold's pass. "We must do anything to get along," he said with nervous laughter. Finding the pass, he handed it to the leader.

With one hand still holding the horse and the other holding the pass, the large leader wrinkled his nose and eyes as he attempted to read it. From the way he slowly mouthed the words, it was evident he was barely literate.

Esau checked the man holding his horse. An ugly sneer greeted him. This was completely different from their encounter with Captain Boyd. At least the captain was literate and a respecter of laws. From the looks of these men, they respected no authority. The man-mountain's response to the pass confirmed Esau's impression.

He cursed Arnold's pass and threw it to the ground. "You said you was a British officer," he shouted. "Get down! Where is your money?"

"Gentlemen, you had best let us go," Andre said, dismounting. Esau climbed down too. "By detaining us, you bring yourselves trouble, for you are interfering with the general's business."

Grabbing the musket from his cohort, the leader jabbed it into Andre's chest. "Where is your money?" he shouted.

"Gentlemen, in truth, we have no money."

"You are British officers and you have no money?" To his men: "Search them!"

Andre and Esau were ordered into a thicket and commanded to remove their clothes. As they did, their abductors rifled through their clothing. The only thing they turned up was Andre's watch and a few Continental dollars given to them by Smith. One of the men ripped the housings from their saddles looking for hidden money.

When Andre's boots were removed, the abductors found Arnold's maps. They studied the maps carefully, trying to determine their value. Esau prayed they would be too dumb to understand what they held in their hands.

Just then, the leader's head jerked up. He stared at Andre and Esau, standing exposed and helpless nearby. "We got ourselves a couple of spies!" he shouted.

"We'll give you the horses, the bridles, the watch, and upon our safe return, my superior will give you a hundred gold guineas, only let us go!" Andre pleaded.

This got the leader's attention.

"We just escaped from a British prison," the leader said, "and don't want to go back to one. How do we know you won't trick us once we're among your friends?"

"You can send one man for the money, the others can stay here and guard us until he returns!" The high pitch of his voice and the speech with which he was talking revealed Andre's growing panic.

"No," the leader said. "What's to stop them from sending out a patrol and taking us all prisoners? It's best that we take you with us. Get dressed."

Just then, four more members of their band appeared. Andre and Esau were prodded as they dressed, then had their hands tied behind their backs once they were mounted on their horses.

"Where are you taking us?" Andre asked.

"To an American fort," the leader replied, sticking Arnold's maps inside his coat. "If my guess is right, you and these maps are worth a lot of money to someone, and we intend to get it."

From atop his horse, with hands tied behind him, Esau glanced over at his friend as they headed back the way they had come. The look on Andre's face sent a shiver through him. It was the look of a man going to the gallows. Apparently Andre had concluded it was all over for them. Esau stared at his friend for a long time, hoping to catch his eye, to encourage him somehow with a smile or a nod, even though he would be offering hope he didn't feel himself. But Andre never looked at him; his friend's head hung low, his eyes were glazed over and fixed straight forward. After a while, Esau gave up and turned away. His thoughts turned to Abigail. He wondered if he would ever see those curly wisps of blonde hair falling in her face again.

The prisoners were taken to North Castle, the nearest American outpost to where they were captured. While the giant leader requested to speak to the commanding officer—a request that was not readily forthcoming in light of the marauder's shabby appearance—Andre and Esau were left within whispering distance of each other. When the leader and one other skinner disappeared inside a building, leaving only one skinner to guard the prisoners, Esau took advantage of the moment.

"Arnold," he whispered to Andre. "Somehow, get word to Arnold!"

Andre's eyes brightened. He nodded.

"SHUT UP!"

From the ground behind him, one of the soiled, unshaved skinners jabbed Esau in the lower back none too gently with the musket barrel, enjoying his momentary authority.

A few more moments passed and the unwashed sentry's mind wandered. This time it was Andre who spoke.

"I've been a prisoner of war before and survived."

"I SAID SHUT UP!" The skinner rounded the end of Esau's horse and was about to deliver a jab to Andre similar to the one that hit Esau when his two compatriots reappeared with an American officer. The self-important skinner thought better of delivering it and pulled back his musket.

The officer introduced himself as Lieutenant Colonel John Jameson.

"Lieutenant," Andre said, "these men have detained us unjustly. If we may have but a moment of your time, I'm sure we will be able to convince you of that fact."

After having spent the last several minutes listening to the ramblings of the head skinner, Jameson seemed clearly impressed with Andre's more literate presentation. The two captives were led into his office.

The John Anderson merchant story was used, the one that worked so well with Captain Boyd earlier. The fact that they had been questioned and released by Boyd came up as well, as an indication that another American officer found their account to be reasonable. And, had it not been for the map of West Point, Lieutenant Jameson would have released them immediately with apologies.

"The map was concealed at General Arnold's request," Andre explained. "A military officer like yourself can understand that such vital information should not be bandied about carelessly."

"But why would you, a merchant, have a map of a military fort?" Jameson asked.

"I'm afraid, sir, I'm not at liberty to reveal that to you."

"Then I hope you understand my dilemma, sir," Jameson said. "I cannot release you without an adequate explanation."

"Nor should you," Esau inserted. "There is only one person who can give you the explanation you need, and that is General Arnold himself."

"Precisely!" Andre said. "It is proper that you inform the officer who signed our pass of our situation. I'm sure he will explain everything to your satisfaction."

Jameson nodded. "That I will do and more."

He sat down at his desk and wrote a letter to General Arnold, informing him that two men had been apprehended with a pass signed by him and a map of importance in their possession. After sealing the letter, he called for a dispatch rider and the message was sent.

To Andre and Esau, he said: "Not only will I dispatch a letter to General Arnold, but I will dispatch you as well." Jameson arranged for an armed guard to transport the two men to West Point and personally deliver them into the custody of General Benedict Arnold.

Spirits were high again as they rode past the guards toward West Point. Maybe the plan to capture the American stronghold would have to be scuttled, maybe not. The important thing now was that they were being delivered into friendly hands.

Andre leaned toward Esau. "It will be good to see Peggy again," he said with a wink.

It was typical John Andre. Here was a man who had the soul of an artist and the volatile emotions to match. His exuberance rubbed off on Esau.

They had traveled less than an hour when a rider from North Castle overtook them with orders for them to return to the fort immediately. Anxious looks passed between Andre and Esau. *What now? Would this nightmare ever end?*

An unsmiling Lieutenant Colonel Jameson stood behind his desk. He introduced another American officer, also wearing a grim expression, as Major Benjamin Talmudge, his second-in-command.

"Major Talmudge has had much greater experience in secret service matters than I," Jameson said. "At his insistence, I had you recalled. You see, he believes that the two of you and General Arnold are all part of a conspiracy."

It was noticeably difficult for Jameson to use General Arnold's name and conspiracy in the same sentence. Against all available evidence, he still didn't want to believe that his commanding general was in secret negotiations with the British. Jameson turned the interrogation over to his second-in-command. Talmudge began by describing the picture as he saw it from the puzzle pieces available. He linked General Arnold and "Anderson" and "Anderson's friend" together in an elaborate plot to turn over West Point to British troops. His analysis was detailed and accurate.

When asked for a reply, "John Anderson" said: "My name is Major John Andre in His Majesty's service. If it would not be too much trouble, I request a paper and pen so that I can write a letter to General Washington, explaining my presence behind American lines."

General Arnold escaped. When Lieutenant Jameson recalled the travelers he'd dispatched to West Point, he neglected to recall the messenger who had preceded them. Upon receiving the news that Andre and Esau had been captured, Arnold fled immediately by boat down the Hudson to the *Vulture* and safety, leaving his family behind.

As news of Arnold's treachery became evident, the colonies and the American army were shocked to the point of disbelief that the hero of Quebec would willingly turn on his country. But the evidence was irrefutable. General Washington burned with rage. The subject of his fury, Arnold, was out of his reach. However, the new nation would not be without satisfaction in the matter. There were still Major John Andre and Esau Morgan.

Washington wanted to act quickly in dealing with this black spot on the American record. A heavily armed detachment was sent to transfer the prisoners from North Castle to Tappan where they would answer to an assembly of General Washington's senior officers.

Once again Andre and Esau found themselves bound and on horses. This time there was no pretense. They were themselves. There was no longer anything to hide. And their fate rested in the hands of one man, General George Washington.

There would be no trial, no court-martial. Although Washington had assembled a board of officers, their capacity would be advisory only. They would examine the prisoners and the evidence and make a recommendation to the general. He alone would decide their sentence. The prisoners' only comfort was that Washington was known as a man of compassion.

"Whoa!"

The detachment came to a halt.

"Will you look at this?"

There was a commotion at the front of the detachment as several officers rode forward and gathered around a group of American soldiers who were traveling the opposite direction on foot. Whatever the commotion in the front, the four soldiers immediately surrounding Andre and Esau were not distracted.

For them, the distraction only served to increase their guard on the prisoners.

The commotion began making its way back to the prisoners. A small entourage accompanied four soldiers on foot. As they approached, a grin broke out on the otherwise grim John Andre as his head swiveled from soldier to prisoner and back again.

"Just like in Abigail's dining room," he muttered.

Standing beside Esau's horse looking up at him was his mirror image and brother, Jacob. All around them, including the formerly undistracted guards, men looked in astonishment from one brother to the other, muttering, "Amazing!" "Uncanny!" "Like looking in a mirror!"

Jacob talked for several minutes to the officer in command, a family man. He requested ten minutes alone with his brother. He gave his word of honor that the prisoner would be returned to him safely. Jacob's word of honor wasn't enough for the commander. One of Jacob's fellow soldiers, who had fought with the commanding officer at Saratoga, interceded for him. He vouched for Jacob's good character. Even then, because of the gravity of the prisoner's offense, the officer was hesitant. Jacob tried another line of reasoning. He argued that this would probably be the last time he and his brother would ever see each other again. The commanding officer agreed to ten minutes.

Esau and Jacob stood beside the Hudson River. Two guards were posted on the ridge above them, their backs to the brothers. The guards were instructed to give the brothers every privacy unless the prisoner attempted to escape, at which point Jacob would sound an alarm. That being the case, the guards were ordered to shoot to kill.

For several moments the two brothers did nothing but look each other over. One in an American uniform and leaning on a musket, the other in civilian clothes, his uniform having been taken from him shortly after his identity was discovered. Esau rubbed sore wrists that had been temporarily unbound.

"You look thinner," Jacob said.

"Army life. You're looking well. Heard you'd been shot."

"It wasn't too bad."

"Have you heard from Father? Is he still in France?"

Jacob shook his head. "He's in Boston."

"How's Mother and Mercy?" Esau surprised himself by how easily he could inquire about Mercy now that Abigail was a part of his life.

"Mother is as well as can be expected, as is Mercy."

"What do you mean, 'as well as can be expected'?"

Jacob's face flushed instantly. "How can you ask that considering all you've done to them?" he shouted. His outburst was so sudden, it caused the guards atop the ridge to look over their shoulders. Upon seeing no cause for alarm, they again turned their backs.

"I have done nothing intentionally to hurt them," Esau said in a calm but firm voice. "I only did what I felt I had to do considering the circumstances."

"How can you say that? You did everything to hurt them! You could have sat down and talked with them—at least with Mother—and you could have corresponded with Father. But no, you sneak into the house, steal the family Bible, and then turn traitor—bringing shame to the Morgan family name for generations to come! Do you realize that my own immediate superior double-checks everything I do after he learned that you had defected to the British side? People don't trust Morgans anymore. They think we're all traitors because of you!"

This was a blow to Esau. It was something he hadn't considered. "I just couldn't lie to myself any longer. I'm an Englishman. I'll always be an Englishman."

"You're a traitor and you've always been a traitor," Jacob replied. "And now you're about to reap a traitor's reward. I pity you."

It was astonishing to both of them. With so many changes swirling all around them, and all of them happening so quickly, apparently there were some things that never changed. The Morgan brothers would never see eye-to-eye on anything.

"I'm willing to accept whatever comes," Esau said. "But in God's name, I ask one last thing of you."

Jacob looked skeptical.

"Major Andre. He's a good man, an honest man ... a friend. He has committed no crime. He was only doing his duty."

"All right, he's a good man."

"Help me to help him escape."

"You're out of your mind."

"Jacob, I'm begging you. Do this one last thing for me. It would be a tragedy if any harm should come to him. Ask the commanding officer to allow him to join us, then ..."

"No."

"... we can create some kind of diversion ..."

"No!"

"... enough so that he can slip away ..."

"I said NO!"

Esau looked at his brother in disappointment. "You'll never change, will you? You're so full of self-righteousness, you have absolutely no room left for compassion."

"That's right! And you know why? Compassion achieves nothing. Those who know what is right and fight for it are the ones who will build this nation!"

"Well, I think you're wrong. And I'm willing to gamble that there is a bit of compassion in you. It may be the size of the proverbial mustard seed, but I believe it's there."

"What are you talking about?"

"I'll tell you exactly what I'm talking about." Esau glanced up at the guards. Their backs were still turned. "I'm going to turn around and run down the riverbank. Somehow, I'm going to find a boat and row out to the *Vulture*."

"Don't be stupid."

"And you're going to let me do it because I'm not doing this for myself. I'm doing it for my friend. If I can reach General Clinton, maybe I can convince him to trade me back for Andre or me and Arnold both—a convincing trade, don't you think?"

"I won't let you do this, Esau."

"I think you will." Esau began slowly to back away from his brother. "That's the gamble. I don't think you'll sound the alarm, because if you do those men up there will shoot me, and I don't think you can face Mother and Father knowing that you caused my death."

"Don't make me do this," Jacob said sternly, but not loud enough to cause alarm.

Esau continued to back away. "Give my best to Mother and Father and Mercy. Tell them I love them."

Jacob glanced up at the guards. They suspected nothing.

The moment Jacob looked away, Esau bolted. He ran as hard as he could. He didn't look back; it would profit him nothing. If his gamble failed, Jacob would yell and he would die. But the longer he ran without hearing Jacob's voice, the greater was his chance of escaping. He pressed forward with all his might. In the distance he saw a small pier with several boats tied to it. Even farther in the distance, sails. The *Vulture?* He ran harder. Still no sound. Just as he thought, Jacob couldn't …

BLAM!

A single shot. Esau felt the flesh rip away from the side of his right leg, as if a pair of hot tongs yanked out a piece of him.

Instinctively, he reached for his leg. It crumpled beneath him, sending him headlong into the cold, moist dirt and wet pebbles of the river's edge. The searing pain was incredible.

From the ground he looked back. Like ants on a hill, soldiers scurried everywhere along the ridge, some of them slipping down the side to the water's edge, running toward him. Behind them, in the stance of a light infantry soldier on a firing line, was Jacob. Smoke swirled upward from his musket.

23

Smoke swirled around everything—around the figures on both sides of the shoreline, making curlicues on the surface of the river, swirling upward around the trees, around the ship ... *Vulture* ... in the smoke, a phantom ship, so close, three steps across the water and you're safe, now disappearing, swallowed by the mist, going home, home to heaven ... BLAM! ... a deafening blast, Jacob, his face up close, dripping wet, laughing, derisive, ugly taunts, now distant, on one knee, aiming ... BLAM! ... hit! ... no, a miss, Jacob missed! ... Mercy beside him, shaking her head, pointing and laughing, handing Jacob another musket ... trying to scream, to run, can't move, shoreline slippery, feet pushing but no foothold, slipping, slipping ... Abigail, on the far side of the river, calling to him, come home, come home, arms extended, beckoning, her lips form words, I love you ... Jacob takes aim again; struggle to get up, run, get away, must get away ... BLAM! ... pain, leg, throbbing pain, reaching toward the wound, above the knee half the leg is gone, not made of flesh, wax, hollow inside, no, no, not right, wax shouldn't hurt ... Jacob coming toward him with a musket, no, a torch, the torch is thrust at the leg, it begins to melt, try to scream, can't, no sound, mouth yells but no sound, must warn Abigail, run Abigail, run, she doesn't hear, torch coming closer, must get away, get away from the torch ...

Esau awoke with a start, his head and pillow drenched with perspiration.

"Esau, are you all right?" A male voice, deep, familiar, but out of place.

"Son, are you all right?"

Jared Morgan leaned forward in his chair beside Esau's bed, his brow furrowed with parental concern.

"When did you get here?" Esau asked.

Seeing that his son was in no need of immediate medical attention, Jared sat back in his chair. "Late last night. They were good enough to let me be here when you woke up."

"How could they refuse ..." Esau's words were coming out garbled; the inside of his mouth was dry and sticky ... "the request of a famous French diplomat?"

Jared reached for a cup of water on a nearby stand and helped his son down a few sips by lifting his head and holding the cup for him.

"Better," Esau said.

"Jacob informed me you were here," Jared said, placing the cup on the stand.

The mention of Jacob's name prompted a thousand questions and thoughts. *How much did their father know? Did he know Jacob was the one who shot him? How much did he know about Arnold and Andre and all the events of the last few days? And if he knew, who did he hear it from? Jacob? The doctor? The source of information would certainly shade the truth.*

"I know what happened beside the river," Jared said.

All right, the topic was raised. But what did he know? Esau didn't respond, hoping his father would continue on his own.

"Jacob did what he had to do."

"So did I," Esau said.

"I know, son. I know."

"So you were able to talk to Jacob."

Jared nodded. "Briefly. He's gone now." A pause. "Reassigned."

There was something about the way his father hesitated before he said the word *reassigned* that caused Esau to believe that his father knew more about Jacob's location than he felt at liberty to say.

"Just tell me one thing, son," Jared said. "Did Arnold in some way force you to do what you have done?"

Esau was disappointed that his father had asked. The very question suggested Esau was weak willed, unable to stand up against a strong personality. But more than that, it meant his father still didn't understand him.

"No one coerced me," he said. "Everything I have done, I've done freely. I believe in England. I believe England will win this war. And when she does, the Morgans will continue to figure prominently in England's future on the American continent."

"But you joined the Continental Army."

"A mistake. I thought armed resistance would force negotiations, at which time the colonies could hammer out a working relationship with Parliament. In that, I was wrong; just the opposite happened and the two sides crystallized. So I went to the side I felt most comfortable with."

"And you still feel after so much bloodshed the Americans and English will be reunited?"

"It will take time, but yes. Once English law is reestablished, the colonies will be safer places in which to live."

"So that's why you stole the family Bible?"

Esau had always thought this face-to-face confrontation would come after the war, after England had won. It would be easier that way. History would have proved him right by then.

"The Bible has always been in the possession of Englishmen. I wanted to ensure that it always would be."

His father sat stiff, his breathing labored, as the subject of the Bible was discussed. The topic was undeniably an emotional one for him. He made every effort to fight back his feelings, but it was a terrible battle and the outcome was uncertain.

"So you took it upon yourself," he said, "to disregard the history and tradition of the Bible's ownership and appoint yourself its guardian."

Esau didn't like the way it sounded when his father said it, but he couldn't disagree with the statement.

"That Bible was entrusted to *me!* And it's *my* responsibility to choose which son will get it next, not you!" Jared's shouting brought angry looks from the ensign who had been posted as Esau's guard.

"I was thinking of the good of the family," Esau whispered forcefully.

"Let me tell you something. I've been looking out for this family for longer than you've been alive. I think I'm fully qualified to do what is best for the family."

"Over the last few years I've watched you drift closer and closer to Jacob's point of view in politics. I just couldn't live with the thought of the Bible going to him."

"Competition," Jared said, cooling down; "that's the way it has always been between the two of you. You would think I'd be used to it by now."

Esau closed his eyes. His leg throbbed. He chuckled.

"What?" his father asked.

"General Arnold. Twice I've been where you are, beside his

bed after he suffered a leg wound. Now when the two of us walk, we can limp together."

"Arnold's on the British side."

This was news to Esau. "What about Andre?" he asked.

"His hearing is today."

"And mine?"

"In a day or two, after your leg has had time to heal."

"That doesn't make sense. I'm well enough to be at a hearing. Why rush Andre's hearing and delay mine?"

"I'm telling you what I was told."

"Get someone in here. I want to speak at the hearing on Major Andre's behalf."

"They're not taking witnesses. It's not a trial."

"Still, I want to be there. Help me get up."

Esau raised himself up on his elbows.

"Stay there," his father said. "I'll see what I can do."

Jared walked over to the ensign and engaged him in several minutes of discussion. Esau watched as his father said something and the ensign shook his head no; several more times Jared said something—each time the response was the same. No.

"Sorry," Jared said, returning bedside.

"Will you go for me?"

"You want me to attend the hearing?"

"Surely you've done enough for this country to warrant a seat in the room. Use Franklin's name or something. I've got to know what happens at that hearing, and I need to hear it from someone I can trust."

Jared rose. "You lie still and don't cause that ensign any trouble. He's the nervous sort. I'll see what I can do."

Jared Morgan was granted permission to observe Major John Andre's hearing before Washington's senior officers. He didn't even have to mention Franklin's name. Alexander Hamilton, Washington's secretary, recognized Jared's name from the many accounts that had been received from France. That, together with the fact that he was representing a friend of Andre's, earned him a seat.

The hearing was convened at the Old Dutch Church at Orangetown, New Jersey. Those sitting on the board included Washington's senior general and legal adviser, Major General Nathanael Green; the Marquis de Lafayette; and Baron von Steuben. The judge advocate general was John Lawrence. Having become more diplomatically astute from his experience in France, it did not escape Jared's notice that Washington was doing all he could to remove suspicion regarding the board's predisposed prejudices by appointing an international board—of the fourteen generals on the board, three had been born in Britain, one was a German, and one was a Frenchman.

The proceedings were surprisingly calm and courteous considering their highly volatile subjects—espionage and treason. It seemed as if the board of officers were separating their feelings for the likable Andre from the treachery of the villainous Arnold. As one of the officers summed it up: He is an honest Englishman suffering for a dishonest American.

Andre himself helped promote this opinion. His defense was based on the premise that frankness was his surest shield. When a lie or a convenient lapse of memory could have served him, John Andre chose instead condemning truth.

Advocate General Lawrence: "When you left the *Vulture*, boarding a boat for your meeting with General Benedict Arnold, did you come ashore under a white flag of truce?"

Andre: "No, sir."

Lawrence: "There was no flag of truce?"

Andre: "No, sir. There was no flag."

This information was given in spite of the fact that Captain Sutherland of the *Vulture*, and General Clinton, and General Arnold all wrote letters to the board insisting that Major John Andre landed on American-held soil under a white flag of truce.

"I was impressed with your friend," Jared said. "He's personable and honest."

Esau sat up in bed. It was early evening and he'd just finished eating. Most of the day he had spent tossing and arranging the bedclothes, trying to find a position that would stop the throbbing in his leg. In reality, much of his discomfort was not caused by the leg, but by concern for his friend. He'd worried, he'd fretted, and he'd prayed. Now, finally, his father appeared to report on the first day's proceedings.

"Who were the officers on the board?"

Jared described the international panel.

"How did Andre's testimony go? Is there any word from General Clinton?"

Esau's father held up his hand to stop the flow of questions. Then he told his son how the day's events unfolded. Esau seemed pleased.

"It's a good start," he said.

"It's finished."

"Finished? In one day? The verdict too?"

Jared looked at his son with tired eyes, knowing full well that the outcome of Andre's trial was a foreshadowing of what was in store for Esau, with one exception—a very big exception at that. The military officers could respect Andre's loyalty to duty, even though he was the enemy. It was different with Esau. He had been one of them first and had gone to the other side. In this way, he was more like Arnold than like Andre.

"Did they render a verdict?" Esau asked.

"Guilty of espionage. It was unanimous."

It was a blow, but not an unexpected one. After all, they were caught in American uniforms with defense plans for an American fortress. Technically, there could be no other verdict than guilty. The question at hand was the sentence. Would the board recommend clemency? Would Washington listen to them and be lenient?

"Did the board make a recommendation?"

Again Jared nodded. "And Washington passed sentence."

"So quickly? What was the sentence?"

"Death, by hanging."

Esau cringed. His head fell back against his pillow. His thoughts turned to Andre. It was the worst possible sentence that could have been passed. Hanging was for criminals, scoundrels. An officer deserved to die by firing squad.

"Any indication Washington's mind might be changed?"

"If I'm any judge of character, no," Jared said. "He's a forceful man. He's doing this for the sake of the country. A sense of justice must be demonstrated. Andre will hang because Arnold escaped."

"And so will I."

Jared's head fell against his chest, his eyes closed, as he fought the emotion rising within him. He thought of Anne and how the news would devastate her. She was a strong woman, but this was her son. Parents are not supposed to outlive their sons, nor hear of them dangling from a gallows. As for his feelings for Esau, of all men Jared could understand what his son was feeling. There was a time in his younger days when he was in jail, convicted of piracy, and sentenced to hang. Not until he was at the gallows and a black sack had been placed over his head along with the rope was he rescued, a daring daylight rescue orchestrated by his older brother and his brother's Indian friend.

"I know how you feel," Jared said softly.

Esau managed a weak grin. "I suppose you do. I remember the story. Funny, isn't it? Until now I never appreciated the danger you faced. When something's in the past, it's nothing more than a story. There's something not real about it. What I'm feeling right now is real."

"Don't give up hope, son," Jared said.

Tears filled Esau's eyes. He shook his head. "I won't, Father. I won't."

N

Esau Morgan's hearing was held the day before Major John Andre's scheduled execution. It took half as long as Andre's hearing before the board was ready to recommend a verdict and a sentence.

The civility and courtesy present during Andre's hearing were nowhere to be seen during Esau's questioning. He was portrayed as Arnold's assistant, a coconspirator in treason. With the same candor as his friend, Esau told his story. They didn't believe him. They were sure his involvement was greater than he was telling them. The way they pieced the speculation together, he and Arnold had begun planning treachery since the Maine expedition, then in Canada, then in Philadelphia; and finally, the time was deemed right when Arnold was appointed to the position at West Point. But looking back on it now, Arnold sought the appointment, insisted on it.

And so it went. Every previous decision by Arnold was reinterpreted as a prelude to treason, and every meeting between Arnold and Esau was characterized as a seditious rendezvous to plot the overthrow of the newborn American government. As for letters from General Clinton and General Arnold calling for leniency on Esau's behalf, there were none; nor was there any statement from Andre, in person or in writing. Esau felt abandoned.

Two highlights stood out in Esau's mind. The first was when

Lafayette questioned him. For ten minutes, the French general continually referred to Esau by his brother's name until someone finally corrected him. The Frenchman explained his confusion, though it wasn't necessary. The second highlight was when his father requested the privilege of speaking on behalf of his son, in the absence of any letters of defense. His notable service with the commissioners in France was acknowledged by Washington, and his request was granted.

"I know I'm going to sound like a father," Jared began. "But in all honesty, the portrait that has been painted of my son today is a gross distortion. If he is guilty of anything, he is guilty of being a loyal Englishman, something most of us once were. I know his heart. He is not a villain. Esau is a onetime rebel who wanted nothing more than to return to his proper allegiance."

After Jared's statement, the board of officers treated Esau with greater respect. However, Jared's statement did nothing to alter their decision. The guilty verdict was unanimous. Their recommendation was death by hanging.

Outside the Old Dutch Church, as Esau was loaded into a wagon to transport him back to jail, he got to chuckling. "Those poor officers," he said, "they were so angry they wanted to kill me twice. They just couldn't figure out a way to do it."

That night, Jared did not come to Esau's cell at his regular time. Although reason argued that his father was undoubtedly detained in some way, a cursed doubt burrowed its way into him that now that he was condemned to die, even his father wanted nothing to do with him.

The lock clanked and the door swung open. Under armed guard, Major John Andre walked in. Of the two men, Andre was the most surprised.

"Esau? Ha! Esau Morgan! When did they catch you?"

Andre was unbound, and the door behind him slammed shut and was locked. The two friends embraced. It was a lengthy embrace, each one holding onto the other, as if by refusing to part nothing could ever separate them again. Finally, reluctantly, they released each other.

Andre laughed. "I was sure that by now you would be at Abigail's, exchanging tearful stories of good old Andre. Where did they catch up with you?"

Esau was puzzled. "What do you mean?"

"Your escape. How far did you get? It's evident you didn't get far enough away!"

"Escape? I never escaped. My brother shot me in the leg. I've been recuperating ever since."

"That's odd. They told me you had escaped. I remember hearing the shot. They spirited me away quickly, thinking it was a rescue attempt. It wasn't until a couple of days later that I heard what had happened."

"I only wish I had!" Esau turned sober. "I know about tomorrow. Is there any hope for an exchange of American prisoners?"

"Or an American traitor?" Andre laughed. Then he shook his head. "Not much hope there. It's British policy. Besides, Clinton gave Arnold his word that if the plot went awry, Arnold's safety was assured. But what about you?"

"My hearing was today. Same verdict, same sentence. Mine is scheduled for the day after tomorrow."

The news seemed to puzzle Andre as much as it troubled him. "How odd! Why wasn't I told you were captured? I would have spoken on your behalf!" The more he thought of it, the angrier he got. "I will write General Washington a letter, tonight—well, of course I'll write it tonight, I won't be in any shape to write it tomorrow night."

It was gallows humor, but it struck them both as funny.

"In truth," Andre said, "I have high hopes that General Washington will change the method of execution from hanging to firing squad. It's the least he can do to show respect for my rank and service. As a favor to me, I'll request the same for you."

"Who better to request a firing squad than a friend?"

Again they laughed.

The lock sounded and the door opened.

"Ah!" cried Andre merrily. "Here is the man who arranged this little meeting. I thought they were taking me to fit me for a coffin or something like that. Instead, I get this wonderful reunion. How can I ever thank you, sir?"

"No thanks are necessary."

"Surely there is something I can do for your kindness. You've done this wonderful thing for me, and I don't even know your name."

"Major John Andre," Esau said, "I'd like you to meet my father, Jared Morgan."

The next day Jared stood at a bend in the road leading to the gibbet. It was shortly before noon. Thousands mulled about him in holiday atmosphere, anticipating a joyous patriotic festivity. Shortly afterward, Major John Andre appeared, escorted by two subalterns. Behind him marched his personal servant, Peter Laune. The servant had been dispatched directly from British General Clinton with a new uniform for Andre. The uniform's bright scarlet color singled him out from the forty-man escort, drummer, and four-fife procession. The mile-long journey from the stone house in which he and Esau were held to the gibbet was crowded with spectators on both sides of the road.

From time to time, Andre would recognize someone in the crowd and would ask permission to stop and "talk with a friend." Such was the case upon seeing Jared Morgan. He approached

Esau's father as if meeting him during a casual stroll down the road.

"Again, I wish to thank you for arranging the time with Esau last night. True to my word, I have written a letter to General Washington on his behalf."

"Thank you, sir. I know Esau values your friendship."

The words caused a crack of emotion in Andre's granite composure. It was quickly repaired. He acknowledged Jared's thanks and turned to leave. Turning back, he took Jared by the hand.

"Sir, do you believe in an afterlife?"

"I do."

Andre nodded solemnly. "Should your son have the misfortune to follow after me, we will most surely be reunited on the other side. Then, it will be heaven indeed."

The condemned man straightened himself and faced the road leading to his execution. Having just rounded the bend in the road, for the first time the gibbet came into his sight. Upon seeing it, he stumbled. He was caught by one of the men beside him.

"Why this emotion, sir?" he was asked.

Andre answered, "I am reconciled to my fate, but I detest the mode. Must I die in this manner?"

Overcome by emotion himself, his escort could only nod.

"How hard is my fate," Andre replied. "It will be but a momentary pang."

A baggage wagon was placed under the gibbet; on the wagon was a black coffin. As Andre stepped onto the platform, he was told preparations were not ready. He stepped back off and waited for the preparations to conclude, kicking a round stone from foot to foot as he passed the time.

A Tory prisoner, covered in black grease to protect his identity, served as hangman. His payment for participation in the event was his freedom.

With preparations completed, Andre stepped onto the platform again. As he did, his knees nearly buckled and he stumbled, but regained his strength and straightened himself without assistance. Calmly, he removed his hat, untied his scarf, and opened his shirt. The hangman was so nervous, he failed in his first attempt to place the noose over the prisoner's head. Andre gently pushed him aside and did it himself. Then, taking a silk handkerchief from his pocket, he blindfolded himself.

The adjutant general read aloud the order of execution and Andre was informed that he had an opportunity to speak. He pushed the blindfold above his eyes.

In a clear voice he said: "I pray you to bear witness that I meet my fate like a brave man."

He replaced the blindfold. The doomed man's hands were then tied behind his back. A drum rolled, ending with a single harsh beat. The wagon was driven from under the gibbet. The first great swing of the rope killed him.

Esau and his father sat in silence. Jared had just finished relating Andre's last moments on this earth, choosing to limit Andre's comment to him to a simple thank-you for the time arranged with Esau. It was late into the night. The two men faced each other, Esau on the edge of his bed, Jared on the edge of a wooden chair.

"I want you to know, I've done everything I could do," Jared said. "Even today, after Andre's death, I went again to General Washington to plead for your life. He said he could sympathize with a father's anguish, but with loyalties unsettled in the southern colonies and mutinies among some of his own men, he had to take a hard position in this matter." Jared sighed. "Tomorrow morning I'll try again. Maybe after he's had a night to dwell on Andre's death, he'll see things ..."

Esau reached out a hand and placed it on his father's knee.

"There's nothing more you can do. Thank you for all you've done."

Silence.

"Son, I wish I could take your place, trade my life for yours."

Tears came to Esau's eyes. "I know you do, Father. But I've made my choices, and now I have to take the consequences."

Silence.

"Tell Mother I love her and that I hope she's not too ashamed of me."

It was his father's turn for tears. "If you think your mother could ever be ashamed of you, you don't know her well. Nothing could ever stop her from loving you or being proud of you."

Esau smiled. "I remember when Nathan Swift died years ago, you remember, the young carpenter in our church who drowned."

Jared nodded.

"I remember Mother comforting Nathan's mother. Referring to that Scripture verse where Jesus says He's going to prepare a place for us, Mother told her that maybe God took Nathan to heaven because Jesus needed help building her heavenly mansion."

"I remember that," Jared said.

"Tell Mother I'll inspect her mansion when I get there. I'll put a chair by the window, and a small table with a Bible, the way she likes it. Tell her I'll be standing in the doorway, so she'll know which one is hers."

Silence.

"Give my good-byes to Mercy and Jacob."

"Next time I see them. Count on it."

Silence.

"Son?"

"Yes, Father?"

"Is there anything I can do for you?"

Silence.

"Don't come tomorrow. I've imagined what it will be like to stand up there and look down and see you." Esau began to weep openly. "I … I don't want you to see me hang. Please don't come."

Silence.

"All right, son. I won't come."

Silence.

"Is there anything else I can do?"

"Will you pray with me?"

Jared rose and went to Esau. Placing his hands on his son's shoulders, he prayed, "Our Father in heaven, You are the Author and Sustainer of all life. Years ago, You blessed Anne and me with two sons. At that time we gave them to You, and we'll not be taking them back now. I entrust my son's life, both now …" Jared's voice broke, "… and forevermore, into Your hands. Carry him as a little lamb in Your arms. Amen."

Jared stayed with his son until nearly sunrise. They said a final good-bye to each other, and he left.

Esau lay on his bed. The color of the curtains on the window grew brighter, showing the first signs of daylight. A painful pulse in his leg kept him from full sleep. He drifted in and out of rational thought.

One good thing about all this, he thought, *at least my leg will stop hurting.*

Gallows humor. Andre would have appreciated it.

Loud laughter and an equally loud voice boomed outside his door. One guard talking to another. The voices sounded young.

Don't they know I need my sleep? I have a busy day today.

"Listen, I'm serious!" the voice shouted.

"You're seein' things!"

"I was walkin' over here when I sees a wagon pulled in. I thought it was supplies or somethin' like that. Two men were sittin' up front, and one of them was sort of leanin' over on the other, like he was asleep or sick or drunk or somethin'."

"I think you're drunk or somethin'. You're ten minutes late."

"What, you want me to swear that I'm tellin' the truth? All right, I swear this is the truth! The driver pushes this other fellow off him and sort of balances him. Then he gets down and a corporal comes out to help him. So they reach up and pull this other fellow down from the wagon, and the man's head falls off!"

"Watkins, you're insane if you think I'll believe a story like that!"

"Wait, wait ... so the corporal reaches down, picks up this fellow's head and says, 'They just don't make New Yorkers like they used to!' Then he sticks the man's head under his arm and helps carry the rest of him inside."

"Get out of here, Watkins. Go drown yourself or something."

"No, listen! It all makes sense. So I goes up to the corporal and tells him what I saw. Behind him, inside the supply house, this driver is pulling papers out of the neck of the headless man ... no, wait, it makes sense, I promise ... it's wax! Don't you see? The fellow next to the driver is a man made of wax!"

By now Esau was sitting upright in his bed. As the day of his execution lit the room, he whispered Abigail's name with longing.

Breakfast for the condemned man came from General Washington's table with the general's compliments. Although Esau would have preferred a pardon, he ate the breakfast ravenously. According to his father, Andre was sent a new uniform by General Clinton. But the British general neglected to send a letter on Esau's behalf to the board of generals, so no new uniform was forthcoming for his execution. An ill-fitting uniform of a British grenadier was provided instead. He put it on. The pants bunched at the ankles, and the sleeves hung past his wrists to his knuckles.

Unacceptable, Esau thought. *I refuse to be hanged like this!*

The lock clicked and the door opened. Two ensigns in uniform appeared. The shorter one announced: "Esau Morgan, we're here to escort you."

"You're early."

"Please put on your shoes, sir."

"Look, I'm in no rush to get hanged."

"Please, sir, put on your shoes."

"Can you tell me where I'm going? I'm not scheduled to hang until noon, and it's barely ten o'clock."

The ensigns exchanged glances. The taller one nodded and the shorter one spoke again.

"Colonel Alexander Hamilton requests the honor of your presence."

"Hamilton? What does he want?"

"The colonel said he wanted to meet Andre's friend."

Esau finished fastening the second shoe. He stood and stomped his feet. Like the rest of his uniform, the shoes were too big; nearly an inch of shoe extended past where his big toes left off. He looked around the room. Habit. As if he had anything to forget.

"This way, sir."

The ensigns motioned him away from the front door, directing him down a hallway to the back of the house. As they passed one room, the door was slightly ajar. Two American ensigns lay crumpled on the floor.

"What?"

"Hurry, sir."

The two ensigns pushed him out the back door.

"Just what ..."

Esau's sentence went unfinished. The two men threw Esau into the back of a wagon. The taller one climbed in after him, pinning him to the floorboard and covering Esau's mouth with his hand. A tarp was thrown over them and it was dark.

The wagon jerked forward.

Esau struggled to free himself. In the dark, a mouth drew near to his ear. "Shut up, sir. We're here to take you back to New York. Compliments of General Clinton." While the wagon bed bounced crazily, the hand on Esau's mouth eased.

"Why didn't you save Andre?" Esau asked.

"We couldn't get near him."

Esau understood the implication. He was the secondary plan. He was saved only because Andre died.

"Thanks for risking your life for me," he said.

"You were a bonus!"

"I don't understand."

"We didn't know you were there until we arrived. It was while we were trying to get to Andre that we learned you were next in line for hanging. I don't mean any disrespect or anything, but we didn't want to return empty-handed."

Although Esau wasn't flattered, neither was he offended. "How can I not respect the men who saved me from a gibbet?"

The ensign next to him said, "Who are you anyway?"

Esau and his rescuer bounced in the back of the wagon under the cover of a tarp for over an hour. His wounded leg hit repeatedly against the wagon bed. The pain was nauseating, but Esau was content to live with it. Pain meant he was still alive.

The wagon slowed.

"Stay down!" the ensign driving the wagon shouted. "An American patrol."

Esau listened as the driver presented a pass, the same way Andre and he had done with Arnold's pass. The American officer wanted to inspect the wagon. The driver insisted he was in a hurry. That only seemed to increase the officer's curiosity.

Moments later, the tarp was thrown back. Against the bright mid-morning sky, Esau and his rescuer stared into the barrels of a half-dozen muskets.

A round, mustached colonel's face stared at Esau in surprise. Bulging eyes looked at his face, then his red coat.

"Morgan!" he shouted. "What are you still doing here?"

Before Esau could answer, the round-cheeked colonel barked orders at two soldiers. "Helwys! Wood! Escort this wagon to Tarrytown." To Esau he said in a whisper: "I thought you went over days ago!" He ordered the two men in the wagon bed covered with the tarp again. Just before the men disappeared under the covering, the colonel said, "Good luck, Jacob!" Then all was dark again.

The wagon sped off, bouncing along the road just like it had done before. The ensign, if that's what he really was, laying next to Esau on the wagon bed, giggled all the way to Tarrytown. "I thought we was dead!" he said. "I thought we was dead!"

Jared Morgan was packing the last of his clothes. There was a knock at the door. It was 11:47 a.m. Jared knew the exact time because he checked the clock every minute, praying constantly, *Dear Lord, Esau has only thirty minutes left to live*, then, *Esau has only twenty-three minutes left to live, Lord, give him comfort*, and so on. Staying away from the site of the hanging, as he promised Esau he would, pushed Jared's self-control to the breaking point.

The person at the door didn't wait for him to answer. An aide swung open the door and in strode General Washington. He had to duck slightly to clear the doorway. In every encounter with the commander-in-chief, Jared had always found him to be a strong man, comfortable with his authority. This occasion was no different.

Without greeting, he said, "Master Morgan, this morning your son escaped."

It was an announcement, not an accusation. In no way did Jared sense that Washington was accusing him of having anything to do with it.

"I see," Jared said.

"From the initial reports, I believe he was assisted by a team of British agents. We had sketchy reports that there would be an attempt to rescue Andre, so we were prepared for such an event. But, as you know, the situation with Esau was different. As far as we can ascertain now, the team didn't know we were holding Esau until they got here."

"Good, that's good," Jared said. He pulled out a chair from the small dining table in the room and sat down. Washington didn't seem to mind. He remained standing.

"Naturally, we're doing everything we can to bring Esau and the British agents back, but they got a good start on us. Unless we get lucky, it looks like the rescue effort will succeed. You understand what this means, don't you?"

"Yes … yes, General. I do."

"I'll keep you informed." Washington was out the door and gone. The aide closed the door behind him.

Jared sat motionless, staring at nothing. His hands trembled. Thoughts, emotions tumbled around inside him. He should feel elated. *Esau was free! Alive!* And he *was* elated. *This was good news! But that means that Jacob …*

With an inhuman moan, Jared's head fell face forward onto the table, his hands clasped over his head, clenched so tightly they shook. "Dear God in heaven … I don't know how … don't know what to pray … how to pray.…"

Jared wept audibly; his body convulsed with great sobs.

"O Lord, help me … help me … to know what to pray. If I pray for Esau's success, I pray for Jacob's death. Yet I rejoice in Esau's freedom ... Lord, forbid that I should pray for his capture, for he would surely die ... but then Jacob would live ... dear God, help me! Help me ... O Lord, help me.... Thy will ... Thy will ... Thy will be done."

24

Before the breeze had time to sweep clear the acrid smell of gunpowder, and while Esau was still clutching his wounded leg beside the Hudson, and while soldiers poured over the ridge descending on the prisoner, the plan had been born in Jacob's mind.

A switch.

It could work, but he would have to act quickly, a daunting task in any military organization. Jacob took the idea to his superior—who took him to Lafayette—who took them both to General Washington. The plan was simple. Mount a search for Esau, giving the impression he escaped. After several days, Jacob would slip across the lines into British-held territory posing as his brother. If the plan worked, because of Esau's association with Andre, the Americans might gain direct and immediate access to General Clinton's staff, depending on the level of relationships Esau had established during his stay in New York. *When would they get another chance like this one?*

General Washington asked Jacob if he fully understood the consequences should his true identity be discovered. Jacob acknowledged that he did. Caught as a spy, he would suffer the same fate as Major John Andre.

"With added vengeance," Washington added. "The British will be looking for ways to balance the scales for the Andre incident."

Satisfied that Jacob was aware of the risk, Washington approved the plan and set the objectives. Jacob was to learn as much as he could about the British spring offensive. He was to relay the information to a contact who was already established in New York. The contact would relay the information to the American side. Jacob was told he would be briefed regarding the New York contact by General Lafayette. He was asked if he understood his mission. He did.

After dismissing the other officers, Washington spoke to Jacob alone.

"My insides tell me not to send you," the general said.

"Why not, sir?"

A heavy sigh. "If the mission should fail, how can I possibly face your father, knowing that I hanged one son and sent another to General Clinton to hang?"

The news that Esau would be hanged was unsettling. The hearing had not yet been held, but apparently its outcome had already been determined in Washington's mind. A sadness crept over Jacob. The emotional barrier that had guarded him against his brother since boyhood days came crashing down. It was no longer needed. A relic. And for the first time he could remember, Jacob felt a sympathetic emotion for his brother—pity.

He cleared the emotion from his throat: "Maybe some good can come of my brother's death. If this plan works, he will have done more good for the American cause by his death than he was able to do in life."

"Your conclusion is sound. However, I doubt your brother would appreciate his contribution to the cause."

"Probably not, sir."

Washington stared blankly at papers scattered across his desk. Jacob had an unsettling premonition. He got the impression the general was reevaluating his approval of the plan.

"If your insides tell you not to send me," Jacob said, "then why are you sending me? If you don't mind me asking, sir."

That did it. Washington's eyes focused. They were clear, sharp, determined. "Because my instincts tell me it's the right thing to do," he said. "The cold calculation is this: The deaths of two brothers, weighed against the value of the information that might be gained, is an acceptable risk." A pause. "Report to General Lafayette. He'll brief you on your New York contact."

"Thank you, sir."

As Jacob left Washington's headquarters, he chuckled at the thought that he just thanked a man for sending him behind enemy lines, possibly to his death.

"Bo, listen to me. I'm leaving now."

Jacob held the boy's head in his hands to keep him from turning away. Bo began this protest the moment they arrived in Boston. Jacob expected it; still it didn't make leaving Bo any easier. He knew Bo wanted to accompany him to New York, and no amount of reasoning seemed to penetrate the boy's obstinate resolve. It was Bo's stubbornness that worried Jacob most. There was no doubt Bo would behave himself in Boston with Anne and Mercy. The thought that troubled Jacob was that one day he would turn around and find Bo standing behind him in New York. The boy was resourceful enough and bullheaded enough to do it.

"I need your solemn word, Bo. Do you understand? Your solemn word that you will stay here with my mother and Mercy until I return."

They were in the Morgan parlor, the room overlooking Boston Bay. Again Bo tried to turn away from him. Jacob held him fast.

"You have to do this for me," he said. "I can't be worrying about you while I'm gone. It would be dangerous for me, do you understand? You have to stay here for me."

There was no visible break in the stony resistance.

"Promise me, Bo. Give me your solemn word that you will stay here."

Eye contact. Tears filled the boy's eyes.

"Promise me! Do you promise?"

Bo nodded his head. As he did, tears spilled onto his cheeks.

"Your solemn word?"

Another nod.

"I love you, Bo."

The boy crashed into his arms and nearly squeezed the breath from Jacob's lungs.

"He'll be fine, Jacob."

Anne and Mercy stood in the doorway. It was his mother who spoke. "I'm sure he'll take care of us. It will be good to have a man in the house again." She wasn't patronizing the boy with her comment. Bo was growing fast, approaching manly proportions.

Mercy held her hands out to Bo. He readily took them. During their brief encounters—in Philadelphia and now here—Bo and Mercy had developed an immediate bond between them, something that surprised and delighted Jacob. He had spent more than one restless hour wondering how Mercy would react to Bo's presence. Still, this was a difficult parting for them. Except for short absences when Jacob was on patrol, he and Bo had been together since the death of Bo's father.

"Take care of our boy," Jacob said to Mercy.

Jacob liked the words as soon as he said them. The smiles from Mercy and Bo indicated he wasn't alone.

His trip to Boston to deposit Bo had been hastily arranged and made. The duration of his stay was a single night, and Jacob spent every moment of it with Mercy. Ever since the Philadelphia reunion, their relationship had grown stronger with each letter, each passing day, each moment together. Jacob loved Mercy with a greater passion than when he married her. In his estimation she was just as beautiful—maybe more beautiful—and there was now a maturity about her, an unselfish self-confidence that only served to increase her attractiveness.

It was during this single night at home that Jacob fully realized how much he had to live for. Before, he had always been motivated by a cause or competition or anger; but now, he was motivated by his love for Mercy and Bo. It was his love for them that would bring him safely home to them. He was sure of it.

The four of them stood outside the front door on the top of the steps that led down to Beacon Street. Jacob kissed his mother.

As she hugged her son in return, Anne whispered in his ear, "Please come home to me. I don't want to lose you, too."

They had talked freely the night before about Esau. Outwardly, Anne was assured that his life rested in God's hands; but there were unguarded moments when Jacob saw pain in her eyes, a deep pain that reflected the anguish of her soul. Jacob kissed his wife and held her.

"You come back to me, Jacob Morgan. We've wasted too many foolish years, and I won't be deprived of the chance to make them up to you."

Bo stood in line for his hug. It lifted him off his feet.

"Now listen to me," Jacob said to him. A hand on the boy's shoulder pointed him toward the end of Beacon Street. "Once a day, you come out here and look down this street, understand? And one of those days, when you look down the street, you will see a rider. That rider will be me. Do you understand, Bo? It will be me. You have my word."

Jacob was walking the streets of New York the same day Major John Andre was hanged in Tappan as a spy. After passing through White Plains, Esau's double was detained by a British patrol and questioned. Having heard rumors that Andre's accomplice had escaped, they believed his story. Still, they were cautious, so under armed guard Jacob was escorted to General Clinton.

A bit of evidence that made his story believable was the nasty musket ball wound on the fleshy part of his right leg just above the knee. The wound was Jacob's doing, a painful necessity that would save his life. At least, that's how he explained it to the reluctant American soldier who was ordered to shoot him.

The theory was that word of Esau's wounding could have made its way to New York. After all, a number of witnesses saw him beside the river holding his leg. And if any one of them was a spy, a healthy Esau would instantly be suspect. So Jacob made arrangements for a similar wound. It was inflicted outside Boston, so that by the time he reached the British lines it would look less than fresh.

Jacob endured the pain with a bit of philosophical reasoning. The good part about the wound was that he didn't have to act like he had a limp, and he never had to remember with which leg he was supposed to limp. The bad news was that it burned unbearably, but better a wounded leg than a stretched neck.

The British patrol delivered him by wagon to General Clinton's headquarters. The trip there was itself an adjustment for him. Along the way, he had never seen so many red uniforms since the Battle of Monmouth, and then they were targets. It was unnerving to him to be surrounded by them. His hands kept wanting to reach for a weapon.

General Clinton was a gentle man with a round face and short, wide nose. Balding on the top of his head, the general permitted the gray hair on the sides to grow about an inch long. Dark eyebrows sat atop kindly eyes that grew moist as the subject turned to Major Andre.

"Isn't there anything you can do to save him?" Jacob asked.

He sat in a straight-backed wooden chair while Clinton leaned against the front of his desk. The general was quick to welcome him as Esau without a hint that he might suspect otherwise. The general even embraced him as a father would a son when Jacob first came through the door.

If only the boys at Valley Forge could see me now, Jacob thought.

It soon became evident during the conversation that the general's emotional behavior was prompted by his great love for John Andre, not from any personal closeness to Esau. The realization allowed Jacob to breathe easier.

"I've done all I can do," Clinton said, his voice heavy with frustration. "In fact, twice I wrote letters to Washington threatening reprisals, only to tear them up. Washington would see them for what they were—the ranting of an overemotional old man. Besides, my blustering is not going to change that buzzard's mind."

Jacob choked back a chuckle when he wondered if he should use the term *buzzard* in his report. Sheer nervousness on his part. He forced himself to be serious. "What about an exchange of prisoners?" he asked.

Clinton nodded, indicating they'd already considered that possibility. "That's how we got Andre back after he'd been captured in Canada," he said. "But it's different this time. In Canada his position was overrun and he was a prisoner of war. This time he was caught behind enemy lines as a spy." Clinton cursed loudly and slammed his fist on his desk. "Why didn't he follow my instructions? You were here when I gave them. The instructions were clear, weren't they?"

"Very clear." The question sounded rhetorical, so Jacob went along with it.

"Very clear!" Clinton repeated for emphasis. "Under no circumstances allow yourself to be lured behind American lines! Under no circumstances wear a disguise of any kind! So why did he do it? Why?"

Jacob was hoping Clinton was asking another rhetorical question, because he didn't have an answer.

The general looked at Jacob with sympathetic eyes. "I know I'm putting you in a terrible position. Your relationship with Arnold is not unlike Andre's relationship with me. But please forgive me, I don't share your admiration for Arnold. He has admitted to forcing Andre and you to come ashore and then to don disguises. That's what makes this whole affair so hard to stomach! Arnold should be the one on trial, not Andre."

"On that we can both agree, sir," Jacob said.

Clinton smiled warmly. "This must be doubly hard for you, son, since both men are your friends. I'm sorry Arnold is not here to greet you. He's indisposed at the moment."

Jacob stifled a sigh of relief. He knew that fooling Arnold would be a much more demanding test, one he wasn't eager to take.

"How's your leg?"

"It throbs, but it'll be fine."

"I understand your brother shot you?"

Jacob laughed. "I didn't think he would do it! Boy, was I wrong. Lucky for me he isn't a very good marksman."

Clinton chuckled. "So what are your plans, son? From what Andre told me, you're anxious to sail to England."

"If you don't mind, sir, I'd like to stay here awhile, until we find out what happens with Andre, and maybe until my leg heals."

Clinton pushed off from the edge of his desk. The meeting was over.

"If there is anything I can do," Jacob said, rising from the chair, "if I can help you in any way, I'd be more than willing ..."

Clinton placed a hand on his shoulder. Three firm pats were dispensed. "I'll keep that in mind. But right now your priority is to heal. I know you were lodging with Andre before you left. Feel free to stay there for as long as you're in New York."

"Thank you, sir, that's very kind." *It would be even kinder if you told me where Andre lived*, Jacob thought. Then he had an idea. His first step toward the door was on his right leg. He groaned audibly.

"Let me bring my carriage around. I'll instruct my driver to take you to Andre's house."

"That would be most kind, sir, thank you." *Yes, thank you indeed.*

※

Jacob moved nervously through Andre's house. There was something disquieting about being there. He almost expected the major to appear at any moment in a doorway and catch him sifting through personal items. The house was definitely an artist's lair—brushes, charcoal, pens, paints, rags, sketches in various stages of completion were scattered everywhere. The majority of the sketches were of people—ladies mostly, fashionable, pretty. In a pile on the sofa there were some sketches of soldiers and some self-portraits. He recognized the self-portraits because they looked like the prisoner he'd seen on the road beside the Hudson.

His heart jumped when he uncovered one sketch. It was of Esau. Only it looked more like him than Esau, especially in the

eyes. His eyes were closer together. It was a difference impercep-
tible to most people, but well known to twins who had gone to
great pains to find ways they were different from each other.

Standing behind the sofa, Jacob lifted the portrait of Esau. He
compared the chair in the portrait to the chair by the window.
Clearly, that's where Esau had been sitting when the sketch was
made. The chair still sat at the same angle to the window. A cold
shiver ran through him. It was like looking at a ghost. Look at the
sketch and Esau's there; look at the chair and he's gone. To think,
not many days previous Esau sat in that chair posing. From the
angle of the sketch, it looked like Andre was sitting on this sofa.
Two friends, sharing an afternoon. Now they were both dead.
Hanged.

From the sketch, Esau's eyes seemed to stare at Jacob, as if
he knew Jacob was in Andre's house. Those eyes, accusing him of
trespassing, of being somewhere he didn't belong, of violating a
private moment shared between friends.

Jacob's wounded leg quivered and failed him. He caught himself against the back of the sofa. The sketch fell faceup on the
floor, Esau's eyes still in an unrelenting stare. Jacob remembered
that as boys, he and Esau would sometimes wonder which of
them would die first. A common birthday was one thing, certainly
they wouldn't share a common death-day. *So who would go first?*

Jacob met the eyes of his dead brother in the sketch. *It was no
longer a mystery, was it?* They knew the answer to that question.

Leaving the sketch on the floor, Jacob pushed himself away
from the sofa. He needed to get outside, to get out of Andre's
house for a while. As he limped toward the door, something familiar caught his eye. On the bookshelf. He went to it. The Morgan
family Bible, the one Esau had stolen. A sense of vindication
swept through him, strengthening him. Suddenly, his mission had
a second objective. The first, to secure military information, was

for the good of his country. The second, to bring the family Bible back to Boston, was for the good of his family.

Jacob lifted the front cover and looked again at the names printed inside, beginning with Drew Morgan and ending with his father, Jared Morgan. The list brought to mind another of the many arguments he'd had with Esau—whose name would be added to that list next? Who would their father choose to give the Bible to—Jacob or Esau? The cover flapped shut with a thump of finality. There was no longer any question, since only one son was left.

The early October air had a bite to it as he stepped from the house. It was late afternoon, and the sun's strength was waning early as it did this time of year. Jacob limped slowly toward the business center, past shops and taverns. New York was a busy city but not that different from Boston or Philadelphia, though each had its distinctive characteristics that made it unique, much like a person's signature.

"Esau! O Esau!"

Jacob turned just in time to be smothered in the arms of an attractive blonde woman. She kissed him once on the mouth, then the cheek, then hugged him until he thought a rib would crack. Then, as suddenly as she had assaulted him, she turned him loose.

"Oh, look at me! I'm acting shamefully!" she said smoothing her dress and coyly darting glances at him. "Please forgive me, but when I saw you just now, I couldn't help myself! All New York is talking about you and Andre! Of course we know what's happening with him, but there was little news about you, and then we heard you had escaped, and ... Esau, I was so thankful ... so thankful ... yet so sad about Andre ... isn't that ghastly? They won't really hang him, will they? I refuse to believe they will. Even for colonials, they wouldn't do such a thing to a man as fine as

Major Andre ... oh dear, listen to me, I'm babbling like some empty-headed ... and you're limping, aren't you? How did you get hurt? Is it bad?"

The blonde woman paused to take a breath and brush a few stray hairs out of her eyes with the back of a hand. Her excited babbling reminded him of Mercy in her earlier days. He was amused. *Had Esau found his own version of Mercy in New York?*

"Well, aren't you going to say anything?" she said in a pouting voice.

Jacob looked at her somewhat sheepishly. "It's good to see you."

"Is that all you have to say?"

"Well, no. It's just that ..." he glanced down at his wounded leg, "I haven't quite recovered from my ordeal yet."

Before the blonde woman had time to run on about his injury, a stylish man and woman passing them in the opposite direction interrupted. The woman, an elderly matron dressed in fine fashion, reached out and touched the blonde woman on the arm.

"O Abigail," she gushed, "your exhibition is ... is ... beyond description! Simply indescribable! It's ... well, it's beyond description!" Turning to her husband, "Wouldn't you say so, Horace?"

"Beyond description," he said flatly.

"Thank you. That's very kind," Abigail replied.

"And so real!" the woman added. "Why, I know the Earl of Chatham personally—his family and mine have been close since the days of Queen Elizabeth—and let me tell you, I thought he was standing in front of me! Right in front of me! Didn't you, Horace?"

"Right in front of me."

The matron frowned at her unenthusiastic husband. Then to Abigail: "Truly, it was remarkable! Quite remarkable! And to think you do it all with wax. Amazing!"

Horace started to repeat the word *amazing*, but a stern look from his wife cut him off.

"Thank you again," said Abigail. "I enjoy working with that medium."

"Well, it is delightful, simply delightful!"

The matron and Horace bid them good-evening and continued on their way. Jacob grinned, partially in amusement, but more in thanks to the couple for the service they had just rendered him. From their gushing he now knew that the blonde woman's name was Abigail and that she was a wax modeler, and he knew one thing more … he knew he had found his New York contact, the one Lafayette had briefed him on.

"You must come and see me, you must! Tomorrow? Promise me you'll come tomorrow, we have so much to talk about!"

Abigail was looking up at him with pleading blue eyes.

"I can come tomorrow," he replied hesitantly. Only once again he didn't know where. Face after face of the few people he knew in New York flashed in his mind as he tried to think whom he could ask for directions to Abigail Matteson's house … at least he had a last name, thanks to the briefing.

"You do remember where it is, don't you? The white house just outside of town, with the green shutters and the …" she leaned closer and whispered, "drooping gun?" She giggled.

"Drooping gun! Who could forget the drooping gun?" he replied with a smile.

Jacob was unable to sleep in Major John Andre's house until he collected all the sketches and shut them away in a closet. Many of them he had to pull from the walls. But once they were collected and placed out of sight, he was able to relax somewhat. Having spent most of the last few years sleeping in crude huts or on the ground, he thought he could sleep just about anywhere.

But every time he closed his eyes and drifted into unconscious thought, Andre's sketches continued to haunt him. That and a throbbing leg kept him up most of the night.

The next afternoon he tried to secure a carriage, but they were scarce. He could only get a horse. Jacob was beginning to realize that Esau's influence as friend and associate to the famous Major Andre had definite limits when it came to available resources. Being an army man himself, this didn't surprise him. At times even generals were refused supplies or resources. He only hoped that the same strictness would not hold true regarding access to information.

When Abigail Matteson's three-story house finally came into view, he was the most grateful man in the world. His leg was in excruciating pain, and he didn't know which hurt it more, riding or walking, because he'd done both on the short trip. The house impressed him. With the afternoon sun striking the front facade, it stood out in relief against the trees and shadows behind it.

Drooping gun? What did she mean by drooping gun? He scanned the exterior and saw nothing that resembled a drooping gun.

Securing the horse to a post, he limped painfully to the front door. A demur Negro woman peeked out in answer to his knock. He was about to identify himself as Esau Morgan when he remembered the kiss Abigail planted on him the day before. That level of familiarity suggested Esau had been out to the house on more than one occasion, so he simply requested to see Mrs. Matteson.

Abigail's cheery voice came from behind the door. "Let Master Morgan in, Missy," she said. "It's so good to see you again, Master Morgan!"

Missy pulled open the door and jumped back. Abigail Matteson stood a few feet back from the doorway with a musket pointed at his chest.

"Or should I call you Jacob?" she asked.

Jacob was speechless.

"Where are your manners? Come in, Jacob." She motioned with the musket to Jacob's right.

Jacob went in the direction the musket indicated. Abigail directed him to a sofa near the fireplace and requested he sit down. She remained standing, the musket remained poised.

"Now, Master Jacob Morgan, do you mind telling me what you're doing in New York pretending to be your brother?"

Her voice was steady and clear, her eyes businesslike; any prior coquettish resemblance to Mercy was gone.

"You're not the same woman I met on the street last night." Jacob smiled politely as he said it. "How can I be sure you're not Abigail Matteson's twin?"

"How can you say that, Master Morgan?" she replied with a playful lilt. Then in serious tone, "Did you like my imitation of Mercy? I thought that might draw you to the house."

The mention of Mercy's name made him feel more uncomfortable than the thought that he had been duped. *What had Esau told her about Mercy?* The age-old jealousy within him was instantly resurrected. But now was not the time for it. He had to get this woman to lower the musket.

"So you know I'm not Esau," he said.

"I knew almost instantly."

"The kiss?"

She blushed. "Well, yes ... that and your eyes are closer together. I'm an artist, I notice those things."

Jacob smiled in spite of the situation. "Then what was that about a drooping gun?"

"I was toying with you. I knew only Esau would understand."

Jacob nodded. "You are the one thing I overlooked in this whole plan. It just never occurred to me that Esau would have a female friend."

"Because he's always been devoted to Mercy in spite of not being married to her," Abigail completed the thought.

Another reference to Mercy. It was unsettling. This woman was cool, in control, and kept him off balance. That had to change. "You can put that thing down now. I know you won't shoot me."

Abigail glanced quickly at the musket's newly installed flint, then planted the musket against her shoulder in a threatening manner. "You think I won't shoot you because you're Esau's brother, don't you?"

"No. You won't shoot me because we're on the same side."

"What are you talking about?"

Jacob folded his arms. "We both work for the same man. The Marquis de Lafayette of the Continental Army."

Now it was Abigail's turn to be unnerved.

"Wild speculation is unbecoming, Master Morgan. The truth is, I could shoot you, drag your body into town, and General Clinton would congratulate me. He would have no trouble believing me when I told him you were not Esau Morgan."

"Every word you say is true, Mrs. Matteson! That's what makes you such a valuable spy."

Her response was to place her finger on the trigger.

"Do you want me to tell you how you do it?"

She said nothing.

"You mold hollow images in wax of various people—soldiers, merchants, tradesmen—and smuggle secret British documents to the Americans inside them. Your wax people have traveled as corpses in coffins, they have ridden in wagons among prisoners during exchanges, sometimes they even ride up front next to the driver. The usual route is through White Plains, then up the east side of the Hudson to Mr. Shaw's ferry, then to General

Lafayette himself. How is that for wild speculation? Am I close?"

Abigail lowered the musket.

"Why are you here? And why wasn't I told you were coming?"

"There wasn't time to tell you. And I'm here to get information on the spring offensive. You're my contact to see that the information gets to the American side. It was General Lafayette himself who briefed me about you. I'm sorry you had to learn about the operation this way."

Indeed, he was sympathetic, for Abigail was shaken. The barrel of the lowered musket dragged across the carpet as she ambled toward a stuffed chair facing the sofa. She fell into it. The musket clattered to the floor.

"Esau ..." she said softly. "What has happened to Esau?" Her tone indicated she suspected the worst.

Using a tone of voice often reserved for ministers when imparting tragic news to loved ones, Jacob said, "He never escaped. General Washington said he would be hanged with Andre as a spy. It's probably already done. I'm sorry. Esau evidently meant a great deal to you, even though it was not wise of you to get involved with him."

Like the sun ducking behind a dark cloud, Abigail's emotion swung just as dramatically from grief to anger. "My involvement, as you call it, is none of your business, Master Morgan!"

"Maybe not, Mrs. Matteson, but it's the Continental Army's business when it interferes with your judgment!"

"How dare you accuse me of poor judgment! For years I have risked my life for the revolutionary cause. I don't have to prove my loyalty to anyone."

"Loyalty, no. Judgment, yes."

"You evidently have something specific in mind, Master Morgan."

"I do."

Her hostile glare made him hesitate. He liked Abigail Matteson, even admired her since before they met. From everything he had learned about her—her creative daring, her lengthy service despite the risk of death should she be caught, the value of the information she was somehow able to obtain—he knew she was a courageous woman. But Lafayette had specifically instructed him to question her about one matter. Knowing that she had close ties to Major John Andre and Esau Morgan, why didn't she inform Lafayette of their mission to meet General Benedict Arnold?

The question took a measure of life from her. She sank back into the chair. For a long time she silently wrestled with thoughts and emotions. When she did try to speak, she had to work through several aborted attempts before she was able to put into words her feelings.

"I intended to ... to inform ... several times ... the message was written, deposited in a figure, prepared for shipment ... but I couldn't ... I couldn't ... Andre was a friend ... he's an artist, not a soldier, not a spy ... he should be designing party invitations, not sneaking around the countryside on covert missions ... he's kind ... not a threat to anyone ... and then ... then there was Esau ... and I knew I couldn't ... couldn't do it ... I ... loved him."

After only several days of espionage Jacob was ready to send his first report to Lafayette. He was scratching it out on paper, sitting comfortably on Andre's sofa using one of Andre's sketching pens, when he was interrupted by an official-sounding rap on the door. It made Jacob wonder if army officers were given lessons on how to knock on doors since the knock was so uniform, so characteristically military. Before answering, Jacob went to the closet and hid his message among Andre's stack of sketches.

The person at the door justified his knock identification. A baby-faced major informed him that General Clinton wished to see him. The general had sent a carriage, much to the delight of Jacob's aching leg.

When the news of Major Andre's death reached New York, the whole military establishment and much of the civilian population went into mourning. Their sympathy extended to his friend Esau, allowing Jacob to move freely about headquarters. The headquarters staff was so busy consoling him, they never thought to ask him what he was doing there. A few surreptitious peeks at maps and documents revealed that the British planned a renewal of activity in the Carolinas, led by General Cornwallis, which made sense since support for the revolution was weakening in the southern colonies. Another location that appeared on several documents was Yorktown. Jacob was in the midst of recording this information for Washington when the carriage came for him.

"Were you informed as to the nature of this meeting, Major?"

The unsmiling officer said, "I can't say, sir."

The young man was serious and curt. Jacob wondered if the same school that taught the officers how to knock also taught them how to keep from smiling.

"Is this a meeting between just me and General Clinton, or will others be there?"

"I can't say, sir."

"I see."

The remainder of the trip was traveled in silence.

"Show him in."

General Clinton's voice came from beyond the door as the aide announced Jacob's presence, calling him, of course, Esau Morgan.

The general was not alone in his office. Seated to one side of the general's desk, a leg folded comfortably over the other, was

General Benedict Arnold. This was the test Jacob had been dreading. *It was one thing to fool people who only casually knew Esau. But could he fool someone who had worked closely with his brother for years?*

"Esau! How good to see you again!"

Arnold rose and extended his hand. Jacob took it. The grip was a superior one. His eyes were gray and penetrating. It was the same man who had reprimanded him in Cambridge, only older, somewhat sadder it seemed. The cockiness that was so prevalent before was gone.

"And it's good to see you again, General."

That was a lie. Arnold was dressed in full military uniform, the scarlet red of a British general, the traitor incarnate, decorated, self-important, free. The sight of Arnold infuriated Jacob.

"Who would have thought, when we were starving in the Maine wilderness for the revolutionary cause, that one day the two of us would be standing in a British general's headquarters and not be under arrest?"

"Certainly not I, sir."

"If I remember correctly, though, the idea of you being here was not that far-fetched. You'll recall, your twin brother warned me about your loyalist leanings."

"In Cambridge. I remember, sir."

"And for a long time I didn't trust you because of that."

"I'm glad that has changed."

There was a pause during which time Arnold's eyes never left Jacob.

"How is Mrs. Arnold, sir? Will she be joining you soon?"

"We're negotiating for her safe passage."

General Clinton interrupted them. Jacob felt a sense of accomplishment. He'd successfully passed the initial phase. Arnold showed no sign of suspecting him to be other than Esau

Morgan. Still, as long as Arnold remained in the room, the test was ongoing.

"Esau, I had you brought here to ask a favor."

It was getting even better. Here was a chance to build General Clinton's trust in him.

"I'm afraid it would require that you postpone your return to England," Clinton said.

Jacob hesitated. He knew this to be Esau's driving motivation and didn't want to appear too eager. "Sometimes personal desires have to be set aside for the greater cause," he said. "If there is something I can do to help, I'm more than willing to postpone my trip."

"That's a generous sacrifice, considering you've never wanted to go to England."

The voice came from the doorway behind him. For Jacob, it was the voice of doom, a voice from beyond the grave.

Whirling around, Jacob came face-to-face with his twin brother, Esau.

Esau arrived at Abigail's house unannounced. The door opened halfway in response to his knock. A head poked out.

"Afternoon, Missy," Esau said.

"Master Morgan." She returned his greeting, with an indifferent, almost cold tone. "You're early. We weren't expectin' you till later."

"You probably weren't expecting me at all," Esau said kindly.

"Sir?"

"Never mind. Where's Abi ... Mrs. Matteson?"

"In her workshop gettin' ready for you. But you're early," Missy insisted.

Esau reached forward and gently pressed the door, forcing Missy to give way. "Is someone else with her?"

"No, sir, it's just that she's not expectin' you yet. You're …"

"Yes, I know. I'm early. Thank you, Missy. I know my way to the workshop."

Missy fussed at him as he walked by. "'Course you know the way, you was here day afore yesterday." Then under her breath, "Sure liked your brother better. He had manners."

When Esau stepped into the doorway, Abigail was fitting a wax figure of a British regular with a coat. She wore her oversized work apron, her hair was up, her hands and arms covered with splotches of dried wax.

Abigail's back was to the door so she didn't see him standing there. She adjusted the shoulders on the figure, then reached up, and brushed back stray blonde hairs that had fallen in her eyes. Esau steadied himself against the door. To be this close to her, when he thought he'd never see her again, was nearly too much for him. While she plucked at the shoulders, he fought a battle to maintain control over his emotions.

She turned halfway and saw him out of the corner of her eye. She jumped, holding a hand to her throat.

"Oh! Master Morgan, you startled me!" Looking at the small clock atop a cluttered shelf, she said, "What are you doing here? You're early." Her tone matched that of her housemaid.

"So I've been told," Esau said. When Abigail jumped and their eyes connected, the same charge that jolted her in fright struck him in anticipation. His heart responded to it by pounding wildly.

"It's just as well," she said flatly, reaching for a wig and plopping it onto the wax head. "Did you bring the papers?"

"No, I didn't."

Hands went to hips. "Did you forget them?"

"No. I just didn't bring any papers with me."

An exasperated look crossed her face. She returned to the

model and fussed with the wig. "I don't have time for guessing games," she said.

Esau didn't want to play games—he just couldn't figure out how to tell Abigail he wasn't Jacob. Informing someone you're not dead isn't the kind of thing you just blurt out.

"Abigail," he said, "could we go into the parlor and talk?"

"Master Morgan, I thought we had an agreement." She worked as she talked. "I'd prefer it if you called me Mrs. Matteson. I am willing to work with you, but I choose not to socialize with you."

Esau closed his eyes and smiled. Abigail had no idea how much those words meant to him. All the way out to the house he reasoned that it was foolish of him to be jealous of Jacob and Abigail. But the two brothers had fought over the same woman for so many years, it was only natural for him to think that Jacob would be attracted to Abigail just as he was. And since Esau had not been permitted time alone with Jacob yet, there had been no way of knowing the depth of their relationship. Until now. Abigail told him. No socialization. Formal names only.

"Abigail …"

Her hands froze at the use of her familiar name. Her jaw was set; her eyes were blue fire. Esau had seen her like this before, and he knew his time was short.

"… I'm not who you think I am."

"You're right," she said through clenched teeth. "I thought you were a gentleman."

Esau laughed. That only made her angrier. His instincts told him to get ready to duck. Then he had an idea.

"Look at me," he said.

A blue inferno blazed in her eyes.

"No, I mean, take a good look at me."

"Master Morgan, I'm warning you …"

Her anger was blinding her. *How could he get past her anger?*

"Do I have to stand beside that wax model of me that you have hidden somewhere—you never did tell me where you put it—before you will realize who I am?"

Like a catalyst, his words sparked a reaction. The anger in her eyes mutated to disbelief and fear. But she looked at him. She studied his eyes.

"You're an artist! Look at me. What do your eyes tell you?"

Trembling, Abigail stumbled backward, steadying herself on the workbench. Her eyes filled; her mouth trembled. "Esau?" Barely audible. "Esau?"

He moved slowly toward her, his arms outstretched.

She whimpered.

"Abigail, it's me. I've come home so you can trounce me at backgammon."

Whimpering turned to sobs of joy.

25

Anne Morgan sat in her chair by the window, her Bible open, her eyes red. The morning sun fell softly through the window, filtered by thin clouds, bathing the table upon which her Bible rested in a holy light. But try as she might, she could not feel God's presence. His words were there for her, but not His closeness. She knew the feeling. It was like reading one of Jared's letters from China. Grateful for the letter, but needing the person. There were days when words were not enough. This was one of those days.

Resting atop her open Bible was a personally handwritten letter from General George Washington. *Dear Jared and Anne Morgan*, it began. *How difficult it is for me to write this letter* ... The general went on to inform them that he had received a dispatch from British General Clinton's headquarters in New York. Their son, Jacob Morgan, had been arrested on a charge of espionage. A military hearing had found him guilty and he was sentenced to hang. The general expressed his deepest regrets. Mercy had received a similar letter from the commander-in-chief of the Continental Army, also personally handwritten.

Beneath the letter was the Scripture passage Anne had turned to in her grief, Isaiah 40:28–29:

> Hast thou not known? hast thou not heard, that the everlasting God, the LORD, the Creator of the ends of the earth, fainteth not, neither is weary? there is no searching of his understanding. He giveth power to the faint; and to them that have no might he increaseth strength.

Words. Like a letter from afar. Paper and ink when what she needed most right now was comfort and understanding. And answers.

Why does it have to be this way, Lord? Why do countries have to fight? Why do young men ... why does Jacob have to die? But then, wasn't it a short time ago she was praying this same prayer, only inserting Esau's name? And though she rejoiced that he escaped death, he was still lost to her for the duration of the war.

She had sensed this possibility, but that knowledge was little comfort in her present suffering. Her thoughts drifted back to the night both boys were home for dinner. They had guests: Dr. Cooper, Sam Adams, John Hancock. Those days of debate were replaced with days of musket fire, military advances, and killing. She remembered the sense of dread that had overwhelmed her that evening, the feeling that the winds of conflict would scatter her family like leaves across the grass. How does one stop the wind?

Lifting Washington's letter from atop the Bible, Anne read more from Isaiah:

> Even the youths shall faint and be weary, and the young men shall utterly fall: But they that wait upon the LORD shall renew their strength; they shall mount up with wings as eagles; they shall run, and not be weary; and they shall walk, and not faint.

Eyes closed, her head fell against the back of the chair and Anne silently prayed: *"Mount up with wings as eagles." That is too much to hope for. "Run and not be weary." Not possible. How can one run while carrying so great a weight? "Walk and not faint." Yes, Lord, oh yes, that would be enough for today. Help me to put one foot in front of the other and not stumble.*

"Anne?"

She opened her eyes. Jared stood in the doorway.

"Priscilla's here," he said.

Wiping her eyes, Anne stood as Priscilla and Jared and Mercy came into the parlor. They huddled together at the semicircle of sofa and chairs near the floor-to-ceiling windows overlooking the bay. In hushed voices, they told Priscilla the news about Jacob. Priscilla moved beside Mercy and put her arm around Mercy's shoulders, offering words of comfort.

To Jared, Priscilla said: "Have you written to Philip?"

"Just finished." He handed it to Priscilla. She would take it to her tavern, and from there the stage would carry it to their brother at the Narragansett reservation.

Bo could be seen through the window. He was standing in front of the house, in the very spot Jacob had told him to stand, peering intently down Beacon Street.

"Does he know?" Priscilla asked.

Mercy shook her head. "Not yet. We thought it best."

Bo was called into the house for morning prayers. Along with the adults, he got down on his knees, propping his forearms on the seat of a chair.

Jared began: "Lord, I have never been much good with words. Just when I need them, they seem to leave me. But You know my heart. And I think now I know how You felt when You watched Your Son go through what He went through. Anyway, You know I'd do anything to spare my boys the pain they're going through right now, but I can't. So I guess we'll just have to ride out this storm and trust You to keep us off the rocks. You've done it before. I trust You can do it again."

"Lord, we hurt so badly for our boys," Anne prayed. "All we have ever wanted for them was to know love and happiness. Yet the world has given them, and us, pain and sorrow. They need You so badly right now. We can't help them, but You can. Work Your will in Jacob's and Esau's lives, please Lord, work Your will."

Bo prayed with his eyes open, watching the others' lips move, picking up words here and there, waiting for his turn.

Mercy: "Lord, for most of my life I have not been the woman or the wife that You have wanted me to be, and I know I have no right to ask anything of You, but I've learned from Anne and Jared to trust You, and I know You can bring good out of this bad situation." She bit her lip and fought back tears. "Dear God, You know my feelings for Esau, I pray that he will find happiness. And You also know how much I love Jacob and how I long to live the rest of my life with him, please bring him back to me...." She struggled to say what she wanted to say next without alarming Bo. "But I know this, we will be together again, if not here, then in eternity."

"God, You have brought us Morgans too far to leave us without hope," Priscilla prayed. "Only You can save the family now. And, Lord, I want to thank You for making Mercy a part of our family."

Bo: "God, please bring Jabe back to me. Every day I look. Please bring Jabe home."

The initial relief Abigail felt when she learned Esau was alive gave way to mounting terror. Jacob had been arrested, her coconspirator. Her position behind enemy lines had been compromised. The gibbet loomed before her. She wanted to cling to Esau forever, but he was the enemy; she had to run, desperate to get away, but she didn't want to let go. In her struggle, rational thought failed, overwhelmed by the rising tide of emotions in conflict. She collapsed in near hysteria.

Esau knelt beside her, his arms tightly around her, lips against her ear whispering soothing words. Just when it seemed his words were having an effect, she would try to shove him away.

"I have to get out of here!" she screamed. "They're coming! Warn Isaac and Missy. Get to safety."

"Nobody's coming," Esau said. "Nobody. You're safe."

"No! Jacob, they have Jacob."

"He won't tell them about you. They still don't know."

She looked up at him. Her eyes wanted to believe, but she wasn't convinced.

"As they took him away, he told me you were safe."

"How could he do that? Someone could have heard him use my name!"

Esau pulled her tighter. "He didn't use your name. He said, 'It looks like that drooping gun is safe in your hands again.' To Clinton and Arnold, he commented: 'Ever since the days when we played with toy guns, we've been competitive.' They interpreted his comment as a reference to a toy we fought over as children, just as he intended."

Abigail was beginning to calm down. "I never explained the drooping gun to him."

"He knew enough to know only I would associate it with you."

She was still trembling. "And you?"

"What about me?"

"You know I'm an American spy. Will you turn me in?"

Esau lay his cheek against her head. "All of my life I've been looking for you. Do you think that just because we're on opposite sides of a war I'm going to give you up now that I've found you?"

One final shudder, then she lay peacefully in his arms.

Theirs was a perfect world, a cleft in a rock in the midst of the storm. Their world had a population of two, a cozy fireplace, and

JACK CAVANAUGH

a backgammon board. Sweet contentment. But like most worlds, this one had been forged in conflict.

Abigail's parlor was their refuge from the war. While nations raged without, Esau Morgan and Abigail Matteson found peace in each other's arms. But the world of hate and war was much larger; more than that, it was jealous of this haven of peace. And try as they might, Esau and Abigail could not stop it from crashing in on top of them.

"How can you say that? How can you build a nation of peace by starting a war?"

Esau stood by the fireplace, his arms swung wide to emphasize the question. Abigail was still sitting on the floor by the backgammon board. He had just gotten up to stretch a stiff leg. His wound prevented him from sitting on the floor very long. Abigail had just won her third game when the conversation turned to their future together. Esau wanted her to go to England with him where they could start new lives together.

"Sometimes it is necessary to fight for what you believe," Abigail replied.

"In defense, yes. But it was the colonies that provoked hostilities. Parliament had no choice but to send troops to restore the peace."

Abigail shook her head. "I don't agree with that interpretation. Parliament could have given us the voice we deserve. Besides, I think we are acting in defense—defense of our freedom to determine our own destiny. To England we will always be a colony, subservient to them and existing only for their profit."

The debate between Esau and Abigail was without animosity. Their love for one another was still fresh and of greater value to them than stale political arguments. The question of their future had prompted the debate. In this, their desire was identical—to live together in peace and relative security.

However, they differed as to which country could provide that future for them.

To remain as Englishmen and fight for needed reforms within the system or to strike out on their own and create a new system based on their treasured values and beliefs. It was a question Esau had debated hundreds of times before—with his brother, his father, friends at Oxford, students at Harvard—but there was something different about this time. It wasn't that he loved the person he was debating more than he'd loved the others, though indeed he did; the element that made the debate different this time was reality. Before, it was theory and speculation, opinion versus opinion. But seated on the floor was a woman—and a beautiful one at that—who had the courage of her convictions. She was risking her life for her point of view. For the first time, Esau considered the possibility that he might be wrong.

"You once told me about your Puritan ancestor," Abigail said, "the one who first settled in Boston."

"Drew Morgan."

"Why did he leave England?"

"Actually, he was fleeing for his life." Esau told Abigail the story of Drew Morgan, how as a young man he sought fame and glory, was enlisted by Bishop William Laud to infiltrate Puritan villages in search of a notorious underground pamphleteer, how he stumbled into the tiny village of Edenford and found a faith and love worth dying for. Having gone over to the other side, he became the bishop's enemy and, to escape his wrath, fled England with the residents of Edenford, coming to the Massachusetts Bay Colony.

"And what did the Puritans hope to accomplish by coming to the New World?"

Esau grinned. "Is this a history test?"

Abigail returned his smile. "No, dear, it's our heritage. Humor me."

"My ancestors—our ancestors," he corrected himself, remembering that Abigail's ancestors were Puritans as well, "wanted nothing more than to build a colony that reflected their belief in God. The Bible was their guidebook in this endeavor."

"Very good! You're my star pupil!"

"Does my recitation warrant a kiss?"

"Don't be silly. I'm trying to make a point."

Esau sat down on the floor opposite her, for no other reason than to be closer to her.

"You once told me that you wanted to continue Drew Morgan's legacy."

"And I do, with you." He leaned closer.

"The Puritans," she giggled, not wanting to discourage him, yet wanting to make her point, "sought freedom to choose their own destiny, apart from the restricting influences of English government. In my heart, I'm a Puritan. I only want what they wanted—the freedom to raise a family according to my beliefs."

Esau pulled back, sitting upright. Her argument had struck a sympathetic chord in him. "I agree with that. Unfortunately," he countered, "that's not what this conflict is all about. It's a matter of politics, control. It's politics, pure and simple. I've talked—argued is a better word—with many of the Boston politicians who stirred up this hornets' nest. And believe me, they are nothing more than ruthless politicians."

"Not all of them."

"Most of them."

"I know one who isn't."

"Who?"

She didn't respond. Instead, she got up and disappeared from the room for a couple of minutes. She returned with a handful of printed newssheets.

"I hid these away when the colonel was alive. They upset him so. But they were my inspiration. It is because of these pages that I decided to do what I am doing to help the cause of the revolution."

Holding the papers with reverence, she began to read:

"We must never forget those stirring days of the Great Awakening when George Whitefield thundered from the pulpit and New Englanders turned the clock back to the time of Winthrop and Cotton. My greatest desire is to restore Puritan manners and morals in New England. Thus, the chief purpose of our revolt is to separate New England from our decadent mother country in order that Puritanism might again flourish as it had in the early seventeenth century. Puritanism is our goal. Revolution is our method of attaining it."

She shifted papers and read again:

"I firmly believe that the New Englander's best security against British tyranny is the Puritan spirit which, although sadly weakened in the course of a century, might again be made a bulwark of colonial liberty."

"This is a Boston writer?" Esau asked.

"Well known."

"He's incredible. Unlike any of the Boston politicians I've had the misfortune of meeting."

"As influential as your family is in Boston, you've probably met this man."

"No, I'd remember a man with such noble goals. What's his name?"

"Samuel Adams. Do you know him?"

※

"Come to gloat?"

Jacob lay on the bed, not bothering to sit up, let alone get up, when Esau was let in. He was being held in the cellar of an old stone mansion. The previous occupant, a revolutionary shipbuilder with a taste for fine wines, had divided it into two sections. The open side at the foot of the stairs was floor-to-ceiling racks that cradled lesser bottles of wine; the far side had been enclosed and secured with a heavy, solid wooden door that was padlocked. It had originally guarded the shipbuilder's best wines. However, with the British occupation, the finer wines were all gone, the racks were removed, and the heavy door now guarded an American spy.

The room was dark, lit only by a single candle, and cold and damp. Jacob wore his overcoat continually to ward off the chill. The only furniture was the bed and a small table that held the light source. Esau leaned against the wall where some wine racks had once been. He chose to ignore his brother's opening comment.

Looking around, he said, "Not exactly spacious accommodations."

"I suppose yours were better."

"I was above ground."

Jacob snorted. "What do you want?"

"Just came to see how you were doing."

Swinging his legs over the side of the bed and sitting up, he said, "Well, let's see. I'm shut up underground in an enemy jail, I'm scheduled to hang in four days, and I think this damp room is giving me a cold. Life can't get much better than this."

"It's good to see you haven't lost your sense of humor." A pause. "I found your letter to General Washington in the stack of Andre's drawings in the closet."

"Another nail in my coffin."

"Would you like me to get word to Mercy? If you wanted to write a letter or something, I could …" He looked at the heavy door. There was no way of knowing if someone was listening, so he was cautious. "… I could see that she gets it somehow."

A glint of acknowledgment in Jacob's eyes indicated he

understood the unspoken reference to Abigail. "I may take you up on that." Then with a finger-shaking warning he added, "Just stay away from Mercy. I'll bet you can't wait for me to die so you can rush back to Boston. Well, I have news for you. She's not the same woman. You'd only be wasting your time."

"My life in Boston is over. And although Mercy will always have a special place in my heart, I have Abigail now. I'm happy."

Jacob chuckled. It was the first friendly sign he'd shown. "She is one of a kind, isn't she?" he said. "I just don't know what she sees in you."

Esau laughed with him.

"What?" Jacob said. "What are you laughing at?"

"It's the end of an era," Esau said. "Do you realize that for the first time since that night in Philadelphia when we first saw Mercy Reed we are no longer fighting over her?"

"Sad, isn't it? It took you that long to realize you'd lost."

The jab stung, but quickly went away. It no longer mattered. The fight was over. Esau said, "Abigail was worth waiting for."

An uncomfortable silence rose between them.

Esau broke it. "I hear you've had a sidekick since Concord."

"Where did you hear that?"

Actually, he'd heard it twice. Mercy told him when they were in Philadelphia together. Esau decided he was on safer ground to mention the second hearing. "Father told me when he visited me in Tappan."

"Did he tell you Bo was deaf?"

Esau nodded. It was interesting the way Jacob's face brightened as he talked about the boy.

"He's remarkable," Jacob said, beaming. "Intelligent, quick with his hands—he can load a musket faster than anybody I know." Jacob laughed aloud. "And he plays the drum! Learned simply by watching another boy play! Do you know how he does it?"

Esau shook his head.

"Vibrations!" The more Jacob spoke of Bo, the more excited he became. "We were at Valley Forge, and I was sicker than anything. Bo was going around the hut banging things, then reaching out, and touching them. I didn't know what he was doing. I had no idea he'd even met this little drummer boy friend of his. Anyway, Bo was driving me mad! My head was pounding and he was banging on things. I figured, he couldn't understand because he couldn't hear what he was doing. But he wouldn't stop! So I threw him out of the hut! Some guardian I turned out to be, right?"

Esau laughed, at the story, to be sure, but also at the sight of his animated brother. He had never seen Jacob like this before. He never dreamed Jacob could be like this. Somehow, this little deaf boy had tapped a well of fatherhood inside Jacob. He was boasting about the boy as if the boy were his own son.

"Anyway, we were at the Battle of Monmouth, and the little drummer boy got hit, killed. Our men were running away from the field of battle and Washington himself came riding up, looking for the drummer boy. He wanted to signal the troops back to battle. So I was in the middle of explaining to him that the drummer boy had been killed, when Bo picked up the drum and beat the call to assembly. Just what Washington wanted! I was shocked speechless! I didn't even know the boy could play!"

Esau felt he was in the room with a stranger. Someone impersonating his brother.

"I'd like to meet this miracle boy sometime."

Jacob's eyes misted over. "I'd like to see him again myself, at least once before I die." He laughed ironically. "If for no other reason than to tell him he doesn't have to look down the street anymore."

A puzzled look on Esau's face indicated an explanation was necessary.

"The last thing I told him when I left him with Mother and Mercy was to watch for me, that I would come back soon. And Bo is so stubborn, he'll keep doing it until he's an old man unless someone tells him to stop."

Jacob sat on the edge of the bed, but the faraway look in his eyes indicated that in his mind he was back in Boston with Bo.

"Is there anything I can get you?" Esau asked.

"A reprieve."

A half smile by Esau. "When Father visited me in Tappan, he reminded me of the time he was almost hanged as a pirate."

"That's right! Quite a tradition we Morgan men have."

Esau laughed.

"And I hope to keep the tradition alive in every sense of the word," Jacob added.

"I don't follow you."

"Father was in jail about to be hanged, and he escaped; you were in jail about to be hanged, and you escaped. I've kept the first part of the tradition, now if I can just keep the second part."

Esau's eyes surveyed the room. No windows. Only one way out. A guard at the padlocked door. A guard at the top of the stairs. Guards in the house.

"That's right," Jacob said, guessing what his brother was thinking, "in my good humor, I forgot I was conversing with the enemy."

"As I was about to say," Esau continued in a more subdued tone, "Father told me he wished he could trade places with me, trade his life for mine."

An amused look appeared in Jacob's eyes. "Are you telling me you wish you could trade places with me? It's possible, you know."

"No, that's not what I was saying at all."

A smirk. "I didn't think so."

"I was about to say, that if Father were here, I'm sure he'd say the same thing to you."

Jacob shrugged. "Somehow it loses its effectiveness second-hand."

Pushing off from the wall, Esau said, "Well, I'll be going. If you get that letter written, I'll send it to Boston."

"Ironic, isn't it?" Jacob took on a philosophical look. "For some time now, Mother and Father have had to live with the thought that the family was going to be reduced to one son. First it was going to be me, now it'll be you."

Esau pounded on the door to be let out. As the lock clicked and the latch lifted, Jacob called after his brother, "A piece of advice. Give the Bible back to Father. Let him give it to you when he's ready."

"I visited Jacob today."

"How is he doing?"

"Not as good as me."

The back of Abigail's head was nestled against Esau's upper chest; his arms encircled her waist.

"That's not funny! And unkind!" She attempted to pull away. He held her tight.

"Sorry, old habits die slow deaths ... I didn't mean that like it sounded, either ... sorry. He's doing all right. He tries to act cavalier about his circumstances, but the reality of the situation isn't something you can ignore for long."

"How about Mercy? What will this do to her?"

Esau sighed heavily. "I honestly don't know. She's changed dramatically in the last few years. More mature. Deeper spiritually. My mother will be there to comfort her. You'd like my mother. Did I ever tell you she's a poet?"

Abigail leaned forward so she could look back at him. "No! You didn't tell me that. Do you know any of her poems?"

"You mean memorized them?"

"Sure!"

"The thought never crossed my mind. I've read them. She's good."

Snuggling herself back into position, Abigail said, "I've always admired poets. They have a way of capturing life's essence in a few words. I'd like to meet your mother someday."

Esau smiled. "I'd like for you to meet her. She'll fall in love with you, I'm sure of it. The two of you have so much in common."

"How conceited!"

"What did I say?"

"You said your mother and I have much in common, implying— not very subtly—that the common element is that we both love you."

"That's not what I meant at all! But I like it. What I meant was that you both are artists. She uses words, you use wax."

"Oh. Sorry."

Esau pulled Abigail against him, his nose and mouth gently kissing her hair. She responded by hugging his arms and burying the side of her face against his chest.

"Esau?"

"Hm?"

"What are we going to do?"

"About what?"

"About us."

He felt a serious discussion coming on, and he was in no mood for anything serious. They were exactly where he wanted them to be—wrapped in each other's arms with no concerns, no troubles, no war, no difficult decisions.

"I don't want to think about it."

"Darling, neither do I, but …" she hesitated.

She tensed in his arms, no longer lost in love. The outside world was crashing into their sanctuary. He wanted to fight it off.

"I got a message from Lafayette today …"

"Yes?"

"Nothing urgent. He just wants me to go over to the American side. He says I've already done more than my duty and he's concerned for my safety the longer I'm over here. Especially considering the 'Morgan affair,' as he called it. He didn't say it directly, but he's concerned that you might find out I'm an American spy."

"He's too late." Esau kissed her head again.

"There's another reason, but Lafayette doesn't know I know it."

"Which is?"

"New York will be the next battlefield."

Esau sat up rigidly. "You know that for sure?"

She scooted away and turned to face him. "He's afraid I'll get caught between the two armies."

The leg was hurting again. It had been throbbing for a while, but the pleasure of holding Abigail far outweighed the pain in his leg. Now that the pleasure ended, the pain seemed to increase. Esau rose to his feet and walked around the room as he talked.

"Come to England with me," he said.

Abigail closed her eyes, as though she'd been dreading this moment.

"I can't," she said.

"Why not?"

"Because I'm an American spy!"

"Nobody in England knows that!"

She shook her head at his lack of reasoning. She'd been in the spy business much longer than him and was more experienced at thinking through all the implications of decisions.

"If I went to England, the Americans would regard me as a traitor. All they would have to do would be to release a few incriminating papers to prove I'd been a spy. When the English learned that, they would not be too sympathetic, no matter how hard I insisted I wanted to be on their side now. Besides, I don't."

"You don't want to come with me to England?"

"I *want* to be with you, darling, but I can't go to England. I could never live in a country that treats its colonies the way it has treated us. In a year's time I'd be arrested for trying to start a revolution over there."

Abigail was being facetious, yet Esau knew she was right. She would never be happy in England.

"Come over to the American side with me," Abigail said.

Esau looked at her like she was crazy. "They have an empty noose over there that I left behind, and they're aching to fill it with my neck!" he said.

"But maybe if I tell them how you protected me, and if you help me get to the American side, maybe they'll …"

Shaking his head, Esau cut her off. "You're thinking with your heart, not your head. General Washington doesn't love me as much as you do."

Abigail got to giggling. "Nobody loves you as much as I do."

They came together, his arms smothering her head against his chest, her arms around his waist.

"I don't ever want to let go," she said.

"Do you think if both armies see us like this, they'll leave us alone?"

"Can't you be serious?" Abigail said, pulling away far enough to look up at him.

He brushed stray blonde hairs out of her eyes. "It's too depressing."

"Will this help make you feel better?" She rose to her toes and kissed him.

Standing before the fire, in their fortress from reality, they embraced and kissed and talked and kissed.

"Is there anyplace in this world for us?" Esau asked.

"We have our fireplace."

"Not for long. The Americans are coming."

Alone in Andre's house, the warmth and closeness Esau felt during his evening with Abigail quickly dissipated into the emptiness of the big room. The only sounds in the house were sounds he made. The only light came from candles he lit. The only movement in the whole house, upstairs or downstairs, was his. The absence of John Andre made him realize how much difference a person's presence makes in a room. When Andre was here with him, the room was alive, warm, friendly, fun, but only because that's the way Andre made it. Same room, no Andre. Now it was hollow, sad, lonely.

Does the same thing hold true for countries? Could England be home without Abigail? Or for that matter, could anywhere be home without Abigail? What were the alternatives? The Ohio Valley wilderness? An artist and an accountant fighting Indians and carving a civilization out of the backwoods? They would never survive. What about the Caribbean? Or France? France had a monarchy; would Abigail start a revolution there?

Like a black fog, a slow-moving depression tiptoed into his mind. He and Abigail were lovers without a country. *Star-crossed. Wasn't that the term Shakespeare used for Romeo and Juliet?* Only instead of the Montagues and the Capulets, he and his love were caught between the Americans and the English. But whether family or country, the result was the same. He and Abigail would forever be hindered from loving each other freely.

There was something inherently wrong with a world that could not permit a harmless soul like John Andre to grow old. There was something wrong with governments when they had to kill each other's citizens to settle their disputes. There was something wrong with existence when two people who love each other could not be together.

His eyes fell on the Morgan family Bible. Esau knew his thoughts were not profound. From infancy he had heard of sin and its consequences in the world, but like the political arguments prior to the revolution, it had been all theory. Now it was personal. The effects of sin were real, devastating.

Esau rose from his chair and retrieved the Bible, holding it close to the light. Inside the front flap was the list of names:

Drew Morgan, 1630, Zechariah 4:6

Christopher Morgan, 1654, Matthew 28:19

Philip Morgan, 1729, Philippians 2:3–4

Jared Morgan, 1741, John 15:13

A short list, Esau thought. *Would it end here? Was Drew Morgan's dream about to die?* The future of the Morgans seemed bleak indeed. Jared Morgan had only two sons, and it looked like neither one of them was going to be producing any offspring.

Jacob had a wife, but had run out of time. Esau sighed. He had time left, but no wife. Esau felt sad for his father. He so much wanted to carry on the Morgan tradition and pass this Bible on to one of his sons. Esau had always wondered how his father was going to choose between him and Jacob. It didn't matter much now. The list would end with no further entries.

The Scripture reference following his father's name caught his attention. He'd heard it before, but couldn't remember it.

"John fifteen … verse thirteen …" he said as he turned the pages to the section with the four Gospels. His finger scanned down the page, "… eleven … twelve … thirteen.…" His finger and eyes reached the verse simultaneously.

"No!" He jerked his finger back as if verse thirteen were on fire. He lifted his eyes heavenward. "No!" he cried. "No!"

Esau slammed the Bible shut and shoved it off his lap, but it didn't stop the words from coming to him, over and over again.

"No!"

His father's verse, now in his father's voice, echoed in Esau's head. A command? A request? A plea. A plea from his father.

The Morgans could be saved. Esau could save them. Only Esau.

"O Lord, no!"

He sank to his knees and wept bitterly. *It wasn't fair. Not now. He'd just found Abigail. It wasn't fair!*

But the words wouldn't stop. Again and again, in his father's voice they repeated:

> Greater love hath no man than this, that a man lay down his life for his friends.

Late into the night, Esau argued with his absent father, like a lawyer pleading a case:

"It's too much to ask of a man! How can you ask me to do this, knowing the things Jacob has done to me? In Boston, he and his ruffians almost had me hanged! He shot me in the leg! If the situation was reversed, do you think for a moment Jacob would do the same for me? Of course not! In fact, when I was in jail, did he come to visit me? No! He saw it only as an opportunity to gain an advantage for the American army! How can you ask me to do this?"

Exhausted, he collapsed onto the sofa, eyes closed, breathing heavily. In his mind, a picture appeared. It was in Tappan. His jail.

His heart was heavy from the death of his friend, and he was to die the next day. His father sat across from him. And in all earnestness, his father said, "Son, if I could trade places with you, I would."

If I could, I would … if I could, I would … if I could.…

Esau found no rest that night until he realized that the names listed in the Morgan family Bible were not there out of privilege; they were there because they had earned the right to be there.

26

A steady stream of tears poured from her eyes. Abigail wiped them away angrily.

"No! How can you even think of doing it? God spared you from death for me! And now you just want to throw your life away! I don't understand you."

Moments earlier she had bolted from the sofa when she understood what Esau was telling her. The Morgan family Bible lay open to John's gospel on his lap. Esau had brought it with him to help re-create the sequence of thoughts that had led him to this course of action the previous night. He was beginning to think it was a mistake trying to convince Abigail that this was something he had to do. It would have been easier just to do it and explain himself in a letter. But he chose the harder way because it was the right thing to do. Somehow, he had to make Abigail understand what had become so clear to him.

"Abigail, I believe that God spared me in Tappan for this."

"He spared you to kill you?"

"Well … yes, I guess He did."

"Esau Morgan, the wax figure of you sitting in the corner of my bedroom has more brains in his head!"

So that's where she put it! It wasn't important, but the thought pleased him that she woke up every morning and saw his face.

"Sparing me for this moment makes sense!" he insisted. "In Tappan, my death would have been senseless, without meaning. But now, Jacob will be saved, and he and Mercy can perpetuate the Morgan family line, if not with their own child, maybe through Bo ... you really ought to see Jacob's face when he talks of Bo; I've never seen my brother so proud of someone like that ... Abigail, can't you see? By doing this, I can save my family's future. I'm the only one who can!"

"But what about us? What about our future?"

Esau had given this much thought. He knew Abigail would ask it. It wasn't a selfish question on her part; it was a confession of love. He closed the Bible and set it aside, rose, and embraced her. "The future *is* ours," he said softly, "we just don't have a present. This is not our time."

With her head buried against his chest, her voice was muffled. "You're not making sense," she said.

He thought for a moment, then said, "I have no doubt in my mind that we were meant to be together, but not here, not now. We've been through all this before—where can we go and both of us be happy? All we have is this fireplace, but not for long."

"So what are you saying—we'll be together in heaven?" A tinge of sarcasm shaded the question.

Esau said, "Last night, after I finally accepted my destiny, I began reading some of the chapters surrounding my father's verse. I read a passage that told of the night when Jesus informed His disciples He was leaving them to die on the cross. They of course objected. He told them He was going to prepare a place for them, a place where they could be together forever. Funny, I thought of this in Tappan too, but of course I didn't have any way of knowing it would pertain to you. Abigail, I'm going to prepare a place for us, and someday you will join me, and no one or nothing will ever come between us—no war, no army, nothing. That will be our time together."

She looked up at him, the fire flickering in wet blue eyes. "Do you really believe that?"

Esau's eyes grew moist. He gently kissed her lips. "I couldn't do what I'm doing if I didn't believe that with all my heart. It came to me so clearly. We have been mistaken in thinking that this is the only life there is. God has promised us more life after this, a life that is clearer, cleaner, brighter, better than the life we know right now. And in that new world, you and I will live and love each other forever."

She squeezed Esau tightly. "I want that life with you," she said, "but I want this one too."

"I know," Esau said. "So do I."

Softly, reluctantly, she asked, "When will you do it?"

"It has to be tomorrow. He's scheduled to hang the next day."

"Will Jacob go along with it?"

Esau laughed. "Why wouldn't he? How many people turn down a reprieve?"

"I won't help you," she said, looking up at him. "But I won't stop you either."

He pulled her closely to him, laying his cheek on the top of her head. "Jacob and I can do it. There's no reason for anyone to suspect we'd attempt something like this …"

"Of course not, because it's crazy!"

He smiled and completed his sentence, "… so we should be able to handle it alone." Esau got lost in thought for a moment, the thought being he and his brother working together toward a common goal. Abigail was right—it was crazy—it was crazy that it took so long for them to do something together.

"So what do we do now?" she asked.

"You can tell me you love me."

She reached up and grabbed the sides of his head. "I love you," she kissed him on the mouth, "I love you," on the tip of his nose, "I love you," on one cheek, then the other. Then they lost themselves in each other's embrace and kisses.

Through the night and into the morning they sat before the fire, holding each other. Little was said. They were together; that was all that mattered. Outside the house the revolution continued—soldiers on both sides walked late-night patrols; generals lay awake on their cots, rethinking battle strategy; the volunteer hangman awoke with a start when he dreamed of the hanging; and death waited near the gibbet for the war's next casualty. But on this night, in each other's arms, Esau and Abigail were oblivious to these things. For them life was reduced to one man and one woman and the promise of heaven.

The sun was well above the horizon when Esau and Abigail said their final good-byes. Esau rode back to Andre's house where he would change clothes and then to the stone mansion wine cellar where he would change places with his brother.

"Did they send you to torture me?" Jacob asked, sitting up on his cot.

The rough wooden door slammed shut behind Esau, followed by the familiar locking sounds.

"You should be nice to me," Esau said. "I'm your only friend in New York."

"Then I *am* doomed!" There was no humor in Jacob's voice.

"It's hard to see in here, but you look pale."

Jacob held out his hands and examined the back of them. "They're just aging me, like a good wine. Tomorrow, they'll pop my cork and celebrate."

Esau noted that even though the words were light, his brother's tone was flat, cynical. He remembered the encroaching hopelessness he felt at Tappan, similar to the penetrating chill of this wine cellar and just as cold.

"Abigail sends her regards."

Jacob acknowledged them with a halfhearted shrug.

Now that he was in Jacob's holding cell, this close to his brother, Esau wasn't so sure he wanted to go through with his plan. In his mind, he had idealized his brother in a way that didn't match reality. Seeing him face-to-face like this, hearing the dark sarcasm in his voice, feelings from the past rose up and shattered his idealism. Esau still didn't like his brother, and it was becoming increasingly evident that Jacob's nearness to death hadn't softened him toward Esau either. Strange, it wasn't fear of dying that was giving him second thoughts; it was a lifetime of animosity toward his brother.

Esau pushed aside his feelings. "Do you remember the last time I was in here?"

"It's all I've thought about," Jacob said sarcastically. "I still have nightmares."

"I told you about Father visiting me at Tappan ..."

Jacob showed no sign of remembering.

"... how he said he wished he could exchange places with me ..."

An empty stare.

"... you know, how he would be willing to die ..."

"I remember, I remember! What of it?"

"And you joked about me trading places with you?"

No response.

"Do you remember?"

"Of course I remember. You declined. So—let me guess—you've reconsidered and you want to exchange places now."

"That's right."

"Not funny, Esau."

Jacob swung his legs back onto the cot and lay down, ignoring his brother.

"I'm not joking. Listen ..." He glanced at the locked door. Cautiously, he lowered his voice. "This is the plan. We exchange clothes. You walk out of here and go to Abigail's. She'll see that you get back across the lines to the American side."

Jacob's eyes were closed. He showed no sign of having heard his brother.

"What do you think?" Esau asked.

"Get out of here."

Esau moved closer to the cot so that he was standing over Jacob. "Take off your overcoat." Esau began to unbutton his overcoat.

Jacob rose up from the cot so quickly, Esau had to step back or get knocked over.

"What are you trying to do?" Jacob yelled at him, his arms widespread. "If you're trying to make me more depressed than I already am, you've succeeded. Now get out of here."

"You're not making this easy for me," Esau said.

"You want easy? Call the jailer and walk through that door and never come back. How's that for easy?"

Esau reversed himself and rebuttoned his coat. "Fine. Die. That's what you want." He moved toward the door.

"That's what I want!" Jacob yelled. "I've always wanted to die, and I'm not going to let you take this chance away from me!"

Sarcasm again. Esau realized he still wasn't being taken seriously. To Jacob it was still some kind of ruse or joke. Esau couldn't leave this way. Jacob had to know he was serious.

"You have always been the slow one," Esau said. "How can I get this through your thick head? I'm serious. I came here with every intention of exchanging clothes with you. You can walk out of here in two minutes' time. Free to return to Boston, to Mercy, to Bo. I'm willing to die for you."

It was the mention of Mercy and Bo that penetrated the wall of resistance and scored a direct hit.

"Why? Why would you want to do this?"

"What if I told you I wanted to do it because you were my brother?"

Jacob scoffed at the remark. "That's the last argument I'd believe."

"Well, indirectly, that's the reason."

"What's the direct reason?"

Esau folded his arms and leaned back against the door. Looking at the floor, he said, "Because you and Mercy have the best chance of carrying on the Morgan family line."

"What? Abigail's thrown you out already?"

"We have no future. She can't come to England. I can't stay in America."

Jacob studied his brother skeptically, still not believing Esau was being forthright with him. Then he laughed. "I get it ... ho, boy! Now I get it. Your conscience has been bothering you, hasn't it? The traitor now wants to become the hero! And all he has to do to wipe out a lifetime of traitorous activities is to die! Well, I'm not going to make it easy for you. For all of time, the Morgan family will link your name with Benedict Arnold's—the two most infamous traitors in American history!"

"It's hard for me to believe that anyone can be as thick between the ears as you! I am not ashamed of being a loyal Englishman. My conscience has not been bothering me. I'm doing this for the good of the family and for no other reason. Now take off your overcoat. We're exchanging clothes!"

"Not on your life!"

"Then I'll take them off for you!"

Esau lunged at Jacob, grabbing for his overcoat buttons. Jacob knocked his hands away and stepped back. Esau came at him again. The brothers locked arms and circled the tiny cell, Esau pulling at Jacob's clothes, Jacob trying to break his grip.

"Guard! Guard!" Jacob yelled. "He's attacking me! Guard!"

There was fumbling of keys on the other side of the door, then a hasty turn of the lock. Two oversized British guards bounded into the room and pulled the two brothers apart. In a moment of panic, a guard looked at one brother, then the other, unsure which was the prisoner and which was the visitor. Then his eyes brightened as he looked at their overcoats. Both wore civilian coats, but Jacob's was soiled and wrinkled; Esau's was fresh. Jacob was shoved onto the cot while Esau was escorted out of the cell.

The door slammed, and the guard apologized to Esau for the incident. He explained that until now the prisoner had shown no signs of hostility, but assured Esau that Jacob would be punished.

Esau wiped a trickle of blood from the side of his mouth. "Don't punish him," he said. "His anxiety is understandable. He's going to die tomorrow. What could be worse than that?"

The guard chuckled crudely. "Right you are, Master Morgan. Stretchin' his neck will teach him a thing or two."

Esau thanked the guard for rescuing him, and he left. As he walked back to Andre's house, he evaluated what had just happened. He hadn't expected to have to work so hard to get hanged. But the guard had given him an idea—a way to save Jacob in spite of himself. But he would need Abigail's help.

N

Esau was so absorbed with his plan, until Abigail's door swung open, he hadn't given any thought to how his sudden reappearance would affect the woman he loved. She had opened the door herself.

"Hello," he said rather sheepishly.

"Jacob, hurry in before someone sees you."

She pulled him inside and closed the door.

"Abigail …" There was something in the way he said her name that caused her to take a second look at him.

"Esau?" Hands flew to her mouth. "Esau?" She fell into his arms, pounding him on the chest. "Why are you doing this to me?" she cried. "You're tearing me up inside."

Holding her close he explained his dilemma with Jacob. She wasn't surprised at Jacob's reaction and couldn't believe that Esau was still intent on going through with the plan. She insisted she wouldn't help him. He explained his plan to her anyway, including the supplies he needed and what he needed her to do.

"Where am I going to get that?" she asked.

"Do you know a doctor or pharmacist who might have some? General Arnold owned a pharmacy before the war, and he used to tell me about all sorts of unusual things he carried."

She said she might be able to get him what he needed, but still refused to help directly, insisting he was asking too much of her. The more she resisted, the more he persisted, until finally he wore her down.

With her cheek against his chest, she said weakly, "Really, Esau, I don't know how much more I can take."

᠁

It was late afternoon by the time Esau and Abigail reached the stone mansion that was Jacob's jail. The guards were not at all pleased to see Esau again. They reluctantly agreed he could visit his brother one more time, but only with a guard present. That wouldn't do, he insisted. This would be the last time he would see his brother alive, and he needed to make amends with him. It was something that had to be done privately. He assured the guards that he would call them if he needed help and that if anything unforeseen should happen, he would vouch for them that they had warned him.

They finally agreed and let him in. Entering the cell, he turned to Abigail and said he would be out shortly and they would go to dinner. She smiled sweetly and said she would be waiting.

"You again." Two words. That was the extent of Jacob's greeting.

"Have you thought about my offer?"

"Offer? Is that what you call it? I call it soothing a troubled conscience."

"Will you stop thinking about how much we have disagreed and hated each other for just a moment and think about Mercy and Bo? Are you willing to deprive Mercy of a husband and Bo of a father out of sheer stubbornness?"

Jacob stood and faced his brother. "For the last time, get out. I don't need your help."

"All right!" Esau threw up his hands. "I can't force you to do this."

"For once, we agree."

"Then, this is good-bye."

Jacob looked skeptically at his brother. Then, relaxing, he said, "It is, isn't it?"

Esau turned to leave.

"Esau?" Jacob said.

His brother turned around.

"I know you can't go to Boston right now. But this war isn't going to last forever. And, well, if you see Mercy or Bo, or Father or Mother, will you tell them that my last thoughts were of them?"

Esau nodded. Once again he turned to go and turned back again as a thought occurred to him. "You know, Abigail's outside."

"She is?"

"She was going to take you back with her if you agreed this time. Anyway, she gave me ..." Esau reached under his overcoat, under his shirt, to his waistband, and pulled out a flask. "... she gave me some rum ... to keep me warm in here. I told her how cold and damp it was. Well, I just got to thinking, maybe you would want it."

He held out the flask. Jacob took it and looked at it greedily. A shiver went through him just thinking about the cold.

"Oh, you don't know how cold it's been in here," he said. "Do you mind?" He removed the lid and raised the flask to his lips, then pulled it away. "You wouldn't be trying to poison me, would you?"

"Poison a man who is going to hang tomorrow? Why waste a good poison? If it will make you feel better, I'll take the first drink ..." Esau held out his hand for the flask.

Jacob smiled and said, "After me." He took several large swallows.

"As it should be," Esau responded.

Within thirty seconds, Jacob's stomach was cramping. His eyes bulged in horror as he fell to his knees, holding his stomach with his arms. "You wretch!" he shouted. "You ... are ... poisoning ... me!" He rolled to his side, curled up in a fetal position, and passed out.

Esau kneeled down beside him. "No, Jacob," he said. "Just saving your life."

He unbuttoned Jacob's overcoat and tugged at his shirttail, pulling it out; likewise, he pulled at the sleeve from the shoulder so it was bunched up in the sleeve of the coat. Then he took Jacob's shoes off and replaced them on the wrong feet. Finally, he hid the flask in the small of his back, pulled at his shirt around the waist, bunching it up near the waist, and ran his fingers through his hair, tossing it out of place.

"Guard! Guard!" he yelled, pounding on the door. An anxious jangling of keys responded, and the door flew open.

Esau pointed at Jacob on the floor. "He just passed out! One minute we were talking, the next, he fell over clutching his stomach! You've got to do something!"

Both guards rushed in and knelt over the prisoner.

"You need to get him to a doctor or something!" Esau said, his eyes wide with fright.

The guards scooped Jacob up from the floor, one under each arm. Esau held the door open, his eyes darting anxiously from the prisoner to Abigail to the steps leading out of the cellar. He held the door open for the guards, but refused to look them in the eye.

"Hurry! Hurry!" Esau cried. "I'll go get a doctor myself. I know where one is!" He started to walk past Abigail to the stairs.

"Hold!" a guard bellowed.

Esau continued toward the stairway.

"Guard! Guard!" the jail guard yelled.

Immediately, an armed guard appeared at the top of the stairs, his musket at the ready. Esau stopped.

The guard in charge looked hard at Esau, then at Jacob whom he was carrying.

"Let's set this one down over in that chair," he told the other guard.

"My brother's very sick!" Esau pleaded. "He must get attention quickly or he'll die!"

"If he does," the head guard said, grunting as Jacob was lowered into a chair, "it will be only hours before his time anyway. So why the concern?"

"He's my brother!" Esau cried.

"Yes, and if all brothers behaved like the two of you, the world would be populated only by women. Come over here."

Esau hesitated, glancing at the guard at the top of the stairs.

"Come here!" the guard shouted.

Once Esau was in front of him, the guard studied him carefully, comparing him with Jacob. "I can't tell the difference," he said. "But something's not right here."

"Look at this!" the other guard shouted, pointing to Jacob's shoes. "He put his shoes on the wrong feet!"

The head guard looked at the shoes, then at Esau. "Or this one put the shoes on the wrong feet. I think we've got a switch here. Look at the way the clothes on both of them are bunched up."

"That's ridiculous!" Esau interjected. "My name is Esau Morgan, that's my brother Jacob! I can prove it!"

"How?"

"I have a wound on my right leg where Jacob shot me when I was trying to escape from the Americans!"

"He's got a wound on his right leg too," the head guard said. "He's complained about it often enough."

Esau looked around desperately.

The guard looked at Abigail. "Miss …"

"Mrs. Matteson," Abigail replied.

"Mrs. Matteson, you came here with Master Esau Morgan. Can you tell the difference between the two of them?"

Abigail looked at Esau, then at Jacob. "Yes, I can."

The head guard grinned triumphantly. "Which is which?"

Coolly, Abigail looked into Esau's eyes. It was up to her now. Success or failure. *Could she bring herself to hand over Esau to certain death? Was her hope of heaven strong enough that she would give up the man she loved?*

"I'm sorry," she said to Esau. To the guard: "Sir, he is your prisoner." She pointed at Esau.

"Ha! I knew it!" The head guard slapped his hands. "How could you tell them apart?"

"Their eyes are different," she said. "I'm a wax modeler; I notice such things."

A connection sparked in the head guard's eyes. "The wax

exhibit! Of course, I've seen your work."

The other guard was studying Jacob's closed eyes, then looking at Esau. He was obviously unable to see any difference.

"They're set apart slightly different," Abigail offered.

Now both guards studied the twins.

"I see it!" the head guard yelled.

"Now that you mention it, I see it too!" the other guard lied.

Esau considered protesting his innocence more, to add to the drama, possibly even accusing Abigail of lying. But the guards were convinced, and his protestations would only hurt Abigail more, so he stood there and said nothing.

Abigail moved things along. "If you could help me get him to my carriage, I can see that he gets the help he needs."

The head guard yelled for assistance, and Jacob was carried up the steps. Then he thanked Abigail profusely for her help in preventing an escape, expressing his hope that "Esau" would be all right.

Looking at the man she loved as he was led into the jail cell, she said again, "I'm sorry." But her eyes said, "I love you."

The door secured behind him, Esau Morgan ambled to the cot and collapsed onto it. Working out his own martyrdom was hard work, much more so than taking a musket ball for someone or saving them from a burning building, both of which would require only an instant of courageous decision. This was emotionally exhausting. He sighed and lay down, pulling his overcoat tight against the cold. He surveyed the rough beams of the prison cell ceiling. Once again, he was in a jail cell awaiting death.

"God be with you, Jacob," he said.

Streaks of light jabbed at his eyes like daggers. Eyelids clamped down hard, serving as shields against the painful onslaught. Jacob's head pounded with every beat of his pulse. He moaned. Something wet was placed on his forehead. He tried to sit up. Firm but gentle pressure held him back.

"Lie down." A feminine voice. Familiar. "You're safe. Just rest."

Where was he? Jacob braved the daggers of light and lifted the shields. A blurry image appeared over him. Soft white dress, blonde hair.

"Abigail," he said.

"That's right. You're safe at my house."

"Esau ... poisoned me."

"Something like that. Now lie back on the bed, your head must feel like it's about to explode."

Jacob moaned. An understatement. An explosion would be welcomed at this point.

"You were in on this." His voice was dry, barely a whisper.

"Guilty," she said, removing one wet towel and replacing it with another.

He tried to sit up again, but again was no match to her superior position and strength.

"Stay still!" she insisted.

"What ..." he winced at the pain of hearing his own voice, "... what did he give me?"

"A drug we got from a pharmacist. I don't know what it was called. We said we were looking for something to use against wild animals on my property, that I didn't want to kill them, just relocate them. Naturally, the pharmacist scoffed at such a feminine point of view, said poison was cheaper. I made him promise the stuff he gave us wouldn't injure the animals. He said either human or animal could take it and survive. It would cause the one who swallowed it to pass out, vomit often upon waking, be disoriented for a time, and have the worst headache ever, but survive."

Another moan. "So far," Jacob said, "he's right about everything but the last part. I don't think I'm going to survive."

"Don't be such a baby. Your brother saved your life."

His eyes opened fully now. He tried to sit up.

"Do I have to tie you to the bed?" Abigail yelled.

"I'm going back," he said.

Jacob struggled with all his might as she held him down. He was not making any progress.

"Isaac!" Abigail shouted. The volume of her voice was like a hammer blow against his forehead.

The Negro field hand appeared at the foot of the bed with a musket. Jacob stopped struggling. Tentatively, Abigail eased off.

"In all my born days, I have never known two men who were so pigheaded and stubborn and competitive that they would fight with one another over which one of them would get to die! Now you listen to me, Jacob Morgan! You are going back to Boston if I have to pour more rum down your throat and pay blockade runners to ship you back!"

Jacob yielded to the barrage and sank back onto the bed.

He made one more attempt to return to the jail when he was stronger. It was late at night, and Isaac and the musket weren't around, and his strength had revived enough that he was once again stronger than Abigail. She caught him coming downstairs as she was going up.

"Step aside, Abigail."

"Where are you going?"

He didn't answer and that was answer enough.

She shook her head in disgust. "What did they feed you boys when you were growing up to make you so mule headed?"

"This is the last time I'll ask. Step aside."

"Or what? You'll kill me? Go ahead! Dying seems to be in fashion nowadays."

He started down the steps.

"What do you hope to accomplish?" she screamed.

Jacob stopped. "To put things right. I can't let Esau die in my place."

"So it's better that the both of you die?"

"Only one of us will die, and it will be me."

Abigail shook her head. "It's too late for that! If you go back now, they'll kill you as a spy and then kill Esau as your accomplice for helping you escape. Or do you really think they'll believe you when you tell them you went back willingly because you didn't want to be cheated out of your own hanging?"

She had him and she knew it. He stood there in a quandary.

"Shall I burn your family's Bible after you've gone?"

"Burn the Bible?"

"Isn't that what this is all about? The Morgan future, the Morgan heritage? With both you and Esau dead, there will no longer be any sons to inherit the Bible. You might as well destroy it."

"That's not what this is about."

"You're wrong!" Abigail shouted, beginning to weep. "That's exactly what this is about. You and Mercy are the best hope for carrying on the Morgan family line. Esau realized that and is willing to sacrifice himself for that hope. If you go back now, you will not only kill both sons of Jared and Anne Morgan, but you will cut off this branch of the Morgan family for all time."

His head hanging, Jacob pondered his possibilities.

"Do you have the Bible?" he asked.

She nodded. "With verbal instructions from your brother that you are to hand it back to your father with Esau's apologies."

"How can I get back across to the American side?"

Abigail sighed and steadied herself against the banister. "It's all arranged. We leave in an hour."

In the dark of the woods, Abigail gave Jacob his directions. He was to proceed a mile to a farmhouse beside a small white bridge.

There were several loose planks on the backside of the barn. He was to let himself into the barn and wait. When the farmer came to milk the cows in the morning, Jacob was to say to him, "The colonel sent me." The farmer would then smuggle him under a load of hay to the Hudson ferry; the owner of the ferry transported to both sides readily for the right price. Abigail handed Jacob the money he would need. Once on the other side of the Hudson, he was on his own.

"Understood," Jacob said.

She smiled. "Good luck."

Abigail turned to go. Jacob caught her by the hand.

"I knew you were a special woman the first time I saw you."

She blushed.

"I don't mean the kiss," he said, realizing his error. "I was referring to the chances you take for the revolutionary effort. Why don't you come back with me?"

"No, not yet. But soon."

Her evasive glance prompted a thought. "You're not going to the hanging, are you?"

She didn't answer.

"Abigail, you don't want to remember him that way."

"Good-bye, Jacob. When you get home, tell Mercy and your parents that Esau and I were very happy together in the short time we had." She ran down the trail that led back to her house.

Jacob made his way toward the farmhouse as silently as he could for about a half hour. Then, abruptly, he turned around and headed back to New York.

As far as last meals went, Esau preferred the one from Washington's table over the one from General Clinton's table. But he couldn't complain. Both breakfasts were infinitely better than what he was accustomed to fixing himself. Besides, when he was in the Maine wilderness nearly starving to death, he had promised himself if he survived he would never complain about food again. It was a promise he had kept.

The cold damp cell, however, was a different matter. His injured leg was stiff and sore. He was going to be glad to get out into the sun again.

For a man about to die, Esau Morgan was in a chipper mood. Unlike his previous experience of being this close to death, he was feeling good about how things were turning out for him. For the first time in his life he had a sense of purpose that was based on something other than the fulfillment of his own desires. He'd had goals before—getting an education, making his father proud of him, contributing to the family business, pursuing the ever-elusive Mercy, and—his most recent—going to England and starting all over again. Like ships without sails or anchors, these goals drifted aimlessly. But now he had a purpose, an anchor for his life. He was making a contribution—a rather significant one—to the Morgan family, in the tradition of Drew, Christopher, Philip, and Jared, his father. These men made contributions with their lives. He would make a contribution by his death. Let Jacob get his name written in the Bible—mere ink scratchings. For all eternity Esau would know that the Morgan family survived another generation because of his sacrifice.

A fresh American uniform had been delivered for him to wear. He buttoned it with pride. American, British, what did it matter? This close to God's kingdom the differences between the two were inconsequential. He was scheduled to hang at noon. Esau wondered what the significance of midday was to military tribunals. *What is half a day to a person ready to step into timeless eternity?*

They came for him at a quarter before the hour. He dragged his stiff leg up the stairs and emerged into the sunlight. For an autumn day, the sun was warm and the air fresh compared to the dungeon he'd been in. The street was lined with witnesses. Let them gawk, sneer, yell abuses. He wasn't who they thought he was, and they didn't know the mission he was on.

Leaves of yellow, brown, and red were scattered along the ground, their numbers equally divided with the trees—half on the ground, half still on the branches. This fall color spectacle was one of New England's grandest sights. For Esau, it was God's carpeting on the road linking this world to the next. With a British regular on his right and left, Esau walked the road calmly, his hands tied behind his back.

The gibbet came into sight, a singular beam of wood with a horizontal arm supported by a brace. A horse and cart were positioned under it. The hangman, greased in black to protect his identity, stood on the cart with the noose in his hand. The shivering rope revealed his nervousness.

With the help of his escort, Esau was helped onto the cart. As he was stepping up, he saw something that unnerved him. Beside the cart, on the ground, was a black coffin. His knees weakened, and he had to be held up for a second. Up to this point he had been approaching this moment as a simple transition, like crossing over a county line. This black symbol reminded him that the doorway he was to pass through was the grave. The coffin brought to mind all his childhood fears of death—being shut up in a box, buried in the ground, smothered under a mound of dirt.

He steadied himself and turned his back on the coffin, reminding himself of his and Abigail's mansion in heaven ... and of Andre. What a wonderful thought! In just a few moments, he and Andre would be reunited. His friend was probably waiting at heaven's gate for him right now. Esau faced his accusers with renewed courage.

As the charges were read—seditious acts against king and

country—he scanned the onlookers. Not many familiar faces, but then he hadn't become acquainted with many people in his short time there. General Clinton was noticeably absent. Jacob was a common spy, nothing that would warrant the commanding officer's attendance. Then Esau spotted her, leaning against a tree, half-hidden. *Abigail!*

His breathing quickened. He didn't want her to be there. Oh, but she was such a welcome sight to him! A blonde-haired angel weeping for him. Their eyes met.

He frowned and shook his head, trying to tell her he didn't want her here.

She raised a delicate hand as if to acknowledge his message. "I just had to see you one more time." She mouthed the words.

"My brother?" Esau formed the words on his lips in similar fashion.

"Home," came the reply.

Esau smiled and nodded.

"I love you," she mouthed. "I love you!" Then she turned and ran. He watched her until she disappeared from sight.

"Does the prisoner have anything to say?"

Esau was brought back to the task at hand. He cleared his throat.

"In the annals of history, I pray this will be said of me: His death gave meaning to his life. With a confident heart, I now place my life in God's hands, trusting that His promise of heaven is sure. To God be the glory."

He nodded to the hangman that he was finished. The hangman returned the nod, checked the ropes on Esau's hands, and, with much shaking, placed the noose over his head.

"Would you like a blindfold?" The hangman's voice quivered.

"Yes."

The hangman had apparently misplaced the blindfold, for he

searched the cart, and not finding it there, climbed off the cart and began rummaging around some boxes and sacks.

With noose secured around his neck, Esau took a deep breath and waited. During the delay, his eye caught the approach of a British general on a white horse. It was Arnold.

The general pulled back on the reins and repositioned himself in the saddle to watch the hanging. Those familiar piercing gray eyes focused on Esau, and in that moment the condemned man forgot who he was supposed to be. In an instant, memories of their first meeting in Cambridge, the Maine wilderness, the hospital outside Quebec, Saratoga, and Philadelphia flashed in his mind. With a smile and a nod, Esau saluted his former commander and friend.

At that moment the cart rocked as the hangman bounded onto the platform.

A quizzical look passed over General Arnold's face. Then— the last thing Esau saw before his sight was blocked by the blindfold—was the look of recognition on Arnold's face as he raised a hand and guided his horse closer to the gibbet.

"If you would hurry, my dear friend," Esau whispered to the hangman. "Don't make me suffer any longer."

Esau stood in the darkness. He could hear a commotion. It came from the general area in which he'd seen Arnold. The cart shook again as the hangman jumped off.

"Hurry, please hurry," Esau whispered.

"Wait!" Arnold yelled. "Don't ..."

The last thing Esau heard in this life was the sound of the hangman urging his horses forward. Arnold was too late to save him.

In the shadows stood a man who looked identical to the one hanging on the gibbet. He clutched a large Bible to his chest and wept.

Until this moment, Jacob didn't believe Esau would really go through with it. He'd convinced himself it was an elaborate deception—that once he was gone, Esau would somehow prove he wasn't the real prisoner and be freed. Then, with the family thinking he died a martyr, Esau would sail away and happily create a new life for himself.

But there would be no new life in England for Esau Morgan. No Abigail. No children. His body was limp at the end of a rope, a rope that had been reserved for Jacob.

With tears blurring his vision, Jacob pulled the collar of his coat high, though the weather didn't warrant it, and made his way down the street. He had to get to a barn and a farmer who would help him get home.

Looking up to cross a street, he spotted Abigail, the same instant she saw him. Her expression went from surprise to rage.

"You! You with the book!"

The voice came from on high. Jacob looked up into the face of General Benedict Arnold sitting atop his white horse. An entourage of four regulars accompanied him.

"Esau?"

"Sad day, isn't it, General? Not too often a man sees his brother get hanged, not to mention a mirror image of himself. It's left me quite shaken."

"Understandable," Arnold said, "but necessary. Like that time at Gardinerstown when you recommended Stryker and his looters be hanged as an example to the others. I didn't think you had it in you to make such a tough decision."

"Like you said, General. It was necessary."

"What I can't understand is why Esau would let himself get hanged for his spying brother. Care to explain it to me, Jacob Morgan?"

A trick!

Jacob dashed for a general goods store. Some of the men with Arnold drew weapons; others spurred their horses after him.

"Don't shoot, idiots!" Jacob heard as he ran. "There are civilians! Go after him."

Jacob jumped over the counter of the store—to the astonishment of the bald owner and several female customers—and into a back room, slamming shut the adjoining door. He noticed a key still in the keyhole; a quick turn bought him some time. Out the back door.

One step into the alley and he was knocked to the ground by a horse pulling a carriage.

"Get in here!" Abigail hissed.

Jacob scrambled to his feet and jumped into the back of Abigail's carriage as she urged the horses on, ducking as low as she could to avoid detection. The carriage careened around a corner, down another alley, then into the open, heading toward her house.

Poking his head up, Jacob looked behind them.

"Nobody is following us!" he said.

"Of course not! Why should they? They know exactly where I live!"

27

Abigail pulled the carriage around to the back of the house. Running into the house through her workshop, she hollered for Isaac and Missy. Jacob was on her heels. Missy appeared from the kitchen, Isaac from outside the house. They were both wide eyed with worry. Abigail's tone and excited mannerisms alarmed them.

"What's wrong, Miss Abigail?" Isaac asked.

Breathlessly, "This is the day we hoped wouldn't come," she told them.

Tears formed quickly in Missy's eyes, and Jacob knew they had talked about the possibility of discovery before.

"Isaac, do you remember what to do?"

"Yes, ma'am. Go to the abandoned mill, wait until dark, then go to Mr. Jones's farm, the one with the white bridge."

"That's right. It will take you most of the night to walk there. Take the good musket with you."

"But Miss Abigail, won't you be needin' the good musket?"

She shook her head. "Master Morgan will protect me."

Isaac shot a doubtful glance in Jacob's direction.

The big Negro disappeared into the inner rooms of the house, then reappeared with a musket.

"Now hurry up! You haven't much time!" Abigail hurriedly kissed Isaac on the cheek and hugged Missy. "I love you both," she said.

Cradling Missy's shoulders with his arm, Isaac led her out the back door. Passing Jacob he said, "You protect Miss Abigail wid your life!"

They soon disappeared into the woods.

"Up here!" Abigail motioned for Jacob to follow her. She led him up the stairs and into one of the spare bedrooms. "There!" She pointed under the bed. "Prop those in the windows."

Jacob reached under the bed and pulled out four muskets. He started to say something about Isaac's comment of one good musket when he noticed that one of the musket's barrels was drooping. "Wax!" he cried.

"What did you expect in a wax modeler's house? An arsenal? Bend it gently and it will straighten. Place one in each upstairs window!" She ran back down the stairs. Jacob ran from room to room, propping the wax muskets in the windows, balancing each of them between a straight-backed chair and the windowsill. He looked down the road. No sign of anyone coming.

Back downstairs, Abigail just finished throwing a large piece of wax into the back of the carriage.

"What are you doing? Taking your whole workshop with us?"

"I know what I'm doing! Did you put the muskets in the windows?"

"I put the wax muskets in the windows as if that's going to do us any good."

"It will buy us some time."

"Don't you have more real muskets?"

Abigail placed her hands on her hips. "What are we going to

do with a real musket? We shoot at them, they're going to shoot at us! We wouldn't stand a chance. Our best chance is deception."

"Still, I'd feel better if we had at least one weapon."

An exasperated groan. "In the barn. The colonel used to tinker with muskets, there might be one there."

Jacob ran to the barn. Abigail threw up her hands, then hurried back upstairs to get some blankets. She returned with blankets and a British uniform and threw them into the carriage.

In the barn Jacob found pieces of muskets scattered everywhere. One, an antique, was the only piece nearly complete, but it was missing flint. Even if he could find a piece of flint, some powder, and shot, there was no guarantee he could get it to shoot.

"They're coming!"

He heard Abigail's scream as he was rummaging through a box of miscellaneous parts. *Flint!* He opened the jaws of the cock to insert it.

"Jacob!"

The flint was in place, but would it strike correctly? He didn't have time to test it. As he pulled boxes from underneath the bench, one spilled shot all over the dirt floor. He grabbed a ball, found a scrap of paper for wadding. *Powder. He needed powder.*

There! An old horn was strung up on a beam. He grabbed it, hoping it wasn't empty, and ran for the house. Abigail was standing near the carriage. He ran past her into the house.

"Where are you going?" she exclaimed. "I saw them coming up the road!"

"Trying to buy us some time!" he shouted back.

He ran up the stairs to the first bedroom facing the front of the house. Standing to the side of the window, he glanced out. A detachment of redcoats had stopped short of the house. Their lieutenant was pointing to the upstairs windows and saying something to an aide.

"What do you know? They work!" he said of the fake muskets. From his vantage point he could see far enough out the window, down the line of muskets. All in place.

"No," he whispered.

The fourth musket was drooping badly. The lieutenant was pointing at it, laughing. He went to his horse, mounted, and rode slowly to the house.

Jacob pulled out the antique musket rod to load the weapon. He opened the powder horn. Just barely enough for one shot and charge.

"Mrs. Matteson!" the lieutenant called to the house. He had approached the front, still on his horse, his men not far behind.

"I admire your courage, Mrs. Matteson, but we know the guns in the windows are made of wax." Turning and looking at his chuckling men, he said, "One is even melting!"

The redcoats behind him burst into good-natured laughter.

"We understand that you may be confused as to the identity of the man who jumped into your carriage. He is not Esau Morgan, but Jacob, Esau's twin brother! We have come for him and mean no harm to you."

Jacob stepped from the side of the window and aimed the antique musket.

"If you do not come out willingly, Mrs. Matteson, we will have to assume you are being held hostage. In which case, we will attack the house. Can you respond, Mrs. Matteson?"

"Well, Lieutenant, it's time to convince you that at least some of these muskets are real," Jacob said softly as he aimed at the leader. He pulled the trigger.

Click.

"No!" Jacob pulled back the cock and repositioned the flint.

"Mrs. Matteson, I must assume you cannot or will not answer."

Jacob took aim again.

Click.

"All right, Mrs. Matteson. I'm coming in."

The lieutenant climbed down from his horse, drew a pistol, and approached the house cautiously.

Jacob repositioned the flint again. "Probably the powder," he muttered. Throwing the musket to his shoulder, he pulled the trigger.

BLAM!

"It's not the powder," he said with a smile.

The ball zipped past the lieutenant's head and hit the ground in front of his horse. The horse reared and ran off; the regulars turned and retreated a good distance to tree cover. The last Jacob saw of the lieutenant, he was scurrying away from the house casting frantic glances over his shoulder.

Jacob dropped the musket on the bed. Abigail was standing in the doorway.

"That should give us some extra time," he said.

They were downstairs and in the carriage when they heard muskets firing at the front of the house. Jacob grabbed the reins and they sped off.

"Where are we going?" Jacob asked.

"North to Turner Crossroads, then we come back around behind the hill heading southwest."

Jacob looked over at her. "You sound like a military strategist."

"I've had many long nights to think about this should I need to escape suddenly. I just didn't think it would be today." She shot an angry look at him.

"You're right! I shouldn't have come back."

"Then why did you?"

Jacob looked at her sheepishly. "You really don't want to know."

She stared at him.

"I didn't think he'd do it. All right?" His voice broke. More softly, "I thought it was some elaborate deception."

"You really didn't know your brother at all, did you?"

"I'm beginning to realize that."

They reached the Jones barn at dusk without further incident. They hid the carriage in the barn, also the horses and themselves. Mr. Jones, not his real name of course, was well known as a loyalist. What was not as well known was that following the Battle of Saratoga, the American victory ignited a patriotic fire in him and he, much like Abigail, used his loyal standing among the British to aid the revolutionary effort. Also like Abigail, his loyalty had become so ingrained among the British, that he was beyond suspicion. That's what made his place such a successful stopover with the underground traffic that went back and forth across military lines.

"Shhh!"

Jacob motioned Abigail to be quiet, and she quickly doused the little candle that was their only light. Jacob stood at the door of the barn, looking through a crack at the house. Five redcoats had just arrived. Mr. Jones had come out and greeted them. Jacob strained to hear what was being said. He thought he heard Abigail's last name mentioned, but wasn't sure.

Abigail sat on a three-legged stool. The wax she had loaded into the carriage was under her apron. She was working on it when the redcoats rode up.

Two redcoats split away from the rest and began walking toward the barn with muskets. Jacob was just about to motion to Abigail to get into the loft when Mrs. Jones emerged with a tray of drinks. The two inquisitive redcoats were called back.

Whatever they were drinking, it was hot. Jacob could see the steam rising from a distance.

Mr. Jones and the redcoats were having a good time. They were laughing and chatting as if it were social visit. After a while, attention was drawn again to the barn, and the two redcoats began to walk toward it. Jones called after them to stop. He said it was getting a bit cold, but if they would wait for him to get his overcoat, he would come with them and show them where the lantern was located. The leader of the redcoats said that wasn't necessary, ordered his men to return, and seemed to insist that Mr. Jones go back inside where it was warm. The two redcoats who had twice approached the barn shrugged their shoulders and returned. Moments later all of them rode out and all was peaceful again.

Abigail relit the candle as Jacob joined her.

"Our Mr. Jones is crafty," Jacob said. He resumed his position on a pile of hay, his back against an empty stall.

"And kind. Isaac and Missy should arrive sometime in the morning. They'll become his servants now."

"I'm sorry," Jacob said. "I really made a mess of things. It is evident you are quite fond of Isaac and Missy."

Abigail pulled her hands out from underneath her apron and rubbed them. "I'll miss them," she said, staring off at nothing. "But we all knew this day would come."

"Hands hurt?"

She nodded. "When the wax gets cold, it's harder to work."

"What are you molding?"

"Insurance."

She stared at him for a long time, then quickly turned her head.

"What?" he asked.

Tears fell in spite of her efforts to prevent them.

"What? Is it something I said?"

She shook her head. "It's something you are. Don't you realize how much it tortures me to sit here and look at you knowing that Esau is dead? Yet every time I see you, my heart leaps within me as if it's all been some kind of horrible mistake and Esau's still alive. Then I realize it's you and I begin grieving all over again."

"Would it be easier for you if I sat back in the shadows?"

She produced a handkerchief and dried her face. "No, that won't be necessary. If I concentrate on the wax, I seem to do fine."

Her hands slipped back under the apron. With forearms straining and an occasional grimace, she pushed and smoothed the wax.

"Esau had no reason to do what he did today," Jacob said. "That's the thought that keeps coming to my mind over and over. I can't get rid of it."

"What do you mean?"

"We hated each other! Or at least I thought we did. It was a comfortable hate. And I gave him every reason to hate me. So why would he do some fool thing like he did today?"

In the darkness of the barn, now that they had some time to reflect on the day's events, Jacob's emotions began to rise to the surface.

"I mean, we had an unspoken understanding. We would always hate each other. It was dependable, something we could always count on. And I was good at it too! Better than him! You don't know the pleasure I got out of making him hate me! So what does that fool do? He comes to the jail and offers to exchange places! He had no right to do that! He had every right to gloat. That's what I would have done."

Jacob began to weep, his voice deep and heavy as he continued.

"After all the nasty things I've done to him, he should have been the happiest man on earth at my execution. He should have stood at the base of that gibbet and laughed in my face when they put the noose around my neck and cheered when they pulled the cart out and run back to Boston and married Mercy because she'd finally be free, and then he could be Father's only son, and he and Mercy could have children, and he would get his name printed in ... the front of the ... family Bible, just like he has always wanted. Why didn't he do that! So now he's dead and I'm in agony. Why? Why did he do that? I hate him! Hate him!"

His sobs came unhindered.

In words difficult to understand, he said: "He had no right to love me like he did! No right!"

Abigail wrapped her work in a towel and set it aside and went to him. Sitting in the hay next to him, she held him in her arms, his head against her shoulder, and comforted him.

It was past midnight when they set out again. Jacob sat in the front carriage seat, urging the horses on at a speed that was dangerous in the dark. Abigail sat in the backseat amid the supplies she'd hastily thrown in from her workshop. She continued working on the wax figure in her lap while the carriage slipped around curves, jolted in holes, and bounced in and out of ruts.

"Faster!" Abigail demanded. "Faster!"

"We're going too fast already!"

"If you want to live, get this carriage moving faster!"

Jacob shook his head at her stubbornness, but still urged the horse to pick up the pace.

"Tell me if you spot a British patrol! I need to know as soon as you see it," she yelled.

"Why?"

"Just drive and keep your eyes open!"

The moon was cut in equal halves as they raced toward White Plains. The closer they got to the town, the more likely they were to run into a British patrol since it was on the out-skirts of British control. They'd been traveling for well over an hour. The first part of the journey was at a leisurely pace, but for the last few minutes Abigail had insisted they travel at a perilous speed as the road narrowed and they headed into a wooded area. A dense growth of trees on both sides flew past them as the carriage stirred up billows of dirt behind them. The road was getting harder to see with the restricted moonlight. But Jacob stayed the course and speed because that's what Abigail told him to do and the last time he ignored her instructions, it almost cost them both their lives.

Suddenly a British roadblock loomed ahead.

"Looks like a log across the road," he called back to her. "One … two soldiers. That's all I see."

"Don't slow down until the last possible moment!" she shouted.

"I've always wanted to die in a carriage accident," he mut-tered to himself, continuing to let the horses run. He took a hurried glance behind him. Abigail was bent over. Clothes and blankets were flying everywhere.

"What do I say to them?" he yelled.

"Nothing! Just act like you're in a hurry."

"That shouldn't be hard!"

The blockade came upon them quickly. Two muskets pointed at them from opposite sides of the road.

"Halt!" a voice shouted. It sounded like a child's voice. "In the king's name, halt!"

Acting in accordance with his instructions, Jacob waited until the last moment to pull the horse to a stop. The trailing dust caught up with them, enveloping them in a dirty cloud.

The redcoat on the right blinked into the dust, never lowering his musket. "State your business at this late hour!"

Jacob remained mute as he was told. But the muskets were pointed threateningly at him, and the redcoat was waiting for an answer.

Suddenly, from the backseat of the carriage, there was an ear-splitting wail. "I think he's dead!" she cried. "O driver, why have we stopped? We must continue on! Oh, I do believe he's still alive! He's still alive! Driver, hurry or the general will die!"

At the word *general* both soldiers ran to the carriage, one on each side. It was enough to cause Jacob to turn around also and what he saw caused him to stare in disbelief even though he knew better. Cradled in Abigail Matteson's arms was General Benedict Arnold.

The British redcoats gawked in disbelief.

Abigail wailed incessantly. "Are you the ones who've stopped us? Please, sirs, let us through, let us through!" she pleaded.

"What … what happened?" the redcoat on the right asked.

The general's eyes were closed; his powdered wig was slightly askew. A blanket covered most of a red coat, extending down to the floorboard over the body. Jacob had no idea what she used for the body, but it was convincing enough for even him.

"An assassin!" Abigail yelled. "Good sirs, let us through. Don't let an assassin take the general's life like this."

"Hanks! It is the general!" the soldier on the left shouted. Both soldiers were young men; Jacob guessed them to be shy of twenty years. They would have been shaken had a live general appeared at their post, but a near-dead one was a catastrophe.

"He looks so pale," the soldier called Hanks noted.

Abigail let out a wail, as she rocked the head back and forth on her lap. "He's lost so much blood! White Plains is our only hope! The general's surgeon is there visiting family. Please, sirs, in the king's name, let us through!"

The soldier named Hanks sprang into action. "Barnett! Help me get this log aside." To Jacob: "Go! Hurry! I'll catch up with you and escort you the rest of the way!"

Jacob was about to tell the soldier an escort wouldn't be necessary. Abigail cut him off. "Yes, driver, go! Go quickly! I can't tell if the general's still breathing or not!"

"Go, driver! Go!" Hanks shouted.

The log was removed from the road, and Jacob urged the horse to full speed. Minutes later, Hanks sped by them deadly serious. He rode in front of the carriage, leading the way to White Plains. They traveled this way for nearly twenty minutes. Meanwhile, Abigail repositioned the "general" so that he was propped up in the corner of the seat. Then she told Jacob to pull up. He did and, as expected, Hanks circled back to see what was wrong.

The British soldier stuck his head into the carriage. Abigail was waiting for him. His anxious inquiry was greeted with a pistol pointed at his head. Jacob relieved the stunned soldier of his musket. With Abigail dictating instructions, Jacob chased off the soldier's horse and had Hanks strip down to next to nothing. Then they rode away leaving a very embarrassed British soldier standing in the road in the middle of the night. Jacob smiled to himself. There was a general in the backseat, but it wasn't Arnold.

"Is there anything you *haven't* made out of wax?" he yelled back at Abigail after they had traveled a short distance.

She looked at her wax pistol on the seat beside her and shrugged. "Like I said, I've spent a great deal of time thinking about what I should do given this set of circumstances."

They passed by White Plains without further incident and entered the middle ground between the two armies. This was lawless territory, as Andre and Esau had discovered. Jacob kept a keen eye open for renegades from either side.

The sky had just begun its gradual gradation from night to day when they caught their first glimpse of the Hudson River.

Almost home, Jacob thought.

From out of nowhere a team of nearly a dozen riders appeared, encircling the carriage. They appeared so quickly, Jacob didn't have time to ask Abigail if she'd considered this scenario. If they were British, the Arnold gambit might work again. *But what if they were American?* He wondered how fast Abigail could change the features of the face so that it looked like General Washington.

There was no standard uniform worn by the riders. They were ragged and dirty. Skinners. While the rest of the men pointed firearms of all kinds at Jacob and Abigail, a burly, bearded man ambled forward. His self-assured slowness was that of a man who enjoyed being in complete control of a situation, of holding the destiny of other people's lives in his beefy, filthy hands. He was wearing an American soldier's coat with the rank of sergeant.

"Boys, we have caught ourselves a pretty one!" He was leering in the direction of the backseat as he approached. "So what do we have? A lovely tart, her poppa, and ..." looking at Jacob, "... husband? I do hopes you are not her husband, 'cause if you are, I'll have to kill you. I'm not an adulterer. I've got morals." Looking back at Abigail, "But there's nothin' wrong with lovin' widow-ladies."

Jacob recognized the sergeant. Vernet, from Valley Forge. He was the one who cheated Bo out of his rawhide moccasins in a game of toss-up. The resulting fight between Jacob and Vernet had landed both men in front of General Washington's desk for discipline.

Because Abigail had gotten them this far, Jacob looked back

at her for some kind of signal. She wore a look of desperation. No plan. Her hand rested on a lump in the blanket. The wax pistol. Slowly, she moved her hand, slipping it under the blanket for the wax firearm. Jacob shook his head.

Jumping out of the carriage, he shouted, "Vernet! Am I glad to see you!"

The burly sergeant was taken aback at the sound of his name. Thick eyebrows merged together as one as he looked hard at the man who called him by name.

"We were at Valley Forge together! Remember?"

Vernet's brain was trying to work, but from the pained expression on his face, it was failing him. Jacob guessed it wasn't the first time.

"I'm desperately in need of a friend from the army right now. You are certainly a blessing from God."

"I ain't no blessing from God," Vernet shouted.

Jacob didn't doubt it for a moment.

"But I'm no friend of the army, either. Not after what they did to me. I work for myself. These are my men, and I'm their general."

"That's even better!" Jacob sounded delighted. "Because ..." he leaned closer to Vernet and whispered, "That's General Benedict Arnold in the backseat of the carriage."

Vernet's mouth fell open. He stared into the carriage.

"He's deathly sick, and all he wants to do before he dies is to see his beloved wife, Peggy, one more time. That's where we're going right now. To the Robinson house, you know, his former headquarters near West Point. But we need help, and you're just the person who can help us!"

Vernet cursed a vile streak. "I may not be in the army no more, but that don't mean I help traitors! Nothin' worse than a traitor!" He reached for a pistol in his waistband and pointed it at the figure of Arnold.

"No!" Jacob commanded. "We won't get the money if you shoot him now!"

"Money?"

"Why do you think I'm doing this?" Jacob said. "Look, he's dying anyway, so why shoot him now? The way I figure it, the traitor deserves to die. But in exchange for getting him to the Robinson house to see his wife, he promised me all the cash he has stored there! Think of it! All the money he didn't get to take with him when he deserted! It must be a fortune! And if you help us get there, I'll split it with you!"

Vernet was unconvinced.

"I want to hear it from Arnold himself!" the burly man said.

Jacob shot a quick glance at the carriage. Abigail shook her head. "He's unconscious!" She slapped the wax figure on the cheeks. "He slips in and out."

"No!" Vernet shouted. "I don't want no traitor's money. And you …" he shook the pistol at Jacob, "I'm startin' to remember you. I remember the men I punch … Morgan! Yeah, the one with the idiot boy!"

"You've got to help us out, Vernet!"

"Now I'm gettin' it! You're that Morgan fella's twin brother!" Vernet shouted to his men. "Remember that Morgan spy we was lookin' for? This is him! Tryin' to sneak back! And General Arnold too! We bagged some big spies this time!"

"Look, Vernet, just take us to the Robinson house, and you can have all the money. You can get much more money from Arnold than you can from Lafayette. Arnold's rich!"

Vernet sat tall in his saddle, a vision of wealth and glory appearing in his head.

"Who knows how much Lafayette would pay for three traitors? All you would get from him would be a pat on the back. But Arnold's rich! Everyone knows that!"

"Shut up, Morgan!" The pistol shook threateningly at him.

"Boys," he said "we're gonna be heroes! Rich ones at that! Remember how they made all that fuss over them three fellas for capturing that Andre spy? Well, we got three of them! And one's Benedict Arnold himself!"

The more Vernet thought about it, the better he liked his vision.

"Ha! We'll show 'em, won't we, boys? They said we weren't good enough for their army. I can't wait to see the looks on their faces when we rides into Lafayette's headquarters with Benedict Arnold! They'll be thankin' us and writin' songs and stories about us for years! We'll be rich!"

Jacob started to object.

"Shut up, traitor, or I'll blows your head off. Get in that carriage. We're takin' you to Lafayette!"

Vernet didn't trust Jacob with the reins. He ordered one of his men to pilot the carriage. And so, surrounded by Continental Army rejects, Jacob and Abigail were escorted to Lafayette's headquarters.

Two of Vernet's men rode ahead to spread the news of their capture, and as the procession made its way down the street to the general's headquarters, scores of curious citizens lined the streets. Lafayette himself was standing at the top of the steps when they arrived.

Without introduction, Vernet launched into a speech that he'd evidently been rehearsing all the way into town. Lafayette cut him off after just a few words with an upraised hand, more interested in the figure in the back of the carriage. An almost wicked smile crossed his lips as he recognized Arnold. He looked at Abigail, then Jacob.

"Esau Morgan, I presume," he said.

"No, sir. Jacob."

Lafayette gave him a look of disbelief. He gazed into the carriage again.

Abigail reached over to the figure of Arnold and smashed his nose to one side.

General Lafayette jerked back, stared at the nose, then burst into hilarious laughter. "Mrs. Abigail Matteson!" he exclaimed. "I'm so delighted to meet you at last!"

※

The "prisoners" became General Lafayette's guests of honor while the "heroes" became his prisoners. Jacob and Abigail were welcomed into Lafayette's headquarters with much celebration. Vernet and his men were arrested for outstanding crimes against the military.

Lafayette entertained them for about an hour, bringing them cakes and coffee to eat and drink. He'd sent word to Washington by express messenger and was awaiting a reply, if not the commander-in-chief himself, who would undoubtedly want to meet the celebrated Mrs. Matteson personally. In the meantime, he'd been called out of the room on an urgent matter. Jacob and Abigail found themselves alone on a sofa in a spacious parlor with a portrait of King Louis XVI of France displayed prominently above the fireplace mantel. The Morgan family Bible lay between them.

"We made it," Jacob said.

"Little did I realize yesterday morning, I'd be on the American side this morning."

"Where will you go from here?"

"Probably Philadelphia. They encourage and support the arts there. Andre spoke so highly of it."

"You're welcome to come to Boston."

Abigail looked down. "It would be too painful for me there. Philadelphia is where I always imagined I'd be, so I'll go there first. If it doesn't work out, who knows?"

"Another one of your middle-of-the-night strategies?"

She giggled and nodded. "I suppose you'll go back to Boston."

"At least for a while. I have to let them know I'm alive."

The unspoken second part of that thought—*and that Esau is dead*—plunged them into silence for a time.

"Will you travel alone?"

"Probably."

"Then you'll need this." She reached into the folds of her dress and produced the wax pistol and handed it to him.

He laughed, turning the pistol over in his hands. "May I really keep it?"

"If you'd like. Why?"

"A memento. Something to show my grandchildren someday. Are you sure you don't mind?"

"There's plenty more where that came from."

Jacob sat back and examined Abigail.

"What?" she asked.

"My brother was a fool."

"Now don't start that again!"

"No, I mean it. How could he possibly leave someone as incredible as you?"

Abigail lowered her eyes. They grew moist. "He was an uncommon man," she said. "When he told me what he wanted to do, I thought he had gone mad. But the more he explained it to me, the more I was reminded of a verse of Scripture from my father's favorite chapter of the Bible—he called it the chapter of heroes." She looked up at Jacob. "I think that's one reason I loved your brother so much, he reminded me of my father. Anyway, when Esau left me to exchange places with you the first time, I picked up this Bible and found my father's chapter."

She did the same thing now. With the Morgan family Bible open on her lap, she read:

"These all died in faith, not having received the promises ..." Her voice broke.

> ... but having seen them afar off, and were persuaded of them, and embraced them, and confessed that they were strangers and pilgrims on the earth.... They were stoned, they were sawn asunder, were tempted, were slain with the sword: they wandered about in sheepskins and goatskins; being destitute, afflicted, tormented....

She couldn't continue.

Jacob was following along. He finished: *Of whom the world was not worthy.*

Abigail and Jacob held each other as they remembered Esau.

"Promise me you'll come to Boston. My parents will want to meet you."

"And I want to meet them and Mercy and your remarkable Bo."

Jacob Morgan crossed Boston's geographical neck and entered the city by way of the main thoroughfare that changed names from Orange Street to Newbury Street to Marlborough Street to Cornhill Street, the longer one stayed on it. With him he carried Abigail's wax pistol and, most importantly, the Morgan family Bible. He was bringing it home where it belonged, but there was little sense of joy attached to this part of the homecoming. For of the two candidates who would have eventually possessed it, he felt the least worthy.

Familiar sights came into view as he rode toward Beacon Street, giving him a sense of nostalgia. He passed the Liberty Tree, where his brother stood tarred and feathered at a mock hanging, and the Old State House where Mercy and his mother first heard the declaration of the colonies' independence. So much had happened these last few years. Boston would never be the same, nor would the Morgan family, nor would he. When Jacob first followed after Sam Adams, hoping that a war would shortly ensue, he was a cocky revolutionary enthusiast. Returning home, he was just as committed as ever to American independence, but the price of that independence was more than he'd imagined it would be. The Morgan family paid the price of freedom with its dearest blood. And it was up to Jacob to inform his father and mother how that price had been paid.

At last he reached Beacon Street and slowly traveled the yellow- and orange- and red-leaf-strewn avenue. In the distance, in front of the Morgan house, he saw a boy, taller than Jacob remembered him being, standing at the top of the steps.

The boy watched him intently as Jacob got closer. He ran down two steps, looked, then ran back to the top, shouting something inside the house.

Racing down the steps, the boy ran down the middle of the road toward him.

Familiar figures emerged from the house. Father. Mother. Mercy.

Mercy screamed after the boy, "Bo! It's not Jacob! It's his brother!"

Jared ran part way down the steps. He cupped his hands over his mouth. "Bo! Bo!" he shouted. "It's Esau, not Jacob! It's Jacob's brother!"

Bo pulled up as the horse and rider approached him.

"Jabe?" The boy took a tentative step forward. "Jabe?"

Jacob smiled broadly at him. "I knew you'd never give up on me."

Bo was on Jacob before he could climb all the way down from the horse. While Jacob smothered Bo in an embrace, he looked toward the house. Mercy's hands were raised to her mouth in disbelief. Jared and Anne had to steady her. But not for long. Soon she was down the steps, running toward him.

"Jacob? Jacob! Dear God in heaven, is it truly you?"

Bo wouldn't release him. So, dragging Bo with him, Jacob ran to Mercy. The three of them met in the middle of Beacon Street.

"I can't believe it's you!" Mercy exclaimed. "You're alive! You're alive!"

Jacob held Mercy and Bo until his arms ached, never wanting to let them go. Mercy was kissing him, weeping. Bo was hugging his waist and grinning.

"We'd heard you were dead!" Mercy cried.

"I would be," Jacob said, "if it weren't for my brother."

EPILOGUE

America's struggle to become an independent nation lasted another year. Not until British General Cornwallis negotiated for the surrender of his seven-thousand-man army at Yorktown was the American victory assured. When Lord North, head of Parliament since 1770, heard of the defeat, he exclaimed, "O God! It is all over!" Britain began immediately extending peace feelers.

Talks began with the only remaining commissioner in Paris, Benjamin Franklin. Preliminary articles of peace were signed in 1782 and took effect January 20, 1783. That same year, in June, the armed force that had defeated the British was disbanded, and Jacob Morgan came home for the last time.

The struggle for independence from Great Britain that had begun with the Stamp Act in 1765 had finally reached a conclusion eighteen years later. The actual armed conflict, from Lexington to Yorktown, was six years in length. Now that hostilities had concluded, the young nation turned its attention to building a government.

The Morgan house and garden on Beacon Street were alive with laughter and gaiety. It was July 4, 1786, and the Morgan family had gathered to celebrate the tenth anniversary of the signing of the Declaration of Independence.

Anne Morgan breezed from couple to couple, group to group, as the hostess of the party. Mercy and Priscilla had both insisted on helping her, but she sternly refused any offer of help. She insisted that it was Jared's and her party and that they were to consider themselves guests.

"How are you doing, dear?"

Anne put an arm around Priscilla Morgan Gibbs and gave her an affectionate squeeze. Priscilla had been looking at Anne's rose-bushes in the garden. Well into her seventies, Priscilla was just now beginning to lose her fiery red head of hair to a silvery gray. She had been widowed for nearly five years and suffered bouts of depression for which Anne checked on her regularly. Priscilla's husband, Peter, was killed in an ambush near Yorktown as he ferried supplies to Colonel Alexander Hamilton's troops. To keep his memory alive, Priscilla still owned his Good Woman Tavern. It was there she and her husband first met when she led a horse into the tavern during a dispute with a dishonest blacksmith.

"I'm holding up well for an old lady," Priscilla responded to Anne's query. "Looks like it's going to be a fine celebration."

"We have much to be thankful for."

"Where's Jacob? I haven't seen him yet."

"He'll be back shortly. Said he had a surprise for us," Anne said.

"Do you know what it is?"

Anne placed her forehead on Priscilla's forehead in a playful way. "If I knew what it was, it wouldn't be a surprise, now would it?"

Mercy and Bo emerged from the back of the house. Bo was a young man of twenty-one. He was employed with the Morgan's Redemption Company as a dockworker, following in Jacob's footsteps. He was taller than Mercy and had lost all of his little-boy look. He still struggled with his speech, but was making progress. And he still liked to play the drum.

He tapped Mercy on the shoulder and pointed to the doorway that opened to the garden.

Mercy smiled. "Yes, that's who I was telling you about. That's your grandfather's brother."

Ever since coming to live with the Morgans when Jacob went to New York as a spy, Bo had called Jared his grandfather. On this day of celebration, he was pointing to Jared's older brother, Philip, and his Indian wife, Weetamoo, as they stepped from the house into the sunshine. The moment she saw them, Anne was right there hugging their necks.

As a result of spending years in the sun, Philip was nearly as brown as his wife. They moved together with the ease and grace of two people whose souls were knit together. Weetamoo's smile was as dazzling as ever. And Philip had a manner about him that put people at ease the moment they met him.

Philip and Weetamoo had met Mercy once before, but never Bo. The young man had never seen an Indian up close and had been excited about meeting one. After exchanging greetings, Weetamoo took a necklace of seashells from her neck and placed it over Bo's head. She told him it was a present from the Narragansett Indians to him. For the rest of the day, he fingered the shells on the necklace, discreetly, of course, because he didn't want anyone to think he was acting like a little boy.

Priscilla joined them and soon Jared came from the house, and the three children of Benjamin and Constance Morgan were together once again.

"Mother, Father."

"Jacob, you're back!" Anne exclaimed.

"I'd like you to meet someone."

A blonde woman stepped from the house. She squinted

against the bright sun and brushed stray hairs away from her eyes with the back of her hand.

"This is Mrs. Abigail Matteson."

"O Jacob! What a wonderful surprise!"

Anne Morgan went to her and embraced her as if she were Anne's own child. Jared was next in line to hug her, while Jacob slipped back inside the house.

"How can we ever thank you for all you've done for our boys?" Anne said.

"It is I who should be thanking you," Abigail said. "Esau came into my life at a time when I was struggling spiritually. He has been my inspiration as well as my love."

"Hello, I'm Mercy, Jacob's wife."

"There was no need to introduce yourself," Abigail said. "I would have known you anywhere."

Mercy embraced her and whispered, "Thank you for helping Jacob get home safely. I still can't believe the two of you did the things he described."

Abigail smiled sweetly. "Well, you know men. He probably inflated the story a bit."

"And now, I'd like you to meet the other man in my life," Mercy said. She nodded toward the house.

Out came Jacob, carrying a baby.

"Oh! He's darling!" Abigail squealed. "Jacob couldn't stop talking about him all the way here."

Jacob said, "Abigail Matteson, I'd like you to meet Master Seth Morgan."

"How old is he?" Abigail asked, reaching for him.

"Twenty months."

Abigail held little Seth and cuddled him. Then, looking at Jacob and Mercy, she said, "Esau would be so happy for you. He really would."

Mercy put an arm around her husband's waist and gave him a squeeze. "We know," she said.

As with most celebrations, after a time the men gravitated to one area while the women congregated in another. The women spoke of children and households and the prices of foodstuffs in the parlor; the men discussed business and horses and politics in the garden.

"Esau predicted this would happen," Jared said. "One of his greatest concerns about the revolution was the possibility of anarchy. He warned us that it was easy to start a revolution, but how does one stop it?"

"I can't blame them," Jacob replied. "These are farmers who fought for an independent country and what do they get in return? Hard times, tight money, and heavy taxes. Many of them have gone bankrupt, lost their farms, and have been thrown into debtor's prison. I'd revolt too!"

"How many farmers have armed themselves?" Philip asked.

"From what I heard, about a thousand," replied Jared. "Their leader is a man by the name of Daniel Shays. He was a captain during the war."

"At what point does a Christian man take up arms against his own country?" asked Philip.

Jacob chuckled. "Seems we've been down this road before."

"The country is young," Jared said. "We're going to experience some growing pains. If nothing else, I think this just points out the weakness of the Articles of Confederation. We need a stronger system of government."

"It will be interesting to see what happens when the Constitutional Convention meets this summer. If we can't form a lasting government, we may just tear ourselves apart with one revolution after another."

"God forbid," said Philip.

Later that afternoon, the entire Morgan party gathered in the parlor. Chairs were arranged so that they faced the paned windows overlooking Boston Harbor. Small pleasure craft sailed leisurely across the bay. Masts of merchant ships, some of them belonging to the Morgans, lay anchored contentedly in the harbor, some tied to the wharves, all of them bare masted, bobbing peacefully on this day of national celebration.

The family and guests took their places in the chairs. Jared and Anne stood before them. "We want to thank you all for coming today," Jared said. "You are …"

"Wait!" It was Jacob. "Just a minute, Father."

He disappeared out the door, then returned, and, with a servant's help, carried a covered pedestal to the front of the gathering. The pedestal was about four feet high, the draped portion adding two more feet in height.

"I told you there would be a surprise," he said.

"We thought Abigail was the surprise," Anne said.

"She is a lovely surprise, isn't she? But she's only half of the surprise. She brought someone with her."

Jacob removed the drape. It was a bust of Esau. The rendering was so lifelike, it was as if he were in the room. His chin was held high and proud—his eyes were clear and determined—his mouth confident. A powdered wig tied in the back and a tricorne hat completed the wax model.

Anne was in tears. Jared was too, but he tried not to show it.

"Abigail!" Anne went to her. The two women cried together. "Thank you, thank you, thank you."

The eyes of everyone in the room were fixed on the likeness of Esau. Bo's mouth hung open in amazement.

Jared wiped away a tear.

"As I was saying," he cleared his throat, then looked directly at Abigail as he continued, "you're all family. And the Morgan family has a tradition that is linked to this Bible."

He picked up the Bible from a chair and held it up for all to see. It wasn't necessary. Every person in the room, save baby Seth, was familiar with it.

"This Bible was first given to our ancestor Drew Morgan, who fled England and came to what was then the wilderness, hoping to join others in creating a place where his family could thrive and be free to practice its Christian faith. Inside," he opened the Bible and pulled out the lace cross, "is a work of beauty, a lace cross fashioned by his beloved wife, Nell." He replaced the cross. "Together, these symbols represent the Morgan family faith. It's hard to imagine how much the world has changed since those early days of mud huts that were once situated in that area below us near the shoreline."

He paused and looked out over the tops of churches and houses and taverns and miscellaneous places of business.

"Drew Morgan gave this Bible to his son, Christopher, at a ceremony under a tree where the early settlers met for worship. He charged his son with the responsibility of ensuring that the Morgan family faith was carried on into the next generation and told him to pass the Bible on in similar manner in unending succession. It was Drew Morgan's vision that the Morgans would never know a generation that did not acknowledge Jesus Christ as its Savior and Lord.

"For a while, it looked like his dream would die a stillborn death. Christopher Morgan became a missionary to the Indians, and all contact between him and the other Morgans was severed during King Philip's uprising. It looked as if Drew Morgan's Bible was lost to us forever. And if it weren't for our father, Benjamin Morgan, it might have been."

"Just before he died, he stumbled upon Drew Morgan's journal and learned of the missing Bible. Do you remember how excited he was putting all the clues together?"

Philip and Priscilla both grinned and nodded.

"When he was dying, our father entrusted my brother, Philip, with the task of finding the Bible and bringing it back to the family. All the clues that he'd uncovered led to a Narragansett Indian village. And, sure enough, we got the Bible back, but in the process we lost my brother, Philip!"

The family looked at Philip and chuckled.

"Philip not only found the Bible, but he also found the still-living son of Drew Morgan. And that's how my brother came to love a Narragansett Indian maiden and work with the Narragansett people. Together, they teach the Narragansetts to read and write, and they teach them that Jesus is Lord of all races. Which brings us to me."

Jared swallowed hard, then continued. He never did like speaking in front of groups. "In order to ensure the Bible would remain in the mainstream of the Morgan family line, instead of passing the Bible to a son, Philip passed it to me, his brother. And today, in the tradition begun by Drew Morgan, I fulfill my responsibility by passing the Bible to my son. Jacob, would you come stand beside me?"

After Jacob was beside him, Jared continued.

"I chose July Fourth to do this because I thought Drew Morgan would have liked to see this day. He fled the tyranny of England in order to assist in the formation of a society that was free to worship God according to the dictates of this Bible. And today, we celebrate the tenth anniversary of our Declaration of Independence. Our representatives are preparing to formulate a government that will guarantee our treasured freedoms. And we have in our midst, in the person of Seth Morgan, the first Morgan to be born a citizen of the United States of America. I think Drew Morgan would be proud."

A gentle hand-clapping indicated the rest of the family agreed with him.

Jared looked pleased. He opened the front cover of the family Bible and said, "It is our tradition to place the names of those persons who have been entrusted with the Morgan family faith in the front of this Bible. Next to each name is a date and a Scripture verse that characterizes that person's life. Let me read the names that are in here so far:

Drew Morgan, 1630, Zechariah 4:6

Christopher Morgan, 1654, Matthew 28:19

Philip Morgan, 1729, Philippians 2:3–4

Jared Morgan, 1741, John 15:13

"And today, it is my privilege to add a fifth name, the name of my son, to this list and to entrust this Bible to him, as well as to charge him with seeing that the Morgan family faith is carried on through his offspring."

He looked at Jacob with obvious pride.

"Before I read the inscription, an explanation is in order. When I informed Jacob that I would be presenting the Bible to him on this occasion, he made a suggestion regarding the inscription, one that I agree with wholeheartedly. This is what I have written below my name:

Jacob Morgan, Esau's brother, 1786, 1 John 2:10

"For as long as this Bible exists, Jacob and his brother will share this line in memory of the contribution both of them made to the continuance of the Morgan family line. The Scripture verse reads: *He that loveth his brother abideth in the light, and there is none occasion of stumbling in him.*"

Placing his hand on his son's shoulder, Jared prayed, "Lord, there was no happier man on earth when, years ago, You blessed Anne and me with twins. And through these many years, they have struggled and fought with each other, until they learned a better way. And though Esau is with You and Jacob is with us, today and forever they are united in heart. Bless my sons with happiness, Lord. And give Jacob the courage to live the remainder of his days as faithfully as did his brother, Esau. We pray this prayer in the name of Jesus Christ, our Savior. Amen."

Jared Morgan handed the Bible to his son and then embraced him. To those gathered at the Morgan house that day, it looked as if Esau were there with them, watching the Bible being passed to his brother, and approving.

"You're the oldest, you do it," Jared said.

"I've already done it once, it's your turn, you do it," Philip insisted.

"They hear me all the time. It will be a special treat for them to hear it the way Christopher Morgan told you."

"But it's not my place! You're his father. It will mean more coming from you."

Anne and Weetamoo approached their husbands.

"What are the two of you arguing about?" Anne said.

"Telling the story of Drew Morgan," Jared explained. "I think Philip should do it because he's oldest and highest up on the list in the Bible."

"But the tradition is that the person who is handing the Bible on to the next generation is the one who tells the story!" Philip retorted.

"Just listen to the two of you!" Weetamoo scolded. "You ought to be ashamed of yourselves. It's a great honor to tell the history of your family."

"Exactly! That's why Philip should do it!" Jared said.

"No, this is your house, it's your son, it's your turn!" Philip said.

Jacob passed by, carrying Seth upstairs for a nap.

"You two brothers should learn to get along with each other," he said. Nodding to Seth, he added, "What kind of example are you setting for the younger generation?"

The rest of the afternoon was spent congratulating Jacob and celebrating the birth of a new nation. As the shadows grew long and the bay turned a deeper hue of blue, Jared gathered his guests to fulfill one last responsibility as keeper of the Bible.

"I was reminded earlier, that our gathering is indeed unique," he said. "Normally, during ceremonies such as these, there are only two of the Morgan Bible's names represented. Today, however, we have three: Philip, myself, and Jacob. Who knows if the Morgan family will ever see this occurrence again?"

Jared positioned a stuffed chair in front of the others, and he told the story of Drew Morgan as it was relayed to him by his brother, Philip:

"The story begins at Windsor Castle," he said, "the day Drew Morgan met Bishop Laud. For it was on that day his life began its downward direction...."

AFTERWORD

The Patriots is, by far, my most historically ambitious project of the American Family Portrait series to date. Had I used all the research I'd originally intended to use, this book could well be over one thousand pages in length.

The historical characters in this book are more easily recognized than in the previous books. While many readers may not have recognized Bishop William Laud of *The Puritans*, or John Eliot or John Sassamon of *The Colonists* as historical characters, who will not recognize names like George Washington, Benjamin Franklin, and Benedict Arnold in this story?

The familiarity of these names creates a dilemma for some. Having elevated these persons to lofty status, at times it seems to stretch credibility to have everyday characters interacting with them. Works such as this one attempt to bring these legendary figures out of the clouds and place their feet on earth where they rightfully belong. How many times have we heard people who knew a famous personality before that person achieved fame talk about them as if the celebrity was indeed an ordinary person? Such is the case here. With the exception of Franklin, who had gained a great deal of notoriety by this time in history, the famous persons of this story were ordinary leaders in extraordinary times.

At what point does a Christian take up arms against his government? This was one of the dilemmas I wanted to address in this story. It is unjust of us to use hindsight to simplify the dilemma. Good Christian men and women of the time refused to take up arms against England for biblical reasons. Many of them returned to England rather than join the fight against their government. John Adams estimated that at the time the Revolutionary War broke out, only one-third of the people were revolutionaries, one-third were loyalists, and one-third were undecided. That is why the word *patriots* is a fitting title for this book. Men and women on both sides of the conflict considered themselves to be good patriots—some of England, some of America.

Basically, the story followed four historical lines: Jared Morgan was used as an eyewitness to some of the diplomatic events through his association with Benjamin Franklin. Jacob Morgan followed the traditional American patriot history beginning with the Sons of Liberty and Lexington and Concord and then continuing on under George Washington's command. Esau Morgan followed the lesser-known, but no less exciting, course of a loyalist as he reluctantly joined the revolution, sharing the exploits of the infamous Benedict Arnold. The women, Anne and Mercy, represented life on the revolutionary homefront in Boston when battles were often fought in one's own pasture or cornfield. The account of the two women riding out to the army with information regarding British troop movements is based on a true account.

The trio of dinner guests in the first three chapters—Dr. Samuel Cooper, John Hancock, and Sam Adams—is historical. Their characters have been sketched from historical accounts. I found Sam Adams to be a particularly interesting and complex man and have tried to portray him as such. On the one hand, in his zeal for revolution, he practiced that dubious philosophy "the ends justify the means" and felt very comfortable hoisting an ale with the boys at the tavern; on the other hand, he was one of the most deeply spiritual men among those early revolutionaries, to the extent that he has been dubbed "the last Puritan" because of his spiritual desires for the country. It was his hope to continue the spiritual revival begun by George Whitefield through revolutionary means and thus make a final break from England, which he considered a corrupting influence on the colonies. It was difficult for me to understand how he could reconcile his actions with his faith until I considered the inconsistencies of my own life.

Mercy's humorous presentation of table manners was taken from a handwritten document of a lesson all schoolboys were expected to learn. This actual historical document is in the handwriting of a boy named George Washington.

Trade with China in those days was a burgeoning market for adventurous merchants. The pieces described at the Morgan's dinner are representative of the vases and plates treasured by the early Americans.

All good history students will recognize the debate between Esau and Adams as nothing more than a summary of American history prior to the outbreak of hostilities. The hope here was not only to put the story in historical context, but also to remind us that these vexatious acts of Parliament were the everyday conversation of families in that day, just as people discuss politics and news stories today. And the founding fathers were by no means in concert on every issue of the Revolutionary War effort as the historical recounting of the rift between Sam Adams and Benjamin Franklin over the personal letters of Governor Hutchinson suggests.

Esau's tar and feathering is a composite of firsthand accounts. The event demonstrates vividly the internal battle among the colonists and the uncertainty of the times as men and women in America made the conscious split with England at various stages. It also demonstrates how those who made the split readily attempted to persuade some of the more reluctant colonists to join them.

The accounts of the Boston massacre and the annual massacre oration are drawn from historical documents. Modern-day police officers and court representatives have a good idea of what it is like to try to re-create events such as this accurately when they are called upon to re-create the scene of an accident from conflicting testimony. Historians have the same difficulty, only the event occurred hundreds of years in the past.

The events of Lexington and Concord are historical, as are the rides of Revere, Prescott, and Dawes. Adams and Hancock stayed at Rev. Jonas Clark's house and left before the troops arrived, as indicated.

The account of Benedict Arnold's march through the Maine wilderness to Quebec is historical. Considering all the mishaps with resources and supplies during this march, it's interesting to note that life in the military has changed little in the course of two hundred years. The church service and the opening of George Whitefield's coffin is drawn from a firsthand account. It's ironic but true that the Revolutionary War's most infamous traitor was one of its earliest heroes. The Battle of Quebec and Arnold's wounds are also historical.

Life in France with Franklin is taken from biographies of his life. His celebrity status, his relationship with the Brillons, his work habits, and his relationship with the other commissioners are a matter of record. The work of these men in France is a neglected area of study in American history. Without the success of their efforts and the eventual involvement of France both economically and militarily, it is doubtful the revolution would have been successful. Besides, the cloak-and-dagger story of these early diplomatic efforts is fascinating. The preliminary work in Paris, the secret negotiations with Britain, and the resulting preliminary agreement formed the basis for the treaty of 1783.

The accounts of life at Valley Forge and the Battle of Monmouth are based on reality. Gambling in the army, then as now, was a constant problem. The conditions were insufferable. I hoped to provide specific details to what is known generally. For example, the sentry standing on his hat in bare feet is from a firsthand account. And von Steuben's military drilling is well known.

Philadelphia's change in hands from American to British to American yields some wonderful stories—some fact, some fiction. The grand parties were part of the British occupation while the American soldiers endured Valley Forge. The Shippen family is historical, as is Peggy's courtship with both Major John Andre of the British service and General Benedict Arnold of the American forces.

Benedict Arnold's early contacts with the British through his wife all the way to his deserting her at West Point is all based on fact. I didn't attempt to analyze the traitor's mind, simply to include the facts as we know them. Following his treachery, he served as a brigadier general in the British army, carrying out marauding expeditions into Virginia and New London, Connecticut. After the war, he and Peggy settled in England where he was regarded with contempt. Arnold's last years were filled with an obsession with his reputation. The worst thing that ever could have happened to him did—the Americans won their war for independence. For some reason he had convinced himself that they could never succeed without him.

Of great interest to me was the historical character Major John Andre. As the story indicates, everyone liked him. When he was sentenced to die by hanging, Colonel Alexander Hamilton wrote a personal letter to Washington urging leniency. And when Washington ignored all such appeals and Andre was hanged, Hamilton was so outraged, he considered—admittedly only briefly—resigning his position. So well known were his feelings for Andre, the British secret service regarded Hamilton as a possible prospect to follow Benedict Arnold's example.

Abigail Matteson is a fictional character based on a historical one. Patience Wright was a wax modeler and spy who lived in New York and was friends with Benjamin Franklin. Her replicas were as lifelike as this story indicates. Stories of them abound:

One English lady came into a room and spoke to the housemaid. And only when the housemaid would not answer her did she realize it was one of Mrs. Wright's creations.

Mrs. John Adams wrote that she sat observing an old clergyman in Mrs. Wright's studio for ten minutes before realizing he was wax.

And in France, Mrs. Wright was detained by police at a roadblock one night while traveling in a carriage. She was holding the head of a recently completed work. The police arrested her, thinking she was a lunatic who had murdered a man and was on her way to dispose of his head.

When I learned of this wonderfully colorful and courageous woman, the story possibilities were too good to pass up. In creating my fictitious Abigail Matteson, I borrowed Patience Wright's profession and wax-modeling technique, not her personality or life story.

As in the previous volumes, the lives and adventures of the Morgan family are totally fictitious as is their Bible and family tradition.

Jack Cavanaugh

San Diego, 1995

The Word at Work Around the World

A vital part of Cook Communications Ministries is our international outreach, Cook Communications Ministries International (CCMI). Your purchase of this book, and of other books and Christian-growth products from Cook, enables CCMI to provide Bibles and Christian literature to people in more than 150 languages in 65 countries.

Cook Communications Ministries is a not-for-profit, self-supporting organization. Revenues from sales of our books, Bible curricula, and other church and home products not only fund our U.S. ministry, but also fund our CCMI ministry around the world. One hundred percent of donations to CCMI go to our international literature programs.

CCMI reaches out internationally in three ways:

· Our premier International Christian Publishing Institute (ICPI) trains leaders from nationally led publishing houses around the world.

· We provide literature for pastors, evangelists, and Christian workers in their national language.

· We reach people at risk—refugees, AIDS victims, street children, and famine victims—with God's Word.

Word Power, God's Power

Faith Kidz, RiverOak, Honor, Life Journey, Victor, NexGen — every time you purchase a book produced by Cook Communications Ministries, you not only meet a vital personal need in your life or in the life of someone you love, but you're also a part of ministering to José in Colombia, Humberto in Chile, Gousa in India, or Lidiane in Brazil. You help make it possible for a pastor in China, a child in Peru, or a mother in West Africa to enjoy a life-changing book. And because you helped, children and adults around the world are learning God's Word and walking in his ways.

Thank you for your partnership in helping to disciple the world. May God bless you with the power of his Word in your life.

For more information about our international ministries, visit www.ccmi.org.

Additional copies of this and other titles in the
"American Family Portrait" series
and other RiverOak titles are available
wherever good books are sold.

If you have enjoyed this book,
or if it has had an impact on your life,
we would like to hear from you.

Please contact us at:

RiverOak Books
Cook Communications Ministries, Dept. 201
4050 Lee Vance View
Colorado Springs, CO 80918

Or visit our Web site:
www.cookministries.com

RiverOak®
Good News in Fiction